BLOODSWORN

BLOOD SWORN

ASHLORDS BOOK 2

SCOTT REINTGEN

CROWN ♛ NEW YORK

Text copyright © 2021 by Scott Reintgen
Jacket art copyright © 2021 by Sammy Yuen

All rights reserved. Published in the United States by Crown Books for Young Readers, an imprint of Random House Children's Books, a division of Penguin Random House LLC, New York.

Crown and the colophon are registered trademarks of Penguin Random House LLC.

Visit us on the Web! GetUnderlined.com

Educators and librarians, for a variety of teaching tools, visit us at RHTeachersLibrarians.com

Library of Congress Cataloging-in-Publication Data
Names: Reintgen, Scott, author.
Title: Bloodsworn / Scott Reintgen.
Description: New York : Crown Books for Young Readers, 2021. |
Series: Ashlords ; #2 | Audience: Ages 12 & up. | Audience: Grades 7–9. |
Summary: Pippa, Imelda, and Adrian are in the fight of their generation when three cultures clash in all-out war—against each other and against the gods.
Identifiers: LCCN 2020010753 (print) | LCCN 2020010754 (ebook) |
ISBN 978-0-593-11921-1 (hardcover) | ISBN 978-0-593-11922-8 (library binding) |
ISBN 978-0-593-11923-5 (ebook)
Subjects: CYAC: Alchemy—Fiction. | War—Fiction. | Gods—Fiction. | Fantasy.
Classification: LCC PZ7.1.R4554 Blo 2021 (print) | LCC PZ7.1.R4554 (ebook) |
DDC [Fic]—dc23

The text of this book is set in 11-point Garth Graphic.
Interior design by Ken Crossland

Printed in the United States of America
10 9 8 7 6 5 4 3 2 1
First Edition

For Daddio, who taught me how to swing a golf club . . . which is about as close as I'll ever come to swinging a sword on horseback in the Ashlord Empire. You were a dedicated teacher to a stubborn student. Thanks for everything.

CONTENTS

PART ONE: MORTALS

1. CHANGING SKIES . . . 3

2. THE BURNERS . . . 14

3. TO KILL A MAN . . . 25

4. A BLOODY SECRET . . . 38

5. THE FURY'S GIFT . . . 46

6. PROPAGANDA . . . 54

7. BLOODSWORN . . . 63

8. ANOTHER WORLD . . . 75

9. ANOTHER BATTLE . . . 87

10. THE LITTLE PRINCE . . . 97

11. DIVIDED . . . 105

12. THE DREAD . . . 120

13. STRIKING A BARGAIN . . . 131

14. CURIOSITY . . . 140

15. BETRAYAL . . . 152

PART TWO: GODS

16. ACCOMPLICE . . . 161

17. EXPECTATIONS . . . 172

18. GROVE . . . 182

19. THE GAME BOARD . . . 196

20. THE BUTCHER'S STOREHOUSE . . . 206

21. SAIL . . . 213

22. LITTLE FIRES EVERYWHERE . . . 223

23. THE HANDS THAT BUILD DREAMS . . . 228

24. SHORE . . . 234

25. THE CAPITAL . . . 241

26. THE OTHER CAPITAL . . . 250

27. HUNTED . . . 259

28. THE HUNT BEGINS . . . 267

29. FREEDOM . . . 276

30. HOLD THE HILL . . . 280

31. THE TRAITOR . . . 284

32. SURROUNDED . . . 290

33. GODS AND MORTALS . . . 293

PART THREE: FORSAKEN

34. THE CAVALRY . . . 299

35. COLLIDING WORLDS . . . 304

36. THE FURY . . . 310

37. THE STRIVING'S CITY . . . 317

38. A GOD'S OFFER . . . 327

39. DEAL . . . 335

40. THE DREAD . . . 340

41. THE MADNESS . . . 349

42. THREE VOICES . . . 353

43. BALANCE . . . 360

44. HOME . . . 371

45. NEW . . . 379

DRAMATIS PERSONAE

THE ASHLORD PANTHEON

The Hoarder: god of possessions (fox masks)
The Curiosity: god of whispers (hawk masks)
The Striving: god of technology (robotic upgrades)
The Butcher: god of flesh (butcher masks)
The Fury: god of war (bull skulls)
The Madness: god of passage (wolf masks)
The Dread: god of caution (turtle masks)

PART ONE

MORTALS

No stars winked over my birth. No crown
was set on my head. I was born into a
world of possible gods. My name whispers
through the caverns of time because I
whispered it first.

—The Dread,
Cautions and Concerns

1

CHANGING SKIES

IMELDA

A single flame shines in the ghostly fog like a jewel.

I stand there, neck craned, waiting for Bastian to complain about the plan. Wind howls over a sprawl of dunes. The dark sea reaches for us with iron fingers and sand hisses against exposed ankles. I knew the cliffs would be high, but it's actually nauseating to stand in their shadow and dream of scaling them.

Locklin Tower—a supposedly impenetrable Ashlord fortress—hides in the clouds. Only the weathered map in Bastian's back pocket and the glinting flame above us confirm that the castle is actually there. After a long second, Bastian turns back to face me and the rest of the crew.

"You're sure this will work?"

I can hear the way he pitches his voice. Loud enough that the wind will carry his question back to the others. He knows the plan is sound. He just wants them to hear the promise in my voice. Their crew saved me after I escaped the Races—they rode out to my rescue when Martial whispered my plan to the mountain rebels. They are also the crew who gave me my first taste of blood and war at the Battle of Gig's Wall. After riding with them for a month, most of the riders are still learning to trust me, but Bastian knows my words carry a different kind of currency. He's their leader. I am their expert, especially in alchemy.

"It'll be the smoothest ride we've had in weeks."

A few laughs at that. Bastian nods once. "Show them."

The crew circles to stand in front of their ashes. Only twelve volunteered for our task. More than expected, honestly. Bastian didn't spare the cowards on the other crew. I almost smile, imagining them piled in the cargo hold of our stolen carriage, wedged against each other and cursing under their breath. While they approach the castle as luggage, our group will ride in more glorious fashion. I glance around the circle, unsurprised to find my favorites of Bastian's crew.

"So this one's called Changing Skies. . . ."

And it's like I'm back on the ranch with Farian, shooting our next video. Walking out to Martial's barn early on a holy day to make one of our films and hope enough people will watch to pay the bills. That's how I got looped into the Races in the first place. It all feels like it happened to someone else, in some other lifetime.

It takes less than fifteen clockturns to get the group's powders properly settled. Every gust of wind complicates the task. It whips cloaks into faces, snatches powders from palms. Only when the group is finished do I circle, triple-checking their work. The last thing I need is someone dying today because they mixed the wrong ratios into their ashes.

Everything checks out.

Now we wait for the sun to rise.

The Rowe siblings—Harlow and Cora—adjust their belts and weapons, their motions a perfect mirror of one another. Layne tightens her hood and comments on what fine weather we're having. The girl is shaped like a knife and twice as sharp as one. Our eldest member—a man named Briar— laughs at Layne and says it's nothing compared to mountain cold. I thought he was a little boring until someone told me he was a member of the original Running Rabbits. Any man who marched with Gold Man Jones is a legend in his own right. My cousin Luca is with us, too. He hums some mountain song I've never heard. Bastian picks up the notes, tapping a rhythm with the fingers of his metallic arm. I know it's the more dangerous of the two limbs. When I first met him, he was winning a duel with an Ashlord sentry. His prosthetic arm is a deadly weapon, even if right now he's using it more as a glorified musical instrument.

I smile at their talk and pretend I'm one of them.

It hasn't been easy to carve a place in this family. Especially when half of my heart is somewhere else. I miss the way my mother clucked her tongue when I came home too late. The way my father's chair groaned like a ghost in the kitchen whenever he sat down to read the morning paper. Prosper's constant smile and Farian's pursuit of the world. I spent so long trying to leave that town that I never thought I would actually miss the place.

Sunlight finally claws over the western cliffs.

My skin drinks in those first rays, and in the same breath, our phoenixes rise. Out of death and into life. Great bursts of fractured light. I glance up at the tower and am thankful for the fog. A curious soldier might see a speck of light if he looked down, but it wouldn't be enough to raise suspicion. Besides, most soldiers wouldn't look down on this side of the castle. Locklin's never been approached from below. Which is half the point. I learned this strategy from the Races.

Change the game. Make them play by your rules.

"Mount up," Bastian orders. "Low in your saddles. Complete silence until we're inside."

There's the crashing waves, the crunch of sand, our beating hearts. I have to tighten my grip on the reins just to keep my hands from shaking. I try to remind myself that the plan will work. The phoenix magic will not fail us. My nervousness has more to do with how my decisions echo now. Back when Farian and I were filming stunts on Martial's ranch, the only neck I could break was mine. Now there are other lives depending on my choices.

Bastian studies his stolen map one more time before directing us over the dunes. The horses lower their heads, forelegs flexing, hooves flicking sand. We break into two distinct rows. Six riders up front and seven behind. Bastian takes point. Against his wishes, I claim the right corner of the front line. We have argued more lately. But this decision was simple. How could I ever ask the others to put their lives on the line if I'm unwilling to do the same?

We reach the end of the beach. Here, the ocean and cliffs embrace. There's a great smash of water on stone. Spray hisses into the air and scatters into mist. Above, the fog continues to thin. We have a few more minutes to make this a surprise. Bastian aims us at a specific section of stone. There are no handholds. No winding and forgotten stairways.

There is only waiting magic.

"Ride hard," Bastian calls. "Let's make something from nothing."

His eyes lock briefly on mine. There's a fire in them that only surfaces before a fight. I always wonder if I have that same fury buried in my bones. Is it a Dividian thing? Or something burned into the mountain-born? He grew up with a pistol in one hand and a shovel in the other. If he wasn't working the land, he was busy defending it. His whole crew is the same way.

I watch him urge his horse into motion.

My body answers. Great snorts echo. My horse's hooves dig down into the sand. Breath smokes into the air. Less than a few seconds and we're sprinting. Our entire row holds the pace. I smile, imagining some witness farther down the beach. What a sight this must be.

Thirteen horses galloping right at the stone cliffs.

A string of curses sound. Faith always slips through our fingers in such moments. My faith is in the horses, though. I know the magic will work right before we make impact. I know because none of the horses hesitate. Not so much as a flinch from them. There's no fear because they were born for this moment. It's the same summoning I used on the first day of the Races. The one that had me sprinting sideways up a wall, in defiance of gravity, to avoid Thyma's swing at me.

We hit the wall at a full sprint.

Normal horses would die. And we would probably die with them. Instead, gravity snatches us like playthings. The sky trades places with the ground. Our horses sprint straight up the stone rises. I've got a death grip on the reins. Bastian lets out a low whoop as we ascend like gods.

It was one thing to taste the impossible on my own. It's an entirely new feeling to perform this magic alongside brothers and sisters. A glance shows all thirteen horses sprinting to heaven. We are breathless with joy and fear and everything in between.

The only sound is thundering hooves on stone.

Ahead, the fog scatters. Our sprint is no longer hidden. I can see where the cliff ends and the castle walls begin. The blocks of stone are massive, dotted by moss, carved smooth over the centuries. Two guard towers loom on either side of the ramparts. From our angle, they look like dull spears being thrust into the sky by invisible hands.

Both towers are empty. I can't help smiling. The timing is perfect. Our other crew must have arrived. Devlin was assigned the role of the bloody priest. He'll have crashed his carriage just short of the gate. I can imagine him running forward in his stolen monk's robes. The crew covered his hands with sheep's blood. He's supposed to approach them and pretend he's been attacked by enemy soldiers. Locklin's guards won't be foolish enough to open the gates, but every one of them will be drawn forward by the spectacle.

And we'll ride up the undefended back ramparts.

Bastian shifts our formation, urging his horse ahead. His movement draws the Rowe siblings forward as well. Squinting, I can see Harlow grinning briefly at his sister. Another hand signal has them both swinging over in front of me.

My eyes dart to Bastian. He sees the scowl on my face and shrugs once. Fury thunders in my chest. He's been doing this for weeks. Ever since Gig's Wall. That first battle was chaos. My first real taste of war. I was so shocked that I could barely reload his pistols.

Which means he thinks I need his constant protection now.

There's no time to wrestle with anger. We reach the bottom of the castle wall. Our horses gallop through a final curl of fog and burst out into sunshine. The ramparts are empty. Bastian tugs on his reins just as he reaches the top of the wall.

The rest of us follow suit. Momentum carries us over the lip and then gravity slams down on our shoulders again. I almost let out a shout. This is an ancient castle. The waiting ramparts are narrower than we expected. Bastian's horse digs its hooves in and still slams into the opposite wall. My horse skids and the second row of riders almost sends us toppling into the courtyard below.

There's a chaotic press of bodies as we get a glimpse at Locklin. Our view of the castle is elevated. Looking down, there's a courtyard that's been converted into a training ground. Stone staircases lead up the opposite end of the ramparts, and that's where most of the movement is. A pair of Ashlord soldiers stand above the castle's barbed gates. One calls down in an annoyed voice.

More soldiers wait below, listening in on the conversation. Our group takes in the scene, awaiting Bastian's command, when a *tinkle* of broken glass sounds.

Everyone turns.

A guard stands five paces away. His eyes are shocked wide. At his feet, a shattered teacup. Dark liquid carves rivers through the cobblestones. Cora Rowe smiles as she raises her pistol and points it at the interloper. "Well, good morning, sunshine!"

The boom echoes. Gunpowder and death fill the air. Bastian curses once before barking out new orders. Our crew divides into three groups. Two groups circle the upper ramparts, tasked with holding the upper ground at all costs. Bastian dismounts, leading me and four others down the only access ramp in sight. Ashlord soldiers shout their own orders. More gunshots.

Luca is pressed in beside me. My uncle's bulky frame follows. I catch a brief glimpse of someone falling from the ramparts as we whip around the corner. An older Ashlord guard barrels right into us. The impact sends him stumbling back. Bastian shoots before the guard can even ask where the hell we came from. Blood slicks the floor. My stomach tightens at the sight, but we keep on moving and searching and aiming. Our path takes us inside the castle proper.

This is war.

We turn down a long hallway. It's bright with morning light. So bright that we almost miss the Dividian standing at the end of the corridor, his rifle raised. Bastian shouts a clipped warning that has our whole crew darting behind random pieces of furniture. We're barely hidden when the first blast punches a hole in the artwork behind us.

"Ho, friend!" Bastian calls into the echo. "We're here for them, not for you."

A moment of silence. "For who?"

Bastian lifts his head a little. "The Ashlords! We don't kill our own!"

Another blast forces Bastian back down, cursing.

"The Longhands don't take prisoners," the Dividian calls back. "Look at what happened in Vivinia! Your lot burned a sanctuary town to the ground!"

"Do we *look* like Longhands to you?"

There's another shot, followed by a groan. I peek around the corner as Harlow Rowe comes strolling toward us, stepping gracefully around the fallen Dividian.

"If you're done hiding," he says, "we can finish securing the castle, dearies."

It doesn't take long to reach a surrender. Locklin is known for hosting very few troops. The Ashlords have held this castle for nearly two centuries, against any number of attacks. Always they have boasted that the elevated fort could be held with just ten good soldiers.

I guess they should have hired twenty.

One Ashlord soldier makes his final stand in the kitchens until a Dividian cook knocks him out with a skillet. Bastian claps the man on the shoulder as we tie the soldier's wrists. When it's all over, our crew rallies back to the courtyard.

Devlin oversees the proceedings, handing out blasphemous blessings in his robes. Layne is picking the pockets of the dead and taking meticulous notes of our earnings. I see that one is a priest to the gods. He's facedown, but I spy silver mechanics grafted into the back of his neck. One of the Striving's creatures.

Eight Ashlord soldiers are bound in one corner. Dividian servants wait opposite them. Some of us watch the proceedings with drowning eyes. We've freed them, but I know by now it doesn't always feel that way at first. We've upturned their quiet lives here.

Bastian looks ready for his usual speech when Cora crows her way out of the basement living quarters. She's marching men at gunpoint: three startled Ashlords. Two are shirtless.

"Gods below," Bastian whispers.

It takes a second to recognize them. These are not everyday soldiers, nor everyday citizens. Their mouths are shaped perfectly to beckon servants with. Even now—marching as prisoners—they look as if they're on the verge of waving a hand to dismiss the lot of us.

All three are kin. Their father has marked them with a sharp chin and narrow lips. Their mothers, however, have left each of them with eyes of different colors, singular shapes.

Cora offers a mocking bow.

"Might I present the sons of the Brightness . . . some of the lesser ones, anyway."

It's impossible to recall their names, but I've known their faces all my life. Always wearing their regalia on the Empire-wide broadcasts. I can tell Cora is right, too. These are three of the younger children. Not directly in line for the throne, but still, princes all the same.

My eyes find Bastian. I can see the gears turning. He cannot believe our good fortune. Our plan for the war has been simple. We fight for bargaining chips. Sometimes that means stealing Ashlord supply carriages. Other times it's sacking a strategic castle. Everything we win gets sold off to the Longhands. We use everything to increase our resources and free Dividian prisoners.

We came here thinking that Locklin would fetch us a pretty penny, but we never thought we'd stumble on royalty. Bastian's eyes shine like a pair of gold coins. The entire crew are exchanging looks now. He smiles like a man who knows his way around a scandal.

"I've forgotten, Cora. What's the going rate for princes these days?"

2

THE BURNERS

PIPPA

You watch as the men begin to *burn.*

It is not the first time you've witnessed the process. Sometimes the gods will draw too much power from one source. It happens rarely, but every now and again, an Ashlord collapses in the streets of Furia. You've watched as their skin takes on a shine. Almost as if they've swallowed the sun. Their eyes brighten like flames. They scream smoke. All that witnesses can do is watch from a careful distance as they begin to burn.

You were taught as a little girl not to touch the ashes. Everyone always told you such people were cursed. The Longhands coined the term *burners.* In their minds, such deaths were signs of tainted deity. Gods who demanded too much of their charges—or worse, gods capable of making mistakes.

But the men standing in your command tent are not accidents. They are volunteers. You watch quietly as the first grunts of real pain begin. Red flames dance in their irises. One of the men slaps a hand to his chest as the fire inside begins to grow.

"Get them mounted," you order. "Soldiers. Our gods will remember your service today. This final act of courage will echo to their world. Such sacrifices can redeem a lifetime of mistakes."

You're not sure if those words are true, but the troops take comfort from them. Even your hardened guards approach the burners cautiously. Likely they've heard one too many myths. You can see it in the way their hands avoid direct contact with their skin, as if the burning might be contagious in some way. The burners do their best to sit straight as they're placed in saddles.

One of the Curiosity's priests stands beside you, unblinking in the birdlike mask. It was this creature that brought the burners to you in the middle of the night, along with instructions from your mother. It even speaks in a similar voice. A clever trick to use the god of whispers in such a way.

"Do you understand the battle formations?" the creature asks.

"I have studied these formations my entire life," you reply.

There's a brief pause as word travels from the lips of this priest to some other conduit back in the capital. You can almost imagine Mother pacing in a battle room, a great map of the Empire sprawled out before her, covered in tiny figurines. You know there is nowhere in the world more fitting for a mind like hers, even if she checks on you a little too often.

"Don't forget to feint hard—"

But now it's just getting annoying. "Yes, of course, Mother. It is time. Fire and blood."

You turn your back and march out of the command tent, a clear signal that the conversation is done and you are ready. Mother's plan is clever, but as the general, you still must execute that plan. These three men are here to atone for their sins against the Empire. It is their last chance to be invited back into the good graces of the pantheon. A worthy sacrifice, but you've already reduced them to a function. As with every company—every soldier—they are simply tools in your arsenal. It is a cold thought, but there is no room for doubt.

This is war.

"Etzli," you call. "Marching formations. Make sure Bravos knows what to do."

The ever-steady Etzli is already moving. You make quite a pair. When you would risk too much, she preaches caution. Where she might hesitate, you strike the killing blow. It has been a delicate balancing act that's allowed your armies to crush the Longhands again and again. From Inverness to the Gulches, you have not lost a battle.

Outside the command tent, sunlight glints off golden gauntlets and polished breastplates. Your cavalry is mounted. Etzli stands near Bravos, relaying final instructions. The burners are taking their place within his formation. Bravos's dark eyes find you in the crowd. He nods an affirmative.

A small part of you still cringes at his betrayal during the Races. It wasn't long ago that you considered throwing away your future for him. He's been eager to prove his loyalty ever since. It helps to view him as a tool. You are the hand that guides him. That is all there is now between you.

A marching boy leads your horse over. You thank him, mounting to survey the rest of your army from horseback. Each company stands in flawless formation. No one is polishing their weapons at the last minute or shuffling nervously. It is the Ashlord way to be ready hours in advance. Order is the first step toward victory. Mother drilled that lesson into you.

Signal flags wave. As the army begins to move, your eyes drift across the battlefield. The valley below is scarred from night skirmishes. Smoke drifts into the sky from scattered ashes. Beyond the valley, up a narrow rise, is the enemy. A wall of Longhand soldiers, one hundred across.

It's a strategic choke point. Your own outriders neglected to take it because there was an entire city between the Longhands and this pass. You thought that, surely, they would stop and deal with the enemy-occupied city first. But their general—a woman named Tessa Joseph—was cleverer than you gave the Longhands credit for. She ordered her soldiers to skip past Navassa on a night march. They left the fortified Ashlord city untouched, claiming this choke point instead. Cut off from reinforcements, Navassa has certainly since fallen.

It was a clever maneuver that gave the Longhands the high ground.

You could wait them out. It will take another two weeks for western reinforcements to circle the northern passes. All the troops stationed to the east have their hands full with

Adrian Ford. Thinking his name brings back memories. His muscled shoulder pressed against yours, fighting down the final stretch of the Races. The way that Quinn leaped from your horse and tackled him at the last minute. You might have been crowned champion, but the replays of Adrian falling unexpectedly from his horse lit the fires of war. The Longhands cried foul. It's clear from the reports that they'd intended on rebelling all along, but it was your victory that they paraded as their reason.

Now you march against each other.

It takes an effort to dismiss the other memory of him, sitting in that dark carriage. No, you need to focus. All the more reason to keep marching. Every pause allows thoughts like these to plague you. It is better to march and fight and conquer than to give in to doubts.

Besides, waiting too long here introduces risks. Better to break them now, solidify your grasp on the central section of the Empire, and be rested for your inevitable showdown with Adrian's army. "Forward march," you call. "Break them."

Across the valley, the Longhands react to your army's movement. Shields are readied, arranged in their famous interlocking formation. The location is pinched between two raised plateaus, uphill the whole way. On both rises, sunlight flickers across the rifles of snipers.

"General? Make way, please. I'm to speak to the general."

Your guards make way for Prince Ino. It is an effort not to groan. You watch as the man stumbles through the dust, eyes still puffy from sleep. The Brightness assigned his third-born son to your army as an overseeing general. You could not refuse the offer. You are too young and too unproven, in spite of your recent victories. Besides, the Brightness is the closest thing your people have to a living god. He's the official arbiter between your world and the one below. One does not say no to the king. It is hard enough having Mother plan out your every move. At least she knows what she is doing. Giving credit for your success to Prince Ino is a far more difficult proposition.

"Prince Ino," you call in greeting. "The plan is ready. Another genius strategy, sir."

He squints at the battlefield. Last night, Etzli planted a few loyal soldiers at the prince's gambling table. Their efforts provided him a fine winning streak. And the winning streak had him drinking even more than he usually does. You'd half hoped he would sleep through the entire battle, but now you must give him the credit for you and your mother's cleverness. It galls.

"Genius?" He frowns a little, unsure. "Yes, indeed. Taking the high ground back."

Mother would devour this man. She always pressed for talent to be the deciding factor in war appointments, but your people cannot differentiate skill from bloodline. All the nepotism has watered down the chain of command. In all, there are three larger armies. Father's marching with the one to the west. He reports to another royal family member, though at least Crown Prince Rone has actual fighting experience. He was famous in the gladiator circuits. They've been deadlocked with the Longhand forces for months. A second army is stationed along the eastern seaboard. Adrian Ford has made those legions look like little toy soldiers to be moved at his bidding. But the third army is the one that you lead through the heart of the Empire.

Naturally, Mother oversees everything from the capital in Furia. The Curiosity's spies wing information back to her. She snaps her fingers and entire armies turn their heads to listen. Her instructions this morning were rather straight-forward.

"Use the burners wisely. Give us a victory worth talking about."

And that is precisely what you plan to do.

Etzli returns to your side, a calm expression on her face. Prince Ino points to the distant pass. "Are we sure . . . Is this . . . The plan is to take the high ground?"

"Using the burners," Etzli confirms. "Just as you planned, sir."

His face pinches in confusion. He does not remember crafting this strategy, because he did not participate in any of our prebattle meetings. "Right. Just as planned."

Etzli catches your eye. You have to hide a smile. Every day, she gives you another reason to like her. All around you, the command for a forward march is unfolding obedi-ently. As a little girl, you could move your toy soldiers in-stantly. All you had to do was throw them across the room to take on imaginary strongholds. Real armies are much slower, more deliberate. Every man and woman is part of a larger whole. Your commands echo—moving from com-pany to company—until the entire machine has woken. The front lines move at double their normal pace.

Light of foot but well armored, they cross the valley. You know there are at least twenty Longhand snipers on those rises. An older general—someone like Ino—would slow-march them at a traditional pace. But you're not here to waste lives on decorum.

Bravos leads the cavalry after them. His ranks trot forward, following the foot soldiers down the small hill you've camped on. Moments later the reserves release. The bulk of your army pours into the waiting valley like a river of gold and steel. Etzli sits beside you, drinking in the details. Prince Ino is a constant stream of confused questions. You offer clipped answers as the front lines reach the center of the valley.

Snaps of gunfire. An occasional bullet cracks against the front shields. At this distance, it's hard to do much damage. Your eyes trace the flawless progress of your army. Bravos can be impatient sometimes, too eager to spill blood, but his caution is paramount now.

He cannot break too soon. He must keep your cards well hidden.

More Longhand troops move into position. You knew they had plenty of reserves. It's a tight valley that demands vigilance, certainly, but your first handful of probes were wasted. You've lost twenty soldiers to every one of theirs. Now they react to your increased numbers by bulking up their own. It's clear this is not a simple test of their defenses.

No, this is the part where you take what they think is theirs.

Troops are starting to fall on the front rows. Bullets clip shoulders or dent shields. The wounded are helped back through the lines. Other soldiers march past them, filling the ranks easily. Military surgeons trail the procession, at the ready.

The uphill charge begins. Gunfire comes more regularly, complemented by pistol fire from the second row of Longhand troops. It's chaos and blood and smoke. *Necessary losses,* you remind yourself. *There's always a blood-price.* Finally, Bravos breaks. Horses pour through designed gaps. For all their power, the creatures look like they're moving in slow motion. Everything is uphill. This has all the makings of a massacre. Bravos steers the main force to the right. He looks like a man riding to his death.

Until the three burners break from the main group.

All three stop fighting that inward burn at the exact same moment. Even at a distance, you see their skin flash brightly. Smoke ghosts upward. The Longhand generals are shouting out orders to gun them down. Too late. The shine becomes flame. All three men transform into living infernos. You hold your breath as they hit the front ranks with a bone-crushing *thud.*

The first horse is miraculously turned aside. It runs straight into the stone rise on the left with a startled scream. But that leaves a gap in the ranks, and the second horse thunders through it. Instinct forces the waiting soldiers back a step. The inferno scorches. The screams are terrible. It allows the second burner to ride deeper into their ranks. They react the way Mother knew they would. After all, what threat is a burning rider to them? He's not swinging a sword. All he's doing is screaming at the top of his lungs. And so they simply leap out of his way. He vaults deeper into their ranks, dangerously into their ranks.

The third horse collides with their re-forming ranks. Your eyes flick to the right. This is the moment. Bravos has pulled his team short of their pretended target, shields up. The timing is flawless.

Longhand soldiers on the front row look lost. They do not know that each of the burners was riding a horse strapped with explosives to their girths. They do not know the flames have eaten through the protective fabrics, and even now are reaching for the cache of dangerous powders. . . .

The explosions shake the world.

Everyone watches. The first wave of flames is so bright. No one in the blast radius survives, or if they do, it will not be for long. The horse they turned away is surprisingly devastating. The snipers on the wall above are all thrown to their deaths. Others lie unconscious. An entire section of stone is simply gone, and what remains is colored with clawing black patterns. Shrapnel hits their soldiers and ours.

And then the second explosion. And then the third.

Bravos swings the cavalry around toward the exposed half of their front line. They ride through the sudden gaps, vanishing into columns of charred smoke. You know now—beyond any doubt—that the hill belongs to you. Your foot soldiers press the remaining Longhands as the cavalry pins them in from the left. Prince Ino is grinning.

"We'll have to report this victory back to the capital. A wise plan, indeed."

Emotions war inside you. This is true power. To command and win and rule. Prince Ino forgets that you have been trained your entire life for moments like these. Winning the Races was just a taste of your power. This is what you—and every other Ashlord child—trained to become.

The only thing that's buried deeper in your veins than winning is war.

But then you see the dead. The smoke and the ruin. It hits you harder than expected.

"The hill is yours, General," Etzli announces.

You are uncertain how much time has passed. Your eyes briefly unfocus. Almost like you slipped through this world and into another. The smoke is clearing. Bodies are everywhere.

It is a devastating victory. You steel yourself before starting forward. The three burners have atoned to the gods. Their deaths will be honored in the next world, or so the gods claim.

A handful of Longhands survive. These prisoners are herded away. The shock on their faces says everything. Most of them are surprisingly young. There's barely a beard between them. You guess they marched into this war with an eager step. No doubt they heard stories of your kind as children. You suspect their grandparents whispered the lie they believed themselves: *We would have won the war if not for the gods.*

Let them believe that. You know as well as anyone that the gods play their part. But as you consider the blast radius and the destruction, you know that *this* is the true reason your people won the last war. There has always been a willingness to take whatever the gods give and use it with ruthless precision. You won the war because losing was never an option.

"Salvage what you can," you order quietly. "Then clean this mess up."

3

TO KILL A MAN

ADRIAN

I am learning there are many ways to kill someone.

Crush a skull. Nick an artery. Cave in a chest. I have seen men and women fall from their horses. Bullets that slip past raised shields. Explosions that shake soul from body, leaving nothing but bones. I am learning there are many ways to kill someone, and the world taught me to be good at most of them.

We take three villages that night. Our army skips from town to town like a stone over water. By the time their soldiers see the ripples from the first splash, it's too late.

We are there. Knocking at the gates with a heavy fist.

In the northern cities, we faced more resistance. Ashlords took command of the local Dividian population. Everyone answered the rallying cry, dragging out the battles, forcing supply runs. It didn't matter. Those cities burned. And when cities burn, everyone smells the smoke.

The change was not subtle. Dividian soldiers started

opening gates in secret for us at night. The locals would lead us to their Ashlord commanders. We knew it would happen eventually. These aren't city-born Dividian who've benefited from close relationships with their rulers. Most of these men and women have been forgotten at best—trampled at worst—by the Empire's cruelty. Our army grows with every town that falls.

At dawn, we overtake a third village. There isn't even an outer wall. No local militia with guns pointing out of murder holes. The little town goes by the charming name of Sola.

I follow my soldiers down the main street. Old Trask guides me through the population numbers. He's an old hand, one of Daddy's favorites. His son—Forrest Trask—was one of my best friends growing up. Distracted by the Dividian citizens, I'm only half listening as we walk. They've come out to stand on their raised stoops, hands in plain view, their weapons abandoned in the street like forgotten toys.

There are a few crafters—ironworkers, carpenters, herbalists—but most of the town look like farm folk. It's written in the slope of their shoulders and their calloused palms. We saw the fields on our way into town. All well-managed plots with new crops starting to bud. I'd bet good money the Ashlords had them harvest everything, then sanctioned the surrounding towns, using what they took to feed their newly minted armies. Only problem is it left these people starving.

I can see it in the hollowed cheeks of their children and

the razor-sharp collarbones. The thought has my heart beating angrily. Until Capri's words echo in my mind: *You are just like us.*

Glass shatters.

All of us reach for weapons, but the nervous stances settle when Kenly Knox comes into sight. He's a fourth-generation soldier. One of the best swords in my army. Right now, he's balancing a delicate stack of ransacked jars against his chest.

"Flour," he calls, high-stepping through the broken doorway. "Enough to restock."

He does not notice the baker standing to his right. A Dividian woman. She stares at her feet and I can almost hear her calculating her chances of surviving this loss. Another army has come to pick her pockets. In a town like this, I'd bet she harvested and ground the grain herself. And she's probably been using her stores to patiently feed the rest of the town.

"Put them back, Kenly."

His eyes swing to Trask. I know the older general pretty much raised him. I might be the appointed leader of the group, but Trask is our elder statesman. More military than I could ever hope to be in Kenly's eyes. Too bad he's also an old-school soldier, which means he has a profound respect for the chain of command.

"You heard your general, son."

Kenly just about rolls his eyes. Armies have to cannibalize to keep marching. If we don't take from the towns we conquer, it stretches supply lines and demands more of our own factory workers back in the Reach. He thinks I haven't counted the cost, but he's a bleeding fool if he thinks five jars of flour are worth losing the trust of an entire town.

"These people aren't enemies." My voice rises like thunder. "Not after today. We came for the Ashlords. If the rest want freedom, they can take it by standing beside us in battle, not by looking down the length of our swords. I won't tell you again. Return the flour."

Kenly sets his jaw stubbornly before folding. Not for the first time, I wonder what the soldiers think of me. I know half of them are mine. They're fighting to make the world better. They believe my speeches. But the other half came here for a different reason. They ride into battle with the names of very particular ghosts on their lips. Mothers and fathers, uncles and cousins. I don't blame them, either. That was Daddy's argument to me before I left for the Races.

Look how they buried your mother. You are not free, son. You won't be until we win.

Our crew keeps moving. The baker nods her thanks— a ray of light—as we head for the official town hall. My soldiers flank the entrance. Quick salutes see us in. Up two sets of stairs. The roof has been converted into a courtyard of sorts. Another pair of soldiers stand guard over a single prisoner. I was surprised by Trask's report. Only one Ashlord lives in this town.

He's been forced to his knees. Even captured, he looks up with utter pride on his face.

I can't help remembering Capri. His defiance during the Races. The look on his face when he climbed on my stolen phoenix and rode off to a fiery death. I'm learning that these people aren't fearless. No, it's simply a belief that the entire world conspires to favor them.

And I hate them for it.

"What's your name?"

He graces me with a look. "Oxanos."

"You must be very important if they sent you to take care of such a prosperous town."

"And you must be a great soldier to have conquered it."

He looks particularly pleased with himself. This is how all our conversations start with their kind. It gets old. "Ashlords. You have no idea how to act when you lose."

"Lose?" he echoes. "Is that what you think this is? I forgot I was speaking with a child. I actually recognize you. The Longhand who *nearly* won the Races! What an honor. Do you think that makes you a man?" He lets out a dry-throated laugh. "That was nothing. Just as *this* is nothing. You've captured a ghost town. Congratulations. It will not matter. Our gods will answer. We will win. Put me in chains if that makes you feel better, but mark my words, boy. Ten years from now I will be sipping wine on a roof just like this one, watching your kind survive on whatever our gods decide to leave in your broken hands."

His words darken the expressions of both guards. My hands tighten into fists. It would be easy to punish this man, out here in the middle of nowhere. I decide to remind him of that.

"Dead men don't drink wine."

Oxanos laughs again. "Let me tell you how things will go. You'll drag me back to a prisoner camp. I will be evaluated. They'll trace my lineage and determine my worth. A value will be assigned to me. I am a bargaining chip. I'll be held for months. Rations will be intentionally small. I will suffer briefly, but after a time, you will trade me. Or your army will lose and I'll be set free."

There's no trace of doubt in his voice. He even goes as far as looking away, his chin raised. It's as if this conversation bores him. I smile at that. No problem. I can liven things up.

"We did consider that option." I walk to the roof's ledge, allowing the words to hang in the air. Below, Dividian still line the streets. I have learned enough of this man in two clockturns to know the sort of overlord he must have been to them. "Every prisoner comes with a cost. Extra rations. An extra set of chains. An extra set of eyes. We only take prisoners that are worth what they will cost us. Hear me say this: You ain't worth a bag of rice to me."

My eyes drill into his. He's still not afraid. He still thinks this ends well for him.

"You won't be our prisoner." I gesture below. "You will be *theirs*."

His lips open in surprise. Like all Ashlords, he quickly buries any sign of weakness, but it is too late for that. I have already seen the truth written on his face. His first taste of fear.

He pretends smugness. "No matter to me. Eventually, I will be freed."

I nod. "You almost sound like you believe that. Not to worry. I am sure that you dealt fairly with these people. I have no doubt that you honored their daughters, instructed their sons. Treated them like kin. How wise of you to do so. I am certain they'll repay every good deed."

The color drains from his face.

"See you after the war," I say quietly. "Or not."

I am learning there are many ways to kill a man. Sometimes, all it takes is a whisper. Oxanos opens his mouth to protest, but I'm already starting down the stairs. I leave knowing the man on the roof is already half a ghost. Trask waits below.

"We've got company," he says.

"Ashlords?"

He shakes his head. "Are you familiar with the name Martial Rava?"

Down the road, a man approaches on horseback. He's got both hands raised in the air as he guides the phoenix into town with the strength of his legs. Our soldiers are whispering to one another as the famous former champion passes. He's strapped a harness to his horse and there are sacks dragging behind them, kicking dust skyward.

I glance at Trask. "Is there anyone who doesn't know Martial Rava?"

He's one of the few Dividian to ever win the Races. I studied the footage of his year, hoping to learn how an outsider might succeed against competitors who hate him. Martial's answer to that problem was obvious: be faster, be stronger, be the best. Martial broke the first crew of Ashlords who came for him. On the third night, they stopped coming. On the third night, he went hunting for *them.*

There were only two other riders on the final day of the

Races. Martial beat them easily. He's much older now. I can see the gray streaks in his ponytail and the lines around his eyes. But as he reins in his phoenix about fifteen paces away, I can tell this is a man who has carefully carved his body into a weapon. Age won't stop him from taking a swing at the right person.

"Martial Rava," I say in greeting.

He nods. "Adrian Ford. I thought I smelled silver."

I can't help laughing. It's amazing that even now—with his town under occupation—he can stand there and tell a joke. "I finished second because I was cheated by the Ashlord gods."

"Weren't we all?" Martial replies. "We make the most of what they give us."

"Until now."

"I wouldn't mind you bloodying their pretty noses." He tugs on the ropes of his makeshift harness. Both sacks topple sideways. "So I've saved you the trouble of looting my ranch. These are all the useful wartime powders. It's most of my stock. I've kept what I need to support the town. You can ride up to the ranch and double-check, but I thought I'd save us both time."

I signal. Two guards step forward. Martial tosses the ropes to them.

"Oh. You'll also find the corpses of five Ashlord soldiers about four hundred paces north of the city. Furia sent them our way a few weeks ago. I thought one Ashlord in town was plenty."

Not hard to figure out what happened to them. A glance at Trask makes it clear that he's thinking the same thing that I am. Someone like Martial Rava would be very useful to our cause.

"Come with us," I offer. "Plenty of noses to bloody where we're going."

His features sharpen, like a creature that's unsure if it's being threatened. Maybe he thinks it's my intention to force him into enlisting. But after sizing me up, he shakes his head.

"My people are here. I know enough about war to know what happens in towns like this one. Soldiers get bored. We heard about what happened in Vivinia. . . ."

He lets that name hang in the air. We've all heard about Vivinia by now. At the start of the war, both sides agreed to several sanctuary locations. Soldiers aren't supposed to touch them. Sanctuaries are places that the innocent can travel to and find refuge. Armies skip over those towns no matter what happens during the war. Except someone put Vivinia to the torch in the middle of the night. Most of the victims were completely helpless.

And most of them were Dividian.

"That wasn't us."

Martial squints. "You're sure about that?"

I don't reply, because no one is sure. Antonio Rowan commands the Longhand army on that side of the continent. His soldiers claimed a group of Ashlord outriders were responsible. A day later, the Ashlords spread footage of the town burning and blamed us instead. Both sides have spent the past few days trying to leverage Dividian support from the atrocity.

Martial's reaction makes it clear that he doesn't trust either side in this war.

"Look, I promised our mutual acquaintance I'd protect these people."

That catches my attention. "Mutual acquaintance? And who would that be?"

"Imelda Beru."

His answer surprises me. "The Dividian from the Races?"

Martial lifts an eyebrow. "Kind of thought that was why you came here. Didn't you know? This is Imelda's hometown. She trained with me at the ranch. That's her house right over there." He points down the road. "Not that she's in it. I'm surprised you didn't know. . . ."

I shake my head. "We're just securing towns as we march south. I had no idea."

"Then . . ." Martial frowns now. "Honestly, I came here hoping for a trade. All my powders for information. I thought you'd have some news about where she is now."

His words leave me feeling even more tangled. "Didn't she jump the barrier during the middle of the Races? Rumor was she fled to the mountains."

"And in the process, she baited an Ashlord army for your father's right-hand man. Antonio Rowan followed her to Gig's Wall. Imelda set the whole thing up without knowing it."

"We heard those rumors," I reply, nodding. "Didn't see any mention of it in the official reports, though. Antonio just said they had help from mountain rebels. Nothing more."

Martial looks worried. "Imelda was supposed to join her uncle in the mountains after the battle. He never wrote. I've been hoping for news ever since."

I shrug. "If she's smart enough to pull off a heist like that one, I'd put good money on her being alive and well. No need to worry."

Martial nods. "If you get word—"

Before I can promise him anything, there's a distant shout. I turn to see smoke pouring out of the front entrance of the town hall. Two of my soldiers stumble into the street, hacking and coughing before dropping to their knees. I have to squint through the smoke to make out the third figure. A shadowed form mounts an abandoned horse.

Gunfire echoes from the opposite end of the street. Most of the Dividian have scrambled back inside their homes. I start forward on instinct. The horse darts through the smoke in our direction. There's a rider pressed low against its back. A familiar, proud face.

"Oxanos."

He must have decided he was going to die if we handed him over to the town. It confirms my guess. He was a monster to these people. The phoenix works its way into a gallop at his urging. My walk shifts into a light run. There's only one main street, which means he's vaulting right at us. Martial sits his horse, but I left my own mount outside of town.

A clear disadvantage.

Oxanos grits his teeth, forcing the phoenix toward an inevitable collision. He's about fifty paces away when I see his goal. Even mounted, he won't risk meeting me head-to-head. It has my body pulsing into motion. My arms pump faster. My feet dig deeper into the dust.

Every precious second counts.

He tugs the reins, forcing his horse into a turn. I forgot there were two roads. A simple intersection—one that runs north to south and the other east to west. The horse skids slightly at the sudden adjustment. I reach the spot at the exact moment he makes the turn.

Oxanos urges his horse to the right. Its hooves find purchase. One more stride will put them out of reach, vaulting down a road my crew didn't bother to cover. It'll turn into a chase. Oxanos on the run. Our team pursuing. We'll waste time on a fool.

My eyes lock on him. There's a crate pressed against the side of the corner building. Before Oxanos can pick up speed again, I angle in that direction. A leap brings my left knee to my chest. The opposite foot lands on the waiting crate. I kick off hard, nearly snapping the wooden slats, and momentum vaults me through the air.

Oxanos looks up. It's the only reason the move works. My leap carries me overhead, but that stolen glance gives me the chance to reach down. Right as our paths overlap, I snatch him by his riding hood and drag him to the ground with me. We both hit the side of a building. Hard.

I'm expecting the blow. Oxanos isn't. We roll through the clouds of dust, his horse letting out a startled scream, Oxanos pinned beneath my weight. He struggles until I slam an elbow down into his jaw. His head rebounds off the ground. The sharpness of the blow leaves him dazed. It takes a second to catch my breath and rise, one hand tight on his collar.

There's crowing from the nearest soldiers. Martial smirks. I'm not sure if he thinks what I did was unnecessary, or if he's just happy to see the streets drinking Oxanos's blood.

I smile back at my soldiers, catching my breath, when

I see movement. An open window in the nearest house. My eyes land on a boy—maybe a year or two younger than me—who's watching the whole exchange through the lens of a camera. He notices me noticing him and darts back into the shadows. I'm still staring at the empty window when Kenly approaches.

"I'll take him, General."

I shove Oxanos his way. When I look back at the window, there's nothing but shadows. Trask dusts off my shoulders.

"Hell of a leap. You feel okay? Didn't take a knock to the head, did you?"

I shake myself.

"Fine. There's . . . someone was watching me. From that window."

4

A BLOODY SECRET

IMELDA

Bastian wisely suggests that we interrogate each prince separately. He also suggests sending scouts down the road. The princes clearly came here in secret. Only the gods know what kind of army the Ashlords will send if they find out we've captured them.

The oldest prince offers nothing. He claims this is a safe house. A place to settle a few of the royal family members during uncertain times. Bastian spins that logic against him.

"Clever, really," he says, voice full of disdain. "Protect the royal children by sending them to an active border zone, in the middle of a war, within shouting distance of their only known enemy. I can see why your family has ruled the Empire for centuries."

The second prince offers a little more insight. "We are here for sanctification."

"Hmm. Try talking like a normal person."

The boy scowls in a way that only Ashlords can scowl. So

full of contempt that I'm surprised the stuff doesn't splash out onto the floor. "Our family has traveled here every year for the last two hundred years. You stand on holy ground. We were simply paying our respects."

Bastian nods. "You were still drunk when my crew entered your room. They said you didn't even wake up. Sounds like you have a very deep and abiding respect for this holy pilgrimage you're supposedly on."

The third and youngest prince is the one who breaks. Bastian pretends to have one of his brothers tortured in an adjacent room. It's really Harlow Rowe, screaming into cupped hands every few seconds. But I can see the terror growing on the boy's face with every new echo.

"There goes a finger," Bastian says calmly. "Or maybe just the fingernail?"

The boy stammers. "Please . . . please stop."

"I made promises," Bastian replies. "Surely you can tell that I'm a man of my word. A missing finger for every time your brothers lied to me. I counted *at least* twelve lies in that last conversation. Guess that means we get to take some toes, too."

There's another scream.

"Please. In the stables. Check the stables."

Bastian raises an eyebrow. "We already did."

"Not *those* stables."

And there's the golden thread we've been looking for. Bastian throws me a glance. He's been playing the hard-nosed interrogator. Now it's my turn. I keep my voice intentionally soft.

"Show us where they are."

The boy sniffs before rising. He insists that we stop the torture in the other room first. Bastian knocks twice. The cries go silent. The Empire's youngest prince has been trained in the Ashlord way. He stands straight-backed, chin raised, both hands folded in front of him. Only the sniffling and crying betray his age. I'd bet he isn't a day older than my own little brother, Prosper. Bastian keeps a hand on the boy's shoulder as we march into the courtyard. My stomach twists a little at the thought of some soldier doing the same thing to Prosper on the other side of the Empire. Little prayers whisper in my mind for him, for all of them.

Please be okay. Keep him safe, Mother and Father. All of you stay safe.

"It's this way."

The little princeling marches us to the coastal wall of the castle. I wait for him to aim us at the ramp on our right or the doorway on our left. Instead, he walks straight toward the stone exterior. He pauses in front of the wall and heaves a sigh. "The stables are in here."

Both of us stare. It's a blank wall.

Bastian laughs. "You know, I didn't think you actually had the stones to mess with us like your brothers did. Unbelievable. This is going to be a very, very long—"

But the boy doesn't laugh. He holds out his hand. "I need a knife."

I frown now. There are no signs of a keyhole. What good would a knife do?

"For what?" I ask.

"The entrance requires blood."

His answer sends a shiver down my spine. It doesn't

sound like something a ten-year-old would say. It's almost as if his ancestors are speaking the words through him, an echo of the generations of Ashlords who've stood in this very spot and proclaimed the same dark truth.

Bastian slides a knife from his belt. "If you make even one wrong move . . ."

The boy takes the offered blade in steady hands. It's clear he knows the edge of a knife. He slides it quick and clean across his upper palm. Blood flows. The kid doesn't even wince as he presses the bleeding wound to the waiting stones. An answer comes with frightening speed.

A howl splits the air.

The ground around us trembles. I hear a gasp of air— like an ancient tomb opening—and the wall in front of us begins to *move*. Bastian's hand slides to the grip of his pistol. It takes a second to see the pattern behind the movement. Stones slide like pieces on a game board. Up and left and down. Each one makes room for other stones that seem to appear out of thin air.

It takes half a clockturn for the entrance to emerge.

The prince tugs open a door that looks like it's from another age. It groans on ancient hinges. There's an impossible amount of space inside. I've walked the ramparts. These walls are five or six paces wide at the most. There should be cliffs in front of us. Instead, there's a spacious entryway that leads to eight separate stalls. Each one contains a set of ashes.

Bastian whispers a warning. I realize I've forgotten the prince and, without even thinking, have stepped around him, deeper into the chamber. He's right. It could be a trap.

But the smell within is not of torture. It's the rich scent of alchemy. Powders are slowly burning. I can't resist crossing the room and eyeing the first stall. There are powders I recognize. I can smell the pinches of Revelrust. Circles of onyx overlap one another. One is filled with a pile of Pearlknot powder. The other is accented by gypsum. I can't help but admire the artistry of each one. This is a particularly *beautiful* summoning. Not to mention a complex one. I count at least ten components involved.

There's only one I don't recognize.

A garnet-colored substance placed at the very center of each set of ashes. I walk from stall to stall, examining them in turn. All are identical. A little less finesse here or there, but still the same. My eyes return to the entrance. It's difficult to locate the prince at first. Most of our crew has gathered to witness the strange discovery. I find him, though, forgotten in the crowd with Bastian's knife clutched in his hand.

"What's the rebirth?"

He shakes his head. His eyes are wide now. His skin is as pale as I've ever seen from an Ashlord. He's finally realized what he's done. I ask the question again but he offers only silence. It draws a smile to my lips. I start searching the room. Supplies are scattered. Components stored in traditional racing cubes. On the far wall, someone's pinned a slip of paper to the wall.

I curl down one corner to read. The ingredients are all listed. Instructions, too. The name of the rebirth stares down from the top of the page.

"Bloodsworn," I read aloud. "What does it do?"

Now the prince looks properly terrified. He's too young

to think about anything but the safety of his brothers. He thought this secret would keep their heads on their necks. The false wall and his reaction to the rebirth being named have me thinking these horses—this particular recipe— were never meant for our eyes.

Which has me thinking they're going to be a *lot* of fun.

I cross back over to the first stall with a grin on my face. There's just one detail that's still digging into my skin. There's no roof in here. No skylights, either. How do you summon the sun into a place like this? I squint back at the angles, wondering if first or last light might sneak over the castle walls and reach the interior somehow. But no matter how hard I crane my neck, I know these ashes are too deep in the room to be reached that way.

"So how . . ."

It doesn't make sense. And if there's one thing I've learned, it's that the Ashlords have a reason for everything. These stalls exist for a purpose. There's a reason the ashes were set in this exact location. It takes me some digging to see what I missed inside the stalls.

I was too focused on the ashes.

"Latches."

There's muttering now. It's mostly coming from Bastian. I ignore his whispered cautions and step around the ashes in the first stall. My hand finds a single smoke-black latch. I have to stand on tiptoe to reach the thing, but it gives way with an audible click. A wooden barrier releases, sliding downward in one smooth movement.

I'm forced back by the sudden burst of sunlight. I shield my eyes but the answering pulse is blinding. A phoenix is born. It takes a moment for the light to fade. We take in a new creation.

The horse's base coat is like one long shadow, a moonless night. It has a silver mane running down its neck like the first gasp of a river. But it's the pulses of light that catch my attention. Like strikes of lightning coming from within. Streaking patterns flash—brief and luminous—under the creature's skin. My eyes try to trace them, but the afterimages scatter as the horse moves.

My heart leaps into my throat. I wasn't thinking. Opening the stall to let in the sunlight, I removed the only barrier between the summoned phoenix and the cliffs below. The creature steps forward without a thought. I lunge, too late, as it steps into thin air.

And vanishes.

My hand falls short of a rump that's no longer there. The summoned phoenix is gone. Wind whips through the vacated space. Salted air touches my lips. All I can do is stare at the impossible emptiness in front of me. Gasps echo from the entrance. Bastian is drawn forward.

"What the hell? Where'd it go?"

Horror trades places with excitement. There are pieces of a puzzle finally fitting together. Three of the royal princes came here in secret. Ashes were prepared here in secret. A horse that should have fallen to its death just vanished from existence.

My mind is racing.

Bastian sees the look on my face and groans.

"Imelda," he warns. "No. This really isn't . . . We need to just play it safe. We need to—"

He's too late. I'm eyeing the other stalls hungrily. When I finally speak, I make sure my voice is iron. No one will deny me this. I've spent my whole life searching for these mysteries.

"I'm going. Who wants to come with me?"

5

THE FURY'S GIFT

PIPPA

You dream of Quinn.

It has been seventy days and seventy nights since your friend vanished at the end of the Races. The gifted spirit returned to her world—the realm of the gods—with a grin on her face. Every time you dream of her, you also dream of charcoal plains. In that dream world, the mountains have no majesty to them. Rather, they look condemned, cursed to watch over their lifeless valleys. There is no sun in those dreams. The slate sky looks more like the lid of a coffin. Once you spied a distant herd of horses, stirring up dust like a storm. Always Quinn is nearby. You have witnessed her climbing roofs and lowering herself into dark caverns. In this particular dream, she rides a horse that's the color of blood and her foes tremble at her coming.

You wake with a strangled cry.

It was just a dream. You rise and wrap yourself in a

heavier cloak, slipping out of the command tent. You trade the nightmares you can't control for those of your own making. The smell of burning flesh still hangs in the air. As you reach the overlook, you slip a hand into your inner coat pocket. Mother taught you this lesson. A strange thing to pass on to a daughter. You remove a clutch of lavender petals and hold them to your nose. The delicate flowers become a shield.

Down in the valley, lights dance like fireflies.

Your outriders are playing in their new territory. Revel chased down the Longhands who escaped your first attack. Bravos was bleeding but begged you to allow him to go and prove himself. You permitted it. Now they play with their food. Anything between here and Navassa will burn. It is an art form. Poking the giant and retreating before it can bring a fist slamming down on their heads. Revel is a natural.

And what about Vivinia?

That doubting voice echoes in the back of your mind. News reports reached you before the last battle. One of the sanctuary cities in the west was massacred. Thousands of innocents claimed by war. It's possible that an outrider like Revel—under a general like you—was responsible. Intelligence reports claim the Longhands are guilty, but you know your people's cunning. It is not beyond the most brutal warmakers to use the city's destruction against the Longhands.

Look at how merciless our enemy is! We will protect you! Hide under the heel of our boots. . . .

You have to shake the thought away. It helps to remember that the valley below is not full of innocents. Bravos and Revel are chasing down Longhands who volunteered to fight. It takes a moment, but your breathing steadies. This is war as it was intended.

"General?" It is Etzli's voice. "You have a visitor."

The words are spoken in a strange tone. It has you turning out of curiosity.

"Can our visitor wait until morning?"

"He is not one to be kept waiting."

Interesting. There are only so many in the Empire who can demand your company this way. In fact, you can count them on one hand. It has your mind racing. You take a moment to fasten the bone-wrought buttons along the front of your jacket and smooth the collar down.

"How do I look?"

Etzli clears her throat. "Nor is he one to care about looks, General."

Excitement dances toward dread. It is to be one of *those* visits.

"Lead me."

Always so steady, Etzli turns and marches you into the waiting jaws of a god. She does not tremble. Her head does not bow. You drink her confidence in like an offered cup. The camp is quiet. Your usual sentries have abandoned their rotations. This is clearly to be a private meeting.

As you round the command tent, a wave of power strikes you in the chest. It hits hard enough to steal your next breath. Etzli raises an arm to shield herself. You do not show the same weakness. Instead, you grit your teeth, raise your chin, and march into the clearing.

The Fury watches you.

Most of the other gods are subtle. Your people have studied them for centuries. You know that each god has hundreds of priests, but it is only on rare occasions that the *actual* god steps into those priestly vessels, occupying them with their power. Out of caution, most of the gods do not like to reveal themselves. You imagine there would be dire consequences to dying inside the body of one of their priests. A temporary setback, at the very least. But you've learned to see the difference between an empty vessel and an occupied one. The slight glow circling their eyes. The proud set of their shoulders. Small signs that mark the presence of an actual god.

The Fury does not believe in subtlety. He is the god of wrath and war. It is likely no one has ever taught him the concept. Power pulses from him like rays of light. It draws the beat of your heart up into your temples. Every pulse a punch of thunder. It is not easy, but you steady yourself by focusing on the human vessel the Fury occupies.

A shirtless priest, his chest darkened by constant sun. He wears the traditional bull's skull like a broken crown. There are puckered scars where godly bone knits into human flesh. He stares back at you, eyes like lightless pits. "Greetings, fire-child."

"Welcome, Fury. Join our fires. Call them your own."

The god offers a skeletal smile. "As ever, child. You have done well here. You are ever your mother's child. That was a clever use of an ancient tool. The pantheon smiles upon your success. None more than me. I would favor you now with a reward. A gift for what is to come."

Your breath is stolen a second time. The gods have always

offered gifts in wartime, but they do so with great care. The men and women who've received those gifts make history. Raised as golden standards, or whispered as dark warnings. Their gifts are not to be wasted.

"I would welcome your gift, Fury."

The skeletal figure looks amused, as if anyone would dare reject him. He gestures. You were so consumed by the Fury's presence that you didn't notice the strange piles. The sight has you squinting for a closer look. They are ashes. Row upon row of piled ashes.

Your heart skips.

Could it be? You know the phoenixes were gifted centuries ago. A new creature that turned the tides of our war with the Dividian. You stare at these piles and can only dream of the boon you're about to be given. Will it be a new breed of horse? Some brighter power?

Your voice is hungry. "What are they?"

"Revenants."

It is not a word you've heard before. The Fury smiles.

"It means 'one that returns from the dead.' Centuries ago, we gifted your people with a similar creature. The phoenixes live and die and live again. One hundred horses were given into your care. Now we gift you one hundred revenants. All born on this hill will be loyal to *you*. They will march at your side, fight with your army, obey your commands."

You find yourself nodding, as if you deserve such a gift.

"What kind of creatures are they?"

The god watches you with those burning eyes. "Look for yourself."

Overhead, the clouds part. Moonlight rushes into the clearing. You are not ready for the sudden gasps or the stirring clouds of dust. You have to shield your eyes as moonlight presses down in the same glinting way that sunlight often will for phoenix births. Forms stumble free of their spinning ashes. Your eyes fight through the churning debris to get a glance.

The answer stuns.

These revenants are not creatures. They are people. Men and women stand in the pale moonlight, their lightless eyes fixed on you. Each one bears a resemblance to the next. You watch as they form up flawless ranks. Their uniforms are pristine. It almost reminds you of the first time that Quinn appeared. The strange paleness of her skin. These revenants have that same colorless quality.

"What am I supposed to do with them?"

There's a pulse of power. The Fury's voice is streaked with impatience.

"You can think of no use for such a tool? Women who can march without stopping to rest? Men who do not need to eat? Soldiers who do not fear their enemy's sword, because they *know* they will rise again the next night? If you do not see their value . . ."

"No, I understand." You speak quickly, not daring to risk losing a gift from the gods. "I'm sorry. I was thinking of my own soldiers. How do we explain this? Watching people rush to their death over and over again . . ."

The Fury's horned head twitches in the soldiers' direction.

"Do they not watch their horses do the same?"

It is the kind of question only a creature from another world would ask. One who does not understand the fears of mortals. "It's not the same. We are taught that the phoenixes die because it is their nature. They do not suffer. It is what they were born to do."

That dead, rattling laughter sounds. "Oh, fire-child. What do you know of how they suffer? If that logic helps, hold to it. The revenants are the same. It is their *nature* to die and rise again. It is in the very word that defines them. Your soldiers will understand."

No, they won't. Not easily, but you know better than to press back.

"I accept them gladly."

The Fury nods. "Use them well."

You avoid meeting their empty stares. It is difficult to not search for Quinn in their lifeless faces. Are these soldiers the same as her? Gifts from below? Somehow, Quinn was always more alive than this. Even feeling unsettled, the general in you sees their utility. Soldiers who cannot die. New soldiers breathe to life in your mind. There are so many possibilities.

"What happens to them after the war?"

The Fury considers that. "I suppose you could breed them? Like the phoenixes."

A shiver runs down your spine. *You could breed them.* It is not the first disconnect you've felt with the gods. It is not in their nature to care about humanity. You forget that they exist in a realm ruled by blood and bone and worse. But you have not forgotten that it was their cruelty that won your people the Empire. Where would you be without them?

Somewhere better.

Your eyes widen. The Fury stands in silence. The revenants are still. Etzli stands at the edge of the clearing, well out of range. Who spoke? What was that voice?

It takes effort to center yourself. Your eyes fix on the skull's moonlit horns.

"Do not fear. I will find a use for them."

The Fury cannot see your unsmiling face.

6

PROPAGANDA

ADRIAN

I've heard plenty of stories about Imelda Beru.

One of the most gifted alchemists in our generation. We didn't do a ton of prep work for her before the Races, but I studied a few of her homemade videos. Forgotten rebirths were her specialty. Ancient combinations that had slipped through the cracks of time. I watched the footage after the Races, too. It won't be long before her Changing Skies rebirth becomes a wartime staple.

But it was on the third day that she revealed her best trick. She became the first person in history to actively escape the Races instead of trying to win. Centuries of riders, but she was the only one who'd ever thought to steal a belt full of the Empire's most valuable components. Always thought she gave up a few days too early. She was clearly talented enough to compete.

As I take a seat in her family's home, the decision makes more sense. Their kitchen is small. Four mismatched chairs

surround a table with a scarred top. Cabinets have missing handles. The couches are worn thin by family members
always looking for a place to rest. I can see there's beauty
in this place, the warmth of family. But it's also clear why
Imelda decided to take what the Ashlords never planned on
giving her.

Something out of nothing. I can respect that.

My soldiers march six people out of two bedrooms.
Imelda's mother and father. The mother keeps a firm hand
on the shoulder of Imelda's younger brother, a feather of a
boy named Prosper. I'm surprised when the kid waves at
me. I just barely catch the words he whispers to his father.

"It's *actually* him."

That has me smiling. Flattery never hurts. Next is the
face from the window. The boy with the camera. He's followed by a man and a woman who must be his parents,
judging by how many of the same features echo from face
to face. I take note of the defensive postures. One of my
soldiers leads the boy to the table. He's forced to take a
seat, a little rougher than necessary. Old Trask already confiscated his camera. I can hear the soldiers in the street,
watching the footage, making a ruckus about it. Martial
tried to explain who the kid was, but I prefer to do my own
digging.

"What's your name?"

"Farian Rahm."

I'm a little surprised by the edge in his voice. I thought
the kid would be nervous. I was wrong. He doesn't lower
his eyes, because he's not nervous at all. He looks downright mad.

"We need to know why you were filming. Want to make sure you're not a spy."

He folds his arms defensively. "You got me. Trained by the Quespo. I'm a sleeper agent that they planted in this town. I've been waiting here my whole life just to spy on you."

A throat clears behind us. I glance back. Both of the mothers look furious with him. The fathers, on the other hand, look a little proud. My eyes cut back to Farian.

"You've got the same attitude as Oxanos."

The accusation lands. Farian looks away, shakes his head.

"Look. I was just filming. It's what I do. It's what I did. Before the war."

I nod. "Martial told us you worked with Imelda."

"Martial talks too much."

There's so much rage beneath the surface that he can't even pretend to like me to save his own skin. It's honestly a little refreshing. Even in a marching army, the politics get tiring.

"I'm just trying to clear you," I remind him. "You don't have to like me. I know my people haven't done you any favors. Not yet at least. We just have to make sure you're not with the Empire."

He makes a disdainful noise. "You're no different. Look at what happened in Vivinia."

I shake my head, trying to sound certain. "That wasn't our army."

"And you can prove that? Longhands. You like to pretend we have a common enemy or something. The Dividian aren't welcome in the Reach, either, are they?"

He sits there, waiting for an answer. I consider lying. Throwing back the same propaganda we've put out since the start of the war. The Reach is our home to the north. Every pamphlet and radio broadcast claims that Dividian people like Farian can go there and start a new life, as long as they swear off their allegiance with the Ashlords. But I know that the new life we're really promising is a spot on the front lines of the next battle. I know that most Longhands look down on the Dividian people. They always have.

"That's what I thought," Farian continues. "I've seen how you treat us. We're just another piece on the game board. I saw what you did to Imelda during the Races, too. Do you seriously think we're partners or something—"

Farian's mother interrupts. "Please, Farian. There's a time and a place."

He lowers his eyes again. This time the quiet holds. I'm trying to figure out what to say when the front door opens. Trask peeks inside. "A word, Adrian?"

Farian doesn't meet my eye as I slide free of the chair, out into the street. Trask closes the door behind us. There's a circle of soldiers around the camera. Kenly Knox is the first one to look up.

"That was one hell of a tackle, General."

There's a chorus of agreement. Trask snatches the camera from them. I observe as the soldiers scatter back to their posts and he resets the footage. "Watch."

"I was there," I complain. "It's me in the video."

"Just watch."

It's a bright opening shot. The lighting is flawless. I stand in the street with Martial Rava. Farian's footage captures the moment I turn, the exact moment Oxanos escapes from my two soldiers. I have a feeling most photographers would have changed their focus. Scramble to film what was happening down the road. He resists that temptation.

His camera fixes on me.

I've never seen myself in this moment. It's strange to see the change that echoes through my face. The darkness that forms in my eyes. The promise of violence. The sight makes me shiver.

Farian slows the frames down. His camera captures everything. The way my feet dig into the dusty street. The sudden flexing of my arms. The way my eyes hone in on their target. Farian speeds the footage back up for my sprint. It has the pleasant effect of making me look like a strike of lightning. But then he freezes the footage again as I make contact. It's brutality in its purest form.

"That footage is worth five hundred soldiers," Trask whispers. "I would trade every town we've captured this week for what you hold in your hands."

I frown. "It's well made, I suppose."

Trask almost laughs. He gestures to the nearest soldiers. "Footage like that can win wars. Look at the reaction of your own crew. Kenly was rolling his eyes at you about thirty clockturns ago. And now? He's singing your praises to the rest of the company. It's easy to forget what you pulled off in the Races. War can do that to a man, Adrian. We lose things along the way. All the reasons we marched out in the first place start to slip through our fingers. Until we're reminded."

A little chill works down my spine. His words echo what

Daddy has always said. That was the point of sending me down to the Races. *Show them what we can do.* And unspoken behind those words: *even if it means you don't come back alive.* Trask nods at Imelda's house.

"We need to get this footage out. As soon as possible. Soldiers will rally around moments like that. Anything that gives us a reason to be brave the next time we ride into battle."

After a moment of thinking, I nod. "That's fine. Send the footage."

Trask signals the nearest soldier. "Oh, and I have one other suggestion. . . ."

I march back into Imelda Beru's house. I think about the girl I stood beside in the Hall of Maps. She was sharp-eyed. Was she already planning her escape then? I wouldn't mind someone like her working with us in all of this. Martial claimed she's working with the Longhand army up in the mountains, but I'll have to send some letters to see if there's any truth to that.

For now, I focus on the people she left behind.

"Farian. I have a proposition for you."

He looks up, a little curious. Good. I can work with curious.

"Your footage was brilliant. I've cleared you . . . so that you can come with us."

Curiosity echoes into surprise, only to be drowned in annoyance. I know the last thing he wants to do is march off with a company of Longhand soldiers. Trask suggested

I appeal to his sense of family. Offer their lives in exchange for his services. I knew that wouldn't work. It'd just hammer his bitterness down a little deeper. There's a better way.

"I want to hire you. Film our battles. The footage will be viewed by a national audience. We don't have much common ground, but I think we can both agree that the Ashlords can't be allowed to rule us the way they have all these years. Someone has to put a stop to the Empire they've created. This is your chance to say something about that. I'd offer to put a switch in your hand, but let's be honest, it'd be a waste. This is the weapon you'll do the most damage with."

I set his camera down on the table.

"Up to you. We march in an hour."

As the ranks re-form, it's no surprise to see Farian striding out to join us. A soldier checks his packs, signals approval, and leads him to the phoenix that we confiscated from Oxanos. I'm surprised how uncomfortable he looks as he mounts. How could someone spend that much time filming Imelda Beru and *not* know how to ride?

Orders sound. The march begins.

We're trotting past farmland when the second piece of Trask's plan falls into place. He noticed what I didn't. An affection between Martial and Farian. For some reason, the old champion acts like the boy's guardian. Martial's shouts reach us before he does.

"Farian! What are you doing?"

The nearest soldiers reach for weapons. I give a quick shake of my head. Pretty sure that'd only stoke the flames.

Martial can't kill an entire company, but I'd bet good money he could hack through four or five soldiers before we put him down.

Besides, this isn't our fight. This one belongs to Farian.

He calls back. "They hired me to film the battles."

Martial is furious. "You can't be serious."

"No one ever thinks I'm serious!"

"You're marching into a war! People are going to be shooting at them. Which means people are going to be shooting at you. This isn't some stupid alchemy tutorial, Farian. It's your *life*."

And Martial makes his first mistake. It seals Farian's decision. I can see the way his face hardens into stone. "Exactly. This isn't just another *stupid* tutorial. This is my chance to make a real film. No more reading Ashlord histories and pretending that's how it happened. I get to tell the real story in this war. Leave it alone, Martial. I'm going."

The determination in his voice is iron-struck. Martial must hear it, too, because he takes aim at me instead. "What the hell did you tell him? What'd you say?"

"All I did was give him a choice."

Martial curses under his breath. He looks ready to take a swing at me. It doesn't matter, though. The kid is coming. Now it's time to see if Trask was right. I play our final card.

"You have a choice, too," I remind Martial. "Want to keep him safe? Come with us."

There's another string of hissed curses. The old champion paces his horse behind us in silence for the next few turns. I decide not to push him too hard. He knows the cost of his decision, the weight of all this. It's up to him now.

I hear a firing get-get. Martial races up on our right. I watch the way his body perfectly matches the rhythm of his horse. All these years later, and he's still a champion through and through. Can't teach a man to ride a horse like that. Either you're born with it or you aren't.

He passes us and I can't help shouting after him.

"What will it be, Martial?"

He pulls out of his gallop. Just long enough to throw a brutal stare in my direction. There's an unspoken agreement in that look. I can almost hear his voice in my head.

If the boy dies, I will kill you.

The words he speaks are slightly less violent.

"It'll be good to see the capital again," he shouts. "I'll fetch my switch."

7

BLOODSWORN

IMELDA

Our little prince won't stop crying.

I almost pity him. I know what it's like to open a door you can't close. The moment I jumped that barrier during the Races, Imelda Beru ceased to exist. From that point on, I was always going to be the Alchemist. An outlaw who stole from the Empire. A wanted criminal.

I can't go back. And neither can the prince.

His tears are a confirmation. We stand on the doorstep of history. Only the gods know where that first phoenix went. The creature should have fallen to its death. Instead, it walked out into thin air and was suddenly, impossibly *gone.* One secret usually leads to another. The little prince is heaving sobs in the castle courtyard because these secrets were never meant for the likes of us. I'm so excited that I have to pace around the room to keep from shouting.

Bastian is my opposite. He broods silently in the corner of the room. He's removed his hardware arm. I watch as he patiently polishes every gear and piston. I've noticed that he only does this when events are spinning out of his control. It's a bone-deep fear that drives him to perform a task he knows he can finish.

I keep trying to catch his eye. I want to tell him that everything is going to be fine. This is more than worth the risk. Except he won't look my way. It's only when Cora Rowe bumps my shoulder that I stop waiting for him to act like an adult.

"We're losing daylight, kid," she says.

I don't point out that we're the same age. Instead, I nod an all-ready. We cross over to our assigned stalls. It took a lengthy debate to settle on a proper plan. Bastian decided three riders should go. He's got the right idea. A crew that size can make a stand *or* make a run for it, depending on where the horses go. After all, we might end up traveling straight into enemy territory.

Anything could happen. My smile widens. That's half the fun.

The third person joining us is Briar. Bastian volunteered first, eyes avoiding mine, but the crew drowned that idea in an uproar. No chance. Losing him risked all our connections. Besides, no one is going to let their fearless leader die before they do. No honor in that.

When he realized he wasn't going, his eyes burned in my direction.

"Fine," he eventually said. "Briar will go."

Briar's an old hand. He's been rebelling since before most of this crew was born. Neither of Bastian's choices are particularly subtle. Cora Rowe is the quickest pistol in the group. Briar is the kind of man who knows twenty ways to kill a person. Once, I heard the old man claim he dresses in black because he's always on his way to someone's funeral. If I'm to walk into unknown territory, might as well do it with dangerous folks at my side.

"Let's get on with it," I announce. "Blood first."

It took all morning to figure out how the rebirths work. The first piece that fell into place was the realization that most of the ashes weren't *complete*. The prince refused our questions after his first mistake, but it was too late to matter. This is my specialty. Hours of research went into every video that Farian and I created. Hand me the original sources and I'll find the answers.

A little digging led to the one missing ingredient: blood.

I take my place at the edge of my chosen stall. Briar stands on my right, Cora on my left. It was Cora who figured out how to prepare the blood. She noticed the matching notches in the sidewall of each stall. Imperfections have no place in typical Ashlord design. A tug on the notch revealed their purpose. A device for siphoning blood, hidden in the wall.

More secrets.

Now each of us lowers our devices from the wall. The room is silent except for the scrape of ancient stone. They remind me of the fold-up tables that cheap restaurants use to save space. Only these aren't cheap. They were designed with great care. The top edge kisses the opposite wall, leveling the table perfectly at hip height.

Each table has two distinct features. The first is the siphon. Gravity pulls the metal contraption downward. It aims the device at the very center of our gathered ashes. A second slot sits in the right corner. It's the size and shape of my thumb. Nestled inside, a delicately beautiful knife.

Briar makes an appreciative noise as he picks his up. "These are probably worth a fortune."

"Finders keepers," Cora reminds him. "Do we just cut anywhere?"

I recite from memory. "Horizontal, across the tip of your right forefinger."

"Ho!" Briar crows. "That's sharp."

"It is a knife, dear," Cora says.

Her brother—Harlow—adds from behind us, "Aren't you a famous outlaw?"

Briar lets out a low laugh. "Remind me to show you how sharp it is, Harlow."

I take up my own knife and make a careful slash across my finger. Briar's reaction failed to prepare me. It is pure fire. The blade slips mercilessly across. I give my next instructions through gritted teeth. "Now, hold the blood over the center of the siphon."

"Really?" Cora replies with false surprise. "I'm so glad you're here to instruct us, dear. I was just going to splash the blood all over the walls."

I smile at the dig. A few days ago, they'd only talk to me if they needed help with alchemy. It's kind of nice to be in on the joke, even if it's being thrown my direction.

"At least five drops," I instruct. "Then put the siphon away."

The quiet holds as we make our counts. I note the discolorations around the rim of my siphon. Centuries of blood dripping down. To what end? Once it's done, I push the siphon table back into the wall. There are echoes from the other stalls.

"Bandages now."

We turn away from the ashes. The stolen journal was firm on this point. It was a handwritten note, added later. It read simply: *Do not offer them more blood than you must.*

Hell of a warning. I decided not to share that particular line with Bastian. It would have led to more questions than answers, and I am here for answers.

Cora's brother wraps her finger, laughing about the fact that she's always got to be the first one to do anything. Devlin—still in his monk-like robes—attends to Briar's wound. He pretends he's giving last rites. It's a surprise to see Bastian striding forward to help me.

His voice is quiet. "I suppose there's no chance of talking you out of this."

"There could be treasures. Countless riches. Ever think of that?"

He nods. "Countless riches. Or unspeakable horrors. The Ashlords glitter in sunlight, Imelda, but underneath . . . they are brutal people who worship brutal gods. Don't forget that."

Bastian takes my hand. He sets it against the base of his metallic arm, then uses the other hand to dab away the drips of blood. He winds a bandage carefully around. His eyes are fixed on his work until they aren't. Until we are looking at each other with a bare-bones sort of honesty, less than a breath apart. I do not look away.

"I am not as helpless as you think I am."

His mouth shapes a grin. "Trust me, I know. That's half the problem."

The rest of the crew waits on us. He releases my hand.

I pretend to eye his work. "Passable."

The wounded face he makes has me laughing.

"Just snacking on you." And then in a whisper, only for him, "I'll come back."

He bites his lip and for just one lightning strike of a second, he is a boy. A helpless boy with tangled hair and wide blue eyes and far too many scars. This boy can't be an outlaw. He's too young. We're too young. Far too young to storm castles and defy gods and fight in wars we never asked for. He notices the way my eyes settle on his parted lips. His grin widens a little. Half the time I want to kiss him. The other half I'm tempted to kick him in the shins.

Sometimes I want to do both.

Bastian nods once. I force myself to turn away before I do something as stupid as tell him how I feel. I can hear his steady breathing—a match with my own heartbeat—as I step inside the stall. It takes a moment to gather my thoughts. I need to stay focused.

"Now, sunlight," I command. "Mount up."

I repeat the same motion from the day before. There's a catch on the front of the stall that groans before letting the barrier slide down and out of sight. It slams forcefully beneath my feet as sunlight slashes into the stall. I have to shield my eyes as the brightness catches my ashes for the first time. A contained storm thunders to life. Great gusts whip at my clothes. Sunlight fractures in blinding patterns. I don't look up until I hear the gasp.

My phoenix comes to life.

Like the first horse, his base coat is midnight. Glowing patterns flash in and out of existence like lightning shaking down from the sky. I didn't notice it the first time, but there's an undeniable strangeness to the creature. It looks wilder, somehow more raw than other horses I've ridden. Almost as if the rebirth has forced the creature back to what the phoenixes once were, before we spent centuries grooming and training them. The strangest part, though, is that I can feel its heart beating in time with mine. I find myself nodding. It must have worked. My blood has tangled with the ashes, merged in some unspeakable way with this creature.

Bloodsworn.

Cora's voice draws me back. "Should we start?"

My throat is dry. "Yes."

I'm quick with the bridle and saddle, fearful the phoenix will bolt off without me. He doesn't even twitch, though. He's patient, as if he's done this a thousand times before. Maybe he has.

A connection curls to life between us. It is stranger than what I've felt with most phoenixes. Less like a thread and more like a river. Something deeply powerful, something dangerous. Either we will swim together or drown trying. As I tighten a final strap, the bright lightning flickers across his back and the image holds. It's like seeing the future. I swallow that thought before speaking.

"Everyone ready?"

Confirmations sound. I hear fear and excitement in their voices.

"See you on the other side."

A little suggestion from my knees. The phoenix raises his head and begins. Fear snakes through me. My heart pounds in my chest. What if I got something wrong? What if adding the blood somehow messed everything up? It's too late for fear. The horse steps out into thin air.

I can't help imagining what it would be like to *fall*. How the bright sun would chase our spinning forms and how the ocean would rise up to smash us on impact. We do not fall.

Instead, an entire world slips through our fingers.

And something else bursts to life. It's a full-on assault of the senses. The lighting changes first. Our gold-spun coastline traded for a drowning gray. Then the scent of the sea replaced by the smell of something burning. At first, I think I can still hear the waves against the cliffs. . . .

"What is that?"

The sound takes form. Hundreds of wolves howl at once. Somewhere in the distance? In my head? I start to turn before remembering that I'm mounted. A moment later, the sound dies. My horse takes in the new setting with disturbing calm. The blue pulses under his skin are even brighter on this unlit plain. It's an intense relief to see Cora and Briar appear. Both of them look disoriented. Cora scrambles to take out her pistol. Briar doesn't panic. He turns his horse in a careful circle and drinks in the strange landscape.

"Where the hell are we?" Cora asks.

No answers come to mind. The landscape has no familiarity to it. I see mountains rising in the distance, their peaks digging into the gray. They bear no resemblance to the Gravitas Mountains. There's no color or life to them at all. Dark clouds churn in a sunless sky.

That thought startles me. I can't remember the last time I saw a sunless sky.

Our bright red plains have vanished, too. Every trotting step of our horses kicks up charcoal dust. Briar speaks my thoughts. "It's almost like our world . . . but dead."

Cora gestures in the distance. "Guess we're heading there?"

It's south of us—or north? I didn't notice before, but there in the shadow of the distant mountains is a sort-of castle. The gates stand open. The towers are unlit. There's no movement.

"Sounds like a plan," I say. "Where's Bastian's flag?"

Briar fishes through his knapsack. Bastian thieved an Ashlord marching flag from our first battle together. The Empire's emblem is blacked out. He always does that with confiscated goods. It's a reminder that we're breaking the world they've made for us, one piece at a time.

It takes a minute for Briar to actually jam it into the ground. The top layers cough outward at his touch, more like ashes than soil. He presses down until the flag takes.

Now we have a marker of where we came in. "There's our origin point."

Cora nods. "How long do we have?"

"Until the sun sets in our world?" I reply. "Let's see if anyone's home."

The distance is deceptive. Overhead, lightning flashes. I'm nervous at first by how exposed we are, but the storm appears to be *above* the clouds. It's a small comfort. We start down the first slope. Still no signs of life. It's only as we reach the next hill that the castle walls begin to loom upward. The gates are still open. Cora has her pistol out. Briar is empty-handed, but I know the knife on his hip can become the knife in his hand in less than a wink.

Our horses snort nervously outside the castle walls. There's still no movement, and we finally see why. The city is full of corpses. A string of bodies guides us in like a bloody constellation. They are sort-of men. Patched together like odd puppets. It's hard to tell exactly what they are with how much the decay has already taken from them. Each one lies in a pile of ashes. There are great beasts among the fallen, but each one is abnormal. The heads of dogs attached to the bodies of hawks.

The scent of death only thickens as we move deeper into the city. I'm forced to pull my bandana up over my nose just to keep the worst of it out.

Some of the fallen were never alive. They're more like mechanisms. Strangely human, with arms and legs, but made from wooden clocks or re-formed engines. It is the strangest battlefield I've ever seen. Every new corpse leads me to the same conclusion. My stomach twists.

"I think I know where we are."

Either the others do not hear me or they're too shocked to respond. The dark streets lead us toward a city center. There are lifeless fountains, abandoned halls, empty balconies.

And the dead.

Cora breaks the silence. "Are you sure we should keep going? Whatever did this . . ."

Caution would be wise, but as we reach the main courtyard, I can see there's one last place to explore. Up a set of cobbled steps is the main building. A sort-of palace. The columns do not match. The windows are all a little off. Briar mutters something, but I can't stop myself. I have to know if I'm right. The final clue is waiting inside these walls.

Evidence of explosions darkens the halls. There are gaping wounds that expose the interior to the sky. All that gathered gray guides us on. "Imelda," Cora warns. "We need to get back."

We were never supposed to see this. I want to know why.

A final corner. There's a throne room. Of course. It is a palace, after all, no matter how makeshift. One look down that carpeted length and the final piece of the puzzle falls into place.

The secret room. The prince's fear. The way the horses *vanished* in front of our eyes. Our final clue sits on a distant throne, clinging to some final shred of life.

Cora curses. Briar's face is colorless. I'm the only one who keeps walking forward. This is where the battle was thickest. A defense of the throne room. I'm not sure who did this—or rather, who would *dare* to do this. Great creatures have been cast aside, jaws hanging open, rows of dagger-sharp teeth wasted. Each one is an oddity. Built from parts of this and parts of that.

My guess was right. The man on the throne has always been known in our world as a *collector.* The stories say he can find a use for anything. He's also known as the weakest of the Ashlord gods.

Blood pools at his feet. His eyes struggle to follow us. It's remarkable how much he looks like his priests. I wonder if that is a part of the magic. Does the symbol they take on change them over time? In our world, his priests wear the mask of a desert fox.

Cunning creatures that savor every morsel. Misers that bury and collect and gather. In this world, however, he is just a man. Armored strangely. Clawlike gauntlets extend from both hands.

He would look every bit a god if not for all the blood.

"We're in the underworld." My voice doesn't shake. "And that is the Hoarder."

The god favors us with a bloody smile. A final word rattles up his throat.

We watch as he takes his final breath.

8

ANOTHER WORLD

PIPPA

Daylight stretches over the valley and crowns the distant city with light.

Navassa.

It looks quiet from here, but you know the pearl-white walls hide their chaos well. Longhand soldiers will be storming every home, raiding every pantry. All the food stores will be counted up and locked away. An order of strict rations will follow. It is the only way to survive a siege. You stare at those distant walls until the crunch of boots announces a guest.

"General, might I request an audience?"

Bravos stands at a respectful distance. You know that he's been waiting for a private moment. There's always been soldiers marching around, or Etzli on hand to discuss battle formations. All the commotion has made it easier to ignore his intentions, but now there is no excuse. You turn around. He's dressed in his armor. Spots of dried blood decorate his gauntlets. You have not forgotten that he is beautiful, built for battle. He is the very prototype of what an Ashlord should be, from head to toe.

"Granted."

Bravos takes a deep breath. "I made a mistake."

"Out in the field? Feel free to file it in your official report."

"In the Races," he says firmly. "It was a mistake to betray you. I've known it since the day that I met you, Pippa. You are . . . better than me."

He bows his head. It is not false humility. He's admitting the truth that always sat between the two of you, a dark creature you tried to ignore. It is no small thing to confess.

"You are the better rider," he says quietly. "A better strategist. In the art of war, I am not your match. I might have a small edge in hand-to-hand combat, but overall, you are my superior. I thought I'd accepted that. Even if I had to live in your shadow, I thought it would be enough to be the person who stood at your side."

You are not sure how to reply. It is not the Ashlord way to be so honest, so open about one's faults. Nor is this some calculated effort. He simply wants your trust again.

"I know we are over," he says. "But I would prove myself loyal again. I am your soldier. I am yours to command. Every time I swing my sword, it is for you, General."

A cruel part of you whispers revenge. Leave him this way. March past him and let the wounds of his meekness fester. But you hear Quinn's voice in the back of your mind. You see her going back for Etzli, rope in hand, prepared to save the life of someone she didn't even know. And who are you, truly, if you have not learned how to reach down and help others back to their feet? Quinn would expect so much more from you.

"It is forgiven," you whisper. "It is forgotten. Mark this day, Bravos. We begin anew."

It is an old oath. Once, it was what kings would say to blood traitors. It is the closest thing you can summon to absolution. Bravos presses a fist to his chest. He knows the significance of your words. It's written in the way his shoulders straighten.

"We begin anew."

You stride forward and clasp his forearm. "Now, let's sack a city."

All morning, you've been discussing strategy with Etzli. At first, you were tempted to skip Navassa altogether. Set up a strong garrison in the passes and then keep moving north. Etzli was wise enough to dismiss that strategy. There are too many enemy soldiers inside the walls of Navassa, and no city to the north would provide you the same foothold. Win here and you'll have a base that allows you to lower your shoulder against the entire northern half of the Empire.

It will also give you an opening to cut off Adrian Ford's south-marching army. The move will leave him pinched between you and the larger force stationed near Furia. As long as they can hold him off a little longer, your most dangerous enemy will be forced into the jaws of an inescapable trap. Your armies will pin him there and bleed him until he's left lifeless.

Until the war is won.

But first Navassa must fall. Your eyes flick over the valley again. Bravos quietly explains what he and Revel accomplished last night. There were seven watchtowers between your camp and the city. Four have been burned to the ground. The other three fly the Empire's colors. All their evening play has forced the Longhand army back inside the city gates.

Now it's just about breaking their defenses. You sent Revel north. Around the city to do some hunting. Any desperate supply caravans must be routed. You know the Longhands will have sent their panicked requests back after losing the valley passage. Smuggle in one more shipment and they'll be able to last three times as long. You will not risk that happening.

Especially not when you are aiming to take the city in *days.*

Bravos follows you eagerly. Etzli stands at the entrance to the command tent.

"Come, let's look at the city maps again."

All three of you enter the command tent together. Prince Ino sits at the far end of the table, yawning while looking down at the maps. You hoped he would not bother to wake up for the meeting, but he's waiting and prepared to be a thorn in your side. Bravos takes the seat beside him.

The only other figure in the room is Mother's mouthpiece. The Curiosity's servant waits there, sharp-eyed and silent. You've been tasked with making the first draft of a plan. And she will make any minor corrections needed.

Four maps are sprawled across the command table. You can't help praising the Brightness's provisions. Five years ago, architects were hired to collect geographical data. You remember hearing about it at the time, but you were too busy training to pay attention to the details. The hired hands created blueprints of every major city, even a few of those firmly in Longhand territory. Naturally, the Ashlord generals are the only ones with access to the maps.

"Pretty standard defenses," Etzli notes, her finger tracing an exterior wall. She's a little shorter than you, slighter of frame. A finger-thin scar runs down from the corner of her right eye and narrows to a point. In the light of the sun, it looks like a glinting blade. "The northern gates are all sturdier. It's an Ashlord city, after all. Naturally the fortifications facing the Reach are the strongest. Everything on our side of the city is more exposed. Our only issue is the actual gates."

Bravos grunts. "Livestone."

"Updated three years ago," Prince Ino confirms, stifling another yawn. "The Striving's temple is the largest one in Navassa. She has even more patrons here than the Fury does. Aside from the capital, it is the most modern city in the Empire. There are livestone gates and sentry cannons. It's all very advanced."

"How did we lose a city with livestone gates?" Etzli asks the right question, as always.

"From the inside," Ino answers, a little annoyed. "There was an established network of spies. The Reach knew what they were doing. I believe they put most of their resources into Navassa. Must have known it would be a crucial swing city. It wasn't *our* fault, really. . . ."

You do your best not to roll your eyes. Any royal of a

proper age is assigned a role in the Empire. Prince Ino has long worked with the question police—or the Quespo. The Empire's network of spies and informants. Much good that his work did in *this* particular city. He forgets that Ashlords do not make excuses, or mistakes for that matter.

"We might do well to hold the central pass," Ino concludes. "Post a solid crew there and march the rest of the army back to the south. We'll be more useful that way, and the Longhands stationed in Navassa will be wasted."

You're already shaking your head at that plan. The Fury did not give you a gift so that you could retreat. His timing is significant. You are intended to move forward, to win Navassa.

"Etzli, show me the tunnels."

She came up with the idea after the Fury delivered his gift. Now it's just a matter of selling Prince Ino on the one thing he believes in more than all else: the providence of the gods. One of the commissioned maps details the sewers and industrial tunnels beneath the city. Most lead down to buried chambers well below the surface. Impossible to access. But by Ashlord law, there is one tunnel that breaches the surface.

"This location is to the west," Etzli notes. "I would never send normal soldiers down there. The four pipes are stacked together. According to the annotations, each one is about this wide." She holds up her fingers to display the width. "I would barely fit, and I am slighter than most. Combine that with the distances this requires one to crawl through the dark, breathing in those fumes . . ."

Prince Ino frowns. "No one would survive that. Not for long."

You correct him. "Etzli said no *normal* soldier would survive."

Bravos glances over curiously. He knows you well enough to know this is all setting up something larger. Prince Ino takes the bait. "Are you in possession of a different type of soldier?"

You smile. "We had a visitor last night. He left me a gift."

You take some satisfaction in the prince's shock. The emotions flicker over his face in perfect sequence. A little joy, a touch of jealousy, and then hunger.

"Which god?"

"The Fury."

Bravos rattles his knuckles on the table. His face is split in a wide grin. A soldier like him knows all the stories. Your people are raised to repeat history, because history has always favored you. His excitement is contagious. Like a boy preparing to open presents on Sacrifice Day.

Ino's enthusiasm is more polished. "Show me."

You lead the way through the back of the command tent. Bravos lets out giddy laughter. You're reminded—briefly and painfully—that he once laughed with you that way. It's a thought that you burn. That world no longer exists. He is your soldier now. You are his commander. There is less than nothing romantic between you. Only the sound of your voice issuing a command and the obedience of his body. Nothing more.

"The Fury called them *revenants.*"

Your gifted army waits behind the command tent. All night they stood statue-still. You thought that might frighten your actual soldiers, so you asked them to pretend to go about camp duties. Their preparations look forced, but it's better than the empty stares.

Sunlight doesn't help the facade. It only serves to expose their strangeness. They move like normal soldiers. They are dressed in the same uniforms. They wield the same weapons and tools. At a glance, you might believe they were an average battalion, going about the business of preparing for the day's march. But a closer look reveals the colorless eyes. Skin like wax. Even their movements are telling. There's a brief delay, almost like the pause between a string's flex and the moment the puppet raises its arm. You do not know how these revenants were created. You do not intend to ask. The only thing that matters now is that they're yours.

So you own them now? Do you truly believe that?

That voice echoes in the back of your mind, full of doubt. You frown at how much it sounds like Quinn. It takes a moment to refocus. This is how you will win Navassa.

"How many did he give you?" Bravos asks.

"One hundred."

Ino frowns. "A strange gift. In the Helio Wars, the magic of our gods swallowed entire cities. The Fury would ride into battle with us on the back of a giant sunwolf. These are just one hundred of them. Won't they just die?"

"They will," you answer. "But each night, they'll rise again. Like the phoenixes."

Ino's next complaint dies on his lips. His eyes widen at

the possibilities. Bravos is laughing like a maniac. Etzli's voice is calm. "A useful tool."

You find yourself nodding. "Especially in my hands."

Only one opinion *actually* matters. You turn around to the Curiosity's priest, who has been hovering in the background all this time. There's a brief delay before the eyes light with power once more. The deity speaks, and you can hear your mother's smirk in the voice.

"It is a good plan. Make sure to have the cavalry paint their shields black. Otherwise, you have the Empire's approval. Well done, Daughter."

It's satisfying to hear those words, although you should have thought of the paint. Always missing one little detail. Prince Ino asks another question, and you're a little surprised by the distance of his voice. It's like someone calling from the other end of a valley. You turn. Ino is there one moment and then he's gone the next. You feel the world spinning in violent circles. Your first instinct is poison. Who would betray you?

But as you look around . . .

. . . you find yourself standing in an entirely new world. It is the world from your dreams. The charcoal plains and the starving mountains. Looming gray clouds overhead. And the face before you does not belong to Prince Ino.

It's Quinn.

In every dream, the girl moved and spoke, unaware of you. Even when you called out to her, she would never turn. Quinn's mismatched eyes never locked on yours. Until now. She offers that familiar, lopsided grin. "It worked."

"What worked?"

"You're here."

Here. You do not like the taste of that word, especially the more you look around. It is the colorless world of your dreams. This is not a *here* you would ever agree to visit.

"What is this place?"

Quinn grins. "Your people have many names for it."

It takes effort to focus. You trace back through the conversations you and Quinn had during the Races. Your parents raised you on memory exercises. You were trained to never forget a word. All those quiet moments with Quinn rise to the forefront of your mind.

"This is the Realm of the Gods."

"The underworld," Quinn supplies. "Your gods call it Heaven. My people call it Hell."

You're considering her words—and the idea that you might *actually* be here—when you finally notice what Quinn is doing. She's spread out what looks like a pile of ashes. She traces strange patterns in the pile, and the substance in her palm is finer than sand, as dark as . . .

"Is that blood?"

Quinn nods. "The final ingredient."

You're having trouble breathing. When the Races ended, you accepted that you would never see her again. The girl was a gift. It did not matter how much you admired her. The Madness was always going to draw her back to this world. Quinn's final words confirmed it. She was coming here to run her own race. At the time, you didn't understand what she meant.

"What are you making?"

"A storm."

You can't help shaking your head. The girl has never made any sense. It reminds you of the first time she appeared. You asked how she got there and she told you that she rode the lightning. Her strangeness amused you at the beginning. Now it worries you.

Quinn gestures in the distance. You thought the plains empty, the mountains vast and unpopulated. But as your eyes trace the path of her finger, you can see that isn't true. There are buildings. Or rather there are ladders. Elaborate ladders stretching down from the clouds. And there—at the very top—you see a city hammer-struck into the sky.

Impossible. "What is that place?"

Quinn doesn't answer. She's finished her crafting. You watch as she leans over the piled ashes, her lips forming a quiet circle. Air whispers out. She blows so softly that the answering roar nearly lifts you off your feet. Lightning forks down from above. Wind whips your riding hood against your neck. Quinn stands, watching with satisfaction, as a storm is born.

"We'll see each other again. Soon."

She doesn't look back. You shout after her—desperate for an explanation—but she marches toward that sky-strung city like a hopeful conqueror. The storm thrashes and dances and follows after her like a pet. You're trying to understand what is happening, why you're seeing this, when you hear another gasping sound. The noise draws your attention back to the ashes. You're standing well clear of the figure as it appears. The boots come first. And then the rest of his body colors to life.

It is a body you know well. A body you have dreamed about.

His arms are bronzed, darkened from marching under the Empire's sun. His shirt grasps at his arms and chest, slick with sweat. It has been a while since you last saw him. Not at the finish line, but in the dark of a shared carriage. You recall the heat in your hands. The rise and fall of his chest.

You have forgotten what it is like to stand on even ground with him. He is colossal, a statue of a human being. It is like watching a god come to life. A god who's leading armies against you.

As he steps clear of the ashes, your hand settles on the grip of your switch.

Adrian Ford blinks to life.

And his eyes settle on you.

9

ANOTHER BATTLE

ADRIAN

I'm walking down the hallway of our borrowed headquarters, about to enter the command room, when something massive *crashes* into my side. It hits like the punch of an anvil. Arms snake around me, tightening like a vise, and all the breath sucks from my lungs. A roar sounds in my ears. It is a familiar roar.

"Adrian Ford! I dare you to get out of this one!"

I can hear my attacker already panting. I let out a laugh, but his choke hold strangles it. His grip is solid, his footwork is good, but he forgets that I'm no longer a boy. A flex of my shoulders widens his grip just enough to snake an arm through his headlock. I break the hold, clasp his forearm, and twist around. There's a sharp yelp of pain as I come face to face with a grinning bear of a soldier. My guards are farther down the hall, unsure if they're supposed to help. After all, they've spent their whole lives taking commands from this boy's father.

"Forrest Trask." I pin him against the wall. "What is that hideous thing on your face?"

He grins back. "It's called a beard. You'll eventually be able to grow one when your—"

I twist again, cutting off his sentence, and both of us break out laughing. The moment I release him, he rushes forward to wrap me in a bone-crushing hug. After tackling Oxanos, I'm a little bruised, but this is a reunion I don't mind. Forrest Trask is my oldest childhood friend. We stole horses and raced them. We explored the neighboring mesas, nearly getting attacked by sunwolves once for our troubles. Now we're both a few feet taller, a pair of boys forced to play the part of soldiers.

"What are you doing here? I thought you were heading for Navassa."

He shakes his head. "We got cut off. The Ashlords were already through the pass."

That's bad news. Pippa is moving faster than expected. I nod once before clapping a hand on his shoulder. "At least it brought you to us. It's good to have you, Forrest."

"I know command is waiting for you, but we need to have a drink later. You and I have a great deal to catch up on, old friend. What do you say?"

That has me laughing. "A drink?"

Forrest shrugs. "Several drinks."

I laugh again. "We're marching at dawn."

"All the more reason to enjoy ourselves tonight."

This is the Forrest I remember. Always up for an adventure. Always ready to take risks. Even all these years later, that grin on his face is the one I saw a thousand times as a child.

"Drinks," I agree. "But we have to get through this meeting first."

"And by then, we'll need a drink anyways." He claps my shoulder in return. "Come on. It's been too long since I had to listen to these old crones talk of war."

Half smiling, we enter the command room. It's a gathering of some of our greatest generals, but Forrest's point is not lost. Some of these fighters are old enough to have marched in the last rebellion. The room falls silent. I gesture to Forrest, who recounts his news from the center of the Empire. It does not take long for debates to break out.

"I can't believe she has Navassa under siege. . . ."

"Tessa will hold her off for a while."

"And if she doesn't?"

"Then Antonio harasses her from the west. His crew already took Locklin."

"Locklin? I thought it was unconquerable."

"It *was* the unconquerable castle. If she wins Navassa— and that's a *huge* if—she'll have to march north of the delta to cut us off. That's a long way from home. She'll be exposing Furia. If we swing inland quick enough, she'll never make it back in time for support. Besides, our intelligence says the capital has its hands full right now. Dividian soldiers are on the verge of a strike. Didn't take the Vivinia news well. And they heard we pay more in our army, so they wanted to leverage that. . . ."

I nod and listen, nod and listen. Forrest was one of

several messengers to arrive before sunset, their phoenixes bursting into flames as they dismounted. Half the problem with fighting a war is information. By the time news of a victory reaches us, the same army might have already suffered a crippling defeat. One scout says Pippa is stymied outside of the Steppes. But Forrest tells us she's knocking on Navassa's gates. The whole thing is a mess.

The Empire uses broadcasting to relay some of its news, but they know better than to risk passing sensitive military information through the Chats. Even the subtlest messages can be decoded and weaponized. It's an ongoing battle for information, against misinformation.

It is the one arena I do not care for. I'd much rather face my foes with a real weapon in hand. After more bickering, Old Trask attempts to point the conversation back to our original argument. "We've got our own decision to make. Furia to the east. Grove to the west."

The coastal town of Grove isn't more than a slash of ink on the map. It's known for being the home of the biggest armada in the Empire. All twelve ships of them. When the Dividian arrived centuries ago, their fleet numbered in the hundreds. But the Ashlords defeated them and only the best ships were kept. The rest were set on fire. Rumor has it that you can dive into the coves off the coast and find the charred masts dragging the sea bottom. Buried reminders of the very first war.

Now the city is a thorn to us. We know the army stationed there isn't formidable. A bunch of merchants' sons. But the ships could sail them up the coast. It wouldn't take much effort for them to land somewhere north to cut off our supply lines *and* our path of retreat. If they timed it right, they could force us to fight on both fronts. They've held their ground for now, according to our scouts, but the second our banners start marching that way, they'll slip off.

Either way, it's a waste of our time and our people.

Forrest catches my bored stare and offers a wink. He leans into the conversation, perhaps hoping to liven it up. "I say we take Grove. Make it quick and clean."

It won't be quick and it won't be clean. I know that much. I smile at his enthusiasm before glancing over at Old Trask. The two are clearly kin. Forrest's beard is thick, but it can't hide the long nose and narrow eyes he's stolen from his father. I'm glancing between them when something strange happens. My vision distorts. Old Trask's nose loses its shape. The silver in his beard fades. His hair grows longer and his skin darkens a shade.

I can feel my heart rising into my throat when the entire world snaps clean away. It's like a fire whispering out of existence. Ashes. There are ashes everywhere. Overhead, the sky sips on darkness. Empty plains stretch out in every direction. Lightning flashes. A storm wall rises in the distance. I have to fight to keep my breathing steady and get my bearings.

My eyes find Trask. Except it isn't Trask.

"Pippa."

Her name whispers from my lips. She stands just ten paces away, already in a fighter's stance, her switch transformed into the standard Ashlord blade. Her dark hair is up in a soldier's knot. It hasn't been that long, just a few months, but I can see how war has touched her. It is in the dark regard of her eyes. The cautious tilt of her chin. The way every muscle stands ready for a fight.

I have not forgotten that she's a weapon. Her entire life has prepared her to ride and to rule and to put soldiers like me in the ground. But I'm too curious to reach for my own switch.

"Where are we?"

She returns with her own question. "How did *you* get here?"

My vision briefly doubles. I get a brief glimpse of a room full of tired generals discussing boring strategies, and then Pippa is standing in front of me again. More real than any of them.

I shake my head. "Something . . . it felt like someone pulled me here."

Pippa's eyes narrow. I can see the gears turning in her head. She knows something that I don't, but she doesn't exactly look eager to exchange notes. Makes sense. I'm not here to offer her advice, either. We're enemies, born and bred. She's marching an army against my people. I am marching an army against hers. We have no business to discuss. No common ground.

So why am I here? And where is here?

My eyes roam the surrounding nightmare. Maybe that's what it is. Could I have fallen asleep at the table? The colors here are all wrong. The landscape is dreadful.

"I must be dreaming."

Pippa lifts one eyebrow. "Am I often the subject of your dreams?"

Her words dig under my skin. I can't help scowling at that suggestion. I do not dream of my enemy. But I haven't forgotten the last time I saw her. We sat across from each other, even closer than we are now. In an unlit carriage, she stitched the wounds she'd given me at the end of the Races. I'd thought it a rare mercy. An Ashlord noble caring for a lowly Longhand.

She'd corrected that notion. I remember her explaining it was an ancient tradition. The champion tended the wounds of the defeated as a reminder that they'd been victorious and could win again if put to the test. The thought of that conversation has me smiling.

"I meant this place. It's too strange not to be a dream."

I reach up and slap a heavy hand against my cheek. I shake myself, trying to wake up at the table I left behind. It doesn't work. Pippa looks at me like someone who's spent too long in the sun.

"It isn't a dream."

I offer a slight grin. "A nightmare, then?"

"One would think so, considering that gods-awful smell."

I sniff the air. "It smells like ashes."

"I wasn't talking about *that* smell."

She offers no smile with the joke. It's more of a barb, and it takes a stretching moment to find the mark. I've been so focused on marching our army south. Winning new towns to our banners. I fight the heat rising in my cheeks. How long has it been since I had a proper wash?

"Is it really that bad?"

She reaches into a pocket with her off hand and brings flower petals up to her nose.

"Do they not have baths in the towns you're conquering?" she asks.

It's almost fun, this back-and-forth. It takes a moment for me to remember that I'm speaking with one of the bright young leaders of the Ashlord army. Her ancestors buried my mother, my uncles, countless others. Her people want to bury me. The thought sharpens my reply.

"The people we've liberated barely have food. Your army took all of it."

She catches the change in tone. I'm surprised how quickly her expression closes off. She wasn't smiling or laughing, but I hadn't realized how relaxed she was until now.

"And your armies? How do they eat? Did you not harvest your fields before marching? Are you not asking your citizens to ration food? I fail to see the difference."

It's a frustrating argument. One I've heard from the Ashlords before.

"Our farmers work with the army voluntarily. The Dividian aren't your citizens—they're your *servants*. Always have been." I can feel my pulse quickening. "Vivinia proves that."

Anger flashes on her face. "Vivinia wasn't us."

"Blood and fire." I aim her people's words back at her. "That's always been your way."

Before she can respond, another strike of lightning cuts the sky. It's so bright and loud that our argument is briefly swallowed by it. We both look up at the flash, and I finally notice the city. A series of towers in the sky, but as I trace their crescents downward, I notice they're not built on anything below. Ladders reach down from the walls, but there's no foundation.

And the storm hammers against the gates.

It takes seeing the impossible castle to understand. "No way I could dream that."

Pippa's eyes are on the storm. Her voice is quiet now.

"I told you. It is not a dream."

A shrill cry sounds. The noise sends shivers down my spine. I only hear it because of how high-pitched it is compared with the storm. All that thunder and boom. This sound is more like the crowing of a large bird. As we watch, darkness blooms above the city walls.

The entire sky grows black. I confuse it for a cloud at first.

Pippa's voice corrects me. "Birds."

And she's right. Thousands of birds are taking flight. Lightning thrashes at the first flock, bringing a few spiraling down. Hundreds more fly forward to fill the gaps. I watch their patterns, all that movement, and realize this is the scene of a battle. They're flying in formation. Against who?

I turn to Pippa, but the dream slips through my fingers.

A heavy hand slaps down on my shoulder.

"Adrian?" Forrest Trask is frowning. "Lost you there for a second. You all right?"

I nod to him, but my stomach turns. I press both palms against the wooden table to keep them from shaking. It takes concentration to look at Trask as the rest of the room spins. I'm aware that all eyes are on us. I keep my response short because I'm not sure how the words will come out. My mind feels like it's still dancing between this world and the other.

"Just thinking."

Old Trask smiles. "Enough of that for one night. Didn't you hear Kenly?"

My eyes swing to the entrance. Nausea threatens again. There's a figure standing by the door that looks soldier-shaped. I can't actually focus enough to see his face.

Trask speaks again. "It's your father. He's just arrived."

I smile at the words and pretend the room isn't spinning. It takes all my effort to rise. I look around at my generals, faking confidence. "Good. He can do the thinking for us."

Their laughter hides my slash of pain. Each step is a blow. I march over to the door, as steady as possible, and offer Kenly another smile. He leads me into the next room. My vision slowly settles. I can hear Daddy outside, already halfway through a story. I dig my feet into this world, trying to get rid of the nightmare vision that's still chasing me.

Daddy turns his trademark grin my way. The sun is setting over his shoulder. I do not glance upward, but as Daddy strides over to give me a hug, I catch a brief slash of that other world against my senses. A sky darkened by an army of birds. The throaty battle cries.

Somewhere below us, a war is raging.

10

THE LITTLE PRINCE

IMELDA

The god stares at us with lifeless eyes.

"Imelda," Cora is begging. "We need to leave. Now."

Briar is pacing the throne room anxiously. "She's right, Imelda."

"But this is one of their gods," I protest. "And he's *dead.*"

I can't keep the wonder out of my voice. I've only ever seen their priests, walking our world in their horrible masks. It was hard to imagine those creatures as powerful. My mind would not believe them actual representations of actual powers, even if I knew all the lore. We were all taught about what happened during the old wars. How their magic swallowed cities whole. How the gods offered the Ashlords gifts in exchange for their blood.

They've always been the difference. A great weight on the scale that tips everything in the Ashlords' favor. We have been kept in line—forced into servitude—because of them.

And now that we finally get to see one of the gods face to face, he's dead.

And if one god can be killed . . .

"Who killed him?" I ask, turning. "Who killed his servants? We have to find out."

"We have to stay alive," Cora replies. "That's all that matters right now."

"Agreed," Briar says. "We're running out of time. We can discuss this later, Imelda. What if one of the other gods comes? Better if we are not here. We need to get back to Locklin. Report this to Bastian. Otherwise, what we've seen dies with us."

It's the logical decision. Briar is right. If we die here, no one knows what really happened. That's one of the Ashlords' most popular tactics. Always controlling the story, writing history in their hand. We can't allow that to happen.

But thinking about going back to Bastian has me grinding my teeth. He won't let us return to the underworld. Not when Cora describes the bloodbath we saw. Or when Briar tells him about an actual deity gasping his last on a throne of bones.

"We'll have to convince him," I say, thinking. "Make him see how important this is."

Cora makes an impatient noise. "Look. I've tried being nice. I am asking you politely. Bastian gave *us* instructions. If you had so much as a scratch on you, he promised to skin us alive. So pardon the point of my pistol." My eyes widen as she brings the barrel up. "But I'm going to need you to march the hell back to your horse or I'll knock you out, pick you up, and carry you."

Briar's voice is calmer. "No need for that, Cora. Imelda was just leaving."

I nod quickly. "Right. Let's ride back."

Cora holsters the pistol and marches off. My heart is thundering. It's the first time someone has pointed a gun at me at that range. I try to shake the fear away as I follow Briar. The two of them pick up the pace, jogging back through the strange hallways. Our phoenixes are right where we left them. The bright pulses are coming less often now. It's another mystery, but we don't have the time right now to puzzle that one out, too.

Our pace out of the city is far faster. We've already witnessed the carnage. There's no need to linger now. Besides, I have a feeling these images will not leave us for some time.

Off to the west—or maybe the east—there's a storm forming. It makes me think about all the stories the Ashlords tell of the underworld. Most of them are supposed to be fictional—tall tales—but my mind traces through them now. Maybe something is hidden inside them.

None of the stories are for the faint of heart.

There's the young soldier—a trickster—who finds himself in the Butcher's stronghold. He guiles the god into trading several valuable possessions, then leaves at midnight, escaping without giving the god his due. His plan works, until he returns to our world and realizes the Butcher secretly stole his organs. The first step he takes back into our world is his last.

I remember a children's story about a boy and a girl who are lured into the Striving's palace and beg to use a new tool she's created, hoping to have it before anyone else. The god grants their hearts' desire. Only both of them wake up in our world and find themselves aged, an entire life having passed them by, but with the clever tools they sought in hand.

Every story goes that way. Cruel gods. Words of warning. Each memory stokes the fear rising in my chest. We are not explorers here. It is a world even harsher than our own. Ruled by the most powerful creatures to ever walk the known worlds. We need to get home.

Bastian's flag waves from the next hill. Briar and Cora have gone quiet, eager to leave as well. There are no signs of danger, other than the distant storm, but that doesn't mean we're in the clear. A shiver runs down my spine. It feels like eyes are watching us. When I look back, though, there's only the empty plains and the abandoned city. No one is here with us but the dead.

"How do we get back?" Cora asks.

I realize she trusted me enough to come here without knowing how to return. She thought I'd know. Even after having a gun pointed at me, I count this knowledge as a step in the right direction. "Wait for the horses to die, or ride back through the entry point."

Cora nods once. She digs her heels in, picking up speed. She aims her mount right at the flag, but a burst of light cuts her off. Before she can reach the entry point, someone else bursts through the gap between worlds. Cora screams, veering out of the way, as another horse stomps into existence. I'm expecting Bastian—no doubt angry with us—but the figure barrels on without hesitation. I realize the only reason he's not disoriented is because he's been here before.

It's the little prince.

He vaults away from us. His horse transitions from trot to gallop in a matter of strides. Briar shouts after him. Cora aims and fires, but the shot misses. I can see his hands are still bound. That doesn't stop him from riding like he was born on the back of a horse.

One thought pulses in my mind: *He can't escape.*

If he tells the gods, if he tells *anyone* what we know . . .

. . . we will be hunted. Slaughtered one and all. My horse senses my urgency, feeds off that instinct, and thunders down the hill. Cora fires her pistol. Briar shouts again. I ignore both of them. I have to catch the little prince.

Open plains roll ahead of us. It takes a second to match my phoenix's rhythm. I shape my body to fit with his movements, arrowing after the escaping prince. He rides well. No surprise there. But that doesn't change the fact that his hands are bound. It forces his upper body into an awkward relationship with the horse, especially as they push their speed.

I'm gaining on him.

He makes the mistake of looking back and loses another few paces. His eyes widen when he sees I'm on his tail. Did he expect us *not* to give chase? Maybe he thought he'd have help in this world for some reason? He aims for the valley to the right of the city. I'm not sure what his destination is, but it's odd that he doesn't ride for the Hoarder's city.

We reach the flattened plains. I spy movement to our right. My eyes trace the distant shapes and my heart beats faster. A herd of horses. It takes another breath to see what I didn't at first. None of the horses have riders. I thought the prince might have help coming. But he doesn't ride that way, so neither do I.

Now it's a game of gaining one length at a time. The slightest anticipation of his route. Angling to cut the barest corners. It has me about forty paces back and closing on him. A second glance shows the prince the truth. He will not escape.

I'm surprised how decisively he acts. He draws up out of his riding pose. I watch him raise his bound hands to his mouth, but the movement is hard to follow from my angle.

Will he turn and face me? I brace myself for contact. It's the only time I'd actually feel confident battling an Ashlord, even one so young. Zion was several years younger than me, and he danced circles around me during our training session. But this Ashlord's hands are bound.

And he's weaponless. I can beat him. I have to.

There's a jerking motion. It's almost like he's trying to rip the bindings with his teeth. He lets out a grunt of pain before spitting something out. Even in my focus, I frown. What is he doing?

The wall appears out of nowhere.

I'm just twenty paces back when an actual wall slams up between us. The speed with which it forms is impossible. Less like something built, and more like something that's growing out of the ground itself. It stretches left and right, cutting me off from the prince entirely.

Is this the gods interfering?

I don't hesitate. My eyes seek out the one weakness in the wall. Every proper gate has an entrance. There's a servant door built into the right side of the structure. I swing my horse that way, lowering against his neck. And then I urge him straight through it.

There's a scream. Wood splinters. Blood sprays, but the horse pushes on, smoke breathing from his lips. We're through the other side in an instant. The prince is twenty paces away, moving slower because he thought he'd escaped for good. His reaction is too slow this time.

He sees me right as I leap from my horse. My arms wrap around his shoulders. Momentum carries us over one side. We hit the ground hard, ashes pluming upward as I pin him beneath my weight. The knife at my hip finds its way to the base of his throat. My eyes burn a warning.

"Do not move."

I see his terror. It has me pulling back on the knife, shoving up to my feet. I forgot how young he is. All I saw was what he represents. I'm lucky I didn't break his neck with that tackle. I watch his chest heaving in the dust and realize his haircut looks like Prosper's.

That detail hits me hard.

"Calm down," I finally say. "I'm not going to hurt you."

He's almost hyperventilating. His horse watches without concern. My own mount has circled back around curiously. I'm not sure what to do with the kid now that I've caught him. I glance back.

No sign of Cora and Briar.

The wall is in the way. My eyes comb the structure. It's a strange sight. Half formed, as if someone tried building a wall but didn't have the material to finish it. The upper ramparts have gaping holes. It stretches seventy paces in both directions, ending in the same unfinished patterns. I should walk him back, get home, but I can't help asking the obvious question.

"Where'd this wall come from?"

He's breathing too hard to answer. I realize he's bleeding. There are a few scrapes on one side of his face, but most of the blood is pouring out from a massive gash beneath his thumb. It's a pretty nasty-looking wound.

"Let me take a look at that," I offer. "I have some bandages."

"*No!*"

He throws the word at me the way a toddler would. I'm reminded of when Prosper was younger and didn't want someone to play with his wooden horses.

"I was just trying to help. Come on, we're—"

But the worlds are dancing again.

I'm ready for the change this time. My vision shifts. Only the prince remains the same. He's kneeling before me, tears streaming down both cheeks. Overhead, the clouds vanish. It's night in our world. But even at night, our world feels brighter than theirs. All those stars glinting and winking from above. I can feel my breathing ease, too. It's almost like the air in their world was laced with smoke. Our mounts are gone. Replaced by two piles of ashes on the edge of a cliff.

Our raised position offers a glimpse of a distant city.

I reach for my knife again. "Where are we?"

But the crying prince doesn't have to answer. I realize I *know* this city. It's the only big city I've ever visited. I still remember the way those golden lights swam from one side of the valley to the other like a lake of gold. All those shimmering towers and bone-dark temples.

"Furia," I whisper in disbelief. "We're outside Furia."

11

DIVIDED

PIPPA

War is an exercise in division.

Etzli has led half of your revenants west. Right now, the lifeless creatures are worming their way underground, infiltrating the city's sewage system. The other half march along the front lines. You have assigned them to attack Navassa's southern livestone gate. It will be their duty to suffer the blows and spare your soldiers during the first feint.

You've also divided your cavalry. Half of them circle north with Bravos. You want the Longhands inside the city to understand: There is no escaping. Let them feel the weight of being cut off, divided fully from their fellow armies for the first time. Let them taste a day without a clear path home. Isolation offers no nutrients.

And then there is one surprising division.

It runs like a fault line through your heart. It was strange to speak with Quinn. Stranger still to see Adrian there. He didn't understand where he was, but you knew as soon as you inhaled that infernal air. It was the underworld. You knew Quinn would return there after the Races. Not a day has passed without a thought of her. But you believed the dreams were your mind's way of comforting you. False glimpses of the girl you'd come to care so much about.

Now you fear they were not dreams, but visions.

Quinn is alive. She is more than well. She is summoning *storms.* You watched as she marched against that sky-spun castle and realized two very important things. First, it is your blood powering her efforts. You could feel the connection, deeper than bone. Next, you determined her target. Quinn is hunting the gods. The very deities that are supposed to help your people win a war.

What if she succeeds? Your fates are linked once more.

None of that explains Adrian's presence. You've been thinking about him a lot lately. After all, he is in every report you read. Leading armies, winning battles. Daily you wonder what it will be like to face him when the time comes. Now his words dig under your skin. *Blood and fire.* You are not sure what to believe about Vivinia. The report claimed it was the Longhands, but now there's a sliver of doubt in your mind. Father is stationed west of Furia. You make a note to ask him for more information when you have a moment—

"Excuse me, General?"

Etzli has settled in beside you. How long has she been there? She watches you with the slightest trace of concern. You clear your throat and nod. "Did all go as planned, Etzli?"

"The revenants moved faster than expected," she answers. "I issued your command and they moved without question. I thought it would take at least thirty clockturns for them to enter the sewage pipes. The entire crew was gone in half that time."

"And do you think they truly understood the schematics?"

"I think their entrance will be frighteningly effective either way."

You nod at that. Their effectiveness will mean the difference between taking the castle in a matter of days or being forced to starve Navassa's defenders for months. Months that your army simply cannot afford. You pray the creatures have a proper sense of direction.

Etzli lowers her voice. "Are you . . . well? Earlier, when we were showing the revenants to Prince Ino . . . and to Bravos. Your personal matters are not my business. It is my business, though, to keep you in your best condition. It is my business to attend to your every need. Do you find his presence difficult? We could always reassign him."

Her words come as a relief. She has the good graces to probe cautiously, but thank the gods she jumped to the wrong conclusion. She clearly saw your distraction in that moment. Only she has no idea you slipped briefly into another world. Her suspected culprit is heartbreak.

"Bravos is a soldier," you reply. "I speak and he obeys. There is nothing more."

"Of course, General."

Silence follows. Her eyes are fixed on the city's distant walls. Etzli's presence soothes you. There has been an unshakeable bond ever since you saved her in the tunnels. It was Quinn who forced you to go back and lower a rope into that dark pit. Her decision saved Etzli's life. You suppose this is the reward for finally sacrificing your own needs to save another. Such kindness breeds loyalty. It is uncommon among your people, and it has become a currency you do not know how to spend. You must start somewhere, though, so you start with honesty.

"Etzli, I am grateful for you."

She blinks in surprise. "Grateful, General?"

"Grateful," you repeat. "I could not have done any of this without your help. On the amateur circuit, there was a nickname for you: Ever-Steady Etzli. Not all nicknames are fitting, but I've found that one to be quite accurate. You are steady, organized, focused."

She nods in return. "Thank you, General. I know that was not my only nickname."

You are aware of that as well, though you do not say the other names aloud. Some newspapers called her Ever-Trembling Etzli, a knock on her caution. Other riders secretly referred to her as Silver. In fact, they even went as far as spreading a joke that she must have had an older sibling, for she only knew how to come in second place. You hate to admit that you enjoyed those nicknames. Each one was a quiet nod to your own success.

"It is the only one that matters now. Caution is a rare trait among our kind."

For a long time, Etzli is silent. You can almost see the gears turning in her head as she weighs what to say and what to keep private. Her response is an invitation.

"It is a quality that was built into me."

"How?"

Etzli purses her lips. "Have you heard of scorched earth?"

Normally, you'd never admit to not knowing something. You shake your head.

"It is an ancient custom," she says. "Most parents do not use it anymore. The idea is that when faced with a massive loss, a child will be pressed forward into maturity. Burn what exists and see what grows in its place. The method demands one of two outcomes. Either they're destroyed by the loss or they become something more."

Her voice steadies as she continues.

"I was five when my parents faked their own deaths," she explains. "I was told that they'd drowned at sea. Their bodies were not recovered. This was the scorched earth. All that I'd ever known—their love and teaching and affection—was gone. I was forced to take over their estate. I had help, of course, but all their responsibilities fell on my shoulders. That year was intended to be my test. Would the grief of losing them destroy me? Or would I rise?"

It is a cruel way to teach a child, but it also sounds like something an Ashlord parent would entertain. Strength through pain. Purification through fire. It is your people's way.

"And you survived."

She nods. "It took nearly three months to reorganize the estate to my liking. Mostly, I simplified their dealings, opting for a more cautious approach. I was so devastated by their deaths that it was the only way I knew to be, cautious and calculating. At the end of the year, I'd managed to turn a profit in most of their businesses. I didn't cry when they came back and revealed the truth of their absence. My heart was already hardened toward them. I'd become exactly who they wanted me to be. I was ready. For the Races. For war. It worked, but it was never the same between us after that. I didn't trust them."

It sounds like a tall tale, and yet you've never read this in any articles about her. Nor did she talk about this in any pre-race interviews. "That story would have gotten you a lot of press."

Etzli nearly snorts. "My parents said the same thing. 'Use it! Build your fan base!' I refused. Call it caution. Or maybe just a young girl not wanting to relive the worst year of her life. I became who I am then. Yes, cautious and organized and thorough, but also untrusting. I have never trusted my parents again. I have never made friends easily." She glances over. "Until the Races. Until you saved me."

Such a direct confession has your cheeks brightening. You do not want to lose the momentum of this breakthrough, though. You do not simply want a good lieutenant. You want someone you can trust for the rest of your life.

"It was Quinn. She showed me a better way to live."

Etzli considers that. "Better than the Ashlord way, you mean?"

It is dangerous ground, nearly blasphemy, but you nod.

"We can be more than what we were taught to be."

She meets your eye, and an agreement passes between you. It is an unspoken promise. The two of you will carve a new way forward. Not the cutthroat path of your ancestors, but with Quinn's mercy as one of your guiding stars. It is a relief to know that another Ashlord can feel the same way that you've felt since the Races ended. You decide to broach the other topic your people do not like to discuss. If you cannot trust Etzli, then who?

"Do you ever think of the Realm of the Gods?"

Your change in topic is a surprise to her. She considers the question thoughtfully, but you can tell she's also searching for the purpose behind what you're asking. In answer, you gesture to the revenants on the front line. "Those creatures are from the underworld, no? It is where the Fury lives. Along with the rest of the pantheon. Do you ever wonder what that world is like?"

A sunless sky. A brewing storm. A desolate plain.

"I haven't given it much thought," Etzli confesses. "Until Gregor."

You'd almost forgotten. Quinn was not the only spirit who entered the Races.

"He was your spirit?"

Etzli nods. "You and I attended all the same preparatory schools. We were taught only what we needed to know. The proper rituals. The blood sacrifices. Which gods deserved what praise. But I spent a lot of time talking with Gregor during the Races. He offered a new perspective. I'd never thought of them existing in the way he described. I mean, I know they exist." She makes a standard warding gesture. "I just mean that I never imagined them living as we do. In an actual place."

Her words bring the floating castle back to the forefront of your mind. *An actual place.* Now you've been there, seen it with your own eyes. It was not hard to guess which god called that home. Before appearing back in this world, you saw an endless flock of birds take flight. The Curiosity has a thousand eyes, they say. Her servants watch this world, they say. The thought of that dark tower sends a chill down your spine.

"I have met two of the gods. The Fury, of course, and the Madness. If I'm not mistaken, you've been introduced to both of them as well."

Etzli shivers. "One does not forget a visit from the Madness."

The god of passage was certainly memorable, and for all the wrong reasons. Your mother invited him to meet you in secret. She had the best intentions. You can still feel that sharp blade sliding across your palm. The howling that came from every direction. The frantic slavering. You know the Madness made arrangements with you, Etzli, and Revel. And his gift was Quinn.

Realization thunders through you.

The thought leaves you breathless. Of *course.* What have the gods always wanted? The very thing Quinn asked of you before she departed. A gift you gave her gladly.

"Blood."

Etzli lifts an eyebrow. "Pardon, General?"

"Our blood. What do they . . ."

The girl looks uncomfortable with where the conversation is heading. You understand her reaction. Many are the rumors surrounding the gods. It is difficult to say what is true, but always there has been a concept of reverence. Speak no ill of the gods, or else risk their wrath.

You decide it's better to focus on the task at hand. Leave more digging for later.

"Let's begin the march."

A signal. Flags rise. The lieutenants rouse their companies, ordering them into marching formations. The larger
body of your army grinds into motion. Everyone is still in
no-man's-land. There's a fine stretch of red-powdered hills
between your troops and Navassa. The goal now is to hit
their exterior defenses with minimal casualties. Your army
is only a distraction.

Prince Ino watches from behind, up in one of the raised
towers. He agreed to the plan, though if it does not go well,
you know he'll pretend to have suggested some other option.

Smoke curls up from Navassa's ramparts. A few early
shots from their snipers. You even see a few arrows cut
through the blue. Wasted ammunition and overeager trigger
fingers. You imagine a Longhand general striding behind his
soldiers, scolding them for their bad judgment.

Another order echoes through your ranks. Shields are
raised. You urge your horse into motion as the back line
moves. More shots ring out now. As soon as they're in range,
your soldiers double their pace. Every thirtieth troop carries
a ladder instead of a shield. It's ferried along by the soldiers
directly behind them as well. All standard siege protocol.

The bulk of your false attack aims for the southern gates
while the rest of your circling army will attempt to scale the
walls to the left and right.

"Trumpets," you call. "Get our front lines sprinting."

The bugles answer. Etzli joins you on a hillside that's just
out of range for their snipers. From here, you have a perfect

view of the southern gate. Your front lines are half running. No breaks in the formation. This is an Ashlord maxim. Perfection even in the face of death.

What have you to fear with the gods at your side?

Gunfire thunders, dropping the occasional soldier. Inevitable losses, you know, because even someone like you cannot capture a jewel like Navassa without casualties.

About fifty paces from the gate, your revenants finally break into a sprint. Even from this distance, you can see there's a strange loping quality to their movements. That does not make them any less the Fury's creations. Their formation angles like an arrow fired at the heart of the southern gate. The rest of your army follows cautiously with raised shields.

And the revenants reach the livestone.

You have never seen the gates in action. The design is pristine. Two gleaming doors, rising nearly three stories high, their surfaces like lakes of mirrored silver. As you watch, the depths stir. The right door breathes to life first. A great warrior—twice as tall as any man—cuts off the approaching revenants. He is a living and moving statue, rendered in pristine stone from head to toe. His eyes glint like diamonds as he looks down at his unwelcome guests. There's glee written across his stone features. This is what he was created to do.

Defend Navassa.

The livestone soldier raises a warhammer. He caves in the skull of the first revenant, a sickening *thump* that you're sure they can hear all the way back in Furia. Battle cries sound on the ramparts as a second livestone statue leaps out of the surface of the right gate.

This one is not a man. A desert tiger roars in warning, jewel-like teeth flashing. Two revenants lash out with their spears, but the tiger slides past them with deadly grace. Claws rake the first revenant's throat. Stone jaws tighten around the jugular of the second. The creature tosses its prey aside like a rag doll. It's a brutal sight.

Silver light tethers both creations to the wall by magic, but that doesn't seem to limit their range. The knight swings his hammer in a savage arc. The tiger moves with a hunter's ease. Overhead, Longhand soldiers add their own long-range fire. All you can do is watch as one of the Striving's creations work against you.

Your soldiers work feverishly on either side to raise ladders. You're pleased to see them holding up shields the whole time. Very few of your living soldiers have fallen. Only the dead are meant to die today.

"Any moment now," Etzli whispers beside you.

The Longhands concentrate on taking down the ladders. Their livestone gates are defending themselves well enough, so they take aim at any soldier daring enough to begin the climb. Several soldiers are shot down just moments after grasping the first rung.

In front of the gate, revenant bodies are piling up. But the Fury's troops aren't without skill. They adjust their tactics. Long spears pin the tiger back toward the gate. You watch the beast swat away their spear tips, growling with menace. It looks contained until the stone soldier disengages with our left flank, bringing his hammer into the backs of several enemies.

"There."

Etzli's voice draws your attention to the ramparts. Shouting. Cries of command transform into cries of panic. The barrage of gunfire slows down as their soldiers have to focus on what's happening inside the city's walls. You imagine the other half of your revenant army pouring into the waiting courtyard.

Your order was simple. Forge a path to the livestone gate. Fight hard. Their success is confirmed by the stone warrior. Distracted, he turns away from your front line and marches into the surface of the gate. His absence offers an opening.

The tiger is alone. Your fighters flood forward—both the living and the dead—purposefully hemming the creature in, away from the center of the gate. You smile with satisfaction as your soldiers plunge their swords through the gap between the doors. Every strike weakens the magic that binds both creatures—and both doors—together. There's no chance of breaking the bond completely right now, but weakening it will set up the rest of your plan.

"Get ready to order the retreat," you command. "Make it look good."

As intended, your fifty revenants do not last long inside the city walls. You suspect they fight valiantly, but there are nearly two thousand Longhand troops inside Navassa. It will be a slaughter. All you care about is *where* they die.

Order slowly restores itself. You suspect the Longhands believe they've withstood your cleverest tactic. Their engineers will examine the sewage entrances and seal them off.

Your one great ruse has fallen short. They will think that your best hope now is a long siege.

A smile steals over your face. Let them believe that.

As the stone warrior reappears, your soldiers are already retreating. Only the final dozen revenants keep fighting, keep falling. The Longhands cheer as your army retreats.

A bright victory in their eyes.

A necessary loss in yours.

"Begin preparations for tonight."

Darkness edges over the plains.

The southern gate boasts a pile of corpses. Fifty dead revenants on this side, and fifty more lying within. You've put on quite a show. Berating your troops. Appearing to lick your wounds. The entire army has been drawn back into camp. You order them to settle in for the night. Except the rest of your cavalry has slipped north. And your sleeping troops are fully dressed for battle, eyes closed as they wait for the sound of horns.

Tonight, the city of Navassa will fall.

"Light the third fire."

A whisper from your lips to Etzli's hands. From Etzli's hands to the eastern hills. There, a third fire appears. Bravos will see the signal. He will rouse his troops and charge the city from the north. Your eyes trace the dark sky. Stars peer through the black like eyes winking down. From an appointed hillside, you watch moonlight stretch over the plains.

Torches are staggered along the ramparts. A city under

siege sleeps with one eye open. You cannot see them, but you'd guess there is a general there, sipping coffee, eyes pinned on your quiet camp with suspicion. And that's when the shouting begins.

Horns blow. Bravos is coming. Your view is cut off, but their scouts are undoubtedly looking out right now in fear. Five hundred horses are barreling down on their northern gate. Shadows weave in and out of one another along the ramparts. You know the Longhands are shifting their troops to answer the attack.

But you also know their scouts are still watching your camp, wondering if you'll double down and attack from the south as Bravos hits the northern gate. Eyes drawn to your camp, the Longhands do not see—and have no reason to expect—the enemy at their gates.

Moonlight feasts on the fallen.

It is one thing to be told what will happen, and quite another thing to see *how* it happens. One by one, the dead rise. Pushing to their feet in silence. Forgotten. They all gather up their discarded weapons. Even from here you can tell the soldiers above have no visual on them.

The angles are just so.

More horns sound.

You smile, because you know the moon has wakened the dead within the city. At that exact moment, Bravos will be dividing the cavalry charge into two. He will not hit the northern side at all. You hold your breath in anticipation as the livestone gates shudder open.

Only a few soldiers would be assigned to such an easily defended area. Your revenants have made quick work of them. Now the gate is yours. The Longhands rally to take it back, but fifty more soldiers force their way inside. Your command to them was simple.

Stand your ground. Defend the gate.

Right on time, the cavalry circles in from each side. Their formation is flawless. Bravos leads them, knifing through the open gate. There's a promise of blood in the way his horse snarls, in the arc of his sword. Your heart drums in your chest.

And you can't resist the invitation. You want to taste the battles waiting inside those gates. A firing get-get has your horse thundering forward. Etzli calls out orders before charging after you. The cavalry has breached the city. Your revenants follow, cutting down shocked Longhands.

You know they'll fight like dogs, but it isn't easy to defend streets that were never yours. Let them try. Let them face you now. As your horse plunges through the southern gate, you lift your sword. Blood pulses in your temples. The city already belongs to you—this is a fact—but now it's time to have a little fun.

12

THE DREAD

ADRIAN

Daddy looks properly dusted. He sets his hat down on the table between us, brushes the hair he has left to one side, and offers a smile. It's a tired one.

"Hard to believe how long it's been."

Before the war. Before the Races. We said goodbye with our feet planted in the dust of my mother's grave. I haven't forgotten that day. I haven't forgotten all that followed.

"It worked out. We got our war."

He nods at that. "You started a revolution, son. You made our people believe."

I meet his gaze. I've spent so long worshipping him that it's hard to accept the flaws. Not just the exhaustion riding his shoulders, but also the seeds of doubt the Dread planted. *Victor or martyr, your father gets his war.* I'm still not sure how much of that was true, but this is the first time I've had to look him in the eye since those doubts surfaced. It's harder than I thought it would be.

"I didn't win."

"That doesn't matter," he says, waving away the past. "You gave us a war to fight. The chance we needed to rise. And now? The Ashlords are on their heels. Antonio's secured the western coast. You've conquered most of the eastern seaboard. All we have to do is squeeze."

It's not that simple. It never was. "The gods haven't involved themselves yet."

"I'm not so sure about that."

He looks over my shoulder. I smell the wash of salt before my eyes can fix on the shadowed figure in the corner of the room. I didn't see him when I walked in, but that's his way. He appeared in my hotel room in secret, too. There one second, gone the next. He is the god of caution. The Dread.

This time his chosen vessel is a woman. She marches out of the corner to claim the only empty chair at the table. She's dressed plainly, clothes stained with sweat. She's as thin as most vessels, their mortal bodies ignored as they serve immortal gods. Like all servants of the Dread, she wears the mask of a great iron turtle. It's sewn over her head at the neck.

"Adrian Ford," the Dread rasps. "We meet again."

Daddy watches my reaction. He knows the god visited me—it was his idea—but does he know what the Dread told me? In every promise and offer to me, this god spoke against him.

"I thought I was pretty clear about where we stand."

Those reptilian eyes watch me, unblinking. Daddy can't resist knifing through the silence. "We're working with the Dread, Adrian. He's offered protection. It's a mutually beneficial relationship. Everyone agreed. If we're to make a stand against the rest of the pantheon, we'll need one of their kind on our side."

My jaw tightens. "What's the price tag?"

Daddy's a little too polished to scowl, but I can tell I'm testing his patience. He's grown accustomed to being right, or at least to having everyone nod in agreement when he speaks. I was as guilty of that as any. It wasn't too long ago that I'd have marched to his commands without a second thought. But I've learned to think for myself ever since the Races.

"The price is blood," he answers. "It's a simple trade. One product for another. He doesn't need our worship. That's all that matters to us. Our ancestors did not bow. Neither will we. The Dread requires our blood for his purposes in the world below. We get his protection in the world above."

The world below. My mind reaches instinctually for the faded vision. A dream that wasn't a dream. Pippa standing below a city in the sky. Thousands of birds taking flight. I'm not sure what I saw, but the experience has me feeling uneasy. Nothing good can come from it.

I eye the Dread. "I'm not interested in your protection."

Daddy makes a disbelieving noise. The god smiles.

"It saved you once."

"And you did that out of the goodness of your heart? Please. You were trying to gain my favor. I'm happy to be alive, but I told you then what I'll remind you now. There's no bargain between us. I owe you nothing. Your kind always have their reasons. I'm not a fool."

Daddy intervenes. "Adrian, you don't have to give the

Dread *your* blood. We've got plenty of sacrifices. The pact between us is sealed. I'm just asking for you to accept the reality of this. The Dread is our ally, has been all along. How do you think our spies remained hidden in Navassa? How do you think we surprised the Ashlords at Gig's Wall? Both were gifts from the Dread. Both were signs that we can trust our new ally."

It takes effort to bite back my complaint. Daddy looks set on this path, and he's even more stubborn than me once he gets his heels good and dug in. "Fine. We've got a god on our side. Have it your way. But you're forgetting that the Ashlords have six gods on *their* side."

"Actually, just five." Daddy's smile stretches into a grin. "The Hoarder is dead."

That catches my attention. I look to the Dread, who nods confirmation.

"The temples are empty. His vessels all burned to ash. One of the gods has fallen."

My mind is racing. The vision of Pippa echoes back to me. I can't stop myself from breathing out the same truth I saw in that world. "A storm is coming."

"So it is," the Dread replies. "My spies know little of what happened. Sometimes the gods will exile their own, as we did with the Veil. The Hoarder is a strange case. He has grown weak over the centuries. The other gods see themselves as brothers and sisters, but the Hoarder is more of an estranged cousin. It wouldn't surprise me if they used the war to sever ties with him."

"An odd cousin," I muse. "What does that make you? Is there a family term for traitors?"

I'm surprised the blow actually lands. The god's reptilian jaw clamps down with a violent *clack*. Clearly, I've found a weak spot in all that well-constructed armor.

The Dread speaks after a moment. "I am all but forgotten by them. That means I am well positioned for our cause, both in this world and the world below."

"One god down," Daddy reminds us. "Five to go. We'll keep our focus on the Ashlords, but if other opportunities arise, we'll take them. For now our goal is to keep winning battles across the Empire. It won't be long until we've pinned them down in Furia."

I nod to him. I wish the Dread wasn't here for this discussion. Better if the fate of our people didn't depend on an ancient enemy. "Our generals are discussing the next move."

"You will march on Grove," the Dread says.

"I don't take orders from you."

"What about from me?" Daddy asks quietly. "From your lead general? The Dread is right. We will move against Grove. We'll feint inland first. The bulk of our army marches in the morning. Long enough for their scouts to report that we're moving on Furia. But you'll take a small company north. The Dread's magic will veil your movement. At night, the rest of the army will double back for support. Grove will wake up to an army at its door. And when they try to send their ships out, you'll be waiting for them."

It's not a bad plan. Except for one thing. "Is the Dread offering us ships? And sailors to control them? None of my fighters know a thing about boats. How are we to stop them?"

Daddy smiles. "You're not just a fighter, nor just a rider.

You're an alchemist, too. Can you think of a combination that might help five hundred soldiers attack by sea?"

I find myself nodding. "The River's Light rebirth."

"Sharp as ever. Make sure you bring the photographer," he says. "It will be glorious. Five hundred horses charging over the waves. Grove surrenders. And leaves Furia exposed."

I can't help smiling back at him. It's a damn fine plan. I just wish we could pull it off without the Dread's help. Our people exist because of a distrust in the gods. We abandoned Furia centuries ago when the gods demanded we bow to them. We always say the Reach was born free.

A part of me thinks that Daddy doesn't fully grasp our situation. He's got no idea how much the Dread will ask for when he tallies up our final tab. The god's smiling like she knows how all of this will end. Even if I've got a bad feeling about it, I know we need to take Grove.

"When do we leave?"

"Tonight," Daddy commands. "The rest of us march tomorrow."

He rises from the table, signaling the conversation is finished. I'm surprised when the Dread remains seated. Clearly, the two of us still have matters to discuss.

Daddy reaches the door and sets his hat back on his head. He now looks like the man I grew up worshipping. The kind of man who could make a deal with anyone. He's taller than me but not quite as wide at the shoulders. There's gray in his hair and in his beard, but I doubt there's too many people who'd want to stand across a battlefield from him.

"Adrian. I'm proud of you. Always. I've been plotting

this war since they buried your mother. Not a day passes that I don't think about our family. The three of us. If they'd had the decency to just leave us alone . . ." The pain in his voice is like a dry wind sweeping across an abandoned valley. These words are carved into his bones. "But that's not what happened. The Ashlords took her, and I promised I'd take everything from them. You opened the door. The rest of us are just storming in behind you. We won't stop until we've buried them all. We'll just have to find a graveyard big enough."

He tips his hat before slipping out of the room. I've always known this part of him. The soldier who failed to protect his family. It's the reason no man or woman would ever dare to say my mother's name in his presence. I've tried to take his revenge and make it my own. The Ashlords will answer for their crimes. I've whispered that to myself before every battle. But I'm starting to see what he can't. War buries the best of us. All of this? It's blood for blood.

Even if we win, there's a boy in Furia who will grow up fatherless. He will whisper *our* names before he falls asleep each night. It will be our hearts he aims for in training. Winning doesn't put an end to that. It just means the cycle will begin again. War and blood and death. My eyes trace the nearest maps and find the little dot out west that I know represents Vivinia. Underneath, the word *sanctuary* is written in cursive. I think about all the innocents who died there and wonder if the cycle is already beginning again . . . and if it will ever end.

No one ever really wins these wars we fight. Except the gods.

My eyes swing to the Dread. She's watching me with a guarded expression. I'm not prepared for the first question she asks. "Were you the one who killed the Hoarder?"

It's so blunt that all I can do is stare. Did I kill the Hoarder? It's the kind of question that comes hand in hand with a few important truths. I do my best to focus, dust them off, and sort them out. First, the Dread believes I'm capable of killing a god. Can a mortal truly slay one of their kind? I'd never considered that to be a possibility until now.

The second realization shivers down my spine. I'm not sure how, but it's clear that the Dread knows where I've been. I choose a simple, truthful answer.

"I've never met the Hoarder."

"But you've visited the underworld."

I nod. "Yes."

Those reptilian eyes narrow. She waits patiently for an explanation, but I feel like we're suddenly playing a new game. I want to know the rules before I make a move.

She breaks first. "How did you get there?"

"I'm not really sure."

The god's face twists unpleasantly. She thinks I'm hiding the truth.

"One does not enter that world by accident. There are very few passages, and most require a god's invitation. But there's no denying it. I can smell it on you. You visited recently."

I nod again. "It was an accident. More of a glimpse than anything."

"A glimpse," she repeats. "Of what?"

Now we're back on unsteady ground. What do I tell her?

What does she already know? If she can smell that world on my skin, it's possible she can smell even more. I weigh all my options before deciding to tell the truth. Sometimes honesty leads to honesty.

And I've got a few questions myself.

"I saw a city in the sky."

The Dread's eyes gleam. "How curious."

"You know the place?"

She nods. "I am a god. I know everything."

"You ask a lot of questions for a god who knows everything."

She smirks at that. "I can't see inside your head. That is not my gift. My expertise has always been protection. But trust me, boy, there are gods who could set you on a table, crack your mind open like an egg, and sift through everything. Your memories, your dreams, your futures. Do not forget that. You are standing against the oldest creatures that have ever existed."

It's a welcome reminder. I'm not afraid of them, but only a fool pretends his enemies are less than what they truly are. Poor assessments lead to poor planning, and poor planning leads to lost battles. I might not trust the Dread, but every piece of information helps.

"What else did you see?" the Dread asks, impatient.

"Not a whole lot. I appeared outside the city. There was a storm raging against its walls. Thousands of birds took flight. That's all I saw."

And Pippa. I'm not sure what makes me withhold that knowledge. She's my enemy. Leading armies that will stand against my own. But the quiet voice in the corner of my mind urges me to not mention her to the Dread. I trust that voice—that instinct—above all else now. Knowing is living.

"You have not visited any other gods?"

I raise an eyebrow. "I barely talk to you."

"And you've not given your blood to anyone?"

"Only the desert."

The Dread smirks. I smile back, but the god's words finally strike. It's like a bolt of delayed lightning. *My blood.* I didn't give it freely, but there was that moment after the Races. In an unlit carriage, Pippa tended my wounds. The warmth of her flooded around me. Those bandages had plenty of my blood on them. Could that be the explanation? Was it Pippa who pulled me to that world? Unaware of my thoughts, the Dread stands.

"Tell me if you travel to that world again."

I put steel in my voice. "Sure, you'll be the first to know."

Those scaly eyes narrow again. "You misunderstand me. The gods have always taken great comfort in their barriers. If a man like you can walk freely into their world . . ." She allows those words to hang in the air. "That could be very dangerous. For them. You were right about one thing. The gods have not come into play. I've heard whispers of a few gifts, but not what was given during the last war. Entire cities burned. Spirit armies marched alongside the Ashlords. If you have access to their world, we would be foolish not to make use of that."

It's so alluring. The way the Dread says *we* and *us.* Like we've been on the same team all along. "God of caution. You're awfully trusting."

Her eyes glint. "It is simply a matter of trusting the right people."

There's a slash of magic in the air, followed by a bright mist like the spray of seafoam. I raise my arm to shield my eyes, and by the time I blink them back open, the Dread is gone. I sit there for a while, considering all that I've learned, and then I head off in search of Forrest Trask. He was right. We have a long march ahead of us. Longer than I realized.

Might as well join him for a drink while I still can.

13

STRIKING A BARGAIN

IMELDA

I will be lucky to survive the night.

"You could let me go," the little prince says for the hundredth time. "I won't tell."

There's a childish part of him that believes that. He's just a kid. Right now, he thinks he can trade his freedom for silence. I know better. The second he's safely inside his father's palace, they'll begin prying information from him. *What happened? What did he see? Who was to blame?*

"Be quiet, please. I'm thinking."

He whimpers in response. I can see his pouting expression by the light of the stars. Furia offers its own distant glow. It's farther away than I initially thought. Distance is hard to gauge with something so massive. But that doesn't mean I'm safe. I've already watched one company of soldiers march south. Nearly within shouting distance of our elevated hiding place in the cavernous hills.

One mistake is all it would take for me to be captured,

especially this deep in enemy territory. Which makes the question rattling around in my brain even louder.

"How did we travel this far?" I ask. "We were on the western coast of the Empire. Hundreds of leagues from Furia. This shouldn't be possible."

He looks up with watery eyes and shakes his head. "I'm already in so much trouble."

I can work with that. Prosper hated getting caught by my parents, too. He was always the child who asked permission, not forgiveness. One of our many differences.

"What's your name?"

He looks up again, and this time there's a little bit of shock in his expression.

"You really don't know it?"

I have to stop myself from rolling my eyes. "Should I?"

"I'm a prince!" he complains. "A son of the Brightness."

"I don't really follow politics. Aren't there six of you?"

"Seven," he corrects. "I'm the seventh! You didn't even know I existed?"

I shrug. "Did you know I existed?"

"You're Imelda Beru!"

My heart sinks. I'd kind of been hoping he didn't know my name. I wanted him to think a band of outlaws were responsible. The Ashlords might piece together the clues and figure out it was us, but they wouldn't have a direct link to my name or any of the crew. Unfortunately, the kid clearly knows who I am. Every child in the Empire watches the Races, and I'd bet this particular child had front-row seats for the entire event. It wouldn't surprise me if he was there on the night they unveiled the map. I know his father was.

"Are you going to tell me your name?"

He lifts his chin proudly. "I am Asha, seventh in line to the throne."

"If you want to live long enough to sit on a throne, you need to listen to me."

To my surprise, he bursts into tears. I'm staring at him, fumbling for words, wondering what I did wrong. He speaks in between heaving sobs. "I'm. Too. Young. To. Die."

"Oh, calm down! I'm not going to kill you."

He points a trembling finger. "But you have a knife!"

Scowling, I toss the weapon behind me. He's firmly bound, and his horse is just a pile of ashes set out on the distant cliffs. He eyes the abandoned blade, still sniffling.

"I am willing to negotiate with you," he says, just like a proper diplomat's son would.

"Thought you'd come around," I reply. "The deal is simple. You answer my questions and I set you free. When our horses are born in the morning, you can ride back to Furia."

His eyes narrow. "How many questions?"

"As many as I need you to answer."

"But you're only letting me go *once.*"

"Do you think your life is worth just one question?"

He considers that. "Depends on the question."

I roll my eyes. "You're wasting time. Do we have a deal or not?"

"Deal."

My mind traces back through what happened in that other world. There are so many questions I'd like answers to, but I have a feeling he'll shut down if I dig too deep too fast. Better to start simple and work our way into more important territory.

"How did we travel this far?"

He considers his answer carefully. "The two worlds are different sizes."

"Explain."

"That is the explanation."

I almost reach out and bop him on the forehead the way I would Prosper. I grind my teeth instead, reframing the question. "So our world is larger than the world of the gods?"

He shakes his head. "Just different. The shapes aren't the same. There are parts of our world that don't exist in their world. So you can kind of . . . skip them."

Interesting. It makes some sense, I suppose. I chased the prince across a solid distance. We were traveling in the world below from one point to another. If we reached a location that didn't have any connection to our world, it might bring us back to the closest overlap.

And that offers several intriguing possibilities.

"Are the horses the only way into the other world?"

His face pinches in thought. "They are the easiest way."

"But there are other paths?"

"The gods can take you there."

A little shiver runs down my back. I imagine those priests, masks sewn over their heads, leading someone down a winding, endless staircase.

"What were the three of you supposed to do there?"

It's the first question that he greets with silence. After a few seconds, I raise an eyebrow.

"Answers for freedom."

He nods slowly. "It is a wartime tradition. We negotiate with the gods."

"For their gifts."

Another nod. "The three of us were sent as a show of good faith."

The look on his face doesn't match the sentence. He looks proud of the role he's been given. Likely he heard his father speak those words, and he's parroting them back to me now.

"You're a ward?"

He shakes his head. "No, I'm a negotiator."

"You said that you were sent as a 'show of good faith.' Do you know what that means?"

He nods but the doubt on his face is clear enough.

"If two sides make an alliance during war," I explain, "often they'll seal the deal with wards. It's an old practice. A son or daughter goes to live with the ally. It's a promise that both sides will honor the terms of their arrangement. Should one side break faith, they risk the lives of the wards."

Asha's eyes widen. "That's not true."

"That's what a show of good faith means, kid."

I can see the foundation crumbling for a moment. It doesn't take him long, though, to double down on his faith in his father—in their gods. "I don't believe you."

"Not believing in something doesn't make it less true," I reply. "What about the Hoarder?"

He frowns. "What about him?"

"Why didn't you ride toward his castle?"

"The Hoarder wouldn't have helped."

I frown. "Why not?"

"He's not really involved in wars. He comes after. To collect things."

Even more interesting. I don't know as much as I'd like about the pantheon, but everyone knows the Hoarder is one of the stranger gods. A purveyor of sorts. That was confirmed as we walked through his slain guardians. Every creature was a piece of this, a piece of that. Patchwork creations of his own design. The prince doesn't think the Hoarder is involved in the war, but clearly the god was involved in *something*. His entire city was put to the sword for it.

"I have one more question."

Asha actually smiles. I know he won't want to answer this question. Which means I have to position it perfectly. "I haven't asked you to reveal much. Just what I need to know to get back home. That's all I want. You want to go home? So do I."

He nods. "Ask your question."

"Where did that wall come from?"

His jaw tightens. His eyes sharpen into blades. He's trying to close himself off, and he unconsciously scratches at his bandage with one finger. My eyes flick to the spot.

"If you want to go home . . ."

He speaks, but his voice is a whisper. His eyes dart around nervously and it's clear that he thinks someone might hear us. Not a passing soldier, either. He's afraid his *gods* will hear.

"It was blood."

His answer makes no sense. "What was blood?"

He raises his bound wrists. "I used my blood."

I can't help laughing. "Come on, kid. You can't make a . . ."

But the realization lands. My mind struggles to accept it. *I used my blood.* Isn't that what the gods are always demanding of them? Our people have always found the ritual strange. The blood sacrifices the Ashlords offer in their stone temples. Priests ushering vials down into the underworld for whatever reason. It has long been the exchange between them.

Gifts and protection in this world traded for blood in theirs.

I have to be careful now. I need answers, but which ones matter most?

"What do the gods use your blood for?"

He shrugs. "How should I know?"

Curious. He knows how to use his own blood but has never thought to ask *why* the gods demand sacrifices from them. If this little boy could summon a wall with less than a thought . . .

"Just imagine what the gods can do."

"What?"

"Nothing." I shake my head. "Last question."

"You already said that!"

"Last one. The gods. What instructions did they give you? For using your blood?"

He turns that question over and doesn't seem to see the harm in answering.

"Only in life-and-death circumstances," he says. "Never in their presence."

I pretend the information bores me. I hope Asha forgets this discussion, or at least that he forgets most of it. But my heart is thrashing in my chest. Pieces of a larger puzzle are nestling into place. He doesn't understand—or else he wasn't told—how all of this works.

The gods demand blood. And in their world, blood is power. An eleven-year-old boy summoned a wall with a few drops. How many sacrifices have the gods accepted on their altars? How many vials of blood? It would offer them stunning amounts of power. No wonder they're so eager to bring the Ashlords gifts. Every sacrifice fuels their grip on the world below.

But my final question reveals a deeper truth. The gods have taught him—and likely the others—not to use their blood. *Never in their presence.* Every instruction carries weight. Rules come to exist for a reason; entire societies observe certain traditions because of what they've experienced. It is not random. The gods have ordered their sacrificial partners not to wield their own blood, except in the worst circumstances?

An order like that speaks of fear.

What would happen if the Ashlords decided to use their blood in front of the gods? Or worse, what if they used it *against* their gods?

"Hello?"

My heart jumps. I turn, searching the cliff face, but it's just me and the prince. He's looking at me, and I realize I was lost in thought. "What?"

"You said I could go home."

I look to the western sky. The slightest traces of pink are appearing. I point that way.

"When the sun rises."

He eyes the horizon appreciatively before settling his

back against the cliffs. I can tell he feels like he got the better of me in this negotiation. Such a little prince. I hope history does not blame him, and I hope his father does not execute him.

This morning he handed us a path into the underworld. Now he's given me the key to destroying their gods. Sunrise can't come soon enough. I count the vanishing stars, eager to return and tell Bastian what I've learned. We can win this war by going to the one place we never thought to go, and using the one weapon we never thought to use.

Our blood.

14

CURIOSITY

PIPPA

You are the proud owner of a new city.

A city that should have taken months to conquer, but alas, you are *you*. Soldiers raise their glasses as you cross the banquet hall. The chorus of cheers rises in a thundering echo. You imagine the captured Longhands in the dungeons below, listening as their defeat fills up the city.

It is another gem in an already glinting crown.

You took the pass everyone thought impregnable. You captured a city that your people shouldn't have lost in the first place. You are quietly making history.

It is strange, then, that you cannot keep the smile on your face. Even as your generals raise their glasses in your honor and welcome you to the high table, a feeling of dread sits in your stomach. You should be celebrating, but you know something is wrong.

You stay only as long as decorum dictates. Long enough to avoid concern. And then you rise, signaling the nearest

servant. Your generals offer their salutes. Etzli throws a con-
cerned glance in your direction. You nod that you will be
fine, even if it doesn't feel that way. Prince Ino isn't with
them. You were told that he took an armed escort back to
the capital to report your success to the Brightness. Undoubtedly, he will report that success as being influenced
by him.

At least you'll be free of him for a few moons.

The servants lead you away. You ask them to ready a
steaming bath. Navassa is as modern a city as Furia. It
comes with the Ashlord comforts you've grown accustomed
to back home. Hopefully a warm bath and a warm bed will
settle the strange feeling.

Quiet is a good start. You are led into a new building, up
several flights of stairs, and into the privacy of your assigned
quarters. The former occupant was tasteful. Marble floors
accented by patterned rugs. A stretch of floor-to-ceiling glass
windows overlook the rest of the city. You glimpse fires still
burning in the streets below. Groups of unlucky soldiers
move in shadow, assigned to systematically clean up the
corpses and sort them into groups for burial. You make the
mistake of looking closer.

The Butcher is there.

His priests glide alongside your soldiers like ghosts.
Their bloodstained aprons cinched at their backs. Carving
knives held out. Those ruby-red masks veil smiles their pa-
tron stole long ago. The Butcher is the only deity in the
pantheon who prefers the sacrifices of the dead to those of
the living. Watching their bloody work has your stomach
turning all over again.

"Curtains, please."

One of your servants slips obediently toward the windows. The other guides you into an adjacent room. It's far darker inside the baths. It was designed traditionally. No windows. Brick walls pressed tight on each side. Braziers placed every few paces. You smile at the steam rising off the water's glass-like surface.

"Leave me."

Each servant bows. You fumble out of your clothing, shrugging off the rust, ignoring the splashes of blood on your gauntlets. Slipping into the steaming water is like an answered prayer. Thousands of knots untangle. There's been so much unspoken pressure. It is the same as it was before the Races. An entire society set on your shoulders, the only option victory.

War is just a bloodier, longer game.

It is a welcome feeling to slip beneath the surface of the water and away from those troubles. You do not want to plan the next march. You do not want to suffer the scrutiny of the gods. You only want to feel weightless. For a time, it works. No one calls for you.

And then a scream.

You surface, eyes searching the room. "Hello?"

Quiet. The servants are outside. Your eyes land on the abandoned pile of clothing and armor. Your switch is tucked into its customary place on your belt. Wary of an intruder, you rise from the bath. Cold slithers over your skin until your hands find the nearest towel. You work to dry yourself off, quickly and quietly, before gliding over to your clothes.

A pity to put the day's filth back on, but there's another scream.

Down in the streets?

You slide back into your leggings. Tighten your belt. One hand clutches the grip of your switch. The other reaches for your leather jerkin and riding tunic. It's gone quiet again.

Except the world—your world—begins peeling away. You're ready for it this time. You take a deep breath as the trade occurs. New colors, new scents, new *everything*.

You are standing at the entrance to the strangest hallway you've ever seen. It matches the tunneled appearance of the bath. Great, speckled stones circle overhead. The gaps between each piece are packed with wispy needles and faded leaves. A feather floats down to the ground.

It looks like a massive nest.

Another scream. Only this time you recognize the voice. "Quinn."

A flick transforms your switch into a sword. Your clothes are still clutched in your other hand. This is the reason for the dread in your gut. The connection to Quinn was gnawing at you across worlds. It is clear now. She is here. She is in trouble. She is about to die.

Desperation has you moving down the strange hallway.

You flinch again, though, at an intruding voice. "Pippa?"

At the entrance of the tunnel is Adrian Ford. He looks lost. He takes in the strange nest of a hallway before staring at you. His eyes widen and his cheeks go bright.

"Are you naked?"

Of course you're not . . . but then your eyes widen, too.

All you managed to put on before the change is a pair of leggings. The bunched clothing covers your front, but still you spin around, finally feeling the chill of the room run down your spine.

"Well, don't look!"

It's a childish request given the circumstances. You start to shove your head through the tunic when you realize that you've foolishly turned your back on your greatest enemy. You spin around, half covered and half not. Adrian hasn't moved. And to your delighted surprise, he's studying the stone patterns of the floor like an architectural student.

"Are you going to attack me when my back is turned?"

His cheeks are flames. "I—Well, you told me not to look!"

Cautiously, you pull the rest of your body through the shirt. All the while, your eyes watch him for even the slightest trace of a threat. He glances up and you burn a look back.

"I said not to look!"

He fumbles for an answer. "I was just making sure you weren't going to attack me!"

"Sure you were."

Now you can't help smiling. His chin is pressed into his chest like it's been drilled down. It takes you a moment to adjust your sleeves, tighten your breastplate. You draw your hair up into a tight knot before clearing your throat. It would be a kindness if, in the future, you were summoned here looking your best.

"It's okay. You can look now."

He smiles up at you, in spite of himself.

"I swear, I wasn't trying to . . . I didn't mean to come—"

A fourth scream cuts him off. This time you feel Quinn's pain like a lash across your back. Someone is hurting her. Your blood boils at the thought. Adrian senses it, too.

"Who was that?" he asks. "Where are we?"

There's a decision to make. You have only seconds to make it. A friend has called you in a time of need. Quinn is down those halls. You can feel her heartbeat slowing. You can taste her fear in the air. You do not know why Adrian appeared, but you are sure of one thing.

"I need your help."

There's a flash of genuine shock on his face. "So I was right. You called me here."

"I didn't call you."

"But the blood . . . I could've sworn—"

"Look. My friend is in danger. She's not an Ashlord. She's not even from our world. If we don't do something, she will die. Either you're coming with me or you aren't. Choose."

A breath passes. You cannot believe the request you're making. You—of all people—are asking him—of all people—for help. No Longhand would ever . . .

. . . but Adrian Ford is full of surprises. He offers a nod.

"Let's go."

There is no time to question his intentions. You turn and march down the hallway. He quick-steps to catch up, until the two of you are matching each other's strides, gliding down the hallway of a god. You know that much. The last time you saw Quinn, she'd used your blood to summon a storm against the Curiosity's stronghold. That is where you must be now.

Inside the skyline keep. And something terrible has happened.

"Any idea what we're up—"

A screech cuts his sentence in half. Two birds swing into the hallway. Their wings widen to slow their descent, claws splaying, and a twist of magic has them landing not on talons but on feet. The birdlike bodies shift into something human and you're caught gawking as a dark spear juts out.

Adrian cuts the weapon in half on a downswing. His right shoulder lowers into the first attacker, then he twists. A perfect plunge into the heart of the second. There's a burst of feathers as the creature dies. Another strike, another screech, another death. His eyes find you.

"Are you just going to stand there?"

You tighten your grip on your weapon. "I thought it was a bird!"

"Don't these things serve one of your gods? Can't you ask them to stop?"

You scowl at that, skirting the bodies, leading him on. The next room is a vast chamber. Wind howls in greeting. It takes a moment to realize the entire room is exposed to the elements. A great dome arches overhead. It's decorated with ledges and bars. Nooks are built into the elevated spaces for birds to settle and nest. This is what you saw during your last vision.

Thousands of birds took flight. It's a massive aviary. And not all the birds are gone.

Adrian's voice is a whisper. "Are they sleeping?"

You're too busy counting them to answer. Adrian just

made quick work of two of these creatures, but this is different. There are nearly fifty above you. He's right, though. They do look like they're sleeping. Feathered heads tucked into the folds of dark wings. Soft cooing.

Adrian gestures. On the opposite end of the room, there are three separate tunnels waiting. You can feel Quinn in the distance. You point to the far left. Both of you quietly pick your way across the room, navigating between slender towers that branch out above your heads like faux trees. There are abandoned bones and feathers and waste piled everywhere.

Halfway across, you freeze. There's a little nest within arm's reach of Adrian. You thought it was empty. A smaller bird rustles out of sleep. You stare—heart pounding in your chest—as the little creature wakes. Little golden eyes blink wide. You've never seen something so adorable in all your life. Adrian's hand tightens on his sword. Before you can scold him for considering hurting a harmless creature, it arches its neck and lets loose a hair-raising screech.

"Dammit."

Dark heads rise. Colorless eyes open. Wings stretch.

"To me," you order him. "Now."

Adrian's already moving, though. He has his sword held out, his eyes trailing upward. He adjusts until his back is pressed against yours. Heat flashes between the two of you.

"There are too many of them," he says.

"Let me try something." The birds are fluttering down to lower ledges. Some circle the air above. It will be a coordinated attack. Unless you intervene. You pitch your voice as loud as you can to the surrounding creatures. "I'm a servant of the Curiosity as well. From the other world. I was drawn to this place by her command."

The only answer is a bloodcurdling shriek. Three of the birds dive.

Adrian mutters, "Well, that didn't work."

All three forms twist at the last moment. You don't get caught flat-footed this time. Your sword turns aside the first spear and disarms the second. Adrian's back presses against yours as he lashes out at his own attacker. More birds dive. Your thrust drops the first. You sidestep, slashing the throat of another. Instinct has you backpedaling to Adrian, who ducks a blow before dropping his own target.

One of the birds lands on Adrian's back, screeching into human form. He roars, spinning to free himself, and you step into his absence. A surprised bird-man's mouth goes wide as your sword slides between his ribs. Three others land as the creature falls. A curse slips from your lips.

The two of you will not survive this way for long.

Adrian carves a path back to you. It takes some shuffling to get into position and face the next onslaught. Your arms aren't tired yet, but now there are four spears penning you in from all sides. You sweep the tip of one away and kick out. It catches that bird full in the chest.

The others answer. A spear grazes your neck. The tip of one lands on your left shoulder. Pain lances out from both blows, dragging a little grunt from you. But pain doesn't stop you from dropping another bird and another. Only, the ranks never falter. There are always more of them.

Spears on your left and on your right. Birds circling the

air above, shadowing the fight with their wings spread, waiting to transform and join the fray. It doesn't matter how many you've killed.

You get caught on a lazy strike. One of the birds darts underneath your jab and drives the butt end of its spear into your nose. The force of the blow shocks you. You hit the ground hard, and the only thing that saves you is Adrian's wild swinging. Your vision spins. Blood rushes down.

On the ground, you have a moment to take in the strange scene. All those ashen creatures, birdlike men and women, circling. You finally see their faces. There is no menace there. No firm resolve that one sees in a soldier doing their duty. Not even the hungry look of a warrior as the taste of blood comes. No, all of them are weeping. It is the strangest sight in the world.

Adrian shouts, "Get up, Pippa!"

He lashes out again and again, but there are too many of them. Far too many for you to stand your ground. Your hand flutters up to your nose. Your fingers come away covered in blood. Is this truly how your life will end? Here in some other world, surrounded by bird shit?

"Stop."

Your voice echoes. It is just a single word, but something unexpected happens. You startle at the power that laces in and through the command. That booming echo barrels out of you like a cannon. And to your surprise, every single one of the birds obeys you. Adrian's chest is heaving. He looks around, as shocked as you feel.

"How . . ."

You do not know. Half of the birds were already dead.

Corpses cast aside in a sloppy circle. The other half are very much alive, but all immobilized. Birds hang in the air above you, their wings outstretched and frozen in place. The nearest attackers wear those sad expressions painted on their faces. A spear tip hovers within arm's reach, unmoving. Jaws are flexed. Arms extended. Feet set.

Nothing moves.

"Come on," you manage to gasp. "We have to find Quinn."

"But they're just—"

"Come on."

Your mind is racing. You pick your way carefully through the frozen creatures. It is impossible. You spoke a word, breathed it like the final request that it was, and it actually happened. It is not just that the birds obeyed. They did not set their spears aside and apologize. Your word *stopped* them against their will. Your voice *was* power. But that doesn't make any sense, either.

You tried to stop them before the fight. You told them you'd been sent by the Curiosity. That accomplished nothing. There was no difference in your tone, no weight in your voice. Adrian follows you down another hallway. The screams have stopped. Your heart is pounding.

Blood runs down your nose. You use the back of your hand to wipe it away.

The hall gives way into another domed room. The wind does not howl here as it did in the aviary. This must be the heart of the Curiosity's sanctuary. It is an arching room of glass. The rising dome is decorated by uneven latticework. There's no sense of proper architecture. Some of the bars run horizontal, some perpendicular. They cut both wide and narrow paths. The effect creates thousands of mismatched windows, some larger than a horse, others the size of your thumb.

One step into the room and you realize it is full. Not with people, at least not in the traditional sense, but with whispers and glimpses. Every window offers a vision. You see men and women from your world. All of them living their lives under a watchful eye.

In the distance—standing over a familiar and lifeless form—is the god of whispers.

The Curiosity.

15

BETRAYAL

ADRIAN

Never seen a place I've liked less.

I follow Pippa into the strange amphitheater. Two people are waiting in the distance. One is lying on the floor, motionless. I can only assume it's the girl Pippa came to rescue. All my attention, however, falls on the person towering over that prone form, the one I know is a god.

The Curiosity is a woman. She's cloaked in black, shaped like a scout in our world. A set of wiry muscles layered over a bird-thin bone structure. But that very human form is framed by a monstrosity. Great wings sweep wide behind her, at least ten paces back from each shoulder. I thought the black material on her head was a hood. I was wrong. It is the head of a creature.

Red eyes stare out from darkness—seven of them— each one hiding a world of secrets within. Talons clutch at the god's bared shoulders, and it takes a moment to realize they're punching straight through skin. Dried blood leaves a stained pattern on human collarbones. I can't help wondering how long this monster has perched there on the shoulders of a deity.

And then there are the whispers.

Voices from our world. Glimpses, too. Each window confirms my people's darkest fears. The gods are not dormant powers from our past, but active agents who spy on our every move. At least, the Curiosity does. She watches our world more closely than we could have ever imagined.

The storm we saw from the plains managed to batter some of the frames, but most of the windows were left unharmed. Through one, I can see a Dividian roasting meat at a fire. Through another, an Ashlord shaving with a bone-thin razor. Yet another reveals Longhands riding across an empty plain. Each window, another life. I can't catch Pippa's eye, but it's odd to note that we're *all* being watched. Not just Longhands. Her people are monitored, too.

"Curiosity," Pippa calls, striking a tone of reverence. "I beg an audience."

I'm surprised when she bows. I stand a few strides back, unsure what to do. The Ashlords are so fond of saying they only bow to the gods, but Longhands don't even do that. I stand in the background and do my best to look inconspicuous. No easy task for a man covered in feathers and blood.

At the sound of Pippa's voice, the god turns.

Both woman and creature *behold* us. It is just a glance, but it cuts deeper than bone. It's like a million tiny blades, digging into flesh, hands sifting through memories and thoughts and dreams. All I can do is grit my teeth and shove back. The feeling briefly fades, but not without a sense that the god has taken something valuable and personal. Her attention swivels to Pippa.

"Sun child. How strange to *see* you here?"

Pippa's head remains bowed. I keep silent. I am thinking of ways to kill the Curiosity. How can I get close enough to strike a proper blow? This is their god of secrets and whispers. Not to mention she's watching our entire world. If the Ashlords are ever a step ahead of our armies, she is the reason why. Kill her and the war changes. . . .

"Goddess," Pippa intones. "I would make a request of you."

The creature's dark wings flutter wide as the god's eyes narrow.

"Ask, then, child."

Pippa finally lifts her eyes but does not look directly at the Curiosity. Instead, she gestures to the discarded form at the god's feet. "I would claim the girl," she says. "The interloper. She used my blood against my gods and against my people. It is an embarrassment to me. I would give an answer."

Her words echo into the quiet. My heart stutters. I can't believe what I'm hearing. Is this why we came here? I thought she wanted to save the girl, not take revenge against her.

"She has many sins to answer for," the Curiosity replies. "This girl killed the Hoarder. A favor to the rest of us, honestly, but coming to my tower was a mistake. This stronghold has stood for centuries, and I have stood with it. She has killed my servants. Trespassed in my halls. Do you think your claim stronger than mine, sun child?"

Pippa bows her head again. "She accomplished all that

with *my* blood. I am the beginning of all this. I would humbly claim her, Goddess."

Those words draw a smile. "You do not do anything humbly, child. That is what we like about you. Do not change
that now. I have heard your claim. Take her. She is yours."

There's a satisfied look on Pippa's face. I've seen it before. A sense of dread knots in my stomach. It was so easy
to trust her. The girl who bound my wounds after the Races.
The one who begged for me to help her when I appeared
in this world a second time. I was foolish enough to think
our connection was the reason I'd returned. I looked into
those dark eyes and believed every single word. I glance
to the nearest tunnel. It's clear I'm alone now, standing in
the inner sanctum of one of the Ashlord gods. All thoughts
before were of attack.

Now I just want to get out of here alive.

"Finish the girl," the Curiosity commands. "Then we will
attend to your other guest."

All those eyes fix on me. My jaw clenches as the prob-
ing fingers try to dig into my mind again. It's impossible to
hold them off. Push back here and they press back there. I
can see the Curiosity's lips curl into a smile, as if she enjoys
breaking me this way. Pippa glances back.

"I brought him as a gift," she says. "In exchange for her."

The red-eyed bird lets out a throaty screech. "A worthy
gift, indeed."

It's almost impossible to resist her gaze *and* move at
the same time, but I slowly backpedal. Moving toward the
tunnel. One thought hammers through my head. This was
all a trap. One more step. Another. Pippa has reached the

platform. The Curiosity moves aside to allow her forward. Pippa rolls the unconscious girl over with the toe of her boot. Her skin is pale. Her dark hair is matted to her forehead. She lets out a pathetic groan, but her eyes do not open as Pippa sets the tip of her sword over the girl's chest.

The Curiosity is watching me. Digging past my defenses. Whispering in my ear. It's impossible to resist. *Set your sword down. Take a seat here on one of my cushions. Rest your head, child.*

"No," I grunt back. "I'm not . . . I can't. . . ."

And she breaks through my last defenses. It's like water rushing through an opened gate. I can feel the god's fingers curling around every thought. My greatest fears. Quiet dreams. Secrets. Helpless, I fall to my knees.

I feel like I'm looking through someone else's eyes as I watch Pippa reach up to her nose. The back of her hand comes away slick with blood. Suddenly, power blooms. Something brighter than lightning. Something louder than thunder. The room becomes a storm.

Her sword rises into the air.

I have been trained in combat my entire life. It's hard not to notice her mistake. The footwork is all wrong. The slight twist of her back heel makes no sense for a plunging blow. It provides no leverage and offers no strength. That small detail is the only hint.

Her blade falls short, a breath away from Quinn's neck. Pippa's back foot pivots. Her hips swing around. Her left elbow tightens to her side. The silver tip circles, following the perfect angle of her body, no more than a blur of silver. It aims instead at the unsuspecting goddess.

But the great creature on the Curiosity's shoulders is too instinctual. It reacts faster than Pippa can strike. I watch the black wings sweep backward. It's trying to take flight, and that single step of retreat nearly draws its master to safety. Until more power thunders into the room. I watch the impossible. Pippa's sword extends. It reaches out just far enough to gut the god.

The Curiosity collapses, blood spilling out. I feel the vise around my thoughts lift immediately. It's like surfacing a moment before drowning. I heave in deep breaths, eyes wide.

And as she falls, the creature takes flight. Its black body twists away. A gust from stretching wings knocks Pippa back. I'm still staring in disbelief when Pippa shouts my own words back to me.

"Are you just going to stand there?"

I remember the weapon in my hand. I trace the creature's escape route. Two long strides carry me directly into its path. All seven eyes widen. It screeches as my sword crushes down into its skull. A thousand whispered voices trumpet into shouts. All followed by deafening silence.

The corpse crashes into my shoulder, claws twitching and grasping. We both go down. I scramble out from beneath the squirming creature to find Pippa staring at me, her chest heaving. The Curiosity is dead. Her monstrous bird is, too.

"You were lying to her," I gasp. "About all of it."

"Well, obviously!"

I'm stunned. "Why not tell me the plan?"

"And have the Curiosity pluck it right out of your mind? No thanks. Get me a med kit."

My hands are actually shaking. It takes a second to dig through her knapsack and find the kit. I've been through battles. I have stared death in the eye, but this was the first time I truly felt like I was going to die. We stood in the throne room of a god. And we won.

I can't help hitching on the word *we*. I look at the girl who summoned me here. The dark-eyed girl with fire under her skin and secrets in her heart. Are we actually working together?

Pippa takes the med kit and begins working. As she kneels, I realize I've seen her patient before. Hidden in that flash of blue, there was a face. "The girl at the end of the Races."

"Her name is Quinn."

"And you came here to save her."

She's too intent on her work to respond. I watch as she patches every wound carefully. I can't help remembering the way she took care of me in that dark carriage. There was a tenderness to it, as there is a tenderness now. There's also a disturbing truth looming in the room with us. A corpse that is already beginning to turn.

"You killed a god."

Pippa drops her needle. I realize her hands are shaking, too. Her eyes search the strange room before finding mine. Now her voice trembles with fear.

"What have I done?"

PART TWO

GODS

Deity is sleight of hand. A daily act of
distracting the puppet from its strings.

—The Striving, Our Bright Futures

16

ACCOMPLICE

PIPPA

Adrian Ford circles the throne room.

You are very studiously avoiding the looks he keeps throwing in your direction. Quinn has steadied under your care. She's woken up a few times, long enough to discuss your strategy for what is to come, but now she is sleeping. You're confident she'll fully revive. A glance across the room confirms the Curiosity will *not* be reviving any time soon. You and Adrian dragged a pair of obnoxious curtains into the throne room and covered the corpses as well as you could. Too bad they can't also hide the foul scent of the dead god and her dark-feathered pet.

After nursing Quinn, you sat there in shock for a while. It was all you could do to take one breath after the next. It was just so strange. You'd not imagined that a god could die so easily. Just a single stroke of your sword and a little bit of . . .

Blood.

Eventually, that was the thought that forced you back to your feet. You made sure Quinn was well, and then you set about the task of finding answers. You left no stone unturned. You wanted answers to questions you'd never thought to ask before. And where better than here?

The god of whispers called this place home for centuries. The very stones breathe secrets. You searched and searched, and now the only problem is that you found answers. Now you must decide what to do with the knowledge you have. Your eyes flick to the Longhand.

"Could you stop *pacing*?"

Adrian frowns. "You're literally pacing! Right now."

You look down at your feet and realize he's right. When you look back up, that grin is waiting for you. Before the Races, you thought it was a look of pure pride. A rebellious boy who needed to be put in his place. Now, though, you see it's his way of dealing with stress. He prefers to turn everything into a joke. At least it's a pretty smile.

"Whatever. I have a good reason to be pacing."

He laughs. "Because your people's history is so embarrassing?"

"It's not *embarrassing*," you reply. "It's . . . All right, it's embarrassing. But it's not just *our* history. It's your history, too."

Books are sprawled everywhere. The two of you have been working together, quietly combing through the Curiosity's private library. It was a delicate balance over the past few days to keep returning to this world. In between searches, you've returned to the real world to meet with your generals and even paused your army's progress in

Navassa, under the guise of restocking supplies for the next march. It's given you the window you've needed to keep rendezvousing with Adrian in the Curiosity's tower. Doing so while marching would have been risky. Servants would have noticed your absence. Here it is well-hidden. Which makes it even more impressive that Adrian's worked with you while his army's been on the move. The poor thing looks exhausted.

It was good that you had time, because the Curiosity's record-keeping was extensive. In fact, there is a book for every person who has ever existed. You found the names written on thin, white-spined journals. Each one contained notes, taken by the goddess and her messengers. The first decision you and Adrian made was to burn the copies with *your* names on them.

It didn't take long to find far more important secrets.

In the library's oldest section, there were histories. One of those texts detailed the first meeting between your people and the pantheon. It was not what you expected.

"Are we sure we can trust this information?" you ask. "What if it's fictional?"

Adrian shrugs his broad shoulders. "It's written in the Curiosity's own hand. Nor does it read like a story. It's a historical account, Pippa. She wasn't expecting anyone to read what she'd written. We have no reason to question its validity."

You secretly enjoy the sound of your name on his lips, even if the other words are all far less welcome. The book in question sits on the table between you. It's thrown open to a page that will change the entire course of history. Or rather, a page that illuminates your people's *true* history. A single leather-bound volume, and it just might be the most dangerous weapon in the world.

"Ashlords," you mutter. "The truth was written in the name they gave us."

Adrian nods. "It makes sense. We were the gods."

Both of you read the account at the same time, shoulders pressed together, discovering the impossible. The Curiosity was the first to name us Ashlords. That initial meeting was historic for them, and her writing makes it clear how they viewed your people. You were powerful beings who ruled over their world of ashes below. Your footsteps were their thunder. Your fights were their lightning. It was believed that when you wept, it rained in their world. The supposed "pantheon" saw *your ancestors* as their gods. Until one of the cleverest among them asked a simple question. What if they could turn these heavenly creatures *against* one another?

"Who do you think it was?" you ask. "The god who suggested that first plan?"

Adrian doesn't hesitate. "The Dread."

You nod. That was your first guess as well. It all began with a bold plan. One of the "gods" visited your world. He found that your ancestors were not fully satisfied. They were powerful, of course, but forced to share their power with others. The current pantheon decided to stoke those flames into a proper fire. The first wars began. And the underworld was positioned perfectly. In a battle of equals, who could tip the scales? Naturally, they could.

"Did you see the first gift?" Adrian asks. "On the next page."

You nod. "They sent a stampede of horses to distract an enemy . . ."

". . . in exchange for blood," Adrian finishes. "The first blood sacrifice. The first horses."

And that is how it began. Your blood for their help. Special gifts and extra troops. Always there was a trade. It went on that way—according to the Curiosity's records—for more than a century. The plan worked. The Curiosity notes that over time, the power of the Ashlords grew fainter. Her theory was that every sacrifice weakened your kind as it strengthened the gods. In the world below, your blood is the most powerful weapon. It is no wonder that Quinn wanted some during the Races. She was asking you for a way to defend herself against the gods.

All the infighting also fractured your society. It wasn't until nearly two hundred years later that the pantheon did something even cleverer. "They destroyed us with words."

Adrian nods. "It's just propaganda. Your people did that with the first Dividian census. Reducing all their names to four letters? It creates a new power dynamic."

"I can only guess where we learned that strategy."

The Curiosity details several edicts that were passed. Each one was designed for the interactions the underworld had with our world. They stopped calling their offerings "sacrifices." Far better to call what they gave us "gifts." An agreement was made that no one should refer to us as gods. In all future exchanges, they did not "request" our blood— they "demanded" it.

"Little by little, we forgot that we were gods."

Adrian nods again. "I read one scholar who said that perspective defines existence. If I grew up competing against
a brother who was stronger than me, I might go on forever
thinking myself weak. But if my brother is the strongest
person in the world, the reality is that I might actually be
the second-strongest person in the world. My limited perspective gave me the wrong impression." He gestures to the
textbooks around us. "It's almost like putting blinders on a
horse. The gods forced us to see things *their* way."

He catches you staring at him. The last few days have
been enlightening. You went into the Races thinking him
a spectacle, pure muscle and little else. It has been nice to
discover that he's rather well-read. Bravos never saw the
point to books.

Adrian gestures to the text. "Did you see the Striving's
first title?"

That draws a smile to your face. "The Yearning."

After patiently shifting the power dynamic, the most
elite members of the underworld decided to take on god-
like titles, intent on elevating their status in the eyes of your
people. Most of the names written in the Curiosity's notes
are the same ones we use today: the Fury, the Dread, the
Butcher. Only the Striving's name was different. The Curiosity notes that she eventually changed it because the first
generation thought she was the goddess of sex.

"We shouldn't laugh."

Adrian smirks. "It's the only thing that's funny in the
whole damn book."

He's not wrong about that. The rest of the book is far too
depressing to be humorous. It details how their plan worked.

Generations of our people were born into a lie after that, even if we were allowed to pretend ourselves the true rulers of this world. We didn't realize our blood was their power. We didn't know that we were once the ones that *they* feared.

"So . . . what are we going to do about it?"

Now Adrian grins more wickedly. "We?"

You scowl at him. He likes to pretend that you're not working together, as if you're still mortal enemies or something. Never mind that he helped you carve a path to the Curiosity's throne. Never mind that he's spent the past few days acting like he's your study partner at university. It's almost like he enjoys drawing that scowl out of you.

"I cannot remake the world by myself."

His eyes narrow. You like this side of him, too. It's his serious look. All the pretense fades away because he knows he's facing something that will change history.

"It's not that simple."

"But it is. Either you are with me or you are against me."

"It's not—you're talking about a *completely* different world. I've got soldiers marching to my orders. Generals who've dreamed of nothing but war for decades. It's not that simple."

"If they won't listen to you, who will they listen to?"

It's surprising how hard that hits him. He looks down at his feet and it's like the entire world is sitting on his broad shoulders. You do not blame him for a moment of weakness. Anyone else would have been crushed beneath the weight of these discoveries. He's been steadier than expected for someone who just learned their entire world is built upon a lie.

"How can I trust you'll do what you've promised?" he asks.

"I am the one with the most to lose," you remind him. "If you whisper this to any of the other gods, I'll be hunted. Likely I've already caught their attention. I am trusting you as much as you are trusting me. The plan we discussed is the best way forward. Surely you can see that."

It took a long time to get him this far. If there is one thing the Longhands share with your people, it is their tendency toward stubbornness. We always believe we know better than everyone else. You wait patiently now, because you have been doing this your entire life. One master class after the next of bending people to your will, and that is what you're hoping to do now. Adrian's just a different sort of metal.

"I'll make the first move," he whispers. "I hope this works."

Music to your ears. You stride back through the throne room, aiming for the location where Quinn first used the blood she was given to call you down into this world. Adrian matches your steps. This is how you've been able to travel back and forth. The blood created what Quinn describes as a temporary pathway. It will close—or be closed by the Madness—eventually. But Quinn made sure you knew of other ways to return. Your plan requires it.

As you reach the spot, you eye your new counterpart. It's easy to forget how tall he is until you're standing there in his shadow. It is one thing to see him at a distance, and quite another thing to stand this close. Proximity does not disappoint. As you hold out your hand to shake, you realize that he has something else Bravos lacks. Standing there, you know this is a leader who can keep pace with you. On a horse, in the war, in all that is to come. He's up to the challenge in a way most are not. Your heart thunders as his hand grasps yours.

"Deal?"

He shakes. "Deal."

The moment stretches. He has dark eyes and cold hands and a quiet smile. His chest is punching out through a white riding shirt and his arms barely fit inside his standard military jacket. You can tell he's taking your measure, too. And for once you do not mind.

"Pippa . . ." His voice falters. "If . . ."

You pull away, shaking your head at his doubt.

"We are not making a backup plan. This will work."

The fire in your voice catches. You can see it spark hope in his eyes.

"See you on the other side."

It's like stepping back through a curtain. He vanishes first. That trusting look still painted across his face. You have a final, fleeting thought of Quinn. She's already working on her part of the plan—and you hope she can fully recover in time. All that matters now is whether or not she's up to the task ahead. Next, the world of the gods vanishes. You're back inside the stone baths, the linking point in your own world. It is where you first heard Quinn's desperate scream. After taking a deep breath, you dress in your best armor, cinching buckles and tightening your gauntlets.

All three generals are waiting in your chamber. Etzli is pacing nervously. It is the first time you've ever seen her even slightly unhinged. Revel's staring into a mirror, using a knife to trim his sideburns. Bravos raises a single eyebrow at your arrival.

"Well?" Etzli asks. "What did he say?"

You smile at them.

"Time to burn it all down."

The three of them follow as you march back through the hallways. Servants flock forward, but you send them all away. Outside, soldiers are patrolling the courtyard. Each is one of the Fury's strange creatures. You signal to the nearest and she lurches over to where you're standing. You've noticed patterns among them. This one is something of a leader. She's got a waxen face darkened by freckles that look more like dried paint. Her short hair is dark and spiky.

"I have new orders for all of you."

She watches and waits. That is another thing you've noticed about them. Everything is dead except for those vibrant eyes. It has you wondering about their loyalty. The Fury said that these were your creatures now, but it's possible they still serve him as well. You have to hope that the power of your command sways them.

"Head west," you say, trying to sound confident. "Travel by whatever means necessary. Waste no time. There is a Longhand army near Grove. You must avoid their scouts. Paint your blades black if necessary. Wait for a moonless night."

All three of your generals stand within earshot. You've invited them into your plan. You've informed them about what you've learned of the pantheon. Now you must hope that your trust in them is not misguided, or all of this will go rather horribly for you.

"... and bring me Adrian Ford."

A moment passes. The creature does not ask who Adrian is, because all the god's servants know him by now. Instead, she turns and begins loping toward the front gates. Every revenant abandons its post as she passes, falling in step. You watch with satisfaction as ninety trained warriors obey your command. There is one other person in the world who knows the truth about the gods.

And they're going to find him.

17

EXPECTATIONS

IMELDA

I return to quiet.

It is evening at Locklin Tower. There is no crowd gathered to celebrate my safe return. A pair of lanterns wink at me from the entryway. Our newly discovered passage into the underworld boasts a single guard. I stand in the shadows of the first stall and consider him.

Bastian's chin has dipped down to his chest in sleep. The weight of his hardware arm rests on a stone ledge to his right. Everything that hardens his appearance—the clenched jaw and the piercing eyes and the fighter's stance—has slipped briefly away. His dark hair looks a mess. His lips are slightly parted. Sleeping like this, he's just a boy again.

I cross the room. Shadows dance in the courtyard. A game of cards is happening around a fire. None of the crew notices my return. I stand over Bastian, close enough to hear the rhythmic whispers of his breathing. I can't help thinking about what Cora Rowe told me. The threats Bastian made about returning me unharmed. I watch his chest rise and fall, and I can't help wondering, *What does this handsome boy see when he looks at me?*

As gently as possible, I set a hand on his shoulder. "Bastian?"

He startles awake. It's striking how quickly he transforms. His free hand reaches for a weapon. His eyes sharpen into a pair of blue blades. And then he sees that it's me. He takes a deep breath and leans back in his chair. It takes him a moment to realize my hand is still on his shoulder. His own hand trembles as he reaches up to set it on mine.

"Imelda."

There's so much comfort in his touch. Comfort in the heat that stirs between my hand and his. I know he's bound to be furious with me. No doubt his crew came back complaining about how reckless I was. For a brief moment we pretend none of that matters.

"I'm glad you're alive," he says.

I nod. "That's my preference, too."

His face breaks into a tired smile. I'm about to explain everything—why I didn't return right away and what happened with the prince—when he pulls me closer. It's surprising enough that my feet aren't ready. I stumble forward, falling into his lap. It draws nervous laughter from both of us, but nervousness cannot stop what comes next. His eyes are asking permission in the way they keep darting to my lips. I run a trembling hand through his hair. The other hand has hold of his collar. I give him permission by leaning down and kissing him first.

His neck arches back. His hand tangles in my hair,

pulling me closer. There's magic in the way he tugs at my bottom lip. It takes a little time to learn the steps, but it's a dance I do not mind rehearsing. I shift my hips, kissing him more deeply, when I hear a noise. The slight creak of wood. It's the only warning.

The back leg of his chair gives way and we both crash to the ground. He absorbs most of my fall, but we both end up on our backs, groaning and laughing together. There's a stir out in the courtyard. A few seconds later, Cora Rowe peeks around the corner.

"Boss?"

My cheeks are already a violent shade of red. Bastian's leveraged himself into a sitting position and waves her away. "No worries, Cora. Imelda returned and I broke a chair."

Cora considers our position, the snapped leg, and performs some basic arithmetic. The obvious answer has her grinning as she steps back out of the room. I barely catch the sound of stifled laughter and her muttered, "Something from nothing. Sounds about right."

Bastian looks at me, clearly hoping to pick up where we left off, and I laugh at him.

"That was quite a welcome back."

He shrugs. "I've wanted to do that since I first saw you. Consider it an apology, too. It was my fault you almost didn't come back. I wasn't watching that little bastard for a second. He summoned the horse and rode off without a saddle. We were getting ready to follow him when Cora and Briar returned. I couldn't believe they came back without you."

His voice has a little edge to it, so I do my best to draw his anger back in the proper direction, toward me. "It happened fast," I say. "Don't blame them. I saw the prince escaping. Instinct took over. I thought we'd be in a lot of trouble if he made it back to the wrong people."

Bastian takes a breath before nodding.

"And?" he asks. "Did you catch him? What happened?"

"He's gone, but I learned how to beat them."

He laughs. "The Ashlord Empire?"

"No, their gods."

The laughter dies away. He weighs the look on my face. "You actually want to go back."

I knew this would be the hard part. Bastian's a mountain-born rebel. He's got plenty of spine, but it takes something else entirely to invade another world. Especially one populated by notorious deities. I knew he'd resist and I knew his biggest concern would be my safety. But we can't afford to play it safe this time. Not with an opportunity like this one.

"I don't *want* to go back. I *have* to go back."

He shakes his head. "Imelda, you could have died down there."

"But I didn't."

"This time. We can't go back. It's not worth the risk."

I stare at him. "You don't even know what I learned down there. Is this who you are? A boy who will kiss a girl before he'll listen to her?"

That hits him hard. I can see his mind turning the accusation over. Eventually, he throws that roguish grin my way. "You're right. Go ahead. Tell me what you learned."

"I interrogated the prince. The gods can be killed. One of them is already dead."

Bastian nods. "Briar told me about that. The weakest god. What's that to us?"

"It wasn't an accident. He was killed. If the gods can be killed . . ."

Bastian pushes back. "But we didn't have a hand in it. Briar said you found the city in ruins. The army was dead and the Hoarder was dying. We have no idea who was responsible. No idea if they'd agree to work with us. It could have been one of the other gods for all we know."

Normally, I'd let it go, but this is important. Besides, Bastian's crew has always worked this way. Honest discussions lead to the wisest decisions. I just have to hold my ground.

"It proves the gods are vulnerable. All we need is a weapon."

Bastian takes the bait. "Last I checked, guns and swords don't work on their kind."

"You're right. But according to the little prince, our blood does."

He falls silent, eyes narrowed. "How do you mean?"

"Our blood is power in the world below," I answer. "I'm not exactly sure how it works, but think about it. It's the one thing the gods demand. Every temple takes blood. Why ask for something unless it has purpose? I saw with my own eyes what our blood can do when I chased the prince. He summoned a wall out of thin air."

And now we arrive at the second turning point in the conversation. I am the only one who saw the prince perform his magic. It would be easy to dismiss the story, easy to distrust me. Which makes his next question even more surprising.

"You're certain?"

I nod. "I saw it happen. Our blood is power there. Look, I know this is asking a lot. But that's what you said to me after the battle of Gig's Wall. You told me that mountain folk don't sit on the sidelines when war comes knocking. It might feel more logical to keep doing what we're doing. Knocking off castles. Freeing prisoners. That's all good. But I'm pretty sure *this*"—I punctuate the word by pointing to the stables behind me—"is a path to actually defeating the Ashlords for good. Go down there, sow some chaos, and we'll change the world."

I've been rehearsing these words for hours. I kept hoping they wouldn't sound hollow when I actually said them. Bastian stares for a moment, then surprises me with a grin.

"Rebellion looks good on you," he says. "Let's do it."

I stare back at him. "Just like that?"

"Well, I'm sure it will be quite difficult to ride into the underworld and start knocking off gods, but yes. Just like that. What did you expect me to say? Hard to maintain a reputation as an outlaw if you turn down the chance to destroy a pantheon."

It is such a relief that I lunge forward and wrap him in a hug. I'd already been planning for him to reject the offer. It was my intention to return to the underworld on my own if necessary. The idea of having him and his crew at my side is a breath of fresh air.

Bastian laughs. "All right, you're choking me a little."

"Sorry."

He pushes up to his feet before turning to help me to my mine. "No worries. You should go get some rest. We'll talk through the plan in the morning. The Longhands will be here to negotiate. Once we handle that, we can figure out what to do next."

I start walking toward the entryway before remembering we just kissed for the first time. It's one thing to make a plan to destroy tyrants and gods, but no one's ever taught me the proper protocols for what to do after a first kiss. I turn back and catch him staring after me, still looking a bit dazed.

"Was . . . Do you want to try that again sometime soon?"

He grins. "Sure. I'll pick a sturdier chair next time."

I offer him a final smile before marching through the courtyard. Harlow Rowe looks up from the fire—along with a few others—and crows a welcome back. I wave at them but don't trust myself to form proper sentences at the moment. Instead, I head straight for the barracks. There are plenty of empty bunks waiting. A few of the other crew members are there, some already snoring. I slip out of my boots, wash my hands in the nearest basin, and climb into bed.

It's hard to fall asleep. I'm not sure which I'm most excited about. The prospect of kissing Bastian again or going back to that other world on my Bloodsworn mount. I fall asleep, silently promising to never tell Bastian the real answer to that question.

I wake to the promise of a new world.

It fills my steps with purpose. We will do the unthinkable today. Most of the crew are still at breakfast as I aim for the ramparts. Our two remaining princes are bound in the courtyard with a few of the other prisoners. Bastian will exchange them for Dividian captives and supplies for the

next mission. A glance shows a column of Longhands working their way up the steep slope. Bastian waits for them atop
the ramparts. I cross the walkway to join him.

He smiles. "You could have slept in, you know?"

"I wanted to get started."

Below us, the Longhand generals are about to arrive.
Marching through their ranks are hundreds of Dividian prisoners. I watch them come. There are women who look like my
mother. Little boys who look just like Prosper. Men like Father,
who were forced to march to war alongside their masters. All
of them have been taken captive since the start of the war.

This is why I decided to join Bastian's crew. At first, I
thought he was an outlaw riding into battles for glory, but he
told me the real goal was to free more of our people. Trade
our victories for their freedom. Send them back to the mountains to start new lives. I knew I could never play it safe on
some farm in the mountains while his soldiers risked everything to save other Dividian. We've done that on a small
scale. But today marks the start of something bigger.

Real freedom.

I can see the same fire catching in Bastian's eyes.

"Go ahead and get the ashes ready. We have to finish the
negotiations first but might as well have things prepared. I'll
be down there soon."

I'm thankful that he doesn't want me to stay around for
the negotiations. I've got nothing to offer when it comes to
political bargaining. My real place is in the secret room per-
forming alchemy. I cross the courtyard again. There's chaos
everywhere as the prisoners are prepared for transport. The
door to the secret stall is cracked open. It offers a welcome

quiet. I stand there by the entrance, breathing in those familiar scents, before settling into my work.

First, I set out the ashes. There are nearly fifteen other phoenixes stored here, each one waiting to ride again. Combined with our own number, there should be almost enough to cover the entire crew. I settle them into the stalls one by one, positioning them so they're centered below where the blood siphons will drop down from the walls. After they're all set out, I collect the ingredients for the Bloodsworn rebirth again. Luckily, this is an Ashlord stronghold, which means they've got plenty of every component.

As I work, a shiver runs down my spine. My eyes dart back to the entryway, but it's empty. Everyone else is back at the gates. I shrug off the feeling and keep working. It's a rather intricate pattern. I follow the directions, recalling my memory of the first ashes we found here, and it takes nearly twenty clockturns to get the first three stalls settled.

A break is necessary. My back starts cramping up, bent over in those tight spaces, so I stand and stretch. There's a workspace in the opposite corner. I cross the room and spy the notebooks some other alchemist left behind. I turn to the page that has the Bloodsworn mixture and start working through a few exercises. Flexing my mind instead of my body. This is something I used to do when I worked with Farian. Most of our mixtures were revived from ancient texts, but some of them were my own invention. I never advertised that, because honestly, I wasn't sure if the Ashlords would take notice—or offense. They don't exactly love when people mess with their traditions.

But I learned enough of the science behind the alchemy

to improvise. Horses that were slightly sleeker or brighter or any number of minor adjustments. The Bloodsworn mixture has me more curious than any other recipe. It's the only alchemical combination I've ever seen that uses human blood. I've read a *lot* of textbooks on the subject. Each one starts out with a list of rules. The first rule in every single volume? Never mix human blood with ashes.

It has me wondering if there are ways to tweak this particular combination. Maybe there are other reasons that the Ashlords—or their gods—did not want us to have it. I run the numbers a few times, taking pinches of powder and swirling them into a cube on my belt. There are several intriguing possibilities, but I won't be able to test them out until I'm back in the world below.

Just thinking of that place sends another shiver down my spine.

I recall the bloodied throne room. The dead god that we found. Thinking about that has me curious about what happened next. Chasing the prince through the countryside. The one thing we don't know is where the other gods live. Where are their fortresses? I flip over to one of the blank pages in the journal and start sketching out every detail I remember. There was the valley on our right. Mountains on our left. Anything that might help guide us. I set the writing utensil down and step back, admiring my rough map.

"Hmm. Now we just have to find the gods."

There's a rustle, like the wind. A voice drips into my ear.

"Oh, dear, dear . . . you've already *found* one."

Before I can turn, there's a thud, a sharp slash of pain, and darkness.

18

GROVE

ADRIAN

Dawn brightens the horizon.

I raise one hand, giving the signal, and five hundred horses start forward. A rising wind tosses our cloaks from shoulder to shoulder. Sand crunches under hooves. We press our horses into a trot. A strange quiet fills the air as packed sand gives way to ocean. I tighten my grip on the reins as the horses glide impossibly over the surface of the water.

One horse already waits for us in the distance. Farian pretty much demanded to go out there before we did. Something about the lighting being just right? At this point, he films everything. Sometimes he'll be waiting for me outside the command tent, excited to show off the day's footage. The soldiers are getting used to having him around—with Martial always watching in the background—but right now I'm mostly focused on not falling into the ocean.

I settle into a rhythm and lead five hundred riders out to sea.

The River's Light rebirth was made popular a decade ago. The Empire Racing Board designed a course that featured the Lonely River—one of the country's most famous stretches of water. It forced the riders to summon horses that could run along the surface. All these years later, it's still one of the most beloved courses in the history of the Races. It was chaos. Riders knocking each other off their mounts. The fallen swept downstream, their phoenixes forced to backtrack and collect them along the treacherous stone banks.

I pray no one falls from their saddle today. Not in these waters. A glance shows Farian struggling on his mount, the eye of the camera trailing our progress. Even my seasoned riders look uncomfortable. Salt fills the air, gathering on our skin. Sunlight carves a false road of gold across the blue. We follow it, plunging through the mouth of the cove.

Open sea waits. Gulls wheel overhead. I squint throug the splashes of white seafoam and look south. Grov ships are there, glinting like prizes. Another signal from has the ranks widening. No ships can escape. Our plan take them all. There are thirty soldiers on my right. Ar thirty on my left. Matching rows fall into position bel

Heat scorches the back of my neck. Sunlight gli everything. We're depending on that. Enemy so look north and see only the blinding horizon. O that by the time they spy us, it will be far too la

Our horses snort as the waves get a littl lighted. This is what they were made to i accustomed to riding the waves. My stomac fortably. On my right, Forrest Trask loses h

talked me into evening drinks a few times now, in between marches. *In between visits to the Curiosity's tower,* I think in the darkest corner of my mind. I'm just thankful I declined last night. He wipes at his beard with a gauntlet before looking over at me.

"I'll have to make sure Farian cuts that from the footage," he says. "I have a reputation to uphold."

I grin back at him. "Your reputation is floating out to sea."

He laughs. Several other soldiers are looking green. We return to our silent approach as Grove begins to loom larger. We're about five hundred paces from the bay when Grove begins to wake, like a giant rumbling to life. There are cries from the front of the city. Bells ring in warning. The scouts have spotted our army marching toward them on land. A stolen march in the night brings an enemy to their door.

From our vantage point on the water, we can see Ashlord soldiers scrambling to the docks, boarding the waiting ships. Our guess was right. Their plan was to flee. Avoid a direct battle, sail to the north, cause some trouble. Adrenaline pulses in my chest as I watch.

"Swords!"

All down the ranks, hands drift to belts. Sunlight dances across drawn blades. Our lines hold steady as the first ship pulls anchor and begins making for the open ocean. It's a galley ship. Seventy paces from end to end. The oars are all manned—some twenty on each side—and they tooth down into the water with flawless rhythm. It's expected. These are the finest sailors in the Empire.

Too bad they won't make it out to sea.

We reach the mouth of the bay at the same time they

do. There's no hiding now. Our horses snort. Our soldiers whoop. Our metal shines. The ranks divide around the first wooden hull. Each rower sits low along the railings, undefended. My horse takes the tightest line, hugging the side of the ship, curling around until the first soldier comes into sight. I can hear Forrest whooping as he follows me into the chaos.

The first Ashlord's eyes widen. Captains are shouting orders, but he reaches for the weapon at his hip far too late. My horse hurdles over his oar and I bring my sword cracking down diagonally. It splits him open. There are screams from every direction. My sword swipes another exposed throat, opens a stomach, slits a wrist. Each swing is punctuated by another hurdle over the oars.

I clear the first ship and aim for a second. Other soldiers have ridden ahead to harass their sides. A third ship looms on my left. I see our crew leaping from their horses, boarding in chaotic slashes of steel and bone. All three ships fall into our hands in less than a breath.

A fire breaks out on the fourth ship. Soldiers are down in the water, drowning and wrestling and screaming. A horn blows. Gunfire answers from the docks, but their soldiers pick off as many of their own team as ours. Too much chaos. Another horn blows.

It isn't until I hear Martial screaming that I find the reason.

"Turn around, idiots! Turn and face!"

I whip around in time to see fifty enemy horses storming out of a hidden cove. Their leader has a familiar look. I forgot his name during the Races, but it comes to me now.

Darvin. The son of a famous general. Raised on the coast his whole life. All those details matter less than the most obvious one: He's about to charge fifty horses into our flank.

"Turn and face!" I shout, echoing Martial's order. "To me! Form up ranks!"

Some of my soldiers can't break away. Forrest Trask has already cut a path deeper into the docks. Abandoned mounts circle the ships waiting for their riders to return. One soldier is tangled in ropes and the rowers pull until he falls off his horse. Instead of hitting the water, the ropes go taut and nearly snap him in two.

My eyes flick back to the approaching horses. Their advance is silent. They are halfway to us now. I turn to face them, counting the fighters who have rallied to Martial and me. Only twenty.

"Staggered rows," Martial hisses low. "We just have to keep them busy."

I nod to him. "Two rows. Form up! Full speed!"

The fighters shuffle positions, and then we're darting between ships, riding out to meet the enemy. I take lead of the first row, followed closely by Martial on the second. We're close enough to see the freckles on their faces. The Ashlord soldiers let out a war cry. Darvin beats his chest, eyes locked on me. There's a breath of space between us. Arms flexed, armor bright, jaws clenched.

I raise my sword as our line crashes into theirs. Horses scream. My steel catches Darvin's. The impact shakes me from elbow to hip. Momentum forces us past each other. I turn back a blow from a soldier on his second line, then slip my blade up through another rider's ribs. He falls as I bring my horse swinging around. Darvin's team is doing the same. Abandoned horses stomp and snort between us. Soldiers are struggling down in the water. The dead can only float.

"Again!" I shout. "Swords!"

We thunder toward each other. Martial punches into their line first, his sword cutting bone-deep. Darvin finds me again. There isn't enough momentum to carry us out of range this time. So our horses circle, ears pinning, as we trade blows. A riderless horse jolts between us. I use the brief separation to backhand an Ashlord soldier on my right. He goes reeling from the saddle.

The gap clears. I grit my teeth and block Darvin's first swing. I'm the better swordsman. I proved that once already in the Races. But he is far more comfortable on the water. His horse's footwork is its own kind of magic. The creature dances back on my swings and darts forward on his. It has each blow ringing my forearms. Around us, soldiers are dying. Martial leaps onto someone else's horse. Bells are ringing.

Darvin catches me with a beautiful feint. He stabs high, and I answer by parrying upward. It leaves my blade high and my body exposed. His horse moves with purpose. It dips a shoulder down toward the water. A trained maneuver, because Darvin's body matches the motion perfectly. He drops down and uses the angle to jab upward.

The blade misses. The metal guard doesn't.

Bright light. A feeling like falling. The light sky swallowed by dark sea. The cold sends shocks down my spine. Water soaks the clothes beneath my armor, weighing me down. Instinct has me wanting to fight back to the surface, but I tamp that down and squint through the dark instead. The dead stare at nothing. Hooves dance on the surface.

I stay down, eyeing everything. My horse to the right, backpedaling. Another horse circles and I know it's Darvin. Waiting for me to rise so he can finish me off.

I've got no sword, no upper ground, no horse. It leaves only one option. I sidestroke to the right until I'm positioned directly behind his horse. There's no time for fear. An upward stroke brings me to the surface. I leap out of the water and grab the only thing I can reach.

His horse's tail.

The creature unleashes a violent scream. It tries to kick, but I'm already scaling its rump. Darvin twists in his saddle. I lunge before he can fully turn, wrapping one arm around his neck and the other under his sword arm. We fall over one side together. I lock my hands, tightening around his chest like a noose, as we hit the water.

I'm expecting him to struggle. Instead, he lets go of his sword. His body goes still. I'm blinking in the dark, trying to figure out what he's up to, when the two of us begin to sink. Our combined weight is too much. Darvin's eyes close. His expression is calm. We keep slipping down into darker waters. My heart starts racing. The bay runs far deeper than I knew.

The light of the surface is fading.

Down here, no one can help me. There's no sign of Martial Rava, or Kenly Knox, or Forrest Trask. There's no one but me and Darvin and the darkness. I'm surprised when Pippa's face flashes to the forefront of my mind. The way she looked at me when we shook hands, hoping to build a new world. Will that dream really die with me drowning below the waves?

I can't risk that.

I let go of Darvin and start to kick upward, but he snatches at my waist. His legs twist around mine like a wrestler. I curse—wasting more breath—and try to get free of him. Every time I pry his arms off, though, he encircles me again. I know I'm stronger, but down here it doesn't matter. He's quicker and water-savvy. I have no sword, no dagger, nothing.

My lungs start to burn.

I am going to die. I am going to die. I am going to die.

I'm reaching down for his face, hoping to get my thumbs at his eyes, when his hands suddenly release. I look down and see other shadows circling the deep. I take two panicked strokes upward before I recognize them. There's just enough light to see the massive iron-scaled shells. Giant turtles surround Darvin. Their jaws close around his ankles, dig into the meat of his arms. He screams soundlessly for help, but the creatures are without mercy. I watch until one finds his neck. Blood plumes out. I shove up to the surface in terror.

The Dread's creatures are here.

He saved me again.

Grove surrenders quickly.

Our soldiers come grinning through the front gates. I'm soaked to the bone, heart still pounding. It's the second time the Dread has saved me from dying. The god of caution is not so bold that he walks the city streets with us, but the turtles are enough of a sign. I saw the truth on Darvin's face, too. He knew he'd been betrayed.

It's their own damn fault. Forgotten gods are bound to cause trouble.

We count prisoners and start interrogations. Martial's out in a rowboat with Farian. There are several other pairings navigating the grim waters, collecting the dead or pulling out anyone who's lucky enough to still be treading water. I'm thankful when Forrest Trask comes thundering over to clap me on the shoulder. He's got a gash on one arm, but otherwise looks unharmed. "Killing Ashlords out at sea has its perks," he laughs. "No need to bury them!"

I pretend to smile until another lieutenant pulls me away. Only seven longships survived the attack. All of them are dragged back to the docks. I order the survivors to unload their stock and start setting up skeleton crews. The boats give us another supply route. We'll have them running north in no time.

I'm too tired to do more than nod as lieutenants make the rest of the arrangements. Sleep has not been restful lately. I have Pippa and her friend to thank for that.

My eyes trace the waves. Darvin is down there somewhere. My hands are so calm now, but I know it could have been me who drowned. Turning away, I follow a group of soldiers back into the city. Sunlight has discolored all the buildings. Centuries of wind and salt have slowly peeled away the paint. It has a certain beauty to it, even if the pale stones are splashed with blood.

A group of my fighters walk ahead—Kenly among them—

boasting of their own battles. How many they killed. How close the blades came. I do not speak as I follow them.

We pass the empty doorway of a sacked cathedral. Movement draws my attention. Empty one moment, full the next. A figure looms in front of the shattered glass doors. It's no surprise.

The Dread.

He is a man this time, thin as an arrow. I can count every rib. The vessel gestures for me to follow. My soldiers walk without so much as a glance back. Behind me, the streets are empty. Always the cautious god. I ascend the marbled steps. The Dread turns and leads me within.

I do not fear him. Why save me one moment to kill me the next? It's clear he sees me as a useful tool. I see him exactly the same way. It's getting hard to tell who will come out on top.

"Thank you," I say. "For intervening."

The vessel looks back with surprise. "Finally starting to understand?"

I make no reply. Daddy always used to say there's a big gap between being thankful and being friends. I am not planning to bend the knee, and deep down I think that's what he wants. If not as my god, then at least as my benefactor. The thought spins my mind back to the throne room with Pippa. All the clever strategies she had for ending this war. I know she's another potential ally, but like this god of caution, I wonder if I can fully trust her.

I will simply have to proceed carefully. The Dread would like that. I follow him down the empty rows. It's the first time I've set foot in one of their temples.

This is where the Ashlords come to worship their gods. Blood sacrifices and muttered prayers. A shiver runs down my spine as I think of that other world. The dead god in her throne room. I do my best to bury the thought. No telling what the Dread can hear.

We take a back stairwell. I follow, tired and weary, but curious, too. The climb is brutal. Eight stories up, tight stairwells and suffocating passages. The Dread doesn't speak until we reach the top. An overlook. He skirts a weathered bell and gestures out at the wide ocean. It's quite a view.

"I wanted to show you this."

"The ocean," I drawl. "I've already seen it."

"Is that so? And what is beyond? Out there?"

"Other lands."

Now he snorts. "Only a fool takes joy in not knowing something. Look."

"I am looking, Dread. It's an ocean. I can only see so far."

"And that is by design," the Dread replies. "This is where the Veil came. Do you know her?"

It's an unexpected turn in the conversation. I've seen the abandoned temples in other cities. In the Reach, we learn about the gods. Not who to worship, but who stands against us.

"The Veil is the god who died."

"Yes. And this is where we killed her," he whispers, almost to himself. "Out there. We did not dare let her make landfall. She knew too much. She would have ruined everything. It was an ambush. Seven gods against one. I sensed something was wrong. After all, she could have stayed hidden. That was always her talent."

He stares out to sea. The wind carries up the scent of salt and the dead.

"She chose to hide *their* arrival instead."

I frown. "Who?"

"You call them the Dividian," he answers. "They were her people. The Veil grew tired of enslaving them. She came to love them, and so she set them free. Built boats in secret and sailed from our world to this one. We killed her on this shore. Quick and clean. But then the boats started appearing. Up and down the coast. She had sacrificed herself to hide them."

I can sense him slipping back through time. I keep quiet. One secret usually leads to another.

"The Fury wanted to slaughter them." His voice is a whisper. "The fool. My plan was better. We whispered to the Ashlords that the Dividian had come to conquer. Why not let them do the killing for us? It ended with the Dividian enslaved and the Veil buried. And with her we buried the truth. All the histories breathed our lie. No one knew they'd come from the underworld."

He turns to look at me.

"Until now."

I like the direction he's heading in, but I know I have a role to play. He thinks me impatient and ungrateful. Best if I stick to that attitude. "Get to the point."

"Your father wants you to march on Furia. The Ashlords might tremble, but their gods will not. We've spent centuries perfecting our power here. We come and go as we please. We offer gifts to those we favor. You have no advantage in this place. But down there?"

His reptilian face stretches into a grin.

"Down there you'd be a god."

A series of images swim through my mind. The strange tunnels and secret rooms. Stones that whisper secrets. Pippa's dark eyes meeting mine after we finished reading that groundbreaking passage. The invitation to work together in the throne room of a dead god . . .

. . . and the girl who *killed* that god.

"Explain."

The Dread reaches out unexpectedly. There's a cut on my arm, freshly dried. He uses a nail to scratch away one of the flakes. I recoil as he grins. "Your blood. It's a wonder the Ashlords never figured it out. Centuries of blood sacrifices, and no one ever understood *why.*"

I nod and pretend surprise. Blood is everything. I first saw its power in the throne room below. The way Pippa reached up to wipe the blood away from her nose. She settled the same hand on the grip of her weapon and used her power to gut the Curiosity. Her blade should have missed, but she used the power of her blood to make sure it didn't. Afterward, we read the Curiosity's more theoretical account on how our blood works. The entire reason for the sacrifice system they established. It gave us plenty of ideas.

"So . . ." I pretend to be curious and unknowing. "The blood holds power?"

The Dread watches me with narrowed eyes. He does not ask whatever question is sitting on his tongue. I can tell he's playing a game. He wants to reveal enough to make me powerful, but not so much that I can overpower *him.* This god is too clever by half.

"It is how we have ruled all these centuries," he con-firms. "Imagine what you could do, walking into that world, wielding your *own* power against them. A rising god in your own right."

I offer a thoughtful look before baiting him in deeper.

"It's a sound plan, except I've only ever traveled there by accident. I don't control it at all. You're right. Down there, I could do some damage. . . ."

The words linger in the air. The Dread smiles.

"You do not need to be summoned. Weren't you listen-ing?" He gestures to the ships below. "The Dividian sailed here from the underworld. Do you want to surprise the gods?"

He raises his finger to the golden horizon.

"Go that way."

19

THE GAME BOARD

PIPPA

You watch as the unexpected visitor arrives.

Navassa's southern gates groan open. Your generals stand at attention. There are no foot soldiers patrolling the court-yard. This is to be a private meeting. Dust rises as twenty horses knife through the entryway. A familiar face leads them. Five days ago you took Navassa from the Longhands. Four days ago you killed a god. Three days ago you received an urgent letter commanding all troops to stop marching and maintain their positions. Two days ago you crafted a plan, and yesterday you shoved that plan into motion.

Today brings the first potential obstacle. The rest of the Empire calls her Prama—or Prama the Gifted. You stride forward and call her by the only name you've ever known for her.

"Greetings, Mother."

She dismounts a sleek warhorse. You know the road here

could not have been easy, but she shows no signs of weakness. Instead, she strides forward and kisses your cheek. It is telling that she came—or was sent—to meet you in person. The obvious reason is that all the Curiosity's little birds burst into flame when the god was killed. You can only imagine how that's hindering communication around the Empire.

No more secrets, no more whispers, no more watchful eyes.

"Forgive my lack of professionalism," she says to your gathered generals. "I am a mother who has not seen her daughter in many moons."

She sweeps a lock of your hair behind one ear with a graceful touch. The moment allows her to take your measure, the way she always has. A mother ensuring her daughter is well, or else prepared for the task ahead. It has your stomach tossing nervously. You know that you are not the girl you were before the Races. You will never be that girl again. Now you carry secrets and potential shames that could ruin your entire family's reputation.

You meet her eye, though, because confidence is its own armor. She nods at that display of strength. "Let's get started. There is much to discuss."

You can almost hear the sound of a coin flipping in the air. You are not sure what is about to happen—or who you can trust—but you know your fate hangs in the balance. How much do the gods know of what occurred? What clues do they have about the Curiosity's death? You wish the Brightness had sent Prince Ino back to you instead. Mother

will *want* to take your side, but she's also one of the smart-
est women in the Empire. It will be far more difficult to
trick her.

Inside the command tent, Mother takes the head of the
table. You have not been observing some of the older military customs. It isn't your style, but those lessons are buried
too deep to forget. You and your generals learned decorum
at the age of three. So you claim the seat on her right side.
As your second in command, Etzli sits on Mother's left. Bravos and Revel split up, flanking either side, as Mother's personal guard take up their posts by the doorway.

"You've performed well," she begins. "Taking the pass the
way you did. Brutally executed. We knew Navassa would
fall eventually, too, but after just one day? The Brightness
approves of what you're doing."

You offer a slight bow of the head. "Winning is an expec-
tation."

Mother nods. "Tell that to the rest of our army. The eastern seaboard belongs to the Reach. Grove fell earlier this
morning. Adrian Ford is preparing to move on the capital."

You lift your chin. "Don't worry. I've sent him a gift."

"A gift?" Mother echoes. "What do you mean?"

"I grew tired of watching those propaganda videos. I decided to intervene. There are ninety trained soldiers heading his way. They were a gift from the Fury. Soldiers who
cannot die. Assassins, on their way even now. If we can cut
off the head of the desert snake . . ."

Mother looks briefly surprised. She's never surprised.
You can't help but guess how she's feeling. After all, she is
an Ashlord. She is not immune to the desires your people

have been taught since birth. Secretly, she wishes this gift was given to her. After a pause, she nods.

"The body dies with it. But what are the odds the soldiers succeed? What can they do?"

"The goal is for them to fail the first attempt," you answer. "The Longhands will think they've slain one hundred soldiers. But these soldiers are like our phoenixes. Only, the moonlight brings them back to life. I believe they'll have a fine chance of succeeding on their second attempt. His soldiers won't expect their resurrection, and surprise favors the bold."

"It would be a crucial blow. I pray they succeed. Meanwhile, we make our own plans. The Longhand forces have advanced in the west as well. Locklin is captured. Baybou routed. Aside from your army, the only large contingent has retreated to Furia. We are bracing to be pressed on both sides."

Bravos leans in. "Give us leave to go north. We can burn our way through the Reach. Cut off their supply lines. If it comes to a siege, they'll feel the effects before the city does."

It is exactly what you told him to say. It plays into Mother's idea that he is a fool. She doesn't even pretend to consider this option. "March north? They'll have soldiers stationed at every choke point to bleed you along the way. Besides, the Longhands captured our fleet in Grove. They'll sail boats up the coast tomorrow and gather supplies to feed their army. By the time you get there, it'll be empty farms and abandoned factories. A waste of time."

"We could go east," Revel offers. "Slip north of Ford's army and force him into a battle on both fronts. He sounds like the true thorn in our side. Why not focus on eliminating him?"

"I did not come here to strategize," she replies. "Do you think we have no plans of our own? You are ordered to return to Furia as soon as possible. We will defend the capital."

The other generals all look surprised, but this confirms your worst fear. The gods have grown suspicious. Easier to investigate if they recall all of you back to the capital to figure out who had a hand in the Curiosity's death. That is one of the few missing pieces in your plan. What methods do they have of discovering the truth? How can you ward against it?

Etzli points out the glaring mistake. "Consolidating our forces like that goes against the best practices of war. We're simplifying the target for our enemy. Why do that?"

"Because the gods command it."

Mother's crafty smile returns. The room grows quiet. It is one thing to discuss military strategies with an envoy, and quite another thing to question the pantheon.

"Much has changed," Mother says. "We were so busy fighting our war that we didn't know they were fighting one, too. Some of the gods have decided to consolidate their power."

She lets that news breathe through the room. You can tell she is watching for specific reactions, and you are doing your best to feign surprise. "Consolidate? How so?"

"They've removed the Hoarder. An easy choice. The god played no meaningful role in our world—or theirs. You'll find his temples empty. His priests are gone. It was the second choice that we found more surprising." Her eyes settle on you. "They killed the Curiosity."

This time the shock is genuine. It's honestly such a clever damn tactic. You wouldn't be surprised if Mother was the one who suggested it. Framing it this way to their people, even to their faithful generals, is a genius move. They know the guilty party will not correct them with the truth. Too easy to be exposed as a traitor that way. It also leaves the pantheon looking stable. Strong gods dealing with their weaker siblings. Nothing more than that. This, you realize, is how history has always been written in the Empire. The strongest decide which truth to tell.

Never mind that *you* are the one who killed the Curiosity.

"Can't she just take a new vessel?" Bravos asks. "She has hundreds of servants. . . ."

Mother offers him a withering look. "They killed the Curiosity in their world, boy. Not in this one. All her priests were consumed. Don't you know your histories?"

She glances your way. It's a subtle reminder of her disapproval. That you ever considered letting Bravos win the Races is baffling to her. You are thankful when Etzli changes the topic.

"I'm struggling to connect this news with our change in battle tactics."

Mother nods. "The new pantheon would like to show off their power. The Striving and the Fury have always favored the capital. They will do so again. Our armies will gather around Furia. It is simple *by design.* Our plan is to lure them all to our doorstep. We want the Longhands in one place.

The gods have promised to deliver their wrath. And we will sweep in to finish off those who survive."

The room falls silent again. Etzli has no more complaints. There is no arguing a plan gifted to you by the gods. Revel and Bravos look satisfied. Both of them are bruisers at heart. Blood waits for them regardless of which way your army marches.

Mother stands. "You will leave a garrison of troops here, as well as in the Steppes. If we are agreed, I would selfishly ask for time with my daughter. It has been too long. And please send my general inside. He should have arrived by now."

She smiles warmly and the others quietly excuse themselves. Etzli hesitates for only a moment, her eyes on you, but a quick nod from you has her retreating. The room empties. Mother reaches across the table for a wineskin, hooking her other fingers around a pair of empty glasses. She pours a healthy measure, eyes on the entrance, until the footsteps are distant and the voices faded.

"I need you to tell me the truth." She slides a glass across the table. Everything in the room is made of whispers. "Were you involved?"

You have been preparing for this moment all day. The acting beats come instinctually.

A confused frown. Lean forward. A preposterous answer.

"With Bravos?"

Mother's briefly taken aback. But those famous eyes dig into you again, searching for buried truths. Too bad you're better than her at this particular game.

"Not with Bravos." She scowls. "With the Curiosity."

Set the glass down. Add a touch of confusion. Thoughtful voice.

"You just told us this was the doing of the gods?"

"Answer the question, Pippa. Were you involved?"

"I have no connection to the Curiosity. You were there for the only two tributes I ever offered." *Add a scolding look.* "The Fury was given blood at my birth. And the Madness, as you recall, was given my blood before the Races."

Mother doesn't look fully satisfied by that answer. It's almost as if she can tell that you are avoiding the actual question. You'll have to be a little sharper.

"Pippa, I just want to know the truth. If you tell me now, I can soften the punishment you'll receive. The gods are taking this very seriously. The Brightness sent us out to begin investigations. All of us are searching on his behalf. We suspect that someone at the highest level of our government played a role. The Brightness believes the traitors wanted to establish a new regime. If you know *anything,* suspect *anything,* tell me now. While I can still help you."

Flash a little anger.

"Seriously? I've been marching, Mother. Out here in the middle of gods know where. Winning battle after battle. And this is the gratitude the capital offers? Accusations?"

She takes a deep swallow of wine, swirls the liquid, and sets the glass down.

"You know that I had to ask. Better that I find out now while I can still shield you. The Quespo will be waiting in the capital. Watching everyone and everything. You know the gods have their own methods of discovery, too. The guilty parties cannot hide for long. It warms my heart to know that you didn't have a hand in any of this. I'm honestly relieved, dear."

It is her final effort. She's painting a vision of the threat you will face and offering herself as the last bastion of safety. It is a lure to get you to admit the truth. You can hear the first piece sliding forward on the game board. Mother is not your enemy, but the people who sent her here want you found, imprisoned, and executed.

If only they knew how many moves you'd already made in this game.

"And I will be relieved to be back home." *Offer a small smile. Extend your hand halfway.* "I want to sleep in my own bed. I want to see Father again. I want the war to be over."

Her suspicion finally breaks. She reaches out and wraps your hand in hers. It is the same warmth you always craved from her as a little girl. She offers it now. Warmth and comfort and calm. "Well, I can help you with one of those items. . . ."

You hear the sound of boots at the entryway. A dashing figure enters the room. He's always been so handsome, but in his armor, your father is radiant. Earlier, your mother asked for her "general" to be sent into the room. You hadn't realized Father had returned from the west.

"There's my girl."

He flashes a grin and you can't help rushing forward to throw your arms around him. It's such a relief to not have to be a general, if only for a moment. Mother does not bring this out in you. She's always strategizing, always thinking. But Father is the one who'd sneak onto the roof with you on warm summer nights when you were a little girl and count the stars. He lifts you up now, spinning you around, and it's impossible not to grin. He sets you down and glances over at your mother. You do not miss the exchange. She shakes her head to his unasked question, and the relief on his face is palpable. Both of them feared you were involved in the conspiracy.

Both of them feared the truth you've carefully hidden from them.

"Time to go home," Father says. "But not before we feast. I've had the servants arrange a private dinner for the three of us. Just like old times. Before my daughter became a conqueror."

He winks at you. Mother rises with a slight scowl on her face. "Conqueror? She has a long way yet to go before she can take on that title. Don't you think, dear?"

You smile and nod, because only you know just how far a journey awaits.

20

THE BUTCHER'S STOREHOUSE

IMELDA

I am upside down.

Blood is rushing to my head. I can feel the goose bumps on my arms. I let out a panicked gasp and my breath frosts the air. I am somewhere cold. I am bound hand and foot. There's a single window to my right. Outside, I can see an overcast sky. It's a recognizable curtain of gray. Our world does not look this way. The realization turns my stomach. I've been dragged into the underworld.

"Ahh. My honored guest is awake."

The voice scrapes through the air. I'm hanging from the ceiling. The ropes rotate until my captor comes into view. A man sits in a chair. No, something pretending to be a man. Dark hair slicks back from a ghostly forehead. There are pale stitches along his scalp. A pair of mismatched eyes regard me. It is not just their color, but the size and shape and depth that do not agree with one another. I can't help

shivering. It is like a creature staring out at me from beneath a mask.

His voice is rust. "You were looking for a god. You just
found the wrong one."

He turns away and my eyes are drawn to the wall behind
him. It boasts a series of black hooks. The instruments hanging there send a new chill through me. Carving knives and
bone saws and blunted hammers. All that treacherous silver
gleams bright. He carefully fastens the strings of a smock
behind his neck and I know now which god I've found.

They call him the Butcher.

He is the god of blood and bone. In our world, his servants wear red masks sewn over their faces. They trail the
marching Ashlord armies, collecting the dead. I fight against
the rising panic in my chest. The room smells of carrion. It
takes all my effort to slow my heart rate. I came here with
purpose. *Our blood is power.* I imagine the wall the prince
summoned. I reach inside myself for the same power he
called. But nothing happens.

The Butcher's mismatched eyes find mine. "All that
straining on your face . . . Hmm. Reaching for the power
of your blood? How curious. I wonder who taught you such
knowledge. I'll have to do some digging, some punishing. It
is *very* powerful, but useless so long as it's sitting inside your
veins. I was rather careful about that." He taps the back of
his head. "Blunt trauma. You will not bleed until I *want* you
to bleed."

He reaches for the first tool. It's a crude piece of iron,
about the length of his forearm. He allows the tip to drag

across the floor as he crosses the room. My mind is racing. I hadn't realized the blood's power depended on its being free of the body. It makes sense, though. The prince summoned the wall, but he bit into his own hand first. That jerking motion I saw. The raw wound he wouldn't let me touch. Of course.

The little prince was letting out blood.

"Let me show you my collection."

The Butcher reaches for my shoulder. His touch is ice. He spins me around so that I can see where we are. It's a great storehouse. Vaulted ceilings. The walls are decorated only by stains. Each row runs as far as the eye can see. Every few paces, a rope hangs down. On the end of each rope is a cut of meat. My stomach turns as I take it all in.

"There is no collection in the world like mine." He uses his blade to point. My eyes trace the light that shivers down its length. The handle appears old, but I can see just how sharp an edge it carries. "First row is modern era. That one is a massaged bull. Cows after that. All prepared in their own way. And then bears, sunwolves, brightlings. Any cut of meat you could want, I have."

He keeps talking, but my mind is focused. Drinking in the details. My hands are bound in front of me. I can just barely wiggle my fingers. The rest of my body is tied, too, but a slight adjustment of my position has the rope overhead swinging slightly. My entire body sways.

I can work with that. My eyes fix on the Butcher. The glinting blade and the masked face and the pale skin. He's standing well out of reach. I need to draw him closer.

"This row is water creatures," he says. "Shark hearts are a favorite of mine."

He points with his blade once more, and now his voice drips with pleasure.

"But this row is the crown jewel of my collection. I have worked on this part of the collection more closely than all the others combined."

Light footsteps carry him away. He lets the tip of his blade drag once more. Sparks cut the dark. He walks to the edge of that row, and my eyes finally take in those cuts of meat. I trace their shapes. The familiar forms have me dry-heaving.

"This man died yesterday," the Butcher says. "A heroic death. I claimed him before the vultures could. Did you know that each death has a flavor? Cowardice tastes sour. Bravery tastes rich. I have learned the nuances." He gestures down the row. "I have preserved them. One for every year your world has existed. I have cuts from every century. From the darkest ages, the most heroic times. I have generals and peddlers. Tyrants and intellectuals. Each one with its own subtle taste."

My calm slips away. I'm shaking uncontrollably. I'd been planning to bring Bastian and his crew down here. To a place where the gods are older than time, bent by the centuries they've spent in their shadowed towers. I watch the Butcher admire his own masterpieces—each one captured and killed and skinned—and I can feel my own death hanging in the air like a promise.

"Do not worry. You shall not suffer. My kills are very . . .

decisive. And if it's any consolation, know that they did come to rescue you. Quite brave of them." There's a smile in his voice. He walks to the lone window in the room and looks down. "The boy is pretty. He smells like fear and love, all tangled together. He will blame himself for your death, I suspect. But do not worry. I will make sure his time of mourning is short."

"No!" I shout. "You will not hurt him."

The Butcher does not reply. His eyes follow movement below.

"You have a place here," he whispers. "But not him. He is just a boy pretending to be a hero. I'll feed him to my pets. They have a taste for the lowly."

Fear burns to anger. Anger breathes purpose out of panic. My entire body goes still. I watch the god standing before me. How do I change the game he's playing? What do the gods always want from our people?

"Blood," I hiss at him. "Free me and I'll give you sacrifices."

His eyes find mine. "You would pay me with my own coin? Oh dear, I have your blood. I have your bones. I have your eyes. I have *everything*. It is only a matter of taking it."

Fury pulses inside me. "Let me serve you."

"You will," he promises. "You already do."

"More crew members will come looking for us."

The Butcher nods. "My servants will call it a proper feast."

Now the anger begins to burn. Enough of this.

"I am going to destroy everything you hold dear. When I am done, your collection will be nothing but ashes and bone. I will go back to our world and destroy your temples, too. Stone by stone. No one will remember your name. All of this will burn. . . ."

I keep pushing until I see his calm features sharpen. It's the smallest flash of anger, but it draws him to me like a moth to flame. I do not know much about the Butcher, no more than what I've learned living in the shadows of the Ashlords all my life. But I am certain of one thing.

This is his sanctuary. A threat to it is a threat to him.

Anger has him stalking forward. His misshapen eyes narrow. He points his blade at me, a dark promise on his lips. It is his first and only mistake.

I worm my body forward. My legs and hands are bound. Thick ropes that I could never hope to break, but the momentum swings me like a pendulum. Just far enough.

His extended blade is there.

I stretch my fingers. Light shivers off the metal. The Butcher can't draw it away in time. All four of my exposed fingers slick across the edge. The rope tugs me back, but the blade is true. It cuts deep. Blood rushes out from the fresh wounds.

And the Butcher's eyes widen with fear. He lunges for a killing blow, but the words from my lips come a beat faster. "Get back!"

The command tangles with my blood. And the blood gives answer, echoes power. It is more than I could have ever dreamed. A wave of gold light thunders from my fingertips. There's a sound like the great tolling of a bell. It is a collision of every heaven, every hell. Ripples are thrown outward and the answering wave pulses forward.

An explosion.

The Butcher's hands lift, but I can tell in that moment— in his expression—that I am the predator now. My golden light crushes him. It is strong enough to course around him. The stone wall rips free of the framework. Scorch marks darken everything. Gray light ghosts through the sudden opening.

My chest heaves. I am gasping for air.

The Butcher is gone. Shouts fill the courtyard below. My body turns in a helpless circle until I can look down through the opening. There's chaos as the Butcher's servants flee. In the midst of all that, I finally spot Bastian. He stares up at me with a look of shock on his face. I offer him a bloody, upside-down grin and say the only thing I can think to say.

"I'm pretty sure I got him."

21

SAIL

ADRIAN

Our ship launches in secret.

It is a moonless night. The galley drifts silently through the black. Even the shuffling footsteps along the deck are lost beneath the rhythmic waves. I watch the lights of the city fade away as we carve a path out into the open sea.

Old Trask has command of the army. He'll leave a small garrison inside Grove's walls, but the rest of the troops will march with him to Furia. Let the Ashlords feel the heat of our breath on their necks. And let their gods feel the heat of mine.

It is strange to sail away from certain battle. Even stranger to trust the guidance of the Dread. I wish there was some other way. I have studied enough history, though, to know what happens to people who only ever follow the footsteps of others.

Our first Rebellion started well enough. The Long-hand soldiers were disciplined, our resources vast. My grandfather's legions moved with precision, gaining ground, until the gods ended all of that with an iron fist. Winning will take more than clever tactics.

No, we must carve a new world out of the old one.

Half of our crew works the oars. The others have bundled up, resting before their shifts come. Some look out over the railings, trying to trace stars overhead. The Dread promised to cloak our ship from view. We aim for the underworld in secret.

All my chosen soldiers are eager. I made an effort to recruit the right sort. Forrest Trask grinned at the idea of killing gods. Kenly came with us, too, and gladly accepted a promotion. I even asked him to pick a few soldiers himself. His first selection was a young scout named Nevira Pearce. I could tell she was sharp right away, observant in the way a good scout has to be. I noted she has one blue eye and one brown eye. Kenly joked that's why she never misses a single detail; it's like she's watching the world through two different perspectives.

A lot of the others are like her. Young soldiers who are eager to make a name for themselves. Our task will not seem so impossible to them. Sail to a new world. Stand against the gods. These are the soldiers who will change everything.

Forrest spies me at the railing and approaches. He pretends to be fearless, but even I am unsettled as we get deeper out to sea. Our eyes trace the oily shadows, then the stars above.

"Did you ever imagine this?"

His question surprises me. "Fighting a war?"

"No, not that. I've imagined fighting this war every day

of my life. My uncle was the firstborn in his family. They came for him a few years after the war. Killed him in his sleep. My father still says his name every night before he goes to bed. Wasn't too hard to imagine a war. We all but inherited it." He gestures out to sea. "I meant all of *this*. Sailing a damn boat into the jaws of waiting gods. Aiming for the heart of the underworld. When we used to fight as kids, we always pretended to be the great heroes. Gold Man Jones and Olivia West. Always thought of them as legends. But what we're doing? It's our turn to carve our own legacy."

I eye the dark horizon. "Or die forgotten in a foreign land."

He barks a laugh. "That is the more depressing option, yes. It's a coin flip, really, but I do like our odds. At the very least, we'll bloody some noses while we're down here. Can you imagine it? The Ashlords without their gods."

I've been imagining that for days now. Forrest Trask just doesn't realize that the person who gave me this dream was one of his sworn enemies. Even now, I picture Pippa at the helm of her army in Navassa, plotting the course we decided together. If we're lucky enough to defeat the gods, it will take a great deal to persuade my people not to finish the job and kill their former allies. Forrest is only confirming that fear.

"Forrest, what if I told you there was another way?"

It is hard to know if it's the right decision, but if I cannot trust a man like Forrest Trask, who is there? I've persuaded them all to join me on this journey to kill gods. They volunteered for glory, not knowing that I would ask them to betray their ancestors and join forces with the Ashlords. If we are to build a new world, I will need people willing to take on some of the load. Patiently, I walk Forrest through the plan, through what happened in the Curiosity's throne room.

He's the perfect audience. Asking skeptical questions. Smirking at the parts where I play the hero. Doubting Pippa's intentions. We stand there discussing the truth in whispers until Kenly calls out a rotation. Forrest claps my shoulder again. I don't know if I've won him over until he speaks.

"Our people will go where you lead us. Just make sure you're leading us the right way."

I watch him join the rowers, eager to do his part. My heart is beating fast. I can't believe that it was actually that simple. We both grew up with the same dream: revenge. Now that we know the whole story, though, it feels like such a small purpose. Forrest is a start. I know the others will be resistant, but I will have to teach them to dream of a bigger world than the one their parents wanted. After all, even this little ship is not entirely made up of Longhands.

Farian and Martial stand on the opposite side of the deck. I told Farian where we were going and knew he'd bite. The chance to film another world? It was too good to pass up. Martial looked my way when Farian told him where he was going. That glance was sharper than his sword. He knew the battle was lost, though, so he quietly assented to come with us. I can see him standing in the bare light of the stars and wonder if it was a mistake. One more worry in an already unpredictable journey.

There is one other sailor who is not a Longhand. His presence sends a shiver down the spines of the rest of the crew. The Dread's vessel stands at the prow of the ship like a figurehead. He hasn't moved since we began. I am not sure if he's sleeping or praying or both. My people didn't like the arrangement, but I told them there was no other way to go where we must go.

Our boat rises and falls. After a time, my mind drifts on the waves.

Pippa is out there somewhere. I have not seen her since the tower. It was such a shock to see the body of a god at her feet. Even more of a shock to learn the real history of our peoples. I have to press those memories back as I approach the Dread. I know that if I want to topple the pantheon, I'll need to know more about them.

"Dread," I say in greeting. "Tell me about the land that awaits us."

"You've been there," he reminds me.

"I've seen a glimpse of it. I would know more."

His eyes remain on the unlit horizon. "It is a single continent, much like the Empire. A sunless place. Most of the land is wild. We unleashed horrible creatures in the beginning. It was all a part of our plan. Build strongholds. Make the land dangerous. Offer safe havens. Consolidate power.

"You'll see it for yourself. Most of our servants live underground or behind high walls. We created fear and made ourselves the answers to all their problems. Now only the great cities exist. We will aim to land as far north as we can."

I nod to him. "Where we'll find the Fury's stronghold."

"And the Striving," he corrects. "The two gods are something of a pair. Their twin cities flank a long-dead river. Massive bridges connect the two. They have long been the most popular gods. It only made sense for them to partner with one another."

Another nod. "How many gods remain?"

"The Fury, the Butcher, the Striving, and the Madness."

I quietly note that he doesn't include himself on the list. Either he feels himself inferior or he hopes I'll forget that he is one of the gods we aim to kill. How clever it would be of him to not get caught up in the bloody battles to come. No doubt that is his plan. I will not forget.

"The Madness won't trouble us," the Dread says. "He exists more as a force of nature now than an actual political creature. Like the tides or the glow of the moon. He is there to be crossed or to drown those who dare go where he has not offered passage. It's the Fury and the Striving who deserve our attention."

"Tell me about them."

He shrugs. "I am sure you could guess their natures. The Fury is strength in its purest form. No god has been given more blood over the centuries. The Ashlords' devotion is his armor, their fear his sword. Even wielding your own power . . . I promise you will find him a worthy foe."

I consider that quietly. "And the Striving?"

"She is the cleverest creature in existence," the Dread says bitterly. "The Fury swings his swords, but the Striving aims each blow. She will have a thousand countermoves prepared for us."

The silence stretches. "And how do we beat someone like that?"

His smile is full of secrets. "Make something out of nothing."

I have one final question. It takes a moment to figure out the best way to position it.

"And what of the Dread? Will you meet us in your true form? Guide us?"

He shakes his head. "I will send a messenger, but no, I cannot attend you myself. My kingdom is not with the others. I live on an island that circles the land. It is remote, unapproachable. Always moving. If I were to dock again, the other gods would seek me. It's better this way."

"As you say."

Without anything else to add, I leave him at the railing. If all goes according to plan, the Dread will be our last problem. I have no doubt that his answer is its own protection. It will just be a matter of puzzling out the truth.

Down the line, I find Martial and Farian leaning over a railing. My first instinct is to leave them be and get some sleep. But we're about to walk into the unknown. Daddy would tell me to make sure every single soldier standing on the front line is with me. That no one will back down when the time comes.

"Gentlemen," I say, leaning my arms against the railing. "Thanks for coming."

Martial spits overboard, but Farian is all smiles.

"Can't wait to see how the lighting is there."

"Gray," I answer. "It's a very gray place."

Farian considers that. "How would you know?"

I don't see any reason not to tell them. "I've been there."

Martial doesn't smile. "Is that how you ended up in league with one of their gods?"

"A means to an end."

"Our end," Martial returns. "You don't know who you're dancing with, boy."

Farian leans around him. "So you were saying . . . it's just gray?"

I nod. "A barren landscape. It's nothing like here."

It feels like I'm dashing Farian's hopes at first, but he actually drums the railing in excitement.

"Nothing like here," he whispers. "I'm going where no camera crew has ever gone before. Not even the Ashlord journalists. Can you imagine? The footage . . . I'll win awards. . . ."

"Don't forget to bring a sword," Martial replies. "Hard to win an award if you're dead."

His eyes cut back to me before he pushes away from the railing. I hear him mutter something about sleep as he departs. I'm tempted to find my own hammock, but something about Farian keeps me there with my elbows pressed to the railing, eyes on the lightless horizon.

"I've never sailed before," he says.

"Me neither."

"Never even been swimming in the ocean, either."

"Same."

"I hope the boat doesn't tip over."

I laugh. "I'm more afraid of what happens when we land."

He's quiet for a time. "But you're still going."

"What other choice do I have?"

It's his turn to laugh. "Gods, you're just like Imelda. I swear. It's my luck to get stuck working with the two of you. It's like you don't even question it. Like there's some destiny just waiting to be plucked out of thin air, and you're the only ones who can reach out and take it."

Farian shakes his head.

"I mean, listen to you. What other choice? There were hundreds of other choices! You could have stayed in the Reach. Lived a normal life. You could have steered clear of the Races. Not started a war. You didn't have to ride into battle. You didn't have to pick a fight with the gods. Or sail a ship to their world. Those are all *choices*. But it's like I said. Imelda was always the same way. Both of you don't even see it in yourselves. It's so frustrating."

I consider his words. I'm not sure if I ever pieced it together that way. I've been training for the Races since I was a boy. It never felt like a choice. It felt like something I'd promised the world.

"You know, I meant what I said before. . . ."

I frown at him. "What's that?"

"You're no better than them," Farian replies. "If you don't make the world different. If you rule the way that they do. If you create a world where other Vivinias can burn to the ground. If my people end up with new masters . . . you'll be no better than they are."

I can't meet his eye. I was there when we planned the war. I've been at every meeting, heard the generals at their tables. And I know how we discuss the Dividian. We hoped to turn them on their masters. We never talked about freeing them for good. Never talked about giving them their rightful place at the table. They were always a tool against our true enemy. Farian is right.

"If this works, I promise you. It will be different."

Farian swallows. "That's the thing about you. Imelda is the same way. You're the kind of person who just might change the world. Either that or you'll die trying." He pats the strap of his camera. "I'm here to make sure the world doesn't forget. No matter what happens."

He gives a quiet nod before heading off. Long after he's gone, I whisper those words.

"No matter what happens."

22

LITTLE FIRES EVERYWHERE

PIPPA

You are marching through the Steppes when the fires begin to burn.

Word echoes back through the ranks, but your eyes tell you all you need to know. There are three separate bursts of flame in the ranks ahead. It's dusk, and you can see soldiers scattering away from those locations. You know they're burners. Nothing out in these hills would just burst into flame like that. The gods are devouring their own again.

You're wondering at the timing of this particular burn when a rear-guard scout thunders forward. Mother's guards halt him twenty paces away, but he shouts his message to you.

"More fires behind, General!"

The group pauses long enough to look back down the passes that lead to Navassa. There were three or four burners up ahead, but behind you . . . there are little fires everywhere. You give up counting them because the wind is spreading the flames too fast, and they're dancing into a single mass. You know there's only one group that would follow your army through the hills. It's the same group that follows *every* Ashlord army.

"Those are the Butcher's priests."

Something about the fire has drawn a horrified look onto Father's face. He buries it the moment he sees you looking, but there's something strange about seeing him afraid. Mother is far better at masking her emotions. She gestures to the nearest guards and looks at you.

"I need to go inspect them myself."

You nod to her. "We'll escort you."

Bravos and Revel are riding ahead, but Etzli is at your side, as always. She exchanges a look with you before peeling away from the column to follow Mother. You nudge your horse in pursuit. The fires are burning a good five hundred paces back. Mother is already dismounted, circling the dying flames. She inspects each body patiently. You're not sure what she's looking for but you know *exactly* what happened. Etzli catches your eye. The two of you exchange a nod.

"All the burns are the same," Mother says. "Watch."

A gentle wind passes through. You frown when every single fire snuffs out at the same exact moment. Their dark work is done. Only ashes and bones remain. There were at least twenty priests. Each one has paid the price of their god's final breath. You do not speak the truth, but you know it. The Butcher has been killed.

Your mind is racing because this wasn't a part of your well-constructed plan. You are quite certain that Quinn is still plotting from the safety of the Curiosity's tower. Adrian has taken Grove. His course to the underworld does not involve the Butcher. A few possibilities come to mind, each as unlikely as the next. You do not know the cause, but you know the consequence. Another dead god will increase the urgency of the remaining deities.

Your window of opportunity is tightening.

It does, however, provide you a valuable alibi. Mother has been with you all this time. She will confirm that to the Brightness. It will be quite difficult for them to blame this death on you. You're quite certain they have other means for determining guilt, but this surprise buys you time.

"It appears the Butcher is dead," Mother says, loud enough for her guards to hear. "And finally, the Triumvirate is complete. A god of power, a god of vision, and a god who links us to both. We have entered a new era. Long may they reign."

The surrounding guards nod their approval. Etzli is watching you as Mother signals for the guards to leave. She circles the burning piles, deep in thought. It was quick thinking on her part to credit the gods with the Butcher's death. But now you can see the fear hidden beneath her carefully groomed words. Something is clearly wrong. Something has happened beyond even your own secrets.

Mother points at Etzli. "Do you trust her?"

"With my life."

"This was not supposed to happen. The gods promised their war was over. When I left the capital, the new pantheon had been determined. The Butcher was meant to survive."

It is a testing moment. You know your mother is a genius

at strategy and warfare. She would be an incredible ally in all that is to come. You briefly consider inviting her into what you know. All the secrets you discovered in the Curiosity's empty tower. There's even the assurance that no one is watching. After all, the god of whispers is dead. No one would ferry your words back to the wrong ears.

But the moment stretches, and you hold your tongue instead. Mother has another role to play in your plans, even if she does not know it. Etzli steers the conversation away.

"Do you think the gods lied to you?"

Mother has always been devout. The gods have given her so many gifts over the years. She shakes her head fervently. "I see no benefit to lying about this. The Brightness truly believed the new pantheon had been decided. The Striving reported it to him directly. No, I think this suggests foul play of some kind. Another power . . ."

You do not help her to the right conclusion. You need her to get there on her own, and she's already halfway home. You put on a thoughtful look and wait. Mother has always been clever. And you suspect she has even more information than you first believed, because she arrives at the right conclusion after only the briefest pause.

"The Longhand."

Adrian Ford. Guiding their suspicions in his direction opens several important doors. This is just one of many pieces in the game to come. Now you wait for her to provide an opening. Etzli offers up some rather well-played skepticism.

"But the Longhands don't dance with the gods."

"Adrian Ford does." Mother looks thoughtful. "He is more dangerous than we knew."

"My creatures are making their way to him," you say, taking the opening. "But if they fail us, I want to be on the front lines to face him. Give me permission to lead the cavalry into battle. Adrian Ford has not had to face our best. That is how he's carved his way to the capital. It stops now. It stops when he has to stand against me. Give me that honor."

Mother's still eyeing the corpses. After a breath, she nods.

"I will put in a word to the Brightness."

You hear another piece sliding into place. One at a time. The game is well underway.

23

THE HANDS THAT BUILD DREAMS

IMELDA

Bastian and I stride down a dark hallway, shoulders pressed together. He was the one who busted down the door to the Butcher's dark storehouse. He came in and cut me down. I was glad the rest of his crew waited in the courtyard below, because the moment I was free of those ropes, I started to cry. Bastian held me for a long time, doing his best to shift his body and shield me from the sight of those horrible carcasses. It was easy to be strong as I stared down a god, but that strength hid the fear beneath. I know I'm lucky to be alive.

Now I work with a sense of urgency. A clearer purpose. We enter a room full of huddled survivors and take our seats at a table carved from bone. The Butcher might be dead, but his tastes remain. Everything in this cruel place is shaped to his liking. Amber lanterns glow overhead. I thought they were carved in the shapes of skulls. It took a moment to realize they actually *were* skulls, with candles glowing inside.

A ghost of a smile crosses the boy's face. "Our hands are . . ."

He trails off, searching for the right word. It is not something he has ever been able to say before now, but it is beautiful the way his mind reaches for a new truth.

"Our hands *choose* to help."

The rest of the conversation is logistics. Fissure calls on a few of the older slaves. Some have lived long enough to be sent as messengers between strongholds. Their combined knowledge casts a clearer vision for us. None of it is pretty. This is a dark world. Great valleys separate the cities, each one controlled by one of the gods. The Fury's warriors are without comparison. They speak of the Curiosity as if that deity can hear them all the way across the world. It's hard to tell if the gods are truly that powerful or if these people have simply been forced to believe they are.

"The Curiosity's birds see all," Fissure finishes. "Or so says our master."

"He does not say much now," Bastian reminds him. "Do you have any maps?"

It takes time to put everything together. We're missing a few crucial pieces, but I know this is a beginning. Before leaving, I ask if Fissure will escort me back through the Butcher's stronghold. Bastian shoots me an uncertain look, but I nod to him. I'm strong enough to do what must be done. The dead god boasted that there were samples in his collection from every century. It has me curious. I want to look back at his oldest specimens. I have a few hunches about what I might find there.

I know, at the very least, I will not repeat my first mis-

The bright eyes of various creatures cast their light over the only room in the castle that doesn't smell like freshly drawn blood. I force myself to focus on the boy who's been chosen to lead the remaining servants.

"I am named Fissure."

The boy looks more like a ghost than anything. We found him and hundreds of others locked underground, working a complicated system of factories. All the survivors are pale from lack of sunlight. It doesn't escape my notice that many of them share features with my people—with the Dividian. Brightly colored eyes. Slightly wider hips. I am not sure what to make of that.

"My name is Imelda," I say. "And this is Bastian."

Fissure bows his head. "How can we serve you?"

The question sparks my anger. The Butcher is gone. He cannot harm them now, but the scars from what he did will stay with these people long after today. It falls on us to begin turning back the curse. "It will not be like that," I say. "Your master is dead. You are free now."

Fissure frowns. It is not a concept his god taught him.

"We do have questions," Bastian puts in. "Questions, mind you. Not commands."

"The Butcher's questions *were* commands," Fissure replies.

"Our questions are invitations," I amend. "We want to work *with* you and your people."

Once more, Fissure stares blankly at us.

"How many of you are there?" Bastian asks.

"Four hundred and sixty, but seventeen are now imprisoned, as you commanded."

Bastian tries to keep his voice patient. "As we *agreed*. We imprisoned those who abused their power here. How many of you can march?"

"If the command is to march," Fissure replies, "all will march."

Bastian bites his tongue, gesturing for me to jump in. He's lived his whole life in the mountains. He could never understand their servitude. He woke up in the mornings and rode his horse wherever he wanted. I am more familiar with the taste of a life with overseers.

"Are there elders?"

Fissure nods. "Very few. The conditions below do not promise many years."

"Children?"

For the first time, Fissure's face brightens. Even in this dark place, children are a blessing it would seem. "Four infants, seven toddlers. The rest are forge-ready."

"Forge-ready?"

"All children begin work at the end of their third cycle."

Bastian pales. It is a helpful reminder. I might have tasted servitude in the world above, but nothing like this. I have known open skies. I have ridden horses just for fun. I was not forced into labor at the age of three. I have no idea who I would be in this world under these conditions.

"From now on, there will be no more working like that."

Fissure bows his head. "It will be as the old gods command."

Bastian makes a disbelieving noise, but I keep my reminder gentle.

"Not a command. A promise. Your children a[...] mind is still turning over the strange phrasing F[...] "You said the 'old gods'? Who are they?"

Now the boy looks even more confused. "Yo[...] the world above?"

We both nod.

"Then you are the old gods," he says. "Aren't y[...]

His words make no sense to us. Bastian's impati[...] faces. He wants to focus on logistics, not riddles.[...] other gods keep slaves?"

Fissure nods. "Of course. We are the hands th[...] their dreams."

Anger thrums in my chest again. I can see it f[...] in Bastian's clenched fists. These people have been [...] and painfully bent to the will of rulers even cruele[...] ours.

"My dream is a world without masters." I keep my [...] quiet, steady. "Imagine that world, Fissure. There wi[...] be stones rolled into place to make sure you do not es[...] You will not be kept in underground prisons. No one [...] force your children to labor. If you like the warmth of [...] sun, you can go where it is warm. If you like the cold, [...] can go where winter winds blow. You will only answe[...] each other. The only law will be the rights of all to purs[...] their own hearts."

Fissure's eyes narrow. His answer is a whisper. "I cann[...] imagine such a world."

"But I can. And so can Bastian. We just need some hel[...] building it."

take. I will not walk through this world without a few weapons at the ready. The Butcher's lesson was well taught. I will wield my blood from here on out. After we finish our search, Fissure returns to speak with the other freed slaves about what will happen next. Bastian's arranging for the rest of the crew to join us. Once everything's settled, he stands in the courtyard of a god and meets my eye.

He has that wild look that I first saw out on those bloody plains after I'd escaped from the Races. It is an expression only outlaws and rebels know. He speaks with fire in his voice.

"We're going to burn this world to the ground."

24

SHORE

ADRIAN

Kenly wakes me roughly. "Sir, there's been a fire."

I jolt to my feet. I might not be a sailor, but even I know a fire on board a ship would be pure disaster. The sleeping quarters are bright. We must be well into the day. I thunder after Kenly, up onto the deck, and spy the reason for his concern. The fire's gone out, but there's a dark mass of ashes and bone by the prow. A few of the planks have taken damage, but it's a surprisingly controlled burn. It is where the Dread stood the night before.

"What happened?"

Kenly shrugs. "Your priest told Nevira that we weren't making good time. Muttered a few words and burst into flame. Pearce was the first one to spot the ropes. . . ."

I frown. "What ropes?"

Kenly leads me forward. The rest of the crew are craning their necks curiously. Nevira Pearce is standing at the prow of the ship. Sure enough, there are ropes attached to the front of the ship that were not there before. Hundreds of them. Each one reaches ahead, flexed tight. I follow their paths into the water below.

"Turtles," I say in disbelief. "Are they *pulling* the ship?"

Kenly nods. "Our pace has nearly tripled. I wasn't sure what to do, sir. I had the crew pull up the oars for now. None of us are sailors. Our strokes were starting to slow the ship. Besides, I wasn't sure how long we'd have this . . . boon. Might as well save ourselves for when they fail."

I'm still staring. "There must be hundreds of them. Good thinking, Kenly. Tell the crew to rest. We'll be there sooner than expected."

He nods once before raising his voice, bellowing at the others. I can't help noting how well suited he is to command. He'll need another promotion if we survive this. I circle the charred bones, turning a femur over with one toe. Forrest Trask joins me.

"Bastard melted himself," he says, half laughing. "Never seen anything like it."

I nod. It's obvious this was a trade. The vessel's life in exchange for the creatures and the ropes and the magic. I stare down at the herd of massive turtles ushering us through the water with their steady strokes and doubt the world has ever seen such a sight. It's a fine reminder that our blood carries a powerful magic.

I glance to my left and find Farian a few paces away, leaning against the railing.

"Aren't you going to film this?" I ask him. "It's a bloody miracle."

Farian smiles back. "Already got the footage."

I stand there for a while, marveling at the magic, until my eyes return to the burn pile. Their magic always has a cost. Who died for the protective spell the Dread gave me during the Races? Or the turtles he sent to help me against Darvin? Does every gift claim a life?

No easy answers there.

We make good time. I join some of the crew for a game of cards. Every now and again, some new landmark draws our attention. There are islands out here that no one in our world has ever seen. It isn't until evening that we all start to feel the changes. A shift in the air. My eyes find the pile of bones at the prow and I can't help wishing the Dread were here to talk us through it. His turtles keep swimming. The ship glides on.

The first sign is the temperature. It drops fast. The setting sun vanishes without warning. Overhead, the sky grows dark with clouds. At first, I think a storm is on the way, but then I remember the underworld looks like this. A barricade of clouds that drown out sunlight.

"Back on the oars," I order. "Swords ready. We're here."

Great stones claw up out of the water. We're forced to navigate around them, and it's not a task we manage well. A few scrapes come far too close for comfort. The ship groans with each mistake until finally the shoreline appears in the distance.

It is nothing like our world. My crew marvels at the sight. Our entire eastern coast is lined with white-sand beaches. The substance is so fine that you can let it run between your fingers like an alchemist's powder. Here, a shore of dark stone looms. I'm squinting in search of a proper landing when Nevira Pearce crows down from the upper nest.

"On our right. There's a lantern."

I see it. A jewel glints through the barren fog. I watch as the ropes off the front of the ship swing in that direction. Not all the turtles are still swimming, but those that are know the way. I command my crew to follow their lead. "Keep steady. Hands on swords."

Farian is at the prow with his camera. Martial's a few paces back, hissing for him to move the hell away, but the boy's excitement echoes through our ranks. We're about to land on a foreign shore. We will be the first in history to travel this path. I consider the shrouded landscape and can't help imagining that someone left this place to die long ago.

The glinting light brightens. We close on the location.

And as the fog shifts, I see a single figure waiting. His arm is raised and a lantern is in hand. It is the servant the Dread promised would greet us. His turtles keep the ship groaning onward until the bottom scrapes to a stop along the shallow stones. We're about fifty paces from the shore. It looks safe enough, but I warn my soldiers all the same.

"Everything here will be different. Different can mean dangerous. Move carefully."

It's too shallow for the rowboats. Instead, the rowers throw ropes over the land-facing side of the ship and we all begin the descent. The waiting water is hip-high. Boots splash. The first few people hiss their complaints about how cold the water is. Kenly has them unloading supplies without me saying a word. Most of the boxes being ferried to shore contain phoenix ashes and armor.

We're a kill squad, after all, not a merchant ship.

The Dread's servant stumbles down to the edge of the water and throws up his free hand to halt us. He is exactly the sort of creature I'd expect to serve the god of caution. Everything about him is quiet. His jacket is colorless, his gloves threadbare. A slash of dark hair hides most of his face. He traces our movement with a pair of deep-set eyes. My crew is impatient to make land but he thrusts his free hand even higher as he searches for me in the crowd.

"Hold there. I said *hold* there. I'd talk to Ford first."

I shoulder through. "I'm right here."

He bobs his head. "A little shorter than expected, but fair enough. I just want to make sure you're good and ready. The moment your feet land on this shore, you'll be marked. The forces that call this land home will turn an eye your way. Lord Dread will shield you, but think of it as a clock winding down. There will come a point where Lord Fury and Lady Striving will know you're coming. I'd have you in position well before then. So go on and distribute your ashes, take your formations. All of that. Then come."

My crew glances back at me first. I give them a nod. Preparations begin as the cold water soaks through our boots, biting bone-deep. It's all I can do to stop my teeth from chattering. Forrest Trask laughs and says I should grow a beard like his for a little warmth. Everyone always says it's colder up north of the Reach, but all that means is that there's an occasional breeze. None of us has ever faced cold like this.

"My name is Press," the Dread's servant says in greeting. He almost seems bored by our arrival. Eventually, his eyes find me. "So this is the crew you've chosen to take down the gods?"

I raise an eyebrow. "They are my best fighters."

He assesses the crew again. "I wish my lord would have warned me that he was sending a bunch of green children. I'd have reconsidered taking the job."

That earns a few dark glares from the crew. "We are more dangerous than you know, or else your god wouldn't have brought us."

Press nods. "Let us hope the Fury doesn't string you up from his gates."

Kenly hands me a set of ashes. We're settling into our formations, ready to get moving. The Dread's servant sounds like a pain already, but he's all we have out here.

"You have your job," I remind him. "And we have ours."

"Well, I can promise one of us will succeed," Press replies. "No one's navigated these lands more often than I have. We'll ride hard. You can't burn down here as fast as you do up there, but the horses can still be pushed. Follow me and we'll make good time. Keep your eyes open. Call out anything that seems amiss. I'll not be whipped by my master because one of you gets eaten."

I find myself nodding. The faster we reach the city, the better. I can tell it will take some effort to keep my crew from smothering Press in his sleep. I glance down the lines and see a mixture of emotions. There's annoyance in some, pride in others. Running beneath that, though, is the first small trace of fear. It is one thing to volunteer in a meeting hall surrounded by your fellow soldiers. It is quite another thing to step foot in a new world and face threats no other soldier will ever know.

I have to be the bold voice that leads them.

"We didn't come here for talk. We came here to kill a few gods. Get us moving."

That earns a look of approval from Press.

"Come and welcome," he replies. "Let's see how many of you survive the night."

25

THE CAPITAL

PIPPA

Furia transforms in wartime.

You've never seen it this way, but you've read the old stories and know some of what to expect. The walls are raised. There are designed choke points that funnel enemies toward livestone gates. The lower floors of every building convert into battle stations with window slits for archers and snipers. Drums beat rhythms in every war camp. Soldiers sharpen their swords and ready ashes. Most of them are smiling. Your people have always liked warcraft.

We were taught to like it.

The bulk of your army settles along the western front. You've sent out orders. Most of them will set up inside the city's gates. Foot soldiers will begin digging trenches. And your cavalry has been given very specific orders for the rebirth it'll use in the morning. You wrote down the list of ingredients from memory. It is a rebirth the Longhands will not know or expect.

One of many tricks you have hidden up your sleeves.

Adrian Ford's army is still marching, a few days out at least, but you know the Longhands have night-marched before, and you want to be ready as soon as possible. It is the Ashlord way. Prepare for everything. Bend the world to face you on your own terms. You think about Adrian's army marching inland and can't help wondering how far your revenants have traveled. Will they intercept his army tonight? Tomorrow night? Anticipation runs like a newly carved vein in your heart. Half of your thoughts are of Adrian as the final pieces of the plan fall into place. At first, you kept thinking, *May the gods help him.* But then you realized you need a different prayer. This time, you hope the gods do not see him coming.

Etzli finds you bent over city maps and making final plans.

"We've been invited to a gala tonight. It will be hosted at Ashtaki's manor."

"A gala on the eve of battle. Only natural."

She sets a lettered invitation down on the desk. "We are guests of honor."

You read the letter carefully. It is disturbing, really, that someone took the time to have this printed. The city is days away from siege warfare and they're manning the printing presses? There are thousands of other more meaningful tasks. It digs under your skin. Not to mention you'll be expected to dance your way through a gala instead of resting after a long march. It does, however, give you an idea.

"I want the name of the printer," you say. "See if his press is still open."

Etzli notes the command as you read over the letter again.

"Gods. Ashtaki has commissioned ice sculptures. And there's a *theme.*"

Etzli nods. "Magicians do this. A bright ribbon in one hand to hide what they're doing in the other. We are meant to see the flash but not the fire. This gala will function the same way."

"And we both know what's hiding underneath all that glitter."

"Do you want to alter the plan?"

You almost shake your head, but Ashtaki's name summons a few memories. He's one of the favored cousins of the Brightness. He entered the Races last year and managed to come in last place. He drank his way through the opening galas, blacked out the night of the map revealing, and barely could seat his horse at the starting gates. His opening rebirth comes to mind.

"I have one alteration. Summon Revel."

It does not take long to settle things. Revel heads off to the stables with new instructions. Bravos is conspicuously absent. Etzli trots alongside you through the streets of Furia. An already full city is stretching at the seams. Corner stores have been converted into makeshift hotels. Military wagons rumble past, full of spears and arrows and freshly painted shields. Civilians—mostly Dividian—crowd around drafting stations, waiting to find out if their name will be chosen in the newest lottery.

Your eyes are eventually drawn to the Curiosity's tower. It's not empty. The hawk-masked servants are gone, but you suspect the Brightness sent scouts to fill the abandoned tower after her death. It offers the best views in every direction. Sunlight glints off looking glasses that are aimed at the distant hills. Everyone is waiting for war.

A gathering to your right confirms this. The Fury's temple is full of movement. Parishioners of all kinds wait in line. Each of them clutches a vial of blood, or else a spattered handkerchief. The waiting priests—each wearing the sightless bull's skull—accept their tokens. Some of the worshippers bend a knee at the edge of the temple and whisper a prayer. All are hoping the god of war will bless them in the battles to come. The tokens are tossed into a waiting pit that's meant to symbolize the blood's descent into the waiting hands of the gods.

You quiet your thoughts. No telling what the gods can hear.

A guard halts the two of you outside the Sunlight Quarter. All it takes is a second glance, though, for his eyes to widen. He throws you a salute and waves you inside.

Etzli smiles at that. "Being the famous winner of the Races has its perks."

"You're about to learn that in full. Are you sure you're ready?"

The smile vanishes, but your second in command nods.

"I am not afraid."

"You never are."

A fierce pride blossoms on her face. You are so thankful to have a soldier like Etzli at your side. It reminds you of the story she shared of her parents and their cruelty. It is a common thought among the Ashlord people. A person can be carved into the shape you most desire, if only you have a patient and steady hand wielding the knife. It is a tradition you hope to leave behind in the new world.

"You are more than what they tried to make you."

Etzli nods. "As are you."

The next few days will test the loyalty that's formed between you, but there is no doubt in your mind. Etzli will not fade, no matter how bright the sun burns against her. That assurance has your heart thumping as your horses weave through the streets. Normally peaceful gardens have been commandeered. Guards patrol every rise. These are the Brightness's protectors. You head straight for the largest pavilion. Mother stands there, surrounded by princes and generals.

It is only as you dismount that she finally notices you.

"Pippa. Good. We're going over the latest reports."

Etzli follows you into the crowd. It is a who's who of Ashlord nobility. The Brightness lounges in a raised chair to your right. He's by far the oldest in the group, but he manages to look younger than others his age. His close connection to the gods supposedly keeps him in good health.

His three eldest children stand a step behind him. You know Rone—the crown prince—from the gladiator circuit. He wears the traditional armor, but you know that his right knee was shattered in a famous duel. The man who shattered it was never seen again.

The other two are twins. You are familiar with Prince Ino. He wears the same disapproving scowl that he offered you every day of the march. His twin sister—Mira—is the city's master of coin. A sharp girl with little taste for battle.

Mother stands in as the lead strategist. Four generals

wait behind her. You recognize Carla. A brutal woman who famously tunneled her way into the Longhand's final stronghold during the Last War. There are two younger generals you know only by name. The fourth general catches your eye and offers you a forced smile. Father is a vision in his armor. You can't help noticing how tired he looks, how much this war has taken from him. You suspect you know the source.

There are three other less welcome guests.

All three are priests. One of the Striving's representatives stands on the edge of the group. Her creatures do not wear the animal masks the others do. Instead, their human faces are masked by something more robotic. The Striving's gift has always been technology, and her priests are less than human for it. Painted eyes watch the proceedings from a silver face.

The Madness is also represented. A priest with a three-eyed wolf mask has his back turned to you. He's crouched like a dog, distracted by the fluttering leaves in the distant gardens. And the last priest belongs to the Fury. He stands straight-backed and muscled. You know the Fury himself is not present, because his power is not pulsing against you like a second sun.

You do your best to focus as Mother begins.

"Antonio Rowan has reached the Burnished Valley," she says. "He'll camp there tonight and reach the highlands sometime tomorrow afternoon. I've assigned units to harass him as he makes his way, but they'll pull back the closer he gets. I'd not waste good riders."

You nod at that. The Brightness does, too.

"And Ford?" he asks.

"Marching from Grove," Mother answers. "According to our scouts, we're outnumbered nearly two to one. I want to hit them hard when they arrive. A few cavalry bursts with infantry supporting the effort. We'll do our best to leave a few wounds before retreating into the city. A siege could be problematic given our population, but I trust the gods to make that difficult. . . ."

She dangles the invitation. All eyes swing to the Striving's priest. She offers a nod. Her voice crackles, half human and half machine. "Our efforts will force them toward the city."

"And break them against our walls," the Brightness adds. "Make them earn every step."

Mother is nodding. "Our defenses are not impregnable. Especially given the recent demands of our Dividian soldiers. Even with the pay raise we offered, many have wearied of our command. The word from our spies in the east is that several cities surrendered without even fighting. Our city-born Dividian are more loyal, but when the battle comes to their door, we need to expect some to fade."

"The cavalry charges will dictate momentum," Carla points out. "Who's leading them?"

Mother's eyes find me. "Pippa, you wanted to face Adrian?"

You offer a fearless look. "Give me a thousand horses. I'll paint the hills with Longhand blood."

A few of the older generals nod. Mother glances to the Brightness for approval. He knows what you've accomplished in the north. He remembers how many cities you've won.

"Pippa strikes west," he confirms. "Carla to the east. Make them hurt."

Carla offers you a wicked grin. "Count your kills. We'll see who gets more."

You grin back as another piece falls into place. The discussion turns to draft numbers. Mira walks the group through the population increases, supply costs, and more. She estimates that we would last seventy days on light rations. The generals dismiss that number, too proud to believe their city could ever be reduced to a starving mass. Mother is far too intelligent to act as if the battle is already won. Instead, she takes everything into consideration. While you will lead the first brutal charge, she'll strategize what the army will do based on every imaginable outcome.

As the meeting concludes, everyone is dismissed. Etzli asks to be excused to get ready for the gala. You join Mother and Father, linking arms with both as you walk through the forgotten gardens and back toward your home in the Straylight Quarter. Father is proud of what you've accomplished, though you can see a shadow hanging over him that you noticed on the journey home. There's something about this war that's taxing him in a way that others have not. You only wish there was time to sit down and talk with him. Your plan does not allow that.

Mother fusses, expressing her concerns. She dreads sending you in such a direct charge against such a worthy foe. It is a brief and wondrous thing to feel like a child again. It doesn't last. As you reach the gates that lead home, you glance back toward the pavilion.

A shiver runs down your spine. The other generals are

still there. A few of their servants hustle to and fro. It's a bit chaotic, but in the middle of that chaos, there is stillness. One figure has not moved since you arrived, nor after you departed. The god's vessel remains crouched. You realize that he is staring at the place where you intended to pause all along.

All three eyes are narrowed.

The Madness is watching *you*.

26

THE OTHER CAPITAL

IMELDA

We wait in a valley that was once a river. According to our guides, the two most influential cities in the underworld loom around the corner. Bastian ordered a halt before we moved into their territory. As he goes over some of the schematics, I focus on the alchemy I've been working on for the last few days. Before the Butcher took me, I'd come up with a few theories for how we might use the Bloodsworn mixture. It was too good an invitation to pass up.

I'm carefully mixing the powders when Cora Rowe kneels beside me.

"You're like a little girl in a sandbox," she notes. "What's this one do?"

"Been working on reverse engineering the new rebirth."

Cora snorts. "Make that a smart girl in a sandbox. Reverse engineering. Meaning?"

"I'm not actually sure. It might not even work. But I've been studying alchemical combinations since I was a little girl. This rebirth is the only mixture I've ever encountered that uses human blood. And there's one rule that's on the first page of every single alchemy book that's ever been written."

Cora nods. Even she knows it. "Don't use your own blood."

"Exactly."

Cora eyes the fresh wound on my palm. "You like breaking the rules, don't you?"

I shake my head. "It's more that I want to figure out why the gods made that rule in the first place. The Bloodsworn rebirth is clearly safe to use. My theory is that our blood is powerful and that the gods did not want us learning to use it. If that's correct, well . . ."

I finish off the mixture, swirling drops of my own blood in. It alters the color slightly, thickening the texture, too. I pinch the coarse powder between my two fingers and stand.

"We'll be able to do some amazing things. Ready? I'm going to test it."

Cora raises an eyebrow. "Right now?"

I shrug. "Why not? Stand back a few steps."

Cora Rowe isn't exactly a fearful creature, but this is not gunslinging or riding breakneck into enemy territory. This is an unknown magic. When she's at a proper distance, I take a deep breath. The powder is thick between my thumb and forefinger, snug as a gun. I nod to Cora.

"Something from nothing."

And then I snap my fingers.

At first, nothing happens. Not so much as a whisper. Cora lets out a snort but the sound fractures as it reaches my ears. All my senses flee. The volume of the underworld falls to a muted hush. The colors fade. Everything becomes nothing. Until *our* world shoulders back into existence. I find myself standing in an absurdly beautiful fountain. I groan a little bit because my pants are soaked up to the knees. My teeth chatter a little from the sudden cold. I quietly survey my surroundings. I'm on someone's property. It's a vast estate. There's a manor on a raised hillside to my left. War bells are ringing. Where is this? Furia? The rest of the estate has been converted into gardens. I drink in the details before remembering this is an experiment. It would not do me any good to lose my one path back to that other world. Not now.

I press my fingers together again and *snap.*

Cora Rowe is staring at me, her jaw hanging down. "What the hell was that?"

A nervous laugh escapes my lips. My breathing is a little ragged. Good to know. The mixture works, but there are definitely physical effects to traveling between the worlds so quickly. My head spins a bit as I wipe the powder off my hands.

"It actually worked."

"You *vanished,*" Cora says in disbelief. "You went somewhere without a horse? And . . . why are your pants wet?"

I can't help grinning. "Come on. I'll explain as we walk."

Our crew is ready to move again. I'm still explaining the science of what I just did to Cora when the two cities come into view. Even at a distance, they look impossible to breach. Our approach forces us down a long-dried river canyon. Fissure explains that this waterway once ran wide and deep. Until the Fury dammed the river in an attempt to create a drought in the competing southern province. His strategy worked. We passed a few houses that were little more than dust and memory. The canyon shielded both cities from view for a time, but now they loom on the distant horizon.

It is easy to tell which is which.

The Fury's stronghold stands on the southern banks. The walls are dark and cruel. Spikes run the length, making the city look like a giant barbed mace ready to be swung. From the way the freed slaves talk, I'd almost think the god of war *is* strong enough to swing the whole thing at us.

On the northern bank sits the Striving's city. It is more sophisticated. The walls rise just as high, but they're a clean-cut silver. Futuristic lights beam down from the ramparts, roaming the plains in unpredictable sequence. Bastian notes the one detail I miss.

"The entire thing looks made of livestone."

I've seen livestone gates once before, but never in action. Supposedly, the stones summon statue guardians that can come to life, defending the gate without loss of life. In our world, the gates are quite rare. I'm also pretty sure they don't normally account for the entire exterior.

Harlow Rowe asks the obvious question. "How the hell do we get in?"

My eyes trace the third noticeable feature. Twenty bridges connect the two cities. Each one is bright and marbled, a beautiful contrast to the gray landscape. They span across the dried riverbed below. These look like potential access points, but the longer I stare, the more obvious it becomes. Each bridge has to be at least fifty lengths high. A Changing Skies horse would do the trick, but we're stuck with the rebirths we came on. I grind my teeth in frustration.

Fissure edges forward. "I know of an old slave door. It's close, but likely in disrepair."

"Lead the way," Bastian replies.

It's a little strange to go forward without our mounts, but everyone agreed to leave the horses tied up farther back in the canyon. Too much visibility. Over half of the freed slaves are waiting with them. Fissure and Bastian went through the ranks together, picking out those who could fight and those who shouldn't. They agreed on everyone until the very end. A group of unchosen children pushed forward. The leader of the bunch couldn't have been a day over ten. All of them wanted to fight. Bastian tried to laugh the idea away until Fissure quietly reminded him they were free to choose their own fate.

When Bastian warned them of the dangers, each child flashed bits of steel they'd made themselves, down in the Butcher's sweatshops. "You think you know more about danger than us?" one girl asked. "I've made a hundred blades sharper than you."

Bastian was quiet after that. We left the Butcher's stronghold a short while later, needing only to retrieve our crew. I'd expected resistance from them. After all, the last time Cora Rowe came to this place, she'd been so eager to leave that she held me at gunpoint. But not one of them questioned Bastian's plan. I've learned it is one of his greatest gifts. His beliefs become theirs. They trust him, always. Besides, we were inviting a bunch of rebels to kill the gods. It had more than a few of them grinning.

Now our group clings to the shadows of the northern riverbanks. We are one hundred strong. There are whispers of movement on the cliffs above. Fissure warns us not to get too close to the larger burrows. "Even with the help of old gods like you," he says quietly, "there are some creatures here we'd do better not to wake."

Harlow and Cora Rowe laugh about that until we pass a burrow that's wide enough to ride a horse down. Inside, there's a strange reverberation. I smile watching Harlow's mouth slam shut. The crew steers well away from the spot.

About five hundred paces downstream, Fissure turns down an adjacent canyon. The great rises on each side have slowly pressed together over time. Overhead, there's barely a sliver of gray light. "This is the place," Fissure announces. "It hasn't been used in a long time."

Our crew crowds into the space. The deeper we go, the tighter it gets. I walk forward with Bastian to find a silver circle set into the side of the canyon like a steel plug. Bastian runs a hand down the front, searching for a latch, but there aren't any obvious handles.

"Do we knock?"

Fissure's answer is cut off by a low rumble. Dust shakes down on our shoulders and hoods. There's barely enough time for Fissure to hiss a warning. "Everyone down. Don't move."

The freed slaves drop first. We join them, shoulders pressing together, as something thunders overhead. It takes a breath to realize the noise isn't from one creature but hundreds.

Our angle is straight up. About fifty paces overhead, the canyon walls narrow until there's just a whisper of gray sky in sight. Horses of some kind come rushing past. I can see charcoal hooves and brief glimpses of pronounced rib cages. Dark wings rise from their shoulders. I have never seen anything like them. None of the noises they make sound right, either. Their challenges sound sharper, more like metal scraping against metal.

The herd thunders on. The sound begins to fade. I start to stand, but Fissure pulls me back down by my cloak. I'm about to hiss a curse at him when I hear it. Movement. A shadow slips overhead. My entire body goes still as the shadow takes form.

One of the horses sniffs the air. We're just close enough to see flared nostrils. My heart pounds in my chest as it comes into view. It is a skeleton brought to life. Nestled within blackened bones that form the skull, a strange blue light glows where an eye should be. The creature stares down through the razor-thin gap—looking right at us—for what feels like an eternity. That blue light dances in the socket like a living flame.

It snaps its jaws once—a sharp click—before looking up. Those great wings spread from its bony shoulders and the creature vanishes in a burst of movement. Finally, the canyon goes quiet.

"Undead horses," Cora Rowe mutters. "Just lovely."

Harlow counters. "Looked alive enough to me."

Fissure is on his feet. "Those were hunting horses. We are lucky. It seemed as if they've already picked up a scent. Hunting someone else. We might not have survived otherwise."

Bastian frowns at that. "They're just horses."

"With jaws that can crush a man's skull," Fissure replies. "We should keep moving. You are from the land of the old gods. Your blood will be our passage."

His words shiver through our ranks. Bastian looks ready to complain, so I step forward.

"I'll do it," I say, removing the ceremonial knife from my belt. All it takes is a quick slit on my right palm. The pain is sharp, but it does the job. Blood trickles free. I'm not exactly sure how it all works, but I think back to what happened in the Butcher's storehouse. Focused on getting *inside,* I press my palm to the closed metal entrance.

The effect is immediate. A few of Bastian's crewmates gasp as an intricate series of latches appear. I don't hesitate, working the locks one at a time, until the whole thing groans open. There's a dark tunnel passage. No movement within. Only the distant howling of wind. Fissure looks my way, and I can't help noticing there's a little bit of reverence in his stare. His idea of old gods worries me, but right now all that matters is making our way forward.

"This will take us into the city," I say, just loud enough to be heard by those gathered. Farian would hate that I'm resorting to a disclaimer. "We are knocking on the doors of two of the most powerful gods our people have ever faced. The Striving and the Fury will not welcome us with open arms. If you do not want to come, now is the time to stay behind. I have no idea what happens next. I just know that this is our chance to change the world."

My eyes find Bastian's. He nods his approval. Everyone needs to count the cost.

Taking a deep breath, I plunge into the dark, dagger in hand, blood dripping from my palm. I've got more of the powdered mixture in a container on my belt, too. I will not be caught helpless again. Bastian follows me into the shadows. I do not look back as we weave through the staggered stones and into the unlit warrens. But the footsteps sound like a whispered stampede.

We are many.

And we are coming.

27

HUNTED

ADRIAN

I was wrong about Press.

I will not have to stop my crew from smothering him in his sleep. They will have to stop me. We've been riding hard, and there's scarcely been a moment that he does not fill the air with noise. I have never met someone with so much to complain about.

"Didn't sleep well," he's saying as we trot through a tricky valley. "Never do, really."

Most of the others have faded back. It leaves me as his closest conversation.

"I don't think anyone slept well," I mutter.

Press launches into the reasons he probably had the worst of it. I find my mind drifting. At least we're making decent time. The edges of a city appeared about thirty clock-turns ago. Right now, there's a massive canyon separating us from our target. We're navigating down and trying not to break our necks, which Press promises is a likely outcome no matter our caution.

Farian's finally packed away his camera. He filmed too many landscape shots early on and he's already burned through half of his materials. Told me he didn't want to miss the action when we reached the city. I reminded him this isn't a trip to the cinema. It's real life. Martial grunted his approval at that, but Farian shrugged the warning off.

The rest of the team is in good spirits. I cast a glance back at Kenly, who's become the de facto lieutenant. He rides confidently, encouraging the others, promising the blood of gods. Forrest Trask is all smiles and jokes. It's a good thing to keep things light on the way to death's door. I keep a firm grip on the reins and focus on navigating a steep turn. At least I chose the right soldiers for the task ahead.

"And the gods only know what calls *this* canyon home," Press complains.

We reach the canyon bottom. It's gone quiet. Press has fallen back a few paces. The Dread's scout is silent for the first time in days. His eyes find the distant cliffs. He's got his head turned oddly, like a man listening for a sound just out of earshot. I punch a fist into the air to halt my soldiers. The conversations die away. Our horses crunch to a halt.

"What is it?" I ask.

Until now, Press has been casual to the point of laziness. His shoulders always slump. He manages to make everything about their world seem boring and gray. But some approaching danger sharpens the Dread's servant in a breath. His eyes search for movement as he reaches into one of many coat pockets.

Light shivers over an object that looks like a watch. He presses down on a small lever, and a golden substance mists through the air. It surrounds us, less substantial than fog. Some hold their breath but I recognize the substance. The Dread has used similar magic in our world. His first spell of protection was textured the same way. Press's decision draws my eyes to the cliffs. What danger comes?

"I forgot about the damn horses," Press whispers. "Every-one. Stay inside the protective circle. It is a camouflage of sorts. The creatures will see the landscape behind us. Do your best to keep your mounts quiet. The spell doesn't block sound. Nor will it last forever. Be sure—"

Movement cuts him off. Up on the distant cliffs, winged creatures are setting down. An entire herd of horses. But even at this distance, I know they're wrong. Corrupted somehow. Too thin. Their movements unnatural. I watch the creatures sniff the ground and spread out. It reminds me of the hunting rebirths in our world. Horses that follow scents through life and death.

On my right, Forrest Trask reaches inside one pocket. A plum appears in his palm. It's clever thinking. The others take note. We all search silently. Any soft fruits or enticing treats. Carefully, we spread the bounty between us, leaning forward to feed our mounts. Anything that might help dis-tract our suddenly nervous horses.

Several of the interlopers take flight. The group searches and searches. A few land in the canyon on our left. Another pair land to our right, no more than a hundred paces away.

My eyes trace the golden mist that encircles us. It ap-pears to be holding. Powerful magic to entrust to a servant.

I was going to ask Press about that, but now I find myself hoping that his god did not gift him weak spells. One of the creatures edges toward us. A larger herd wings above, landing on the upper cliffs we came down. I hope they'll follow our trail in the wrong direction, but I also know all it takes is one moment of bad luck to discover us.

The closer this one gets, the stranger it looks. A damn skeleton walking through the world. There's blue light where its eyes should be. Hundreds of questions run through my mind, but I don't dare ask them. Every one of us is barely breathing.

Fifteen paces.

Ten paces.

The creature pauses at the edge of our circle. It sniffs the air. Sharp teeth click together twice. That noise stirs a few of our horses. I can see the veins standing out on the backs of my soldiers' hands. Everyone has a death grip on their reins. No one moves. The horses are scared, but I have a feeling the golden barrier is keeping them from outright panic.

Our unwelcome guest circles. It pauses to stare directly at the front soldier. With a silent crane of my neck, I see that it's Nevira Pearce. Kenly's recruit shows off exactly why he has so much confidence in her. She doesn't even flinch. The creature stares a beat longer before turning, neck arching, in search of other clues. Relief thunders.

And then there's a noise like a gunshot.

It isn't a weapon, but in the silence of that echoing canyon, it's just as loud. Farian's camera clicks and reloads and clicks again. His eyes shock wide. He reaches for his bag to

silence the thing, but he's too late. A skeletal neck swivels
our way. Blue eyes brighten. It lunges for him.

Martial is there. Quicker than I could ever imagine. His
horse darts between Farian and the beast. He brings his
sword up from his belt and slashes diagonally in one feral
motion. The creature's lunge exposes its neck, and even
though there's no skin to split, no muscle to tear, Martial's
blade cracks through bone. The creature's head rolls, growl
dying in its exposed throat.

Press hisses a single word. "Run."

The golden mist scatters. A hundred winged horses turn
to stare. I'm the first one to thunder forward. The others
follow, shouting out warnings, steel rising from belts. The
nearest hunting horse comes barreling in from the left. I
swing my sword and strike a glancing blow off the creature's shoulder. It stumbles away before darting toward another rider.

Death comes for us.

Horses are landing on either side of the canyon. There's
a slit of a pathway ahead, wide enough for our horses but
too narrow for the pursuing pack. I aim us for the spot. I
do not know where it leads or where we're going or how
to survive. Press shouts something. It's too loud to hear the
words. There's stampeding hooves and the sound of metal
against bone.

A flash of color on my left is the only other warning.
One of the skeletal horses lowers its shoulder and crashes
right into my flank. It's a bone-crushing hit that ends both
of them. My horse lets out a horrible scream and I spin from

the saddle. The only thing that keeps me from breaking my neck is the layer of ash on the canyon floor. My upper back takes most of the bruising blow.

Luckily, my body rolls twice, just clear of the other horses thundering past.

Forrest pulls on his reins, circling back to protect me. I even hear him shout my name as I scramble to get my switch off my belt. Two skeletal horses wing in my direction. I deflect a snapping jaw, but it was just a feint. Both horses converge on Forrest instead.

The first sinks dagger-sharp teeth into his horse's neck. It startles on hind legs and Forrest's arms go out for balance. It leaves him exposed. The second horse kicks him right in the chest. The blow caves him in. His whole body punches backward and I can tell from the way he folds in on himself that he's dead before he lands. "Forrest!" I scream.

I hold my sword up, chest heaving, but the creatures both ignore me. Instead, they work to take down his horse. My eyes swivel. Kenly is nearby. He's pinned beneath his mount, swiping at one of the skeletal beasts as his own horse screams in agony.

In the chaos, I forgot that we came here with a weapon more dangerous than steel. There's a wound on my neck. I reach for the blood, coating my finger in the substance, before striding forward. I do not swing my sword. I simply point my hand at the creature and command it to die. The blue lights of its eyes vanish. Bones fall in a discarded pile. Kenly's gasping as another horse scrapes overhead. I point my hand again and a second creature spins into nonexistence.

New power thrums in my veins.

I eye the rest of the battlefield. Martial has dragged Farian to the opposite canyon wall. His sword is raised protectively. Press stands behind them. Most of the other soldiers are rallying to the spot, so I reach down to pull Kenly out from under his horse. I shove him in that direction and stumble after him, feeling a little light-headed.

We form up ranks, our backs to the canyon wall, but it becomes clear we're no longer the target of the attack. The horses ignore the other soldiers. Instead, they rip out the throats of our mounts. Like wolves, they circle and pin and nip at heels until one of them can lunge forward and bring it down for the kill.

I'm about to use the power of my blood again, but Press's grip locks on my arm. He pulls me back toward the group, his voice a whisper.

"It's dangerous to use too much. These are not the foes you should waste your power on." And then louder, for the others. "We should move while they feed. It'll give us time."

The others look horrified, but I know he's right. The creatures have forgotten us. New battles are raging as they fight one another for the choicest meats. My eyes find Forrest Trask's body across the bloody field. One of my oldest friends. The boy who used to test my strength, who helped sharpen and shape me into what I am now. My hand trembles as I point to his lifeless form.

"Who will help me carry him?"

Kenly steps forward. "I'll go."

One of Forrest's cousins, a man named Brannan, volunteers as well. The three of us slip through the feeding ground carefully to gather our lost soldier. He's heavier in death. Press waits until we return to lead the crew across the valley, up through another canyon. It is difficult making our way now, but we push on. Our mounts are dead. We are bloodied, but far from broken. I do my best to keep my head held high as we reach the final rise.

Two cities come into view. My voice forges a path toward them.

"Let's show these gods what the Reach is made of. Let's honor the fallen. Let's win."

28

THE HUNT BEGINS

PIPPA

Bright lights glitter over everything.

You swirl your drink and try not to look completely annoyed. Ashtaki is a few paces away, telling the same story he told you when you arrived, boasting in his loudest voice. He's playing the part of host. Encouraging people to dance. Setting glasses in waiting hands. He wears an absurdly bright cloak that looks more befitting of a traveling circus.

The evening's theme is a *sunset.*

It's clear now that the theme was chosen around Ashtaki's newest outfit. The swatches of fabric transition from top to bottom, mimicking a sun setting on a distant horizon. You are not sure if the fabric actually trades places or if some trick of the dye makes it look so. What stands out in your mind is that the pompous brat had it hand-sewn just this week. While your armies retreated to defend the city, he was fussing with tailors over the right shades.

You might have enjoyed that once. Tipped your own

fashionable cap in his direction and toasted his cleverness. Now you look around at the finest Ashlords in the world, the most celebrated, and feel the weight of the truth. It is long past time for your people to change.

The old ways will not survive what is coming.

"Don't look too enthused," Etzli says, tipping her glass into yours. "I'd hate for anyone here to think that you're enjoying the party."

You smile. "A sunset theme. How fitting."

Etzli does not reply to that. She's locked into the role you've assigned her. The two of you are just tools at this point. Ready and sharp and dangerous. You take a large sip of wine as something across the room catches your eye. Bravos has arrived.

You did not notice him slip into the gathered ranks. He's standing beside Prince Ino. The royal wears his customary frown, but as Bravos continues his story, he doesn't dismiss the outrider. He stands there listening patiently and you can't help wishing you were close enough to hear the conversation. Etzli notices the exchange, too.

It is all going as expected.

"How suspicious," she says.

"Indeed."

A group dance takes over the floor. You smile as Mother breaks away from the other generals and hooks your father's arm. He goes reluctantly to the dance floor. Watching them turn in quick circles, eyes locked on each other, is enough to have you briefly forgetting that a war is knocking at your door.

You know that Mother is nothing like Ashtaki—or some

of the other Ashlords gathered. She will dance tonight, but the strategies will be racing through her mind all evening. She will be counting soldiers, thinking through counter-moves, dreaming of a bright victory for your people.

You take another swallow of wine.

A glance across the room shows that Prince Ino is alone. Bravos is gone. How very curious. You resist the urge to cross the room and speak with the prince. He gestures for the nearest servant and whispers a lengthy request. Your voice is a matching whisper.

"He's got the scent."

Etzli nods. "Come. Let's dance."

She drags you onto the dance floor. It is a marching dance. You know the steps, and you let Etzli lead you through them. Mother flashes a smile at you. Father's laughing for the first time in days. The rest of the room is tipsy and on their way to sleeping soundly for the last peaceful night you're promised.

The Brightness joins the revelry just an hour later. He lifts his glass to make a toast. Everyone echoes his words, and Ashtaki spills wine with his enthusiastic applause.

The sunset party approaches midnight. Desserts are ushered in on golden plates. Some of the most expensive vintages in existence find their way to the dance floor, splashing into waiting glasses. Carla attempts to get Father out on the dance floor, but Mother cuts a look that has the old gladiator lifting her hands innocently, and winking her way to someone else. You pretend and you pretend and you pretend and you might just *burst* from all the bright nothing.

It ends when Ashtaki breaks the front legs of an antique

chair that's worth more than most people's city flats. Everyone takes it as their cue to leave. One of the younger—and more drunken—princes tries to help Ashtaki fix the wooden set, both of them laughing like fools the whole while.

The Brightness pauses the entire group at the entrance.

"Tonight we drink. Tomorrow we go to war. I am not sure which one our people like best, but I'll be damned if we are not great at both. Outside you'll find a surprise waiting. Do not be alarmed. It is a precaution we are taking that will bind our most important citizens to our pantheon's boons. Be sure to walk past the waiting priests. Good night!"

His words sharpen your senses. You find Etzli standing across the room. She nods once and you realize the fateful moment has arrived. The one detail you could not plan for is here. Most of the other guests look slightly uneasy, but it could just be the glazed and tired expressions of half-drunken fools. This is the method by which they'll discover who had a hand in the Curiosity's death. You are certain of it.

It has your heart beating up into your throat.

You gather your cloak around you and follow the others outside. Etzli slips through the crowd until you are together, arms locked in preparation for what looks like a pleasant stroll. If the announcement was unnerving, the sight that greets you is downright terrifying. Ashtaki's property makes your parents' home look quaint. It's an absurd manor fronted by marbled steps. There's a carriage road that circles a fountain before slipping out the front gates, all framed by a courtyard that's larger than most of the city's public parks.

And priests wait on the landing.

They stand in a half-moon barricade. Each one belongs to the Madness. Of course. The god who watches the passages between worlds. You are not sure how his magic will work, but you are certain that he'll have some way of discovering who has gone where they should not have gone. As you descend, the priests keep their hands outstretched, fingers splayed, with only slight gaps between each of them. You see now that you are meant to walk between them. Every attendee will pass through those gaps. Every attendee will be touched—or rather tested—by the priests of the Madness.

Etzli keeps her arm linked in yours as you make your nervous way down the steps. Any attempt at escape would invoke suspicion. A glance shows the Brightness watching from the top step, eyes tracing the crowd. You are not sure how quickly this method will work. Will the creatures know the guilty party on first touch? Or are they gathering clues for later?

It could ruin everything if you are seized now.

You reach the landing. Some of the other guests frown as the outstretched, dirty hands snag their cloaks. Mother and Father cross the barrier ahead of you. On your right, one of the princes offers a playful howl. Nothing can protect you from what happens next. Etzli squeezes your hand and does not let go as she crosses the barrier first. You press after her. The priest on the right does not touch you, but the one on the left lands a few fingertips on your forearm. A howl breaks through the night. Is it in the air? Is it in your mind?

You wait for the priests to converge and arrest you.

Nothing happens.

Etzli looks sideways as you turn down the first street. "I'm going to get into position."

You squeeze her hand once more and whisper good luck. Watching her slip down the street, you cannot help but imagine the little girl, abandoned by her parents for an entire year. You know now that Etzli was too strong to be broken by them. Tonight's plan has her walking straight into the waiting jaws of the enemy. It's possible you'll all be executed. Etzli does not so much as flinch. As she rounds a corner, you think she might be the bravest person you've ever met.

Mother and Father wander ahead. You are not sure how the magic works, what information the Madness's priests are gathering, but you are certain they will come. It takes a quick step to catch up with your parents.

"I'm going to check on one more thing before going to sleep."

Mother smiles back, nudging your father, who is lost in thought. The two of them say their goodnights to you before stumbling on. It wastes precious time but you watch them until their forms merge with the shadowed hedges. You want to remember them this way before it all begins.

And then you're marching in the opposite direction with purpose.

Down through the Stallion Quarter, out the gates there, and into another courtyard. No one seems to be following you, but you double back twice, waiting in recesses for passing shadows. None come. You breathe a sigh of relief as you reach the planned rendezvous location. There's a nook behind the eastern stables that you used to sneak away to with Bravos. The two of you would trade kisses and name the stars together.

Revel waits there with two horses. When he sees you coming, he offers the reins of the one on the right. "Your horse, General."

He mounts his own strider before watching you mount yours. It's second nature to slip your foot up and swing your leg around, settling into the specialized saddle. You test the straps once before sliding back as far as you possibly can in the seat.

"Is it working?"

Revel frowns. "Come into the light."

You nudge your horse forward. There's a slit in the stable roof that casts an amber glow. Revel stares at you for a long moment before smiling. "It works."

"Ashtaki is not completely useless, then," you say. "After all, it was his idea. Let's move."

Revel trots forward, accepts your horse's reins, and starts through the streets. He sets a gentle pace. You clench the sides of the horse with your legs to keep yourself steady. Revel leads the two horses through the empty training yard before turning down a side street.

"How do you know we're doing the right thing?" Revel asks quietly.

"I don't."

He sits tall and proud on his mount, the way he was taught since childhood. Revel is as much a picture of Ashlord prosperity as you. His parents can trace their lineage back to the most royal bloodlines. He spent summers swimming off the coast. His school years were spent in the same board-ing schools as you. It is a miracle that he's with you now, prepared to set it all on fire.

"It is the first time I have felt a sense of . . . purpose," he admits.

You're about to reply when a turn brings the chosen gate into sight. There are more guards than expected. One peels away from his post, striding forward. "Credentials?"

"Revel. I'm the lead outrider with the Second Company. We're on the western gates. I was ordered to bring this stallion over, though. Something about needing more purebreds?"

The guard looks directly at you. His eyes skip down to the horse, as if he knows how to tell purebreds apart. His friend back at the gate clears his throat. "Revel from the Races?"

Revel cracks a smile. "The fastest rider in Furia. At your service."

The other guard grins. "Didn't know third place counted as fastest these days." He offers a wink. "Only joking. You're faster than me, and that's fast enough. Go on and make your delivery."

Revel nods his thanks, urging the horse through. You do not dare breathe as the gate opens and the guards begin a whispered argument over who the fastest rider *really* is. Revel shakes his head. He keeps his voice low. "I *am* faster than you, you know."

You smile in return before forgetting that—like the guards—he cannot see you.

"Whatever helps you sleep at night. It doesn't matter now. We're on the same team."

He nods. "I'm going to head back. You know the way?"

"Yes. I know the way. Thanks, Revel."

"Anything for my general."

He slips back through the shadows, wisely waiting in the courtyard for a while so it looks like he did the job he came to do. You are alone. This part of the city does not get a lot of foot traffic. All you can do now is wait for morning. A howl splits the night. Others follow.

The hunt is beginning.

You smile.

Come and find me.

29

FREEDOM

IMELDA

The way is dark and winding.

Everything down here smells like metal. We pass abandoned forges. Their fires have not burned in ages, but the scent of violence hangs in the air, thick as smoke. Water runs somewhere down in the caverns below. I can hear the echoing rush of it. Fissure passes salvaged torches around and we use their light to keep moving. He insists this abandoned quarter will lead us to something occupied. The Fury's slaves have to be here *somewhere*.

I do not want to doubt him, but each new turn reveals abandoned workshops. Empty rooms. There are no signs of life. Fissure eventually grows quiet, too. Something is wrong.

Around another bend, lights glow. I pause the group, veiling our own fires, and slip forward as a scout. Bastian joins me, hissing something about being safe. We move together, edging through the dark passage until we're close enough to see within.

A dirty living quarters. Bunks stacked dangerously high on the wall. Clothes scattered about, but again, no one is there. We signal back and the others press forward to join us.

"Empty."

Fissure frowns. "It is odd that none are resting. Our work is rigorous. Shifts are the custom."

There's another doorway. We cross the room carefully. I've got one hand hovering over the cube on my belt that holds the newly created powder. On the opposite palm, blood runs from a wound. Bastian sports a matching slash on the top of his forearm. We lead the crew into what looks like a massive factory. But once more the machines are abandoned. The underground is even more massive than I imagined. There are production lines. Weapons and armor of all shapes and sizes gathered in piles.

"These are the gifts," I whisper. "This is what the gods offer the Ashlords. Gifts made by the hands of slave labor. Endless production. There's no limit to what they can make."

Bastian nods. "But where'd all the workers go?"

Fissure starts leading us up, toward the surface. Fearful questions break through my thoughts. *Is this all a trap? Did they somehow know we were coming?*

Cora's got both of her pistols out. Harlow holds his rifle, like that will do any good in these tight quarters. Our group climbs dirty stairwell after dirty stairwell. There are no signs of life.

It's starting to feel like we're on the verge of reaching

the surface. The air grows a little less dense, less laced with smoke. Bastian and I turn a corner into a wider room. And the sight pulls me up short. I snatch at Bastian's cloak to keep him from walking forward, and he nearly fumbles his torch. We both dig our feet in as the people following us run right into us.

The room unfolds into a vast underground gathering space. The ceilings are low, but the room is surprisingly wide. On the opposite wall, there are seven iron doors. A massive group has gathered between us and those entrances. I give up counting them. There must be thousands. Each one holds a weapon. Some wear rustic-looking armor. All of them look ready for battle.

And all of them are looking forward. Waiting in silence to be released through those seven gates. As quietly as possible, I start to backpedal. Judging by the whispered curses, Cora Rowe is right behind me. She takes my cue, though, and as one we slowly move out of the room. I consider the powder in my pocket. Is there any way I could stretch that magic to the rest of the group? Even if I could, I'd end up taking all of them back into Furia. That's enemy territory, too. My mind is racing through the possibilities, hoping we won't be noticed, when I finally spot one face that's turned our way. There's a girl at the front of the crowd.

"Leaving already?" she calls. "You just got here!"

The entire sea of people turns to look at us. My breath catches in my throat. Light glints off all the gathered weapons. We are about to die. How could I have been such a fool?

"Your name is Imelda, isn't it?"

I almost pass out. The stress of all those eyes. Hearing my name on a stranger's lips. Bastian holds my arm to keep me steady. The girl strides through the gathered ranks. The crowd splits to allow her passage. I stare—trying to remember her face and wondering who the hell she is. Cora whispers to Harlow. Something about fighting their way through. Bastian silences them with a look.

The girl stops about ten paces away. She's no one I know. I'm certain of that much. She's pale-skinned with eyes that are slightly mismatched. But it's clear she knows me.

"Did Pippa send you?" she asks.

It's another strike of lightning. I stutter a response.

"Pippa? No, I haven't seen her since the Races."

The girl shrugs. "Happy accident, then. My name is Quinn. Why don't you and your crew come up front? I'd hate for you to come all this way and miss the fun."

30

HOLD THE HILL

ADRIAN

We march across the open plain.

Our path carries us to the front gates of the Fury's city. My soldiers march as confidently as they can. As expected, Press is unhappy with such a direct approach.

"There are secret passages," he points out. "Underground. We should make our way into the city through one of those. This amounts to suicide. We can't just *knock* on the doors and expect entrance. Even with your blood at our disposal."

I make no reply. I've spent the last fifteen clockturns coaching my crew on how to use their blood as a weapon. Forrest's death is fresh in our minds. Anger pulses in my chest. Our duty shifts now. The Dread wants us to sneak into the city like assassins, but he's clearly never met a Longhand. We are not fond of shadow games or poisons. Our place is out in the open.

We are a shield against the dark.

I pick a hill just outside the city. It's the perfect spot. Visible from the ramparts. Defensible. It gives us enough room to make a proper stand, forcing our enemies uphill to meet us. I can't help smiling as I look around at my soldiers.

"This is the place." I gesture to Kenly. "Get the drum going."

Press looks furious. "Drum? What are you thinking? The scouts on the walls will see us."

I nod to him. "I sure hope so."

Some of the soldiers take a breather. Drinking water, resting tired legs. I make the rounds, slapping my hand down on shoulders, whispering words of encouragement. Let them rest. A fight is coming soon enough. Kenly removes a standard war drum and sets it on the ground in front of him. He kneels down beside the instrument before looking to me for direction.

" 'The March of Ashes,' " I say. "Let's give them a taste of our history."

Kenly starts playing. It's a simple rhythm. An easy beat. He makes some small alterations. Only someone who's grown up in the Reach their whole lives would recognize them. This song was crafted by the Ashlords to celebrate our defeat. It is a reminder of their superiority. Kenly's changes undercut the main lyrics of the song with bolder strokes. The unspoken line at the end of each stanza goes: *Only with the help of your gods, only with the help of your gods, only with the help of your gods.*

It does not take long to get the Fury's attention.

Figures appear on the ramparts. Nevira Pearce calls out the numbers and ranks, not missing anything. Even from this distance, I can see the bull skulls with their dark horns. Kenly keeps on playing. My soldiers ready their weapons. Swords and shields and blood.

Press is looking quite pale. Almost on the verge of making a run for it. I smile at that. He's welcome to leave. After all, his task is complete. We've made it to the city.

Now it's our turn.

"We hold this hill," I say. "That is our duty. Hold this hill. No matter the cost. Fight to honor Forrest. Fight to honor your ancestors. Fight for your own lives."

The distant gates groan open. We watch as the Fury's army files out. I knew their number would be vast, but the ranks keep widening and widening and widening. Two hundred on the front line at least. Row upon row marches after them. All their considerable force aimed at us.

I set my eyes on the distant city and wait. The stream of foot soldiers finally comes to an end. I smile when the gates do not close. Instead, a massive creature walks through them.

He might have been like us once. Not anymore. The Fury wears a skull crown. His two-handed hammer drags on the ground, kicking dust into the air. He's a statue come to life. We hear him bellow something guttural and his army begins forward, spears raised.

The Fury does not close the gates. That's the moment I know we're going to win.

"Hold the hill! In Forrest's name! Fight for this hill!"

I reach for my blood. I summon that power into my outstretched hands. Stepping free of our ranks, I sweep my sword through the empty air like a scythe. The motion pairs with my blood, takes purpose from my thoughts. I watch the entire front line drop, cut in half by my amplified blow. The army rushes past their fallen, filling in the ranks.

My soldiers taste the impossible power of our blood. Each of them sees that and takes heart. We dig our heels into the packed mud. Our shields rise like suns. Our swords are echoed light. I shout the words one more time for good measure.

"Hold this hill!"

31

THE TRAITOR

PIPPA

I am not sleeping when the front door opens, or when the footsteps thunder up the back stairwell. It is expected. In our society, there's always someone willing to turn traitor. It's just another way to climb the social ladders. It was even likely that it would be the person whose footsteps sound down the hall. The bedroom door opens. Bravos enters. He's alone, but armed.

"Pippa," he says, chest heaving. "I persuaded Prince Ino to let me talk to you first. You'll be treated well if you don't resist. You can fight if you want. You can curse me to hell and back. But they'll capture you one way or another. Come with me and I'll make sure no one harms you."

I stare back at him and put venom in my voice.

"Come with you and *you'll* get all the glory. Isn't that what you really mean?"

Voices echo up the stairwell. Bravos looks back nervously.

"I'm not kidding, Pippa. I'm the best option you've got here."

"You were a traitor then and you're a traitor now."

He comes forward, though, and I don't reach for my sword. I know there's no point. He binds my hands patiently and thoroughly. I'd forgotten how strong he is.

"For privacy," he says, slipping a sack down over my head. The corner lights of my room dim. There's nothing but darkness. I can feel the wool scratching at my forehead and scraping against my lips. He tightens it a little at the neck before shouting. "Come in. She's ready."

I lash out with a kick to his shin. It's satisfying to know my aim is good. He curses as three more people enter the room. They're just shadows in my vision, but I can hear the wood groaning underfoot. Another familiar voice. I'd know the boring drawl of Prince Ino anywhere. "The others are waiting," he says. "Quit fooling around, soldier."

Bravos circles and sets a firm hand on my shoulder. I'm marched out. It is the end of everything I've ever known. Down the hallway, tripping on the uneven steps, out into a warm night. The wool fabric doesn't breathe. It is almost enough to have me sweating.

There are very few voices. I wonder if they cleared the streets—or if we're being led down the more private roads between estates? I do not have to guess *where* we're going. After all, the Ashlord people are fond of their traditions. We move down a few quiet streets before slipping inside a building.

Down a set of stairs. It grows darker with each step. I

take steadying breaths until we reach a room with more light. Bravos gives me a shove. My hands wheel, but the ground is steady beneath my feet. We stand in a wide room full of golden light. I can see the shadows of the guards spreading out. There are distant figures, faces without detail. Whispering voices. I stand as tall as I can.

We have arrived. I knew they would not dare take me to the Forum. Too public a trial for what I might tell the world. No, we've gone instead to the Constabulary.

It is the building in which the Brightness likes to dispense more private justices. There are seven stone-wrought chairs that form a circle, each representing one of the gods. Except now that most of the pantheon is dead, I can only guess who has the honor of sitting in those cold chairs tonight.

"She does not look so powerful now."

The first voice pulses with true force. I've stood in arm's reach of this power once before. It draws a smile to my lips. The Fury has chosen to join us tonight, as we hoped.

"Not powerful?" The second voice is threaded with gold. Always so polished. The Brightness is sitting directly ahead of me. "She's helped cut away half the pantheon. Are you so ready to taunt her? Let's get this business over with. We've a war to fight and I want our house cleaned out before then."

Prince Ino makes a comment. One of the other princes laughs. It's hard to say how many others are in the room. I know that most of the political dignitaries will be present. They might not want a fully public trial, but they need to make an example of me. That is best done before an audience, however small. I can sense Bravos still standing in my shadow. It's hard to make out anything beyond that. Light and darkness tangle together beneath the hood.

The Brightness speaks. "Pippa, do you know why you are here?"

I clear my throat, searching for the right way to phrase my answer.

"A false accusation, I presume?"

"Spare us," the Fury's voice hammers out. "We know you killed the Curiosity."

Another voice whispers into the silence. It is half woman and half machine.

"Knowledge is power, Pippa." The Striving's voice crackles with electricity. "You have very little power left. Trade it to us for comfort. There are ways to make your death unpleasant."

I lift my chin. "I will tell you all that I know."

My offer is greeted with pleased silence. A throat clears. Someone shuffles in their chair. I take their quiet for assent. "I first traveled to the underworld through Quinn. She was the spirit gifted to me during the Races. The girl took my blood back into the underworld. She summoned me with it. I was fond of her, but I didn't know she'd be able to call me to that world against my will."

It is quiet. I have them right where I want them.

"Quinn killed the Hoarder first. And then she challenged the Curiosity. It did not go well. Out of desperation, she summoned me. I knew she was in trouble. I could actually feel how close she was to death. I walked those halls not knowing exactly where I was—"

The Brightness interrupts. "Prama and Marcos. Stand.

Do not attempt to approach your daughter or there will be consequences."

I take a deep breath as two figures rise in the distance.

"You educated Pippa in Furia. Is that correct?"

Both murmur their agreement. I know they are helpless now. Likely, they did not even know what they were being summoned to witness. Now they can only offer acquiescence.

"And no doubt you read her descriptions of the underworld? Told her the tales of our gods? Is there any reason your daughter would not recognize that world if she saw it?"

A brief hesitation, and then a high, calm voice. "No, Your Brightness."

I nod quickly, hoping to abstain them. "You are right. I apologize. I guessed where I was, but that did not make my decision any easier. Quinn was in trouble. She was also the reason I won the Races. I acted on instinct. The Curiosity's tower was mostly empty. I found her throne room. The Curiosity was standing over Quinn, ready to kill the girl."

The Fury's voice rumbles. "And so you killed her instead?"

That question is an invitation. Now is the moment to give them what they crave.

"Yes. I killed her . . . and then I searched her tower. The god of whispers. I discovered a great many secrets there. The first was the extent of her spying. Our people always knew that she watched the Dividian and the Longhands. We didn't know that she spied on Ashlords as well."

My first accusation is greeted by whispers.

"Not to worry. The Curiosity also watched the other

gods. We found her hidden library. It was quite extensive. A book dedicated to every single person who has ever existed. The Curiosity kept meticulous records of our histories. It took days to search them, but eventually we started looking at the oldest texts. Do you have any guesses about what we found?"

There's another pulse of power. Even in my shadowed vision, I can see a figure has taken their feet. The Fury's priest is on the verge of ending this. All the gods should be nervous about where this story is heading. I'm surprised when he chooses not to attack.

"I found one book written in the Curiosity's own hand. It detailed the very first encounter between our world and their world. Can you imagine that moment? When we first met the gods? How our ancestors must have trembled in their presence."

And now for the first blow.

"Except that isn't what the Curiosity wrote. That is not how our first meeting went. Do you know why? Because when our two worlds met for the first time, *we were the gods!*"

The room thunders with noise. I can see the shadow of the Fury's priest rushing forward. No more than a handful of strides. I could outduel any priest, but right now my hands are tied and my head is hooded. Which means all I can do is brace myself for the coming blow.

And so that is what I do.

32

SURROUNDED

ADRIAN

We rise like gods.

Hundreds of the Fury's warriors have fallen. And yet there is no end to them. We are doing our best to be sparing with our blood use—to respect Press's warning—but at this point it's hard to care about our mortal limits. We are caught up in the adrenaline of survival.

I swing my sword, kick a foe on my right, and use the power of my blood to blast another wave of soldiers back. Beside me, Kenly has donned his power like a second layer of armor. It glows against the gray sky. He gathers the pulsing red substance in each fist and lands blows on anyone within reach.

Martial Rava is a living and breathing storm. His blade looks more like an echo. It is in this throat and then that chest and then splitting that belly. I can scarcely trace its path. Nor do I have time to admire his art. There is only enough time to stand our ground, to hold the hill.

We fight with every breath.

The Fury watches. I know he is not afraid. I can see him every now and again, glimpsed over the piling corpses, pacing the back lines of his army. He's not afraid. But he's not a fool, either. Why face us at our strongest?

Wave after wave will crash forward. Every new fight wastes our energy. The Fury wants the dregs of our power. My eyes sharpen as another flurry of soldiers crashes into us. A spear catches my shoulder. I growl as blood slicks down. A mistake. It is only more power.

"Away."

The blood tangles with my command. Twenty horned warriors are flung through the air by an invisible strike. Our half-moon is holding. The other soldiers stand taller than they ever have in their lives. We are the beginnings of a new kind of power. Not far from gods.

If only we can survive a little longer.

"From behind!"

It's a warning from Press. I turn around. Farian's there, chest heaving. Beyond him, there's a new company of soldiers approaching. I almost sag with exhaustion because until this point our blood has made the difference. But the approaching group wears Ashlord uniforms. They come from our world, and I know they have the same advantage that we do. Likely they know how to wield it even better than we do.

Their leader has dark hair that's spiked in the front. Their formation is oddly stiff, but they close in on our location all the same. I order Kenly to take my position up front, tightening our line, as I turn to face the new army.

There are too many. Their ranks tighten around us. The Ashlords lift their swords.

"Come on, then!" I shout. "We did not come all this way to die!"

But at the last second, the front line splits. I swing my sword at empty air. The Ashlords slide around our ranks and dive into the melee for us. Their front wave gives my soldiers their first break. I let out a ragged gasp at the un-expected gift. All our chests are heaving. My crew looks around in confusion. I'm the only one smiling, because I know who sent them.

"Stand firm! Help is on the way."

others. It is no small thing to watch your entire way of life come to an end. It takes nearly a clockturn for him to regain control of the room. Guards are appearing at all the entrances. Our fearless leader can feel his power slipping away.

"We can examine this *after* the war," he says. "Pippa cannot be trusted. She's shown—"

Now it is time for the final reveal.

"Oh! One last thing." The other voices fade. "I can see you are wrestling with the truth. What does it mean? What is this world? Who are the gods, really? I have kept one other truth from you. It is the last knowledge I have, and as the Striving said—knowledge is power." I pause long enough for them to drink in the words. The moment is flawless. "My name is not Pippa."

The entire room trembles. Gasps run the length of every row as Bravos reaches out to remove my hood. I blink back against the sudden light and fix my eyes on the Brightness. He looks terrified now. I made my voice sound like hers. I bent my words to fit what she would say. We even picked out an outfit that she would wear. Bravos helped us carry the lie, hooding me before anyone else could see the truth.

Now they see that we have them. How we have played them like fools.

"My name is Etzli. I am second in command—and loyal servant—to the only woman left in the Empire who we can trust. The one who learned the truth and started fighting these false gods. The one who would throw off our chains." I find the Striving in the crowd. "And let me be the first one to say that she's coming for you. Let's see how powerful you really are."

And the room erupts in chaos.

33

GODS AND MORTALS

PIPPA

"Hey! Stop him!"

A hundred voices sharpen into one. It doesn't matter. I can hear the approaching footsteps and the sound a blade makes as it cuts the air. Death has come. Until metal catches metal. There's a grunt. Bravos steps between us. I watch as his sword cuts the air. He follows the collective command and buries his sword in the stomach of the Fury's priest. There's a shuddering gasp as the servant slumps to the floor.

I smile in triumph. The crowd is ours now. I know they want to hear the rest of the story. That pulsing power has been snuffed out. The Striving's priest is still in the room, but she wisely sits in silence. A few of the gathered Ashlords debate what to do before the Brightness calls out to me.

"Explain what you mean."

"Ashlords." I do my best to make that word a weapon. "That is what the gods named us. Powerful beings who ruled over their world of ashes below. The pantheon that we know today were not gods at all. Rulers in their world, perhaps, but when the people of the underworld spoke of the gods . . . they spoke of *us*.

"But one of their leaders asked a clever question. What if they turned these heavenly creatures *against* one another? They had no power to match ours. Instead, they whispered war to us. Yes, you are a god, they said, but what if you did not have to share the heavens with other gods? Our ancestors grew greedy when they heard that. In a battle of equals, the underworld offered to help tip the scales. A simple exchange. They would fight for the side willing to give them an exchange of gifts. Just a token of appreciation, really."

Whispers echo around the room. They all know and fear the answer.

"Our blood for their help. That was the first trade. And our ancestors fell for it. As you all know, that has been the exchange ever since. Blood for gifts. Blood for extra soldiers. Blood for new weapons. As the generations passed, our power weakened. Every blood sacrifice drained the source of our power and gave it to them instead. Our society slowly fractured from all the wars. And it was in that moment that the supposed pantheon did something even more clever. Instead of fighting us directly, they turned to propaganda.

"Rules were made for all interactions with the world they once called 'the Heavens.' The first rule was that no one should refer to us as gods. Better to not remind us of our power. Instead, they made everything sound like a favor done on our behalf. Slowly and patiently, they made us the beggars in those exchanges. We began to think of ourselves that way."

I fight to remember the details. We rehearsed this speech for hours. It is necessary that I get everything just rig[ ] have to keep their attention, straight to the end.

"It took them another century, but they destroyed [ ] memory of the way things had been. The most powe[ ] among them took on the titles we use today. Anythin[ ] make them seem like actual gods. It worked. Generati[ ] of our people have been born since that era. Each of us [ ] grown up thinking we are *only* mortals. Know the truth n[ ] friends. Our blood has been taken from us for centur[ ] False gods have drained our power to rule their petty ki[ ] doms in a world that exists *beneath* us. Know that once, [ ] were feared and worshipped. Not them."

The silence that follows is carved in gold. An entire wo[ ] is crumbling at my feet. And when one thing dies, sor[ ] thing better can grow in its place. The phoenixes taught [ ] that much. I hold my tongue now and wait for the inevitab[ ] riposte. Our people are as predictable as ever.

The Brightness answers. "She has every reason to lie. Pi[ ] knows her position. Her life is forfeit, and now she is des[ ] ate. These are the words of a traitor. Where is your proof[ ]

Bravos strides forward. I smile under my hood, bec[ ] this is all part of the plan. They thought he was on their [ ] but he's been trying to prove himself ever since his be[ ] during the Races. He wants to be known as more than [ ] tor. He tosses a book to the stone floor. It lands with a [ ]

"Evidence," he says. "From the Curiosity's tower. [ ]

"Feel free to destroy that book," I add. "We hired [ ] ing press to make additional versions. Those letters [ ] making their way through the city all morning. . . .[ ]

The Brightness's voice is drowned out by the o[ ]

PART THREE

FORSAKEN

A god fears nothing more than being
forgotten. Death would be preferable.
—The Striving, *Musings*

34

THE CAVALRY

THE REAL PIPPA

Dawn reveals the Longhand troops outside Furia.

Their armies are making camp in the western canyons, working to find shaded areas to pitch tents and begin building their war machines. The city at your back is sleeping. But you know that if your plan worked, chaos is on its way. All you can do is hope that Etzli and Bravos survive the roles you've asked them to play. It is your turn to fight a different sort of battle.

Sunlight trickles down the ranks. Phoenix horses come gasping to life. You watch with satisfaction as a thousand soldiers saddle their mounts. The creatures are certainly strange. Something more feral. You suspect these are how the original phoenixes once looked, back when the Fury brought them stampeding into your world.

It is a rebirth you found in the Curiosity's tower. Another stolen secret.

"Instructions?" Revel is nearby. "How should I tell our riders to use the mounts?"

"Ride hard and do not slow," you answer. "The horses will do the rest."

He knows the plan, but the rest of the riders will have to trust you. Your orders echo down the ranks, and it is not long before every soldier is up on horseback. Some wield the longer spears. Others brandish their swords. Every single one of them is hungry for blood this morning.

As you made your plans, timing was the chief concern. You were not sure how or when, but you knew the Brightness would eventually discover your role in what has happened. And you knew he'd condemn you as a traitor. For now, that news has not spread. If your plan has succeeded, they're still interrogating "you." And under the Brightness's own edict, you are allowed to lead the attack on the Longhand camps without question. You only hope that you are not too late to come to Adrian's aid.

You raise the cavalry quickly. Lieutenants organize their sections as you lead them weaving through the city's exterior defenses. It feels good to get your horse up to full speed once you reach the open plains. It's a shared adrenaline. The other horses snort excitedly. Your soldiers let out loud whoops. You lift your sword and aim the cavalry at the heart of the gathering Longhand ranks. Your ancient enemy is no fool.

Their foot soldiers already stand in rows. Pikes are being passed forward to make sure we don't enter their camp without taking heavy losses. Formations are shifting to meet you in the open field. A few of their snipers take aim from the far cliffs, clipping riders.

Most of the group thunders on.

There is no room for fear when you're barreling down on an army, all of whom have marched across the known world to kill you. Fear does come, but it is not fear of the bright spears or the glinting wall of soldiers. You are briefly afraid that you got the alchemy wrong. That your horses will not function as they're supposed to.

Fifty paces away.

Thirty paces away.

And then you sense that familiar tug.

Some of your people sit up in their saddles. You do not blame them. It feels a little like a massive claw plucking you by the shoulders. All your horses sprint recklessly forward but as you reach the front lines of the Longhand ranks, the Empire vanishes.

You know what to expect.

An endless gray sky. An ash-covered plain. But for once, the landscape is not empty. Your horses come crashing into the edges of a battle. Your eyes find a half-moon of soldiers. You breathe a sigh of relief because the Bloodsworn rebirth worked. You breathe another at the sight of your revenants already deep in the fray. *Bring me Adrian Ford.* They've taken that command the way that you intended them to. Defend him. Keep him alive. Make sure we meet again.

You search the chaos and find him. Swinging a sword, sweat-stained and exhausted. There are hundreds of fallen soldiers around the hill they've chosen. He did exactly what you asked him to do. He lured out the Fury's army and trusted you to show up at the right moment.

Now it's your turn. The voice of a general booms out.

"Soldiers! Defend our team! The creatures of this world are in open rebellion against the Empire. Ride to their defense! Slay any who would oppose you."

There's a brief hesitation. You know they are confused, but to be an Ashlord is to obey orders. At least, that is what you grew up being taught your whole life. If ever there is confusion, look to your general. Take your orders. Execute the task. For that reason, your word becomes law. The order takes root. Your right flank forges a path toward the hill, riding to Adrian's defense.

"Revel," you command. "Do you see that open gate?"

He is on your left. He offers a sharp nod.

"It cannot be allowed to close."

You do not need to say more. He shouts a command down that line, and the rest of your cavalry lurches into motion. Revel was right about one thing. No one burns as fast as him. You watch as he launches across the open fields. Even lightning could not keep pace. Your eyes flick to the city gates. A massive figure is retreating into the city.

The Fury.

A glance to the right shows Adrian's team slumping down to rest as your cavalry smashes into the unsuspecting enemy. The Fury's foot soldiers do not last long. Revel is already at the gates. Skirmishes are breaking out on top of the ramparts. You head straight for Adrian.

He's tending to one of his fallen soldiers. The group looks up as you arrive. There's distrust written on every face. All they can see is an Ashlord. But they do not know that their fearless leader planned all of this with you. Every single step has been written by both of your hands. It's impossible to earn the fullness of their trust, but you have to start somewhere.

"I told you it would work."

Adrian smirks. "We've still got two gods to kill."

You know he's setting you up. His soldiers need to hear that you are with them.

"I suspect I'll get to them first," you say with a smile. "After all, I've got a horse."

35

COLLIDING WORLDS

IMELDA

We wait in silence.

Bastian and the others are growing restless until Quinn's eyes snap open. The girl who greeted us so warmly jerks her head to the right and stares directly at the wall. A wicked grin splits her pale face. Something has clearly happened. Something only she can sense.

"It's time!" she shouts. "Get to front gates first! Keep them open no matter what!"

This horde of soldiers is made up of the slaves we came to free. It turns out that Quinn had the same intention we did. She's been freeing slaves ever since she returned from the Races. The crews working under this city are cut from a different cloth. A little more muscled from the Fury's rigorous demands. Fissure found a few relatives in the crowd. Long-separated cousins who never thought they'd see one another again. Servants that the gods traded back and forth and were too lazy to ever retrieve. It is clear the gods have abused them for centuries.

And we get to help with the revolution.

Muscled workers spin hatch wheels on each of the seven doors. Bastian crowds in beside me, turning to his crew. "Let's stay tight out there. I don't want to lose any of you."

Cora crows something about him being a sweetheart. Harlow says it isn't a battle without a little blood. The rest are quiet and watchful, fingers on triggers, as the doors open.

Out into the gray. I crowd forward to keep up with the crew. Some of the Fury's slaves know the city. Others have never actually seen the surface. Born underground, raised underground. All of us blink back against the light. The first few streets are empty. Quinn marches at the front, whispering commands. Bastian paces ahead of me. He knows I can defend myself now, but instinct carries him on. Another empty street.

The Fury's city looks like one big training ground. Great fields separated by rows of squat gray buildings. Everything matches the sky overhead. We pass three makeshift arenas before meeting the first resistance. An actual minotaur turns the corner. Quinn's guards descend on him. Steel sings. The creature grunts before being overwhelmed by the slaves he had kept captive.

More footsteps.

We eliminate stragglers as we go. It isn't until we reach one of the front gates that the enemy's true numbers become apparent. There are hundreds of archers lining the ramparts. We watch from below as they take aim, letting their arrows fly. I can't help frowning. Who are they fighting? Bastian commands Cora and half of the crew up the stairs.

Quinn directs the right wing of her march in that direction. They work their way silently up the stairs until one of the reloading archers spots all the movement. He lets out a cry and gets a bullet in the chest for it. Fights break out overhead.

Bastian shouts something about the actual gates. Quinn keeps us moving through the lower courtyard and we run right into a group of fleeing foot soldiers. The gate looms open behind them. All I can do is stare as one of the largest creatures I've ever seen stomps into view.

He stands twice my height, muscled from the neck down. He wears a glowing skull helmet that cannot hide his surprise. It is the Fury. Quinn shouts for an attack, and her first row of soldiers rushes forward to cut off the escaping soldiers. The Fury watches for a breath, then darts out of sight.

Our freed slaves aren't well equipped. The Fury's guards cut several down, but there's always three more in their place. They keep flooding forward until every one of them falls.

We only reach the edge of the fray. My heart is racing as I think about how to use my blood in this crowded space. And then a scream splits the air. The stones tremble beneath our feet. I look up in time to see the Fury rounding the corner. He pretended to flee up the street, but now he thunders into our flank with impossible strength.

I thought Adrian Ford was huge. Compared to this creature, he is a plaything. The Fury lowers an armored shoulder
into our front line. Several are crushed at once. He steadies
himself, sets his feet, and swings a warhammer the size of a
horse. It's wide enough to cave in two chests with one blow.

Quinn's shouting an order when another wave of soldiers
follows their leader into the fray. Hundreds of the Fury's
hand-chosen guards. No doubt some of his best warriors.
They hit our front line like a hammer. Gunfire sounds above
us. I glance up to see our crew has taken the ramparts. Cora
Rowe fires both pistols, her bullets finding their marks.

But their help can't turn the attack. Bastian lunges forward with Briar to meet a blow that nearly cuts me in two.
His metallic arm turns an axe-head. I watch as he spins,
then plunges his knife into the creature's stomach. Sidestep-
ping, he takes on the next one with a quick jab. His metal
fist crunches a nose. That figure slumps and I follow him
into the fight, reaching for the only weapon I've ever used
with any success.

My blood.

One of our soldiers staggers in from the right and acci-
dentally knocks me down before I can form a thought. His
errant blade nearly cuts my throat. It's an effort to crawl out
from the struggling pile and find Bastian and Briar again.
They're standing back-to-back, cutting down soldiers with
ease.

In their focus, they do not see the Fury coming.

The god backhands someone out of the way before vaulting toward them. Every stride is thunder. I scream as he
raises his impossible warhammer, readying a blow that will

end the man I have come to love. My blood pulses instinctually. I dart through the chaos, between them.

The Fury's expression is twisted into a savage growl. He brings down his great hammer, but I've already raised both hands. My fingers are coated in my own blood. I wield only a word.

"No."

My mind reaches back for the first image it can find. The wall that I saw the little prince summon. It's a raw and unfiltered magic. The creation springs from my palms, crushing soldiers in both directions. Most of them belong to the Fury, but I cry out as one of our own vanishes beneath it. I'm holding both hands to the dark stones as the Fury's first blow fails to land. There's an entire wall between us now. Bastian stares with wide eyes. Even I cannot help gasping at the sudden blossoming of so much power.

But an answering wave of magic hits. The same power I used to create now comes to destroy. I scream as the Fury shoulders through the barrier. Bastian shouts but the Fury is faster. He brings up one of his massive boots and kicks me square in the chest. Death would feel better.

A rib snaps. My body is tossed like a rag doll through the air. I'm launched above the surrounding soldiers so hard and fast that my neck almost snaps from the blow. Everything is pain and pain and more pain. I don't feel my body land, but when the world stops spinning, I open my eyes and realize I'm already slumped against the stones.

Bastian is trying to get to me. The Fury cuts him off. He's forced to backpedal. I watch as the boy that I brought to this world—the boy that I have learned to love—matches the first few blows. But this is the god of war. He is too much for Bastian. I watch my love stagger to a knee. The Fury is about to deliver a killing blow when a war horn blows.

The sound is followed by a rush of movement at the front gates. The Fury turns to face the interlopers. Briar sweeps in to help Bastian back to his feet. They move carefully away as hundreds of soldiers pour into the courtyard. My heart sinks at first. The distant banners belong to the Ashlords. I stare in confusion, though, as Longhand banners sway side by side with them.

Help is coming. Help is here.

36

THE FURY

ADRIAN

Our crew follows the cavalry through the front gates.

It's a bloody brawl inside. The city streets run narrow, but each one leads to wider training yards. Minor skirmishes have broken out as far as the eye can see. Smaller contingents of the Fury's soldiers gather in tight circles, defending themselves against the surrounding chaos.

Revel has taken the tower that operates the gates. His riders have barricaded the spot nicely. As we planned, Quinn has struck in time with us. The Fury's freed slaves are rioting. We didn't know if she'd be able to recruit them, but it's clear now that it worked. Even though the streaming masses aren't well equipped, there are so many of them that it doesn't matter.

The Fury's retreat into the city has been cut off.

Pippa's voice rises. "Break up those pockets. Fight anyone wearing the Fury's colors!"

My crew is still catching their breath. We did our duty.

Lured the Fury's soldiers and opened the gates and gave Pippa an opening. It's clear now, though, that the war is not won. Against anyone else this would be a smashing defeat. We've eliminated their outer defenses, flanked them, and routed the bulk of their foot soldiers. The only flaw in the plan roars down the outer courtyard.

I watch the god of war prove his name. Anyone that large shouldn't be that quick. The Fury defies the laws of nature. I watch his hammer catch a fleeing servant. The man's bones do not break so much as shatter. Above, there's gunfire. I look up to find a group determined to bring the Fury down. Shoot and reload and shoot again. Most of the bullets dent the Fury's ruby-red armor with resounding pings. But it isn't until one ricochets off his horned mask that the god turns. He unleashes a roar, takes three massive strides, and swings his hammer.

It is aimed at the wall below the ramparts. Nothing should happen. The outer stones guard inner stones, all stacked perfectly together. But as he swings, the head of his hammer glows with a piercing gold light. The enhanced blow pulverizes everything. The ramparts crumble. Screams sound. The soldiers try to escape but they're too late. The entire wall collapses.

I do not know when I started walking that way. All I know is that my sword leads me forward. One step follows the next. The Fury wheels around. His eyes find mine. I know this is why we came to this place. We wanted to defeat gods like this, too long in their power. I glance left and find Pippa matching my steps. Her dark eyes are set on the same impossible hope as mine.

Revel walks just a step behind her and to the left. Wisely, he has shaped his switch into a shield. I can see he's using the power of his blood to layer its protections. It's also the first time I've ever seen the burner not want to be first. But still, he's with us.

On my right, Martial Rava.

The old champion looks like he's found a worthy opponent at last. Kenly claims the far flank. I almost command him to go back and lead the rest of the Longhands through the city. But who am I to deny him this fight? We promised soldiers like him revenge at the start of the war. Marching out of the Reach, he probably thought he'd be taking that revenge out on Ashlord soldiers.

But now we stand before the true source of our people's suffering.

The Fury makes the mistake of smiling.

"Little gods," he says. "Come. Measure yourself against *true* power."

Magic flexes. We brace ourselves for a direct blow, but it doesn't come. Something layers in the air instead. The Fury smiles again and I know something devious waits. Our crew fans out until there's a large enough gap for each of us to fight to our liking. One of the escaped servants frees himself from the piles of rubble right behind the Fury. He takes one look at the stage that's set and runs in the opposite direction. My eyes flick toward a group of the Fury's guards. Surprisingly, not one of them moves to join the fight.

The Fury takes a feinting step.

Martial takes the bait. He lunges forward, sword raised. There is nothing old about him in that moment. His sword is a silver streak, made faster by the power of his own blood. The Fury steps in close, though, and backhands the gladiator away. His body hits the stones with a *thump* as Kenly slashes forward in his wake, cutting savagely down on the exposed wrist. The Fury suffers the blow and brings his hammer sweeping around. Kenly just barely dodges it.

I draw on the power of my blood. Pippa is a step faster than me. She darts forward and the Fury punishes her speed, sweeping his hammer in a counterblow that nearly takes off her head. It leaves an impossibly easy opening for me. His right hand is weakened by Kenly's blow. His left arm cannot bring the heavy hammer back in time. I am a strike of lightning. My sword aims for the fist-sized spot above his armor. Right at the exposed slash of his throat.

My blood steadies the blow. Somehow, the blade drives home.

I stagger in surprise. The Fury stumbles back a step as I press the blade clean through. How can it be this easy? I suppose I watched Pippa kill the Curiosity the same way. Gods can be killed. I keep pressing the blade deeper until I realize the Fury's eyes are not wide or surprised.

Over his shoulder, I see one of his soldiers drop. The man clutches a bleeding throat. I'm staring in confusion when the Fury begins to laugh. I do not take my chances. I pull the blade out and strike again, sliding it clean across his throat. Nothing happens. The Fury laughs louder as another soldier drops, her throat slit. Others step forward to replace them.

"Taste *this* power."

The Fury strikes, but I'm more than ready, ducking the

blow and swiping his wrist. It should bleed. It should cut down to bone. Instead, one of the waiting soldiers clasps his wrists with a shout of pain. The Fury shoves me away like an annoyance. His face is bright with power.

"Don't you see? I cannot be killed. Not until *every one of them falls.*"

Pippa barely rescues me. I'm too shocked to raise my sword and fend off the next blow. She deflects his hammer and shoves me back. Revel joins her. Martial is recovered enough to add his sword. Kenly shouts as he lunges. All of them circle the god, using the power of their blood to aid their attacks. I watch blow after blow find the right marks. The damage is not suffered by the Fury, but by his servants. They bleed for him. They lose limbs and take death wounds and I can only watch the horror grow. We have the power to beat him, but I know that power will run out before long.

I'm still reeling from it all when Kenly stumbles to a knee. The Fury sees the opportunity. He shoulders Revel away, clearing a path, and brings his hammer smashing down. Kenly looks up in time to watch his own death. It's like a world ending.

Martial screams in rage. It doesn't matter. The Fury has the advantage now. He presses forward, and I realize there's nothing we can do to stop him. He cannot be harmed.

"Adrian!" Pippa shouts. "Adrian! We did not come all this way to die!"

Her words are not what wakes me. There's a tinkling rattle. It's such a delicate sound amid all the grunting and swinging. A golden sphere bounces into the center of our bloody arena. It gasps silver smoke into the air. My eyes search and search until I find Press. He's cowering behind an outcropping of stone behind us. The Dread's servant shouts.

"Sever the threads!"

I'm frowning until I see them. The gold mist reveals what we couldn't see. Secret threads connecting the Fury to his servants. Each one hangs like a living rope strung through the air. Pippa understands before I do. She lunges from my side and cuts a swath of them.

The effect is instant. Several of the nearby soldiers stagger to a knee. The great ropes fall and dissolve into red dust. I bring my sword down on another set. She does the same. The Fury roars in defiance, swinging around to face us. But that leaves him exposed on the backside to Revel. Pippa's outrider hacks at the ropes the same way we did.

Now the game changes.

Pippa parries, dancing out of range, luring the god around in a circle. She hisses threats and promises doom and the god's pride makes a fool of him. Martial severs more of the ropes. I swing at others. It takes three turns for us to bring all his magic crashing to the ground. Pippa suffers a massive stroke of his hammer, staggering to a knee, but she grits her teeth and holds her ground.

Before the god can finish her, I lunge for his right arm.

I know he is stronger than I am. He keeps hold of his hammer, trying to shake me off. But I reach for the last dregs of power in my blood. The Fury has used all of his.

Now I use all of mine. It channels from every wound. Draws on every drop. I scream as the unleashed energy tangles with thought.

My magic brings the Fury to his knees. I fall with him. It's almost as if the very stones rise up. His entire right arm is encased in stone. My magic holds him there like the statue he is. His hammer falls uselessly away. I stand there gasping, my power spent in the effort of binding him.

The Fury's breath is on my neck. He roars again, but I've left him helpless. We both watch Pippa stride across the dark stones. Her steel flashes. She and I exchange bloody smiles.

I watch as she plunges her blade into the Fury's exposed throat.

37

THE STRIVING'S CITY

PIPPA

The god of war is dead.

You wheel around, expecting his servants to come rushing forward and avenge their lord. But the sight of their god laid low breaks them instead. Every single one of them throws down their weapons. Some of your allies are working their way down the distant ramparts. As you watch, they circle the yielding soldiers and order them down on their knees. You search the roaming masses for a sign of Quinn. It has your heart beating faster. Where is she?

Adrian cradles one of his fallen soldiers. Martial stands next to him. They are both too tired to weep for the boy, who looks so young in death that you want to burn down the entire city. You do not know his name but you whisper a plea for a better world at the sight of his crumpled form. Revel's on the ground to your right, but sitting up and cradling one arm. You go to his side long enough to make sure that he's okay. He thinks his shoulder is separated. Nothing that will kill him. He urges you to keep moving. You unclip a waterskin, hand it to him, and take your feet.

"We need to find the Striving."

It's exhausting just saying the words. Adrian looks pained by the idea of doing anything more. In any other war, this would be the end. All the stories we read as children painted the heroic deeds for us, but none of them mentioned the next fight and the next and the next.

"I've seen no sign of her servants," Adrian replies. "At least, not like the ones in our world."

You nod. Adrian is right. None of the gathered soldiers bear her fingerprint. All of them belong to the Fury. Is it possible you'll have to fight an entirely new army?

Before you can sound the order, a new crew approaches. The strangers navigate their way through the rubble of the exterior wall. A bunch of hobbled soldiers. You recognize immediately that they don't fit in with the other freed slaves. Each of them has been kissed by the bright sun of the Empire. They do not share the pale features of the people you've encountered in this world. It takes you a long moment to recognize the familiar face within their ranks. You almost can't believe what you're seeing.

"Imelda Beru?"

It's her, the girl they call the Alchemist. She's got one hand clutching her ribs. A handsome boy is helping her limp forward. Even injured, the girl looks as determined as the first day you met her in the Hall of Maps. You briefly wonder if she's here to take some kind of revenge on you, but that doesn't make sense. Nothing about this makes sense.

"How did you get here?"

"The Bloodsworn rebirth," she answers, like it's the most obvious thing in the world. "We came to hunt the gods."

You can't help smiling at her boldness. This is the same girl who conquered the Races in her own way. After a moment, you gesture to the Fury's corpse. "So did we."

Imelda's eyes dart from Adrian to you.

"Am I missing something? Why are the two of you here? Together?"

The soldiers in the clearing all look like they're wondering the same thing, as if they've finally realized they've been working hand in hand with their sworn enemy. You lock eyes with Adrian. When you first made this plan together, it felt like the chance to start an entirely new world. If that world is to succeed, you must plant the seeds here and now. It brings a boldness to your voice as you answer Imelda's question.

"We came to fight the real enemy of the Empire. The gods are not who we thought they were. Look to the Fury's corpse as proof of that. We've been lied to, cheated, pitted against each other. We were made to worship creatures who are weaker than us. All this time they've used our blood to rule this world. Never again. Adrian and I came here to carve a new world."

The reactions from the crowd are subtle. Some of the soldiers make signs of warding. Others look shocked. A few of them glance to the Fury's corpse, perhaps thinking of it as evidence that you mean every single word. Adrian adds his voice to yours.

"No more gods," he says. "No more rulers or masters. Everyone on equal footing."

Again, you spy the unsettling effect of those words. The Longhands started a war hoping to bury your people's Empire, but they intended to be the ones standing on the grave as conquerors. Even the Dividian look ready to scoff at the offer. Until Imelda steps forward.

"Count us in."

Silence follows. No one moves. The idea of all three groups working together is so foreign that no one seems to know how to react. The quiet is interrupted by a boy with a camera. He edges around on Adrian's right side, offering a little wave from behind the lens.

"Hmm. I don't know about that line, Imelda," he says. "Any chance you can say something with a little more edge? A little more gravitas?"

A breath passes, and then Imelda lunges across the distance. You're half expecting her to level the stranger, but she wraps the boy in a bone-crushing hug instead.

"Farian! You're alive! And . . . down here in the underworld?!"

Martial Rava strides forward. "Couldn't persuade the fool to stay home."

Imelda laughs. "Of course not. How could he resist this kind of lighting? It's good to see you, too, Martial."

The old champion nods. You do not mean to interrupt their reunion, but it's just one more reminder that the job isn't finished. There is not time to celebrate. Not yet. You glance around the circle of gathered soldiers. "Come on. We have another god to hunt."

Farian nudges Imelda. "See? Something like that! We

need to look good in the documentary. Sharpen up your one-liners, okay?"

Imelda smacks his shoulder as the rest of the crew lets out whoops. Longhands and Ashlords and Dividian. All three groups offer up their own versions of war cries until there's a chorus that will surely make the Striving's army tremble. Revel gathers the cavalry. Martial Rava rallies any foot soldiers who still have the energy to swing a sword. Adrian assigns someone to guard the bodies of the fallen before leading his depleted group forward. They add their numbers to the growing pack. Divided you would not have stood a chance, but as the ranks form up, you realize your numbers are solid. More than enough to face another army.

You're about to call out a command when something wings through the air above, darting through the crude-shaped buildings. Two of the birdlike servants you freed from the Curiosity's tower. Quinn dangles between them. Your heart leaps as they land in the dusty street. The girl wears a determined look as she strides forward and wraps you in a hug. You hold her for a stretching moment, not believing that your wild plan actually worked. She hugs you fiercely back before pulling away.

"We just flew over the Striving's half of the city. It is an odd scene. I'm not sure what to make of what she's doing. Come, see for yourself."

Commands ring out. Adrian sends a sharp-eyed scout ahead of the group. As your heartbeat slows, you're worried the adrenaline will fade. You know some of your soldiers might start asking questions. Their morning began with a charge toward the Longhand camps. And then you dragged them headfirst into another world. Best to keep them hunting.

"Everyone together," you shout. "Be ready for anything."

And for the first time in history, an army of Ashlords, Dividian, and Longhands moves as one. You take strength from that brief image of peace, even as you walk the bloodstained streets. All the smaller skirmishes have been extinguished. A few rogue soldiers are still loose. Those belonging to the Fury either surrender or flee. Those belonging to Quinn join your ranks, adding their number to the roaming host.

The Fury's city is an earthen sprawl. Weathered stones rise up and pretend to be buildings. Great gladiator pits of reddish dirt trade off with grassy training fields. The city streets all lead uphill. The Curiosity's notes described it perfectly. Ever a warrior, the Fury designed his city to be defensible. His soldiers would have the upper ground as they retreated back toward his throne. Except your plan worked. Adrian lured him outside the gates with a taste of blood.

As you reach the city's upper tier, the great bridges come into view. Five on this level. Each one is wide enough to drive three carriages down, all side by side. A signal from you divides the gathered forces. You can't help inspecting your newest allies. Imelda's crew looks like your kind of soldiers. Bloodied, but unbowed. One of the girls catches your eye and offers a quick wink. She's got a pistol in each hand, paired with a bloody smile. You suppose they're not the worst people to have your back in a fight.

The waiting bridges are polished stone. They do not creak underfoot, though you must be some seventy paces above the ground. Your friends used to like visiting rooftop cantinas in Furia. Sipping wine and watching the crawling world below. You never liked such heights, so you stride carefully down the very center of the bridge. Adrian matches your steps.

Another city looms. It is as polished as the other is crude. Each building has efficient purpose. Windows run the length of some, reflecting each other back in infinite loops. Electric light borders everything like the bright veins of a larger body. None of this is a surprise.

It is the waiting servants that are odd. Quinn's concern makes more sense. You are walking through a tableau. The god's creatures stand motionless in the streets. Not lined up for war, but paused in their daily functions. Almost like abandoned dolls.

The first group you pass appears to be unloading a carriage. One holds a crate. The others look like they're in the middle of a frozen discussion. Your army passes them warily.

But the city is full of such scenes. As you walk, you begin analyzing them more closely. Most of the creatures are similar to the Striving's priests in your world. The god likes grafting her little sciences into them, altering them with her clever gadgets. But these servants have been pushed further than those you've met in the world above. Some boast entire upper bodies of metal and clockwork. Others have glowing blue veins that match the surrounding buildings.

It is an eerie sight.

You worry what their stillness means as you follow the main promenade. On instinct, you aim for the one building that is larger than the rest. The Striving might be a genius, but you've learned that most gods are the same. All of them dislike the thought of being outshone.

The building's architecture looks impossible. The glass exterior glints with false light. It rises up and somehow four sides merge into a single point. The shape conjures an image of an electric spear aimed at the underbelly of your world. The bulk of your army follows until you reach a narrowed set of marbled steps. Revel rides over, an eyebrow raised in question.

"Orders?"

"Circle this building," you answer. "Assign a few people to look for secret passages. I do not want the Striving to escape. Although it's possible she already has."

You dislike the idea of having to chase one of the gods through this strange world. Especially one with so many tricks up her sleeve. It has you hoping she's foolish enough to have stayed. Most of the gods have been overconfident in their power. Maybe she will fall into the same trap.

Adrian gestures. "I'm assuming the interior will be tighter than the streets. Let's take handpicked teams inside and leave the rest to patrol the pavilion."

You nod and start sorting out who will come. A throat clears, though, and Imelda approaches. "There should be representatives from all races. If you actually want the world to be equal, we need to be beside you at the beginning."

She is not asking for permission. You smile again at her boldness. The new world will need leaders like her in it. You continue drafting soldiers until the group is just the right size.

"Ready?"

Adrian and Imelda both nod. You take the first step, bracing for another taxing climb, when the ground beneath your feet rumbles to life. The entire concourse begins to rise. Your hands swing out to keep balance, and all you can do is stare wide-eyed as the steps begin chasing one another. A nervous laugh escapes. You're rising into the air without even walking. Adrian takes the step below you, wearing a bemused look. The rest of the troops follow nervously.

Of course the Striving has stairs that walk for you.

It's an odd feeling to be ushered up this way. You start to get nervous as you reach the top, watching the white stairs vanish into some automated loop. It has you high-stepping to avoid being eaten with them. The ground at the top of the pavilion is strange in its stillness. You look back and nearly laugh as the others do their best to tiptoe across the threshold to safety.

Adrian shakes his head. "Such a lazy invention."

You shrug back. "I can see it being useful."

His smile is a promise of a future that is not yet yours. You smile back, but if you want to see that smile in the world above—for the rest of your life—you'll need to finish the job. The group presses on into a pavilion featuring yet another scene. There are guards this time, but they appear frozen, too, their spears set on their shoulders. One is in the middle of reaching up to tug at a tight collar. There's no awareness in their eyes. You exchange a look with Adrian before plunging inside.

The way is dark until your steps draw flickering lights to life. You send scouts down adjacent hallways, but each one leads back to a looming atrium. The atrium funnels into a throne room. More automated steps ferry you up. More of the silent servants. Each one frozen in place. And their stillness makes the distant movement more noticeable.

A narrow corridor introduces a bright throne room. Stretching windows highlight a pacing god. You have always known her as the Striving—the god of technology and wanting.

The god of the future.

38

A GOD'S OFFER

PIPPA

You are surprised by the Striving's appearance.

She is a slight woman, dressed humbly. A simple black outfit with only delicate pearl buttons for decoration. She wears no armor. There are no dark pets lurking. There is only her—calm and controlled—waiting for you like all of this was prearranged. Knots coil in your stomach.

"That is quite far enough."

The Striving lifts a small black device. Light flickers along the walls. You stop. Not because this god has any right to command you now, but because you want to size up the actual threat she poses. Appearances can be deceiving. She looks like an ordinary woman, but you know this is the most worshipped god in recent memory. The creator of every advancement your people have ever enjoyed. It is not her way to be unprepared. It is not lost on you that she offered no resistance to your army's entrance. You're quite certain there's a reason.

"I am ready to negotiate," she says. "Who will speak for you?"

Another click of her device. It echoes into the stones. Your ranks tighten as the entire room shifts. A rumble below. You all watch the midnight black melt away to reveal a floor of glass. You're not sure what you expected, but it wasn't this. The room below is a laboratory of some kind. Your mind summons an image of the Powder Room. All those carefully organized ingredients that you were allowed to choose from before the Races began.

This room is a twin to that one. Except it is full of matching vials. Each full of a dark-red substance. You meet the god's challenging stare. "This isn't a negotiation. We have won."

The Striving smiles. "That's up for negotiation as well. Best to hear everyone's terms, no? I have been kind enough to invite you into my city. I could have bled you. I've three thousand servants at my beck and call. Your force would have won in the end, but I could have exacted the cost for every street you took. Instead, I ordered my soldiers to stand down. Call it an offering of salt and bread. An invitation to my table."

Before you can answer, one of Imelda's soldiers strides forward. It's the girl who winked at you. She looks bored. "No one has time for this."

She raises her pistol, takes aim at the Striving's chest, and fires. The blast deafens. It is so unexpected that you do not even reach out to stop her. So unexpected that it might work. . . .

The Striving does not flinch. A purple light cuts the room

in half. There's some kind of invisible barrier between your crew and the god. You hear a gasp. The gunslinger drops to her knees, lips parted in surprise, a bloody hole punched through her stomach.

"Cora!"

Half of the Dividian soldiers flock to her side. Your chest heaves as you watch them work to stop the bleeding from her ricocheted bullet. A foolish move, but you have no doubt the Striving directed the response of her magic with purpose. She watches you now, one eyebrow raised, the way Mother always did when your foolishness proved her right.

"I am not without some minor defenses," she says. "Self-preservation. I'm sure you understand. Now, can we begin negotiations or not?"

You make your voice iron.

"What negotiation can there be? You are one of the last gods. You are without allies, without power. Back in Furia, there are printed leaflets fluttering in every street. They detail how the gods lied. How you tricked our ancestors out of their own deity and convinced them you were the actual gods. Your lies will be known by half the Empire before the day is out. What possible leverage do you imagine you have? We won. It is over for you and yours."

The Striving smiles again. "Leverage. That is the right word for what I have. Let me tell you what will happen next. We will come to terms. You will retreat into your world, taking your friends with you. I will serve as the new pantheon. Frame that however you must to your people. Tell them I am the only god who did not cheat you, if it serves your purpose. I am to be left alone here. I will rule as I have ruled for these past decades. There will be arrangements for sacrifices to continue. We can adapt the language as needed. Lighten some of the drama that the Dread always loved so much. It can be more transactional if you desire. A simple trade between powerful allies."

"I am still missing the part where you have something we want."

"Ah. Yes. There is that." The Striving waves the device in her hand. "For all my boast of ingenuity, I am a slave to history. As much as all of us. This little toy? It's the most powerful thing in the room. But not on its own. It is powerful because of what it connects to. The Ashlords have always centered their lives around two things. You know the words, don't you, Pippa?"

After a moment, you breathe out your people's most ancient creed.

"Fire and blood."

"Fire and blood," she echoes. "And I control *both*. All the gods are collectors—or were collectors, I suppose. When you live as long as we do, it comes with the territory. You're always looking for some way to mark the passage of time. Some way to remember worlds that are spinning out of existence daily. The Butcher had his storehouse. The Fury has a museum's worth of weaponry. The Curiosity gathered history—though I see now we should have monitored her enthusiasm in that regard. I have collected something far simpler.

"Blood. Look at all of it. Some of these vials belong to the Fury, but most of it belongs to me. I was quite thorough. Each of these vials represents a person. Can you guess how many sacrifices I've gathered over the years?"

Your eyes assess the room below. The rows seem end-less. It reminds you of the Curiosity's library and all her countless books. Something that took centuries to create. Your chest tightens at the thought. You do not like where this is heading.

The Striving answers her own question. "I have nearly one million."

You want that to be an exaggeration, but the longer you trace the cellar's contents, the more certain you are it is the truth. You can see passages to other chambers now. More blood. Ladders lead down into the waiting dark. You do your best to remain strong, in spite of the implications.

"And it will all be wasted when you are no longer here to use it."

Light dances across the Striving's face. You are close enough now to see her eyes are painted an eerie color. Al-most like slashes of lightning set in a porcelain face. It is not the first time you've wondered about creatures like her. Im-mune to time. Powerful beyond measure. How can anything true or good survive such an existence?

"Attack me and I burn them all," she says. "It is that simple. You've seen the *burners* in your world. Nothing but bones and ashes. That is what will happen in your world if I press this button. My defenses might not hold against all of you. I know that much. But I promise that if you cross this threshold in an effort to take my life . . ."

She waves the device again.

"It is nearly a third of the current population," she says. "Can you live with that?"

The girl on the ground is still gasping with pain. Her

friends whisper to her. Adrian is standing frozen on your right. You do not know what he's thinking, or any of the others for that matter. Your mind is racing. You've been trained since birth for all of this. Riding into war. Marching tactics. The steps in a proper duel. No one taught you to negotiate with monsters.

For so long, your people *were* the monsters.

The Striving looks disappointed by your silence. Her attention shifts to Adrian.

"What about you, Longhand? I'm sure you've already realized that *none* of these vials belong to your people. Promise to defend me and I'll reset the entire world. The people who've ruled you all this time. The people who buried your mother. Over half of the Ashlords." She snaps her fingers. "Gone. Just like that. Partner with me and we'll write a new world into existence."

You never imagined this as a possibility. The idea trembles from your brain and to your heart. Ever since the Curiosity's death, you've been aligned. But you know that if your people were in Adrian's shoes, it would not even be a question. Eliminate the enemy. Rule the new world. It's almost logical for him to betray you now.

Which is why it's such a relief when he shakes his head in defiance.

"Working with one god has been taxing enough."

The Striving raises a curious eyebrow at that. It confirms some suspicion she has about the Longhands and their presence in this world. As she searches the room for a new target, you just barely hear Adrian's voice break through your thoughts, quieter than a whisper.

"We need to strike. Force her hand. It's possible she's bluffing. There's no way she—"

Before you can respond, the god's eyes narrow. Her thumb touches down on the device for a fraction of a breath. Less time than it takes to blink. A burst of flame cuts the rest of Adrian's sentence in two. Fire spreads in a far corner of the underground. It's a controlled burst. Just one of the standing towers. Your stomach coils, though, as hundreds of vials begin to burn . . .

. . . as hundreds of *people* begin to burn. You pray Adrian is right. Maybe the Striving is bluffing. Until a scream echoes through the room. The gathered masses turn as one of Revel's outriders drops to a knee. Light glows beneath his skin. Both eyes burn with twin embers. He looks up desperately, searching for help. He looks at you right before he bursts into flame.

Everyone backs away in horror.

The fire burns and burns until the god's dark work is done. You can't help thinking of the echoes this will have in the world above. How many brothers and sisters? Fathers and mothers? Who else is paying their blood-price at this very moment?

"A warning," the Striving says over the dying crackles. "Whisper plots against me again, and I will punish you for it. You just spent seven hundred souls. That price will only grow larger each time. Do not test me again."

You have no answers. No one does. You can see the defeat on Adrian's face. He was made for fighting the Fury. So were you. Out there in the courtyard, strength and quickness mattered. The steps of your feet and the length of your blade. Games like this have never been your province. You are searching for some path forward when the Striving looks to Imelda Beru.

"And what about you, Dividian? Are you truly happy? Standing there between your *former* and *future* rulers? What did they tell you? That everyone would be equal?" The Striving lets out a light laugh. "Do you trust them to actually deliver on that promise? Help me survive this and I'll place your people on the throne instead."

Imelda's face is unreadable. A new fear is born. You realize that this girl is a stranger to you. Sure, you vouched for her to enter the Races, but Imelda is from a town that you've never seen. Some speck on the map that your people long overlooked. Always your people have ruled hers, and ruled through brutality. She will know the histories, if she hasn't experienced those injustices herself. It has your stomach turning nervously.

"I want specific terms set out," Imelda says. "A contract written in blood."

Her reply is a shock of cold water. Even her own crew looks surprised, but Imelda doesn't hesitate. She strides forward. Right to the spot where that protective barrier flashed. You can only stare as the Striving allows her through it. The god of the future is smiling. Your jaw hangs open. Adrian looks on helplessly. Neither of you planned for this. The focus of the room shifts. Paradigms are changing.

For once, you are not in the spotlight.

Instead, it is Imelda Beru who goes forward to meet a god.

39

DEAL

IMELDA

It is not easy to look a god in the eye, but I do my best.

I know this god has had more of an impact on my people than any other. Every advancement she handed the Ashlords came to us secondhand. We always got the oldest versions of whatever gifts she offered them. Quietly, she maintained their superiority. She renewed their power with every new invention and offering. It was so stunning to walk the streets of Furia for the first time and see all that she'd given them.

Now she offers that power to us.

"We want to rule," I say softly. "But I need your assurance. Clearly, you can eliminate most of the Ashlords, but if you want my help, I need to know what you'll do about the Longhands. Their surviving army will be the most powerful in existence. How will you deal with them?"

Shocked whispers echo in the crowd behind me. I ignore them.

The Striving's smile glitters. "Most of the Longhand

army has converged on Furia. Even now they're pressing in on the city's gates. It is a trap. Help me survive and I can eliminate most of their army. It will take a concerted effort for you to maintain control in the coming decades, but that is a balance we can work out together."

I try my best to gauge her sincerity. Gods like to play tricks, but right now I know I'm her only choice. Pippa and Adrian both refused her offer. It gives me a position of power.

"I have other demands."

The Striving nods. "Speak them."

I glance back. Fissure is one of the few freed slaves in the room. He's watching me with curiosity, trying to understand what I'm doing based on all that I've said to him up to this point. I nod so that he knows I have not forgotten him, then I turn back to the waiting god.

"All the slaves will return to our world," I say. "So that they might rule alongside us."

The Striving considers that. "I need the servants who live in my city to remain. Otherwise, I cannot maintain production. But yes, the rest are free to go with you."

I consider pushing back on that point, asking her to free them all, but decide that it's better to make my final request instead. I do not want to push her too far, too fast.

"Fair enough. One last thing. The blood sacrifices . . ."

". . . are necessary. It is the exchange for ruling that world."

"Understood, but I will not end up in the situation we are in now. The idea that you could wipe out half of our population at a moment's notice." I shake my head. "This will not be a relationship built on fear. Not if this is to be a simple trade between business partners. We will select certain families to be the sacrifices. There will be a controlled but steady amount of blood offered. There can be no deal between us otherwise."

The Striving's smile widens. I know it is because she's already thinking of one hundred ways around each of these arrangements. Her only goal right now is to survive. The only deal she's truly making is to save her own skin, to live another day, so that she might slowly unravel our society again. It gives me all the leverage. I can do what Pippa claimed she wanted to do. Carve a new world for my people. After a dramatic pause, the Striving nods.

"Deal."

I smile back. "Deal."

Crossing the distance, I offer my right hand.

Her return gesture is all instinct. I see it written in her face. The way her hand reaches for mine. It is as if part of her body has briefly separated from her careful and calculating mind. Her eyes widen slightly in surprise, because she knows she should not shake my hand. It is far too dangerous to make contact with me. She knows that because she is one of the most intelligent beings in the worlds, but even a genius cannot resist their most natural inclinations. So her hand closes around mine. My grip tightens. I raise my left hand into the air and snap my fingers.

It is not the deal she expected.

We trade worlds.

I can feel her scrambling, trying to free herself, but my father taught me to shake hands firmly. My mother taught me to look a person in the eye. Which means the two of us lock eyes in the moment we leave her throne room behind. An entirely new scene fills in around us. We're standing in an abandoned alleyway. I can tell it's Furia. There's chaos farther down the street. Sounds of war in the distance. Soldiers are darting in and out of view.

No one notices us.

"I always wondered why the gods visit our world through vessels."

The Striving looks horrified. She's trying to pull away, but with each passing second, she grows weaker. I keep a firm grip on her hand. It doesn't take long for her desperation to manifest into something more feral. She claws at my wrist. Her pupils dilate. These are the final signs of a creature that knows—after several centuries—it is about to die.

"I figured it out, though. Our blood sustains you in the world below. Its magic has kept you alive all these years. But the blood has no power here. That is why you visit through your priests. Coming here in your own body? It would mean leaving all that magic behind. In this world, you have no real power, do you?"

The god sags to her knees. I was not exactly sure what would happen, but the reality is far more haunting. I watch as the Striving begins to age. The polite woman who looked middle-aged in the underworld physically fades. Her hair silvers first, before curling gray, then finally rotting from the scalp. Her skin freckles and wrinkles until it is a clasping rag against the bones beneath. I do not let her go. I do not look away. I am a witness.

Breath by breath, I watch the unmaking of a false god.

"You are not the only god with a collection," I say, because it's too perfect. The god of the future undone by something so ancient. "The Butcher had samples in his storehouse. I found your blood there. Even if you were not false gods, each of you had grown complacent. It was past time for new leaders, a new world."

The Striving's voice rasps out, like the flicker of a dying candle.

"I . . . am . . . the future. . . ."

Our world devours the rest of her. I watch until she is nothing more than bones and dust. It is not out of cruelty, but more to preserve the truth, that I answer. "Not our future."

And then I snap my fingers again.

40

THE DREAD

ADRIAN

The entire room is in uproar.

I'm usually the calm in the storm, but not this time. I round on Imelda's crew. The outlaw with the metal arm stands at the front. It's pretty clear he's one of her chief lieutenants.

"What the hell was that? Where'd she go?"

He looks lost. Clearly they didn't plan any of this together.

"She must have a plan," he says firmly. "She always has a plan."

"Yeah? Seems like the plan was to help the most dangerous god in the world escape. Give me one good reason why we shouldn't have you all chained up right now."

"Because you promised her," the outlaw answers. "You gave a speech about being equals. And that starts by trusting each other. Imelda wouldn't betray us."

Farian steps forward. "He's right. She must have a plan."

I'm about to throw back a few choice words when the room falls silent. Farian pulls his camera back up to eye level just in time to catch Imelda's return. She stands at the center of the throne room again. Her back is to us. I watch as the Alchemist dusts her fingers. A strangely colored powder falls to the floor. At first, I think she's alone, but then I see the huddled figure at her feet. I'm still trying to make sense of what's happening when I see the device. It's clutched in a skeletal hand. It's impossible, but the god of the future is at her feet, dead.

Imelda turns and starts walking toward us. There's a smirk on her face.

"What? You act like you've never seen a dead god before."

And the entire room erupts. The outlaw with the metal arm sweeps her up into the air, spinning her around. The rest of her crew start crowing the name "Alchemist" louder and louder. Pippa is the first Ashlord to go forward. She shakes the girl by the shoulders and wraps her in an unexpected hug. It is not lost on the rest of us that she just saved millions of Ashlords. The same people who've acted as overlords her entire life. The mercy she's shown echoes around the room.

It is enough to have all of us hopeful for the world above.

The logistics are a headache, but we all agree to send representatives back to the Empire. It's tricky business. Reports are that Furia is on fire. Daddy's boys have sacked most of the city, except for the eastern keeps. A group of Ashlords have barricaded themselves there and are fighting ruth-lessly to hold them off. More people will die in this useless war if we're not quick about it.

We send messengers back in threes. One Dividian, one Longhand, one Ashlord. Always together. Ready to argue on one another's behalf, no matter who they find waiting for them on the other side. Nevira Pearce is my first choice. For-rest's cousin Brannan is my second. We manage fifteen sets before running out of the right groups. Pippa picks a few of the soldiers she trusts the most and sends them back to talk the Ashlords into an armistice.

Next, we send back those who need medical attention. Imelda's trusted gunslinger goes first. Revel and a few of the other riders follow. I can tell some soldiers are just hungry to go back home and forget this nightmarish place. Farian insists on staying and even pulls me aside to discuss next steps. I find myself smiling at his boldness. He's come into his own down here.

Martial leads an effort to gather the dead. All of them are to be brought back to our world for proper burials. Pippa and I briefly turn back into generals, nodding at our lieuten-ants' requests, discussing next steps. The war will soon be over. There are unpleasant tasks waiting for us back home, but right now we've got to focus on getting everyone back safely.

Quinn's people offer the biggest obstacle. All the slaves who've suffered the rule of the gods. Aside from Quinn, none of them have ever been to our world. They don't feel that natural pull that can drag them back home. Which means we've got to find a way across.

"What about the ship?" I suggest. "We came on a galley."

Press steps forward. He was notably absent during our final showdowns. He shakes his head at the thought of the ship. "It might fit seventy people at the most. There are some three thousand here. No, the best way across will be the Bridge."

It's a long march.

We make our way in a single, unified group. Nothing like us has ever existed. Imelda and a few of her crew come with us. The outlaw—whose name we learn is Bastian—refuses to leave her side. Quinn commands a stream of freed slaves. Pippa's got three hundred Ashlord riders forging ahead, prepared to drive off any threats. My soldiers trudge through the ashen wastes as well. It's miracle enough that we aren't trying to carve each other into pieces.

I ride most of the way at Pippa's side. It's meant to be a show of trust, but at the end of the day I kind of just like being the one beside her. There's something about the way she looks at me that sends shivers down my spine. I've always known she was beautiful, but I thought it a cold beauty. I saw her in the advertisements for the Races and swore she was my enemy. Now we ride side by side as victors, and there's nowhere else I'd rather be. She doesn't smile easily, but every time I lure a laugh from her I feel like I've seen a second sun. It makes all we've been through a little more bearable.

Our scouts hear the howls long before we reach the Bridge. It is something out of legend. We direct our path toward a series of gray spires. Each one is abandoned. The true oddity looms beyond them. A stone bridge crawls through the bruised sky. It stretches out halfway over the dead sea before vanishing into the gray nothing.

The Bridge.

Press does not need to name it. Most of us have heard fairy tales of one sort or another. There's a wolf the size of a shed howling at the entrance. We're close enough now to see it's the cause of *all* the howls. It sounded from a distance as if we were hearing hundreds of them, but it's just the Madness, lost to his bone-chilling duty of connecting the two worlds. There are a series of massive metal stakes driven into the ground. I don't really want to know what they've been used to tie down over the centuries. Our party pauses near them, a safe distance from the Madness.

"So do we just cross?" I ask.

Press frowns. "You won't like the answer, given the Striving's threat. But the Madness will demand a toll. A drop of blood from all who pass."

"You're right," I reply, exchanging a look with Pippa. "That's not an option."

Press explains. "Look at him. He demands the toll because instinct tells him to. He's not a being who thinks like us. He exists as the path between worlds now. More function than being. Giving him your blood won't matter in the end because he has no plans to use it against you."

Pippa looks lost in thought. I'm chewing on the idea. It's Quinn who answers.

"We'll pay the price. Anything to leave."

Press nods at that. I still don't like the idea of a god having my blood, but Pippa's next suggestion diminishes that fear. "We can kill him before we go. The blood won't matter then."

I watch Press's reaction carefully. As expected, his eyes shock wide.

"Kill him? That would be unwise."

Pippa frowns. "Would it?"

"He is more than just a bridge," Press answers. "He is a *balance* between the worlds. That is his entire existence. All the roads connecting our two worlds. Kill him and that balance vanishes. It's like taking out cartilage. The worlds would press together, bone against bone. There's no predicting what damage might happen then."

I watch Pippa. She makes a show of considering Press's idea. I've got to learn how to act as well as she does. It's a useful tool for any politician.

"And this is your master's opinion?" she asks.

Press nods. "If he were here, he'd give it himself."

"But he's not here," I remind him. "Why don't you summon him?"

Press laughs. "My lord lives on an island that circles this continent. It never stops moving. It is peerless in its defense. You do not find the Dread. He finds you."

"I beg to differ."

It's surprisingly easy. His defenses are up against those he thinks a threat, not those he believes he's already fooled. My hands clench around both of his forearms. I use all my strength to bring his arms into the air, well away from his pockets. Press winces at the pain of my grasp. His chest heaves wildly, but his eyes are calm the whole time.

"I've helped you!" he asks. "What are you doing?"

I keep my eyes pinned on his. "Pippa. If you'd relieve Press of his gadgets."

My hands flex to keep his arms in place. He doesn't try to kick, but I can see just the slightest trace of panic trickling into his eyes. Pippa slips several items out of his pockets. Each one matches the gadgets we've seen him using thus far.

"You're a clever servant, Press."

"I am my master's most trusted man. I would hope I'm clever."

"I admire your instincts," I say, ignoring his words. "Noticed that with the horses. You *felt* the threat before they even set down on the ridge. Quite a feat. And then again on the hill. You sensed Pippa's cavalry coming before they even appeared. . . . Felt them, too, didn't you?"

Press stares at me. "I have an instinct for preservation."

"More than an instinct," I answer. "I daresay you've got a godly knack for it."

That word punches him in the chest. He opens his mouth to speak before biting his tongue. I nod now, sure that I have him. "Hello, Dread."

A little snort. He allows himself that same sickening smile his priests are always flashing in our world. "I had my guesses, but it was Farian who pointed it out." I nod to our right. Farian is wearing a satisfied smile. "He picked up on your gestures. Hand motions. Stuff I'd never notice. Told me everything you did in this world matched the priest from the other world."

The Dread nods. "How clever of him."

"What better way to preserve yourself," I say, thinking out loud, "than to be right next to the action. A humble servant sent by a reclusive god. Too bad you gave yourself away."

"You kept almost dying."

"Thank you for your intervention."

Pippa watches the exchange. She doesn't speak, because she knows this is *my* god to deal with. The Dread doesn't struggle. He doesn't attempt to flee or to fight. He thinks he's already won.

"In the Races, I was your shield. In the waters of Grove, I was your sword. How many times have I called on my powers to preserve your life?"

"And you think that earns your passage into our world?"

He nods. "That is often how partnerships work. Your soldiers are here. Watching this exchange. So are all the Ashlords and Dividian you hope to call equals. Is this truly how you reward someone who saves your life? Is serving you so worthless?"

"Fair point. Why don't we tally up the debts . . ."

I move his arms, shifting like a wrestler so they both twist behind his back. I drag him over to the metal post jutting up from the ground. I kick it with one foot, just to make sure it's steady, and look to Pippa for rope. She wraps it slowly around both wrists. Tighter with each coil. When she's done, she produces a second rope and does the same to his feet. All the way up his legs. Only when the Dread is fully bound do I circle back in front of him to put on a show for our soldiers. He's right. We need them to know how we honor those who truly serve us.

"You saved my life. One point in your favor."

Pippa speaks. "You helped us kill the other gods. Two more points in your favor."

The Dread doesn't smile as Quinn strides out to join us.

"You were the first one to enslave others in this world. A strike against."

Pippa looks thoughtful. "You came up with the plan to secretly enslave *our* world. Another strike against."

"You killed the Veil," I add. "She was the first person to try to free Quinn's ancestors."

"You invented the blood-sacrifice system."

"You slaughtered thousands."

"Burned down temples."

"Killed any who opposed you."

The silence that follows is its own thunder. The Dread looks dead already. He knows how this ends. I watch him for a long moment, weighing all that he has done on an invisible scale.

"God of caution. Let me spare you the dangers of our world."

I turn away from him and start walking. The rest of our camp follows. The Dread shouts at us, raging as he calls my name. But without the power of our blood, he's nothing but an animal tied to a slotted post. We leave him there in the dust of the world he helped create.

41

THE MADNESS

PIPPA

Only the Madness remains.

It's hard to imagine the howling creature before us is a god. He sends his dark warnings skyward. The great bridge looms beyond him, half shrouded in ghostly fog. Quinn instructs her people to leave a drop of blood on the stones as they pass. It surprises you to see how many times this passage has been crossed. By people? By the other gods? You're unsure, but the first few rows of stone look stained by wine. All the sacrifices over all the years. Your own soldiers make what you hope is their last blood payment and begin forward. By some unspoken agreement, all the leaders wait.

Quinn is there to whisper encouragements to the freed slaves that pass. You can see the hope on their faces as they walk liberated into another world. Most of Adrian's crew went back as scouts, but those who stayed with their commander now salute him before marching on. You command your outriders to protect them on the other side. Imelda and

Bastian stay behind as their crew crosses over. You smile a little at the way they let their shoulders press together without a thought. The two make a fine pair.

Adrian nods to Imelda. "Sorry again about that knock I gave you during the Races."

She smiles. "I haven't forgotten about it. Let's just say I owe you one."

"We owe each other everything," you whisper. "It will take the rest of our lives to pay off these debts, but today was a fine start."

As the crowd grows thin, the Dread's shouts grow louder. The desperate god watches a world slip through his fingers. None of you look back. Your eyes are fixed on the bridge that leads back to your world. It's hard to accept the coming challenges. It would be easier if a quiet life awaited, but you know that all your effort will be required to carve a new world.

A world better for all.

After the ranks have filed past, Quinn turns. "I suppose this is goodbye."

At first, it sounds like a farewell to this cruel world she calls home. Until you notice that she's looking in your direction. "What are you talking about?"

"The Madness must be killed."

You nod. "Of course. We will do it together."

Quinn shakes her head. "I'm afraid not. I conducted research in the Curiosity's tower, too. The gods all had their theories about the Madness. To kill him is to destroy the paths between these worlds. We can't kill him and make it across the bridge. That passage will cease the moment his heart stops beating. And we can't risk leaving him alive, either. One of us will have to stay behind and finish what we started."

There is no hesitation. "Then it will be me."

Instinctively, you take up a fighting stance. You are prepared to battle Quinn for the right to stay. She's already sacrificed so much, but the girl disarms your intentions by walking forward and setting a pale hand on your bright cheek.

"You have come so far," she says. "And I am so proud. But this god belongs to me. You killed the Curiosity and her whispers. You killed the Fury and his love of war. Take those victories back to your people and kill those same qualities in the Empire. Adrian has left the Dread to die. His people's fear of lurking gods can be put to rest. Imelda killed the Striving. Her people need not fear the god's imbalance being set against them any longer.

"But this god . . . When the Madness dies, this world dies with him. This is where my people knew chains. It is where we have bled and died, often without ever seeing the sun. It is a dark world that deserves a proper knife to the gut. It has deserved that for centuries now. Ever since these false gods made it this way. . . ."

It is perfectly reasonable. Sound in its logic. But you cannot stop the tears running down both cheeks. You cannot keep your fists from clenching in anger. It isn't fair. It never is.

"There has to be some other way."

Quinn reaches up to kiss your cheek. You pull her in before she can slip away. Not with some design to wrestle her away or to drag her across the Bridge. No, you pull her in simply to hold her one more time. The girl who rode the lightning and won the Races and defeated the gods. You wrap your arms around her one last time because she helped you to be the leader you never could have been otherwise.

Her voice whispers out, just for you. "Be more."

You're about to release her when you hear the noise. You have been at war long enough to know the sound a blade makes when it enters a body. It's followed by an animal's angry crooning. Your head whips in that direction. Quinn and the others stare.

Martial Rava stands behind the Madness. He's got one hand on the creature's shoulder. A blade is plunged from behind, up through the god's stomach. It isn't a killing blow but you have a feeling the next one will be. The old champion meets your collective stare calmly.

"It was a good speech," he says, nodding to Quinn. "You have my respect. Go now and give it in that other world. I have lived my life. Not a single regret. Take yourselves across that Bridge. I have one more knife here." He flashes a piece of silver, his other hand still firm on the god's shoulder. "And I do not plan to miss the second time. Get across before it is too late."

The boy with the camera—Farian—starts forward. Martial pins him with a look and shakes his head. "You've got a story to tell. Go. Speak our truth."

Those words stop him cold. Imelda slips forward and draws Farian away on unsteady feet, whispering quiet assurances. Quinn looks stunned but she allows you to guide her. Adrian leads the way. A splash of blood from each of you upon the stones. And then you are on your way, one step at a time, aimed like an arrow at that other world.

The last thing you hear is a long and echoing howl.

42

THREE VOICES

IMELDA

Make something out of nothing.

I walk the gilded halls, unsure if this is what I had in mind. Attendants follow, doing their best to keep the pace as we move through the endless halls of the building known as the Forum. Our route takes us past libraries and lounges. Workers are actively removing artwork from the walls. Prying off the images that our former rulers put there. All the little reminders of our true place in the world. Not anymore. A new world is stretching its limbs.

Two guards shove open the doors into the main trial room. Less than a fortnight ago, the Brightness used a different room to conduct Pippa's secret hearing. I couldn't help admiring the story when I heard it. Etzli beneath the hood, pretending to be her general. All the shocked faces. An entire Empire brought to its knees by one voice. Bravos defended Etzli and barely survived the fight. He's recovering now and will wake up with a better legacy attached to his name.

Our trials are held not in the Constabulary but in the Forum. We want our deeds and words carried out in the light of day. We need every citizen to see how the world can change, how things might be made new.

Pippa is already in her chair, having been chosen to represent the Ashlord contingent. She even led negotiations with her own mother, persuading the final remnant of warriors to set their weapons down. The Brightness tried to rally them, but Pippa's mother would suffer no foolishness. She silenced the deposed king and forced her soldiers to stand down.

Adrian is seated as well. His transition has not been as smooth. The Longhand army suffered less of a blow. They were still a large and mostly intact force after the battle. Talks of peace were not welcome by some in their camp. His own father demanded the throne. The only problem is that they made Adrian the face of the entire war. Now his voice carries more weight than the old leaders of the Reach ever could. The Longhands are coming around, slowly but surely.

Quinn and the freed slaves offered their own surprises. Bastian arranged a meeting with their leaders. It was Quinn who grinned across the table as I presented our plan for equal representation. Four separate groups of people, each of whom would rule the land with one voice. She quietly thanked me for the offer and just as quietly rejected it.

"The terms are fine," she replied, still smiling. "But we do not want to be our own group. Once upon a time, your people and my people were *one*. Undivided. The Veil brought your ancestors to this place, hoping to set you free, but that does not make us any less a people. Even separated all this time, we are one people. After what Martial did . . . we would reclaim you. Let us be one again. Let there be three groups in this new Empire. Call us by that name again. Call us Undivided."

Pippa liked the sound of it. Adrian rapped his knuckles in agreement. I stood there—completely helpless—as they elected me their spokesperson. I'm still shaking my head at the thought as I take my seat on the front row with Pippa and Adrian. Others are gathered in the room. Councilors, generals, and more. It falls to us, however, to pass judgment.

The first day of war tribunals begins.

"Antonio Rowan."

A Longhand general. I know him well enough. He led the troops who relieved us at the Battle of Gig's Wall. And then he tried to pick my pockets to fund his next battle. If only that were the worst of his deeds.

"You are accused of attacking the sanctuary town of Vivinia," Pippa announces. "At the start of the war, certain lands were made into refuges. For the safety of our children and the safety of our innocents. Both sides agreed. Vivinia was one of those sanctuaries. We have evidence that you violated that agreement, attacked the city, and took the lives of innocents."

The massacre happened at the start of the war. There were only rumors then. Both sides accusing one another, trying to leverage my people's hate against the other. Until Pippa captured the Curiosity's tower. She and Adrian chose to watch the footage together. It was then, watching mostly Dividian innocents suffer, that they agreed to change the world.

"How do you plead?"

Antonio Rowan stares his disdain at Adrian.

"Age did not matter when they took our firstborn children," he says softly. "My cousin was thirteen. They cut him down under his father's peach tree. Didn't bother to bury him, either."

I can see the words cut through Adrian. He stares at the man.

"A child for a child. Do you like that trade?"

Antonio Rowan looks him in the eye and nods. "I will not lose sleep over it."

"Sleep is harder to come by in the dungeons," Adrian answers. "You are sentenced to life imprisonment. No terms of release. Are all three governments agreed?"

I confirm the vote. Pippa's voice echoes mine. The guards escort him away, and I hope that the darkness devours him. There are whispers in the audience around us. We agreed that it would be important to hear the hardest sentences come from their own. It was our hope that they would come and watch and whisper that this new government had a care for every soul in it.

The next prisoner shuffles into the room. An Ashlord. His shoulders are broad and straight, but he doesn't hold his head high like they always do. When I saw his name on the list, I knew this would be the most difficult trial. It helps that Pippa has known it was coming for some time now.

"Marcos."

Pippa stares at her father. They have the same eyes. A rich, honeyed brown. Deep-set in faces as sharp as stone. Those two mirrors throw their images back at one another

43

BALANCE

ADRIAN

The cliché goes that you must build an empire brick by brick.

We are finding the same is true for unmaking one. It was not enough to topple the gods. That was just the first step. Treaties are drawn up next. Expert lawmakers—one from each culture—sit down night after night, working out all the details. We are present for the opening discussions. It turns out the fall of the pantheon did not magically summon equality.

Pippa is the first to point out how glaring the problem is. "Our gaps in wealth distribution are massive. My mother owns several properties. I have more in my account than some villages. And that's not even considering people like shtaki. His net worth is triple mine."

Imelda nods. "What do you propose?"

Brick by brick, we unmake the old world to build the w. Pippa calls for sweeping reparations. Maximum val-

as Adrian begins reading the sentence. "You are also accused. Vivinia was a sanctuary town. There were Dividian and Ashlords gathered there, some who were your own kin. We have evidence that your army saw the fires begin. You heard the screams. But you ordered them to stand their ground because you thought those deaths would be valuable ammunition against the Longhands."

Antonio Rowan was not broken by this truth. He did not weep, because he felt no guilt over the dead. In his mind, the scales were simply finding their balance. But Pippa's father shatters beneath the weight of his sins. Tears stream down the former champion's cheeks.

"I am guilty."

That is the hard part of justice. The two reactions could not be more different. One man lifted his chin and cursed the world. The other bowed his head in shame. And yet both are guilty of the same crime. Pippa knows the sentence must come from her.

"You are sentenced to life imprisonment," she says, voice trembling. "No terms of release. As they were trapped, so you will be. Are all governments agreed?"

We echo confirmations. Marcos stands there long enough to whisper to Pippa from across the room. His words are simple and difficult all at once. "Forgive me, dear."

She nods to him before the guards lead him away. It goes on like that for the rest of the day. Few trials have as much weight, but there are so many back-to-back that they feel heavy all the same. There are princes who heard Pippa's claims about the gods and defended them anyway. Each one is convicted of willful treason. There are old generals who refuse our new alliance. They cannot agree with a government that would give the same rights to every person, regardless of race.

We sentence them all.

It is an exhausting day that demands every scrap of our energy. I find myself wondering as the long day passes how we ever thought this was how the world should be. We made murder into our sport and rewarded those with the best swords and the darkest hearts. Most of that was driven by the Ashlords—who were driven in turn by their false gods—but my people craved the same. We did not want to *change* the world; we just wanted to be the rulers of it.

"Next," Pippa calls in a tired voice. Even her perfect shoulders are slumping.

I light up a little bit, though, as Farian enters the room. Most of the brand-new tech in the city has fallen apart. Our guess is that the Striving's death had something to do with that. It shorted out her newest gifts, but the more established technologies still work. Which is why Farian wheels in an older version of the Chat-screens. He looks proud to stand before us.

"I've compiled a full account," he says, "of the Divinity Wars."

Adrian chokes on a cough. "Did you come up with that?"

Farian blushes a little. Pippa nearly laughs. I shake my head.

"Really?" I ask. "And you questioned my creative decision making?"

He flushes again. "You know what, I don't care what you call it. I'm just here to say I've got the footage. This

should be mandatory viewing. I know you don't want to do anything that makes you feel like tyrants, but this tells the whole story. It's not a filtered history. It isn't a watered-down version that favors the gods. It shows everything. Good and bad. It shows the pantheon, falling one by one. It walks through the Curiosity's secrets. All of it. This is the first step to a new way forward, for all of us."

He shakes his head in annoyance.

"But sure, feel free to come up with a better name."

I have to fight back my laughter as he starts the video. It does not take long for us to be swept into silence by what we're seeing. The footage is beyond anything I could have ever dreamed. Farian set his fingers on the very pulse o the war. He interviews foot soldiers. Shows grueling batt scenes. It is all the glory of our kind and all our disgrace side by side.

A voice-over guides us, explaining what we're watc and specifically what happened in the underworld. Hi age of that land is haunting. Like watching somethi people will think we made up. We know the Ma dead now. That world is no more. If not for Farian's it could all have been a dream—or a nightmare.

As the video finishes, all of us sit in mutual si

Adrian clears his throat again. "Divinity V for me."

Pippa nods. "Same."

I offer my oldest friend a smile. "Make th

ues are set for every Ashlord citizen. All possessions beyond that amount are reclaimed. It is tedious work, especially after the scattershot confusion of fighting a war, but most of the Empire's wealthiest citizens call Furia their home. We begin with them.

Naturally, there's resistance. Fools like Ashtaki demand trial by combat. We are not tyrants, so we do not have them executed. No, we are the beginnings of a democracy. As such, we walk them to the city gates, offer them a free horse and food, then invite them to ride in whatever direction they'd like. Most grumble before walking back into the city to claim their diminished estates. There are a few who ride off, and I can't help wondering what will become of them.

It helps that the Ashlords are not the only target of the reparations.

I lead the movement to enact a similar measure for all Longhands. We enslaved the Dividian, too. We abandoned them to the Empire's cruelty when we left for the Reach and grew rich from a war won at their expense. It is impossible to untangle our wealth from their suffering.

Land becomes the most disputed item. Some Longhands own properties that are larger than cities. We split those lands, offering deeds to any of the newly minted Undivided who have a care to move north. A few of the larger farms cause more complications. We don't want to build on the land that feeds us. Instead, we divide their profits to eliminate monopolies. It takes time, especially when we have to defend every decision to jilted owners.

Every single temple is ordered torn down. We will rebuild affordable housing on each piece of land. The sacrificial blood is washed slowly from the stones. Most of Quinn's people claim new homes in those spaces, ready to rebuild from the ruins of the very gods who enslaved them. It is its own kind of redemption.

There are fights, growing pains.

A masked group tries to set one of the larger Ashlord manors on fire, not knowing it will be converted into living spaces for others. One of the former princes holds a secret meeting with designs on retaking the capital. There's even a group that tries to free Antonio Rowan from his prison cell. Our newly established government is vigilant enough to root them all out. The only demand we have is equality. Only those who do not wish the same find themselves at the wrong end of our swords.

After a long evening of discussions, Pippa invites me to join her for a drink. The next evening, I invite her. It dances on like that for a fortnight. We talk about politics or the past or the world below. Anything but the way we feel about each other. I was brave enough to start a war, but every time she dangles her hand at my side as we walk, I'm too scared to take it.

One night, she makes a point to invite Imelda out with us.

"No turning us down this time," Pippa says. "I insist you come. Adrian and I both have something important we need to discuss with you. Besides, you look like you need a drink."

Imelda snorts. "How flattering."

The three of us set off together. Pippa aims us in the direction of our usual restaurant. My mind's tracing back through the day. What did we need to talk to Imelda about?

Something about the Vivinia memorial? Pippa glides upstairs to the rooftop cantina we've been visiting, laughing at something Imelda says. I've noticed that she wears fewer masks now. She was always so polished before, as if she'd rehearsed every possible interaction and prepared just the right answer. It is a fine thing to see her with her guard completely down.

The three of us take seats overlooking the capital we're slowly rebuilding. The bartender arrives with our customary drinks. He was a Dividian and now calls himself one of the Undivided. We've come often enough to know his story. He worked at this bar for most of his life. Took over the deed for it when his owner abandoned the city because of the new reparations. We watch as he fawns over Imelda, then rushes off to get our drinks.

Imelda's cheeks go red. It's the one thing she's not used to yet. She's a natural-born leader. Her knack for alchemy translates well into problem-solving. More than once, she's the one who figured out solutions to our most tangled problems. She still doesn't know how to take a compliment, though. Pippa's always teasing her about it.

"So what did you want to talk about?" Imelda asks.

I eye Pippa curiously. She's wearing her hair up tonight. It sharpens her cheekbones, deepens her eyes. But I frown when I realize she's blushing. Ashlords supposedly do not feel heat. Pippa, especially, seems immune to embarrassment.

"Well, I have a confession."

Now I'm even more curious. Imelda rolls her eyes. She thinks Pippa is dramatic.

"It's possible that I . . . influenced something in the treaty."

My eyes widen. "Influenced how?"

"Influenced what?" Imelda asks.

Pippa scowls. "I may or may not have eliminated one of the nonnegotiables."

"Which one?" Imelda asks. "I thought we agreed. Everything out in the open!"

"It was . . . the second clause . . . in section twelve."

A moment passes. I'm nodding, pretending like I know which clause that is. I made sure to read everything, but the idea that I memorized the individual sections? No chance. It's a surprise when Imelda bursts out laughing. She sees the look on my face, and her laughter doubles when she figures out that I don't have any idea what they're talking about.

"He doesn't know?" Imelda asks in between laughs.

Pippa is staring daggers at her. I sip my drink, feeling a little hot under the collar.

"Care to let me in on the secret?"

Imelda's still laughing. "Please tell him."

"I brought you here—*Imelda*—so that everything *would* be out in the open."

"You brought me here because you love a good show."

"Whatever." Pippa's eyes cut to me. "That edict is about the leaders."

"Viceroys," I correct her without thinking. "Remember? We're calling them viceroys."

"*Whatever.* That edict had a rule about the *viceroys.* It had language that did not allow there to be any romantic

as Adrian begins reading the sentence. "You are also accused. Vivinia was a sanctuary town. There were Dividian and Ashlords gathered there, some who were your own
kin. We have evidence that your army saw the fires begin.
You heard the screams. But you ordered them to stand their
ground because you thought those deaths would be valuable ammunition against the Longhands."

Antonio Rowan was not broken by this truth. He did not
weep, because he felt no guilt over the dead. In his mind,
the scales were simply finding their balance. But Pippa's
father shatters beneath the weight of his sins. Tears stream
down the former champion's cheeks.

"I am guilty."

That is the hard part of justice. The two reactions could
not be more different. One man lifted his chin and cursed
the world. The other bowed his head in shame. And yet
both are guilty of the same crime. Pippa knows the sentence
must come from her.

"You are sentenced to life imprisonment," she says, voice
trembling. "No terms of release. As they were trapped, so
you will be. Are all governments agreed?"

We echo confirmations. Marcos stands there long enough
to whisper to Pippa from across the room. His words are
simple and difficult all at once. "Forgive me, dear."

She nods to him before the guards lead him away. It goes
on like that for the rest of the day. Few trials have as much
weight, but there are so many back-to-back that they feel
heavy all the same. There are princes who heard Pippa's
claims about the gods and defended them anyway. Each one
is convicted of willful treason. There are old generals who

refuse our new alliance. They cannot agree with a government that would give the same rights to every person, regardless of race.

We sentence them all.

It is an exhausting day that demands every scrap of our energy. I find myself wondering as the long day passes how we ever thought this was how the world should be. We made murder into our sport and rewarded those with the best swords and the darkest hearts. Most of that was driven by the Ashlords—who were driven in turn by their false gods—but my people craved the same. We did not want to *change* the world; we just wanted to be the rulers of it.

"Next," Pippa calls in a tired voice. Even her perfect shoulders are slumping.

I light up a little bit, though, as Farian enters the room. Most of the brand-new tech in the city has fallen apart. Our guess is that the Striving's death had something to do with that. It shorted out her newest gifts, but the more established technologies still work. Which is why Farian wheels in an older version of the Chat-screens. He looks proud to stand before us.

"I've compiled a full account," he says, "of the Divinity Wars."

Adrian chokes on a cough. "Did you come up with that?"

Farian blushes a little. Pippa nearly laughs. I shake my head.

"Really?" I ask. "And you questioned my creative decision making?"

He flushes again. "You know what, I don't care what you call it. I'm just here to say I've got the footage. This should be mandatory viewing. I know you don't want to do anything that makes you feel like tyrants, but this tells the whole story. It's not a filtered history. It isn't a watered-down version that favors the gods. It shows everything. Good and bad. It shows the pantheon, falling one by one. It walks through the Curiosity's secrets. All of it. This is the first step to a new way forward, for all of us."

He shakes his head in annoyance.

"But sure, feel free to come up with a better name."

I have to fight back my laughter as he starts the video. It does not take long for us to be swept into silence by what we're seeing. The footage is beyond anything I could have ever dreamed. Farian set his fingers on the very pulse of the war. He interviews foot soldiers. Shows grueling battle scenes. It is all the glory of our kind and all our disgrace set side by side.

A voice-over guides us, explaining what we're watching, and specifically what happened in the underworld. His footage of that land is haunting. Like watching something that people will think we made up. We know the Madness is dead now. That world is no more. If not for Farian's footage, it could all have been a dream—or a nightmare.

As the video finishes, all of us sit in mutual silence.

Adrian clears his throat again. "Divinity Wars works for me."

Pippa nods. "Same."

I offer my oldest friend a smile. "Make that three."

BALANCE

ADRIAN

The cliché goes that you must build an empire brick by brick.

We are finding the same is true for unmaking one. It was not enough to topple the gods. That was just the first step. Treaties are drawn up next. Expert lawmakers—one from each culture—sit down night after night, working out all the details. We are present for the opening discussions. It turns out the fall of the pantheon did not magically summon equality.

Pippa is the first to point out how glaring the problem is. "Our gaps in wealth distribution are massive. My mother owns several properties. I have more in my account than some villages. And that's not even considering people like Ashtaki. His net worth is triple mine."

Imelda nods. "What do you propose?"

Brick by brick, we unmake the old world to build the new. Pippa calls for sweeping reparations. Maximum val-

relationships between the three leaders. I had the clause removed."

Imelda laughs again, although this time it's in reaction to my face. I can feel heat creeping up my neck. Pippa continues on as if the world hasn't started spinning around us.

"I apologize for being so secretive, but it is my intention to court Adrian."

I actually spew a little of my drink. "Court me?"

"Court," Pippa repeats. "I intend to find out if you are worthy of me."

Now my face feels like it's on fire.

"I nearly gave up my future for a boy once," Pippa explains. "It was a mistake. I will not do so again, but I also . . . I happen to like you. I have found you worthy thus far. I know you're the clear favorite to serve on behalf of the Longhands. I'm the clear favorite to lead the Ashlords. I have no intention to give up my future for you, no matter how . . . dashing you are."

Imelda is cackling.

"Don't laugh." Pippa rounds on her. "This is the part where you come in."

"Oh?" Imelda actually wipes a tear away. "Am I officiating the wedding?"

Pippa rolls her eyes. "No, you will be the balance between us. You're the only person strong enough to be the voice of reason. If we're ever playing favorites, speak your mind. If we're bickering, be the decisive vote. I am trusting your shoulders to be the ones on which the Empire finds its balance. Are you up for that task?"

That charge sobers Imelda quickly. She glances between

us. Until now, she's likely allowed herself to believe this role of leadership is temporary. Perhaps she thought she could hand the torch to someone else and go off to live a quiet life in the mountains. But we all know she's the one who will be chosen. After an uncomfortable silence, she nods.

"I'll do my best."

Pippa smiles before raising her glass.

"Let's toast. To a new world."

Imelda politely slips off early in the evening. Pippa tries to tease her about going to see Bastian, but Imelda cuts a look my way and laughs her way down the stairs. It's enough to have my cheeks on fire again. Pippa swirls a straw in her drink, avoiding my gaze.

"So how will you know if I'm worthy?"

"Well, naturally, I will have to test you."

She sets a hand on the table between us. It is an invitation. I take it. There's the usual warmth I feel around her, but a surprising softness, too. She traces my thumb with hers and a shiver runs down my spine. "Good hands. That's one mark in your favor."

I smile and try to pretend that this is normal, that an entirely new world has not sprung into existence. "How many other tests will there be?"

"As many as it takes to prove your merits. All your qualities shall be taken into consideration." She leans across the table, her eyes dark and narrowed. "Both good and bad."

I lift an eyebrow. "Let's focus on the good qualities first. I'm rather tall."

"There is that."

"A good rider."

"Almost as good as me."

"I'm a student of history."

"No complaints there."

"A fair kisser."

"To be determined."

That draws laughter from both of us. It's always felt this way between us, as if the world is holding its breath whenever we're within arm's reach. She's watching me patiently but this isn't how I'd planned our first kiss. It was almost impossible to plan for anything close to this moment. We're like desert flowers blooming out of stone. Nothing should have survived between us. We were fated to be enemies. I told her that in the carriage ride after the Races. I said my children would go on hating her children, and so on and so on.

Forever.

I am glad now to be proved wrong.

"Come with me."

She laughs but does not resist as I pull her down the stairs, out into the streets. I've gotten to know my way around the city. It still feels too busy, too clogged, too much at times. But at least I've learned my way. A few folks nod in recognition as we pass. Propriety tempts me to let go of her hand, but now that I've locked my fingers through hers, I do not plan to let go. We slip through side streets until we're standing in front of a familiar building.

"Spontaneous," she says. "Another point in your favor."

We walk inside the building that was once known as the

Historical. It houses some of the Empire's most cherished relics, but its most popular room is one that we both know all too well—the Hall of Maps. We pass through the gilded ballroom. I eye the spot where I first took Pippa's measure. She stood across the room from me, surrounded by sparkling admirers, and I knew I'd found a worthy opponent. It worried me then to see how poised she was. I knew she was not just a smile or a brand name. She was a hardened competitor preparing for a battle.

Now that poise and determination are a comfort. We do not need a "brightness" to lead us into the new future. We need someone who—beneath all the shine—is made of something more substantial. Pippa has proved to be that and so much more.

I lead her, hand in hand, into the Hall of Maps. Our footsteps echo as we pass by all the dusty relics gathered on those walls. Every single year in the history of the Races. Down at the end of the hallway, we pause in front of the map for *our* race. My eyes trace the passes and hills, the rivers and turns. I find that place where I hid my ashes on that first night. And then the little nook where I first fought Capri. All the way up to the very top of the course.

The final stretch.

"I was trying to figure out when I fell for you."

The words come out bold and bright. Pippa turns in surprise, her eyes slightly narrowed, her lips caught midsmile. I have wanted to tell her all of this for months now.

"It wasn't the first time we spoke. Backstage. Remember what you told me?"

Pippa blushes. "I said that you were an awfully pretty

package and that it was a shame they were going to break you."

I reach out and take her other hand in mine. It has us both turning, drawing a little closer. "Which was flattering, but that wasn't the moment. And it wasn't on the Longest Ride. Bouncing around in that carriage with all the other riders. You didn't look at me once."

She's looking at me now. "I was focused."

I nod. "It wasn't in the carriage after the Races, either. When you took care of me. I remember how gentle your hands were, but it wasn't then." I pull her closer. "It wasn't the time we fought together against the gods or even when we plotted a new Empire. No, it wasn't then."

Now she's close enough that I can smell the smoked cherry on her breath.

"When was it?" she whispers. "Tell me when."

I nod to the map beside us.

"It was down the homestretch. First, that whip-strike . . ."

Her eyes glint. "I knew you liked that."

"It was perfect."

"And then? What happened next?"

She guides one of my hands to her hip. With the other hand, she reaches up and caresses the side of my face. It's an effort to keep my voice steady.

"We came down that final stretch," I say. "We both made the same mistake. We looked up. At each other." Her eyes are darting and searching and asking. "That's the moment I fell for you. I started loving you then. It was the start of all of this. That was—"

Her kiss is the lightning. Mine is the thunder. We tangle

together like the storm we've always been. We kiss again and again and again. Our bodies circle until she presses my back against the nearest wall. I'm breathless by the time she finally pulls away, head nodding against mine, a whisper on her lips.

"Old habits," she apologizes. "You know how much I like coming in first."

Before I can laugh, she kisses me again. I can't help thinking about how every good storm brings rain. It is a promise that the old will be washed away and that something else—something better—can grow instead. I kiss her back and know this is the beginning of an entirely new world. It will not be the world our parents might have handed us. Not the world the gods paved in their false gold. No, this world will be one of our own making.

44

HOME

IMELDA

Our boots set down in the desert. It's dark out, quiet.

Farian walks a little ahead of me. He's been silent the whole way home. I don't blame him. It hurt me to lose Martial, but I think it hit Farian even harder. The old champion had become a second father to him. I kept spotting Martial in all of Farian's footage, too. He was always in the background, watching and protecting. It was the last thing he promised me he would do.

I give the outer gate a shove. Farian closes it behind us. The sun's stretching its tired limbs, getting ready to wake up over the distant hills. We head for the stables. No one messed with the place in his absence. I'd be surprised if it was anyone else's property. Martial Rava, though, was not a man to be messed with. We find most of the stalls empty, but the final three have little boxes with ashes waiting inside. At the end of the row, a door into the dark.

The smells come flooding out. Farian stands there with

me. It's not quite the stock it was before the war—Martial gave most of it away to help the town—but there's plenty to get started.

Without saying a word, we both turn and start walking the grounds together. We pass the rise where I first did the Trust Fall rebirth. My eyes trace the landscape. It's hard to imagine that every single video we made happened inside the boundaries of this ranch. Back then, it felt like it was endless. Now it doesn't look like all that much. But the thought has me smiling. It will look like an entire world to some other little girl, some hopeful rider.

"Mother's right," I say. "I'm lucky I didn't break my neck out here."

Farian laughs. "You came close a few times."

I sigh. "Just a couple of kids messing around."

Farian turns in a circle, drinking in every rise and every valley.

"A couple of kids who changed the world."

It doesn't sound so wild, whispered at this early hour, just between the two of us. We stand there for a while and watch the sun rise. Farian finally looks at me.

"I'm going to live in the capital, I think." He gestures to the ranch. "It feels like a betrayal. Leaving all of this behind. I want to honor Martial, you know? But my career . . ."

I nod. "He would understand that. This was *his* heart. He wanted you to follow yours."

Farian looks around again. "And you can't take care of it. Not when you're one of the future viceroys. Can't exactly run the government from a ranch in the middle of nowhere."

I smile at that. "You can *break* a government from a

ranch in the middle of nowhere, but no, I don't think you can run one. I'll be in the capital with you."

He shakes his head. "It's a shame to let this place go to waste."

"I highly doubt it'll go to waste."

There are whoops by the entrance. We both look that way and have to squint. There's only enough light to see shadows darting around one another. I start walking and Farian follows. His eyes have always been better than mine. He sees them first.

"Horses?"

Bastian comes striding through the gate. My father's at the back of the herd. The two of them agreed to take on the task together, said they had a lot to talk about. I smile at the outlaw I brought back from the mountains. And the smile widens as twenty phoenixes thunder through the gates with them. It was hard to position the request without looking like I was favoring my hometown, but when I mentioned the idea, Pippa wanted to send twice as many horses. Adrian nodded his agreement, because at this point he's too in love with her to do much else.

"Where'd you get them?" Farian asks.

"Former warhorses," Bastian answers. "And now they're the official riding mounts of the Martial Training Academy. Well, as long as you think it's a good idea."

Farian's watching the horses and almost doesn't catch the name.

"Academy?"

I nod to him. "We'll train riders out on the ranch, but we'll build a boarding school nearby, too. Most of the focus will be on new technology. The Striving is gone. We're the ones who have to make our way forward now. This should be a step in the right direction. I'm sure we could have some kind of photography major, if you want. . . ."

Farian's gone quiet. He's watching the horses kick up dust. Sunlight splashes over their bright coats. I glance at Bastian, wondering if maybe I did something wrong.

"And the name," I say. "I had to write something down on the official deed. So it's kind of set in stone. Martial Training Academy. I don't know! I thought it sounded fine. I know my creative decision-making has always been a little questionable—"

"It's perfect, Imelda. Just perfect."

Bastian lets out a little whoop. Farian smiles his before-the-war smile. We all stand there, watching the sun rise and the horses roam. It takes him a few clockturns, but eventually Farian wins me a bet I made the day before with Bastian. I don't even have to push him toward it. He just starts walking the grounds on his own, eyes dancing, imagination running wild.

"So I'm thinking we should make some kind of advertisement video. . . ."

I'm sitting with Mother in the corner of Amaya's bar. There's music playing and the room is crowded and Mother can't stop talking about how good-looking Bastian is. Never mind that I just defied the gods, championed our people, and rewrote history. She is pleased that I brought home a handsome boy. Right now, Bastian and Prosper are in the middle of a good-spirited argument. After a brief inspection of the man in question, I smile at Mother.

"You're not wrong."

She laughs. It is such a joy to be home. The relatives have come from far and wide to celebrate another birthday. Thankfully, it is not my birthday this time around. We raise our drinks and dance and laugh tonight as a new nation is born. The treaties have all been signed and the age of the Third Empire begins. Pippa is getting ready to address the entire nation.

Farian's video has been played in every village. There is—and there always will be—some discontent. Some of our people still carry the scars of servitude and don't think we've gotten our due. There are Ashlords who pass by the estates that once belonged to them and look at the new occupants with barely disguised greed. Longhands who will not bow.

But those people exist in the shadow of something more hopeful now.

The rest of us dance tonight in celebration of a new world.

Even though it's a bright evening, I can't stop my eyes from drifting to the front entrance. Mother takes note. She sets a hand on mine. "Do not worry. Oxanos is not coming."

Father stands behind us, quiet until now.

"Tonight you can dance with whoever you like, Imelda."

I smile over one shoulder. "Is there a deserving man among this rabble, Father? All I see are a bunch of mountain rebels."

He grins in response, eyes settling on Bastian. He watches the boy I've fallen in love with and shrugs his shoulders. "No one here *deserves* you, but I suspect he's as close as we'll get."

Mother nods. "He'll have to get used to being a politician's husband. At least he's pretty."

And that has me laughing. Father joins, his chest shaking. It feels so good to smile ourselves away from all that we've lost. "I think I'll dance with him."

Mother gives me a playful shove to my feet. I cross the room, earning a few toasts as I do, and interrupt Prosper and Bastian. The two of them are arguing over which food ingredient is the best in existence. "Quite a standoff," I say seriously. "Can I steal him for a dance, Prosper?"

Prosper rolls his eyes a little, but nods. Bastian turns to face me. He's traded his deadlier hardware for a false arm that's more elegant. He wears a long-sleeve shirt that covers most of it. I take both of his hands in mine, smiling as he turns me in tune with the music.

"Imelda Beru," he says, drawing me briefly back. "The girl who defeated the gods."

The steps to the dance have me pulling away, a shoulder turning to hide my face, and then spinning in the opposite direction. Bastian matches my rhythm easily. I grin at him.

"I had a little help."

"Just a little."

We spin around, the strumming as our guide, and I catch flashes of his crew. Some of them went back to the Gravitas, eager for quiet and the cold mountain air. Others came with us. Briar is at the bar, telling a story that has Amaya blushing. Cora and Harlow Rowe are organizing some kind of drinking game that involves one too many knives. Several of my uncles stand nearby, searching for a way to get out of the game without looking like cowards.

Bastian pulls me close again.

"Make something out of nothing," he says. "You lived up to your name."

I smile. "It's just the beginning, too. We have a long way to go. I'll be in the city. . . ."

He catches the nervous look on my face and laughs.

"Just ask me."

"It's not like the mountains, Bastian. It's not . . . wild."

"Ask me."

"It isn't . . . There's no good riding there. The streets are packed."

"Ask."

Our eyes meet before he spins me away, spins me back.

"Come with me. I want a pretty face to take to parties."

He laughs at that. "Yes. A thousand times yes."

There's a hoot from off on our right. Cora Rowe has surfaced from their makeshift game and gotten a good look at the two of us. She's still recovering from her bullet wound, but the wrap around her stomach doesn't stop her from crowing.

"Go on and kiss!"

My cheeks turn bright red, but Bastian's there, spinning me close, and I use the next turn to snatch his collar. He leans down and we kiss. For a magical moment, it's just the two of us there, floorboards flexing beneath our feet, an entire world at our fingertips. And then the music sweeps us back to the hooting and hollering, the laughter of uncles, Prosper making faces. I smile because this is the way my first party should have gone.

When the song ends, I call over the crowd. It's my cousin Luca in the corner. We didn't know it at the time, but in so many ways, the two of us started a revolution. A man walked into this bar to put us in our place. Luca strummed the song. I danced the dance. And that man walked out in defeat. It was the first whisper of everything that came after.

"Luca! How about a *new* song?"

He grins back, licks his lips, and settles in over his guitar. The first few notes dance from the strings to our hearts. We stand there, drinking in the rhythm, and spend the next few clockturns making our own steps. Bastian spins me around. Prosper high-steps around us, smiling. Mother and Father sway in the backdrop and it's about as perfect a night as I could have ever imagined. I wait until the song is loud and Bastian is close enough for me to whisper.

"You promised we would . . . find a sturdier chair."

His mouth shapes a grin. I laugh as his eyes dart to every exit in the room. We dance and dance until there's a moment that allows us to slip off into the shadows. It's dark out, quiet. There's only the moon and the stars and us, making promises without saying anything at all. I kiss him again and cannot help enjoying the symmetry of the night.

A few years ago, I danced the first steps of rebellion with Oxanos. Each sway and turn had purpose. My intent was clear. I danced to destroy that world, even if I could never have known what would happen next. All that would come after. Tonight's dance is just as necessary. Bastian and I circled each other and every smile acted as a celebration. We danced the moon into coming out, the stars into shining. We danced to welcome a whole new world into existence.

It is a song that no one can take from us now.

45

NEW

———

PIPPA

The stage lights are on.

You are pacing backstage, nervous for the first time in your life. Adrian stands like a statue to your right. His calm is starting to annoy you. "It's just a speech."

"And an interview," you shoot back. "With *questions* from *people.*"

Etzli is there as well. Her calm is equally annoying.

"The people we now serve," she reminds you.

Quinn grins at the expression on your face. You suggested that she be the one to give the speech. Thought it would be poetic to have someone from another world do the talking. But she just laughed in your face, patted your shoulder, and left the room.

Imelda requested time off to visit her home village before taking up her deserved role as the third viceroy. Adrian wasn't an option after he wisely pointed out how heavily the Divinity Wars documentary featured him. You're not sure if he was trying to be equitable or if he just dreaded being back onstage. And that left you as the only option.

"Whatever. Let's do it."

All three of them laugh as you shed the dark backstage for the bright lights. A man named Whittaker Best waits onstage for you. He spent his entire life in the city working for Ashlord theaters and production companies. His status as a Dividian kept him from hosting prime-time entertainment, but he got plenty of practice on their other programs. He has a well-trimmed beard, a neat suit, and an inviting smile. You cross to center stage as he speaks.

"We're back and we are *live* from the capital! I am your host, Whittaker Best. Tonight is must-see viewing. We are welcoming Viceroy Pippa to the stage."

There's no automated applause. You squint through the brightness to take in the faces of actual, present citizens. The mannequins were removed after the Striving's death. It took several weeks to sequester all that technology and refit the old theater seats.

You wave to the crowd, but there's only light applause from a few corners of the room. That has you taking another breath as Whittaker gestures for you to sit across from him.

"Welcome," he says. "Thank you for taking the time to be with us tonight. We're going to keep things simple. I know you have a statement you want to read on behalf of the Third Empire. We'll start with that before opening up time for questions. It was our hope that this new government's leadership could connect directly with the wider viewership. How does that sound?"

You nod. "That's perfect."

"Well, start us off," Whittaker encourages you. "Let's hear the official statement."

And the nervousness washes over you again. You think it's a good thing that it feels different this time. All your other interviews were about *you* and *your* brand. Now that changes.

You unfold the letter.

"Good evening. I am honored to speak tonight with the voice of all three viceroys. We spent a great deal of time preparing these words, and it is our hope to cast a new vision."

Take a deep breath. Take another. Let go of the masks. Drop the act. Speak with your own voice. Be yourself. No more pretending. No more acting. Speak.

"I was once asked by someone why our phoenixes must die. She had never seen the horses before and did not understand their nature."

I cast a glance to the wings, knowing Quinn is there with a smile.

"My answer to her was simple. The phoenixes die so that they might become something more. We have begun the same process. Over the past few weeks, we have killed an empire. There will be different reactions to its death. Some of you will celebrate. This empire was not kind to you. Others will fear what comes next. And a few will whisper that it never should have changed.

"But the truth is that the world we knew was built on a lie. A group of hungry gods taught us war. They made our world a brutal place, and we were fool enough to believe them. . . ."

I read them quotes from the Curiosity's own journals and walk them through what Adrian and I learned in that dark tower she called a home. How they found our world and slowly stripped our ancestors of their power. The clever deceits and tactics that carved our people out of their deity and into servitude.

"And now that Empire is dead. The world the gods built with our hands is no more. As it dies, something else is born in its place. Something new has come. Something that we hope will rise with tomorrow's sun and burn brighter than all that came before it. The Third Empire is a fledgling creature. Much like a freshly summoned phoenix. A little wild. A little frightened. But with a quiet word and a steady hand, we hope to set the proper course. A land where all are equal. An empire in which everyone stands undivided. And we are honored to help with those first steps."

I blink at the empty page, take another steadying breath, and sit down again. I was not sure what their reaction would be, but applause comes. Thunderous and real and not orchestrated by trickster gods. This is a group of people believing there's something more.

I take heart from the sound.

Whittaker smiles. "Well put. That is well put. Shall we field some calls?"

I nod my approval. It's an older system, so there are no visuals. Only the audio. I can hear the simulated search, then the caller's voice piping through.

"You're on live with Viceroy Pippa!" Whittaker announces. "What's your question?"

It's a woman's voice. Thankfully, it's more curious than accusing.

"How will you regulate land ownership? Are the same inheritance rules in place?"

"I'm so glad you asked. . . ."

The questions go on like that. There are easy questions—some I've discussed with so many experts that I feel halfway to an accounting degree—and then there are the harder questions. Someone asks about the memorial we're planning for Vivinia. Another caller claims there are outlaws near their town already, poaching from local farms. I do my best to address every concern. It does not do to overpromise, but that is also the joy of a new world. Its only limit is the extent to which your people's will, hope, and effort exist. Anything feels possible.

It's the final question that surprises me.

The voice is rather young. A boy, from the sound of it. There's a little rural twang that has me imagining a very small Adrian Ford on the other line. I can't help smiling at that thought.

"Uhh . . . yeah. I just . . . I had a question, too!"

"And what's your question, sir?"

The voice gets louder, as if he's pushed his mouth right up to the receiver.

"Well! All these rules are nice! But I wanted to know when the Races would start again! I'm training. I'm pretty sure I could be—well, when I'm older—I could be a champion, too!"

It catches me off guard. Somehow, this is the only thing we've never discussed. Imelda and Adrian never brought up the Races after the war. I'm smiling, though, because I have a sense of what both of them would say. I do my best to reply in a steady voice.

"We've had many discussions. Lengthy debates. One aspect of the old empire that we wanted to abandon was the idea of *blood* and *fire*. We felt like those concepts were given to us by the gods to turn us against one another. We were sworn by blood against one another. And we don't want to live that way in the new empire. But you know . . ."

And now I smile into the camera.

"I don't see anything wrong with a little speed."

ACKNOWLEDGMENTS

One of the few magics that we still have in this world is the moment that someone sets the right book into the hands of a reader. As I've traveled around the country, I've quickly learned the importance of these wizards (librarians or teachers or principals, depending on which branch of magic they've chosen). For this book, I just wanted to thank all of you for putting my series into the right hands—again and again and again. It truly means the world to me.

So huge thanks to Joann Absi, Emily Adams, Stephanie Adler, Stuart Albright, Katie Alexander, Marlene Allen, Pam Alwran, Jared Amato, Michael Ambrose, Michelle Annett, James Argent, Jennifer Barnes, Jamie Baxter, David Beaumont, Kristel Behrend, Stacia Bell, KC Berggren, Brandon Bogumil, Carrie Bolding, Robin Boltz, Allie Boyd, Carmen Brennan, Deidre Brill, Jeddie Bristow, Heather Bromley, Alyson Browder, Jessica Burnside, Katherine Caflisch, Pete Caggia, Lauren Calihan, Alex Canady, Kathleen Carey, Nancy Carr, Tawanda Carter, Jennifer Cassidy, Melissa Castner, Amy Cawthon, Bryan Christopher, Jennifer Cline, Andrew Coffee, Lisa Andres Cole, Lisa Coley, Amanda Collins, Angela Contrada, Anne Cooper, Janice Cooper, Emmalea Couch, Carrie Courtney, Mitch Cox, Eileen Cramer, Caradith Craven, Beth Crawford, Cris Crissman, Melanie Crumpton, Sarah Park Dahlen, Anne Dailey,

Justine Daniel, Nikia Davis, Sandra Davis, Lauren Deal, Kim DeFusco, Molly Dettman, Jon Dodd, Shana Dols, Veronica Dougherty, Brandi Dowd, Wendy Dragone, Jennifer Dry, Rebecca Dunnell, Mike Eagan, Anne Edwards, Lisa Eichelberger, Kelly Eisenbraun, Niki Ellis, Alainey Embury, Kelsey Eppele, Emily Felker, Nina Fergusson, Nicole Fernandez, Stephanie Fiedler, Amy Figley, Angela Finn, Pamela Fitzpatrick, Lynn Flood, Emma Fox, Angela Frederick, Jenna Garrett, Christina Getrost, Jesse Gore, Paige Gower, Laura Grabowski, Margaret Granbery, Bitsy Griffin, Daniel Grissom, Colleen Gross, Lisa Gurthey, Mrs. Hall, Alex Harper, Deanna Harris, Lisa Harris, Lori Mills Harris, Jacqueline Harsch, Shelley Hartle, Kaleigh Hartman, Brandi Hartsell, Lynne Harward, Angie Headley, Tim Hedges, Darren Heiber, Mary Hewitt, Lamar Hill, Cathy Hirsch, Mollee Holloman, James Hopkins, Leslie Howard, Katie Hultgren, Amy Hurley, Gaelyn Jenkins, Scott Jewitt, Kelli Jones, Regina Joseph, Chrystie Judy, Mandy Kain, Brent Kaneft, Katie Karackson, Julie Kelley, Michelle Klosterman, Marcia Kochel, Sharon Kolling-Perin, James Kornegay, Naomi Kraut, Sean Krazit, Ting Lam, Sharon Lapensky, Cammie Ledford, Margie LeMoine, Alison LeSueur, Susan Letts, Jen Lomelino, Jennifer Longee, Blakely Lord, Jennifer Lowry, Krista Lyons, Kristen Manning, Corley May, Donna McAlonen, Kathy McDaniel, Jen McGeown, Kimberly McGuire, Amber McKinney, Kate Mester, Carissa Metoyer, Janet Miller, Becky Mills, Carolyn Mitchell, Erica Morgan, Angela Morris, Lisa Morris-Wilkey, Paula Morrow, Emily Mountford, Heather Munger, Lori Munroe, Angel Murdock, Mary Jo Naber, John Nantz, M. K. Napier, Gretchen Nash, Julie Neff, Lisa Nelson, Angela Nofsinger, Skye Norwood, Sarah O'Brien, Matt Osborn,

Eva Page, Flora Palmer, Jennifer Parks, Caroline Peterson, Kimiko Pettis, Gina Porcella, Amy Powell, Mira Prater, Kayla Pratt, Kelly Price, Lee Quinn, Patricia Radwanski, Lisa Ray, Emma Refvem, Alice Rehm, Diana Rendina, Patricia Richmond, Diane Ruby, Tyler Sainato, Meghan Sanders, Betsy Schneider, Charity Scruggs, Eli Seed, Nathan Sekinger, Barbara Share, Jennifer Sharp, Rhonda Sixto, Beth Slater, Angelica Smith, Liz Smith, Matt Smith, Claire Smullen, Courtney Southwell, Christina Speiser, Jeana Spiegelman, Rebecca Stacy, Sarah Stanley, Danielle Steele, Stephanie Steele, Cindy Sturdivant, Scott Summers, Peggy Swearingen, Katie Taylor, Leslie Taylor, Ketty Thelemaque, Melody Thomas, Jane Tillotson, Lisa Turner, Carla Tuttle, Greg Tuttle, Leyna Varnum, Amy Venneman, Courtney Walker, Kevin Washburn, Sarah Anne Watkins, Ann Web, Andrea Weber, Angela West, Wendy White, Jason Wilkins, Marcia Wingerd, Sally Winstead, Beth Winters, Katelyn Wolfe, John V. Wood, Emily Yates, Carl Young, Suzanne Zaccardo, Kristen Ziller, and Kim Zito.

If I forgot someone, please know this list was compiled while chasing a two-year-old and holding a newborn. I'm so thankful to have worked with all of you in some shape or form. And a shout-out to everyone who I haven't worked with directly who loved on my books by giving them to great readers without my knowledge. You make the book world go round.

All it takes is one book. One book to transform a hesitant reader into a lifelong reader. One book to give a student permission to write their own stories. We get to make that happen together. So thank you for all that you do. I'm honored to be on your squad.

ABOUT THE AUTHOR

Scott Reintgen is a former public school teacher from North Carolina. He survives mostly on cookie dough, which he is told is the most important food group. When he's not writing, he uses his imagination to entertain his wife, Katie, and their sons, Henry and Thomas. Scott is the author of the Ashlords duology and the Nyxia Triad for young adults, and the middle-grade series Talespinners. You can follow him on Facebook, on Instagram, and on Twitter at @Scott_Thought.

itspronouncedrankin.com